Tillie Cole is a Northern girl through Teeside in the North East of England. Sh her mother, her crazy Scottish father, multitude of rescue animals and horses.

Being a scary blend of Scottish and English, Tillie embraces both cultures; her English heritage through her love of HP sauce and freshly made Yorkshire Puddings, and her Scottish, which is mostly demonstrated by h frighteningly foul-mouthed episodes of pure rage and her much rty jokes.

owing university in Newcastle and subsequent years teaching hool Social Studies around Europe, Tillie was inspired to write st novel. Ever since, she has written from the heart, combining ssion for anything camp and glittery with her love of humour and prooding men (most often muscled and tattooed – they're her iess!).

illie lives with her professional rugby player husband in Calgary, a where she spends most of her days (and many a late night) lost in ing euphoria or in her dream of pursuing a dazzling career as a racing, tasselled-chap, Stetson-wearing cowgirl . . . Ye-haw!

Visit Tillie online at:

https://www.tilliecole.com/

https://www.facebook.com/tilliecoleauthor

https://www.facebook.com/groups/tilliecolestreetteam

Instagram: @authortilliecole

Twitter: @tillie_cole

Or drop me an email at: authortilliecole@gmail.com

SCARRED SOULS
RAZE & REAP

TILLIE COLE

piatkus

PIATKUS

First published in the US in 2016 by St Martin's Press, New York
First published in Great Britain in 2016 by Piatkus

1 3 5 7 9 10 8 6 4 2

A CIP catalogue record for this book
is available from the British Library.

ISBN 978-0-349-41149-1

Printed and bound in Great Britain by
Clays Ltd, St Ives plc

Papers used by Piatkus are from well-managed forests
and other responsible sources.

MIX
Paper from
responsible sources
FSC® C104740

Piatkus
An imprint of
Little, Brown Book Group
Carmelite House
50 Victoria Embankment
London EC4Y 0DZ

An Hachette UK Company
www.hachette.co.uk

www.piatkus.co.uk

RAZE

To music for the constant inspiration.
And to Little Big Town, for inspiring this novel with
your beautiful words.

You roll through life like a roaring fire.
I bring the rain like a thunderstorm . . .
— Little Big Town, "Live Forever"

"They were always meant to be together, one boy and one girl, two hearts split into two, sent to far-off lands on their own. For God wanted to see if true love could be tested. He wanted to see if two halves of one soul could find each other again, even against the odds. Years would pass. They would both be hurt. They would both be sad, but one day, when they least expected it, they would stumble into each other's paths. The question is: would they recognize each other's soul? And would they find their way back to love . . . ?"

PROLOGUE

His heart beat like a drum—fast and hard and loud.

His breath blew strong like a windstorm, his chest contracting with his harsh pants.

Fear seeped from his bones, from every cell of his being, his hands shaking like a leaf and sweat dropped from his hot skin.

"Welcome to hell, boy."

These four words greeted Boy as he was brutally propelled into a dank basement by a hugely built guard. Everywhere was black; the blackest of black. The guards wore black, the walls of the truck that had brought him here were black, the sky outside was black, and the windowless room they now stood in, black. The stagnant air was humid and thick, the temperature in the room, scalding. The stench of slick grease, sweat, and something more putrid burned Boy's nostrils making him retch and his feet stuck to the sticky, grimy ground.

Hell, Boy thought, considering the guard's words. It was a living breathing hell.

Then the guard pushed him again, this time down a steep, slippery staircase, dull lights sunken into the walls. The high brick walls were a browning-yellowing color and ancient fans whined in the background vainly attempting to cool the too-hot air. Overhead pipes steadily dripped raw sewage on the concrete floor and rats and other vermin swarmed around his feet.

The place was a *shithole*.

Once again, a heavy hand pushed Boy's back, thrusting him down a narrow hallway. With every step, Boy could hear his breath echo louder in his ears. With every step, he could feel his pounding heart slam harder in his chest at an almost bruising rate. And with every step, he could hear more and more loudly a raucous cacophony coming from straight ahead, just beyond a thick-looking iron door. People were screaming and jeering, accompanied by the unmistakable sound of metal clanging against metal.

Boy's eyes were wide as he stared at the door, his nostrils flaring with terror. Nothing in this place screamed "safe"; in fact, with every new turn all he felt was pure terror.

The guard reached around Boy; loudly and slowly he knocked twice on the iron door, each knock thudding through his chest like a cannon. Locks unbolted, keys jingled, and finally, the iron door cracked open.

Boy's eyes widened in disbelief as he drank in the scene. Grown men were everywhere in the overcrowded room. There wasn't a spare inch free, sweaty bodies pushing and shoving one another from thick wall to thick wall. The men were drinking vodka, exchanging money, hands waving in excitement as they all faced straight ahead, their focus set on something *just ahead*.

"Move, boy," the guard ordered. Boy dragged his feet, reluctant to step across the threshold into "hell." He couldn't move. He was frozen to the spot, his legs shook and a dizziness spun in his head.

Gripping the scruff of Boy's neck, the guard tightened his hold, making Boy wince as he was steered aggressively through the baying crowd. Grown men stopped and sized up Boy, some in approval, most in dismissal. They all became a blur to Boy, the sight and smells too much for him to process.

Boy felt faint. His lungs burned with the velocity of his short breaths. Boy's fingers trembled in sympathy with his fear, but he shook his head, cleared his fearful thoughts like his father had taught him to do, and he managed to keep his head held high, meeting the owner of each curious stare right in the eye.

As the crowd slowly parted, Boy startled at the scene in front of him—a huge floor-to-ceiling square steel cage, the top wrapped with sharp razor wire. Flashes of movement were coming from within. Pained grunts and spurts of blood escaped the cage, splattering his gray-uniformed chest and bare face. This time no breath came from his lungs at all. He was frozen; frozen on the spot with shock, the tinny scent of blood invading his nose.

Boy couldn't believe his eyes. Could not digest the sight that greeted him: pain, cut flesh, cries, blood . . . so much pain and blood.

Suddenly, a wash of putrid breath blew past his ear. Boy flinched as he inhaled the sickening stench of stale food and acrid tobacco smoke.

"Drink it in, boy. That will be *you* in the cage before too long."

Boy held his breath until his chest could take no more. He exhaled sharply, resisting the urge to cough or cry out.

Boy had been taught from a very young age *never* to show emotion. His father would punish him if he dared complain, never mind cry. He refused to start here and now. Boy resolved to remain composed, lugubrious, and stoic . . . anything he had to be to get through this . . . this, whatever the hell it was.

A loud rip sounded from the cage, the sound slicing down his back and bringing vomit to his mouth. As a huge spectator abruptly moved out of the way smiling in celebration, everything became clear. The fighters in the cage were *kids* . . . boys who looked no older than himself.

And they were fighting . . . to the death . . .

Boy's disbelieving eyes darted around the cage. Weapons of all kinds lined the cage: blades, chains, hammers, axes, to name but a few.

One of the young fighters stumbled back, clutching his stomach, as his opponent circled like an animal, crazed eyes bulging as he concentrated on his prey. Clearly the stronger of the two young fighters, the attacker clasped a long-bladed knife, which dripped blood.

When the prey staggered around to face the crowd, he clung to the thick wire mesh that enveloped the cage. Only then did Boy see that the prey's stomach had been sliced open, blood and guts oozing from the gaping wound.

Nausea fought its way up Boy's throat as he watched the mortally wounded fighter drop in agony to his knees. Boy's stomach tightened to a painful intensity and suddenly, he vomited onto the already filthy floor. Wiping his mouth on the sleeve of his gray uniform, Boy righted himself, only to see the young losing fighter expire his very last breath.

The too-full crowd of men erupted, a mixture of shouts of success or groans of dismay, as wads of money rapidly exchanged hands. The fight was done. The noise in the basement intensified and the men focused on their wins and ignored the victor in the center of the cage.

But Boy didn't look away. Couldn't look away, his eyes were glued to the sight.

He watched as the victor, covered in his opponent's blood and guts, dropped to his knees, all energy drained from his too-bulky body. His eyes were red, his body shaking.

Boy watched as the victor tensed with rage, tipped back his head and screamed out in pain upon witnessing his victim's blood, his *life*, oozing outward.

He watched as the victor let drop his bloody knife as an all-consuming numbness washed over his body.

And Boy watched as the victor's lifeless gaze dropped to meet his, revealing how Boy's future would unfold.

That same rancid breath once again blew past Boy's cheek and he heard, "From now on, you'll be known as fighter *818*, and if you want to live, you'll learn how to fight and how to survive here, in hell."

And 818 did.

With the passage of time, 818 became unrivaled.

818 became death.

A.

Fucking.

Stone.

Cold.

Killer.

1

KISA

Present day . . .

"Fuck, Myshka, your cunt's so fucking tight . . ."

Pinned to the bed, my fiancé's strong hands held me down by my shoulders as he slammed into me, his cock pounding my pussy with incredible force, his strong hips locking me in place.

I tried to move. I pushed hard against his chest, but he wouldn't budge, not even an inch.

It was always like this when he took me—hard, rough, raw . . . totally out of my control.

Alik's blue eyes lit with fire as I fought against him, flaring at my resistance, the aggression he expected me to exude every time he took me in this bed—an aggression he loved, an aggression he craved.

He liked to fuck. Never make love. Just to fuck, hard, so long as he was in control.

His right hand moved from my shoulder and wrapped around the front of my neck, not too tight to stop my breathing, but tight enough to keep me in place as I clawed his back and shoulders with my French-manicured nails.

I bucked my hips, but his thick thighs pinned me down even more, his dick unrelenting and slamming against my G-spot, forcing me to cry out in pleasure. Alik laughed at my failed effort to throw him off, his mouth now an inch from my face.

"Just try it, Myshka. Just try to move me . . . I fucking *own* you," he growled in my ear, and his cock jerked in my channel, making me scream and bite into the skin on his shoulder, drawing a trickle of blood. Alik's fingers tightened on my throat, restricting my moans. His breath blew harder. His chiseled jaw tensed, eyes boring into mine.

"Come, Myshka. *Come!*" he ordered. Thrusting into me three more times, almost bruising my clit with his hand as he did so, I shattered, clenching his cock so tight—whether I wanted to or not.

I hated that he knew my body so well. Hated that he knew how to get me off, make me scream, make me cry out. When I came, Alik saw it as a testimony of my love for him. I just saw it as another way to be used so he could lord his power over me.

Hand moving from my shoulder and wrapping in my hair, Alik yanked hard on the long light-brown strands, his eyes squeezing shut and his mouth hanging open. Then with a deafening roar, he came, flooding my pussy. My chest heaved as my hard nipples brushed against his solid, packed chest.

"Kisa . . . fuck!" Alik groaned and thrust slowly into me, winding himself down, hard muscles flexing and tensing all over his large body.

Without releasing his grip on my neck and hair, he crushed his lips to mine, his tongue forcing itself inside my mouth. I submitted, *as always*, moaning, like he would want, as his lower torso worked against my sensitive clit.

Alik pulled back and amusement flashed across his sharp-featured face. "Myshka, always mewling like a little pussy, huh?" His mouth lowered to my ear and his tongue licked along the outer shell. "Love me fucking you hard? Love me bruising your slit?"

Alik released my neck, only to reach down and squeeze my breast, pulling on the raised nipple. I hissed and cried out, making his smile widen.

"Love fucking you too, Myshka," he murmured. Then abruptly, Alik pulled his still-hard dick out of me, leaving me lying on *his* wide bed in *his* luxurious Brooklyn apartment, trying to catch my breath and recover. He strode across the room, his ripped, tall body all walking perfection, and he ran his hand over his buzz cut dark hair.

Alik grabbed a towel from the closet and wrapped it around his defined waist. I moved myself up the bed and watched him.

Alik had changed so much since we were kids. His large-framed fighter's body was bulky. His skin was lightly tanned. His face chiseled, aristocratic, handsome even. He was Alik Durov—the man who decided to make me his when we were just a couple of Bratva kids trying to wade through the trials and tribulations of a rough mob life. The boy I never looked at as anything more than a friend, until he forced me to look at him as something more.

We grew up together. His father and my father were two of the three "Red" Bratva Kings of New York. My father, Kirill Volkov, was the Pakhan, the top boss, the one who ruled the Russian underground here in New York. Alik's father, Abram Durov, was the enforcer, the next in line to the highest seat, the one who would deal with the darker side to the mob, the violent things, the revenge, the kills, the intimidation. He was sadistic, unforgiving and cruel . . .

Like father, like son.

For years, Alik wanted me. From childhood, he always wanted me close. He was always angry, starting fights and getting into trouble. He would tell me he heard voices in his head, voices that would tell him to hurt people, but when he was around me, he was calm, the voices went away.

I felt sorry for Alik. I always had. Having Abram as a papa would be like living with the devil himself. But I had had someone else, a boy I completely loved, adored . . . was born for the sole purpose of loving. Then a tragedy ripped us apart when I was a teen. Within days, Alik made his move and, in turn, made me his.

We'd been together ever since.

As a *mafiya* prince and princess, all of New York's Russian society looked upon us as the "perfect" couple. Alik would have it no other way. He was *obsessed* with me. He monitored my every move. I was his Myshka—his *little mouse.*

And I dared not look elsewhere. Alik would kill anyone who came between us. And this was no threat; it was what Alik did.

He killed.

His place in this life was *to kill*.

He was a fighter—a death match fighter—but I knew he killed for the Bratva outside of the cage too, killed those the Red Kings really wanted to make suffer.

Alik "The Butcher" Durov was the undisputed five-time champion of The Dungeon. At twenty-five, nearly twenty-six, years of age, he was the most feared man in New York.

I could never, ever leave him. I couldn't even if I wanted to. In the Bratva life, men led and their women followed, dutifully, in their path. It was the essence of Bratva life, one that served you very well if you played it safe.

Sentimental feelings and notions of "true love" didn't matter in this life. It was an underground society based on respect and your ultimate support of the "family."

Alik looked me over and his light eyes flared again in need. He stroked his hard dick under the red Versace towel wrapped round his waist. Slowly, he shook his head, his thoughts clearly at war with his needs.

"I gotta shower, Myshka. I have to be out in ten. Serge is coming to take you home. Can't be deep in your sweet pussy again even if I wanted to." His eyes then softened. "And you know I want you, don't you? Can't ever have enough of you, baby."

Frowning, I gently asked, "So we're not going to dinner? We do have a date, remember?" I tried to act disappointed. But all I felt was relief. Relief that I wouldn't somehow piss him off in public by some arbitrary thing he viewed as wrong, which would warrant being fucked too hard as punishment.

Alik strutted toward me, his packed, scarred abs clenching with the movement, and grabbed my chin, dragging my head level with his, making damn sure our eyes met.

"Got business, Myshka."

"Where? And for how long?" I asked, immediately wishing I hadn't, as Alik's face turned to stone.

His grip on my chin strengthened to ensure I understood I'd overstepped my boundaries. My jaw ached and I winced at the dull pressure and pain.

Alik tutted, shook his head slowly, then said, "Business is business. It takes as long as it takes. It happens where it happens."

I lowered my eyes in submission and tried to nod in understanding, but my intended movement was inhibited by his unyielding hand. Alik sighed long. Next thing I knew, my mouth was latched to his, his teeth biting at my lip, causing me to whimper. He ripped his lips away a second later.

"Fuck! I can't stay mad at you, Myshka. You're so fucking beautiful."

I cautiously lifted my trembling hand to stroke Alik's stubbled cheek. "I love you, Alik," I whispered, tears filling my eyes. He was all I had. He was my only future. And I did love him in a fashion . . . he needed me. And I wanted to belong to someone. I wanted to be loved.

Alik's eyes softened, but only a fraction. He couldn't show any weakness. But I knew he loved hearing those three words from my lips. They calmed the monster inside.

Pressing another hard, bruising kiss to my lips, he stood and made his way to the bathroom.

Heart beating and fighting back nerves, I asked, "Can I give charity with Father Kruschev tonight? He's distributing care packages to the homeless."

Alik halted. He turned to look at me, a patronizing smirk on his face, and joked, "Have at it, my good little Myshka. Go serve God! Go rescue the scum on the streets." His condescending laughter followed him into the bathroom, but I ignored the humiliation and the curt dismissal. I simply felt myself breathe . . . normally.

At church, my father and fiancé didn't send their men to spy on me. No one would dare fuck with the Bratva at their sacred church. It was the one place I felt truly free. The one place I could live in my head with my past, with the memories I held so dear.

Rising from the huge bed, I stared at my reflection in the gold-plated ornate mirror. I hardly recognized the girl before me anymore. She got lost somewhere over the years, hiding away, running for her life. Her blue eyes were dead, her usually tanned skin, pale, and her long light brown hair, limp.

I was a shell of the girl I'd once been.

Small bruises were already forming on my neck. This meant I would be wearing turtlenecks for the next few days, *in summer.* Since my teen years, turtlenecks had been a staple of my wardrobe—a necessity after being "owned" by Alik and all-too-quickly learning of his brutal sexual practices and high expectations of me as his girlfriend.

Dressing quickly, I ran my fingers through my hair, making sure I looked presentable. Alik wouldn't like it if I didn't look perfect.

Moving to the living room, I sat on Alik's great-grandmother's antique chair, which dated back to the Revolution. There, I waited dutifully to say good-bye.

I surveyed the mostly early twentieth-century opulent furnishings in the room. This place screamed status and wealth. My stomach clenched in dread. In under twelve months' time, this would become my home. I would be queen of this penthouse, gaoled in a cell of Tsarist luxury. Bratva convention demanded I couldn't live with Alik until we were married. Ordered directly from my deeply traditional and faithful Russian Orthodox father. I thanked God every single day for that fact.

My father approved of the marriage. It suited our way of life. He didn't see the bad side of Alik, and if he did, he ignored it. He only saw the strong and ruthless man Alik had been molded to be by his father. To my father, Alik's stern and violent side only proved he was a perfect soldier of the Bratva, the perfect man to take the reins and be a good leader to his daughter. My mama died when I was fifteen. My papa had fallen apart, and Alik became my crutch, the boy to look after me when everything had gone to hell. Papa loved him for that.

I clung to the thought that I still had a year until we were married, which offered fleeting moments of freedom, before, of course, adopting the mantle of the perfect Bratva wife to the sole remaining heir of the Bratva. Alik, before long, would control all of the Russian underground, a position he thirsted for, something for which he'd been groomed his entire life.

Hearing the shower turn off, it didn't take a minute for Alik to boom out my name and rush through the living room's double doors to search for me.

His tense face slackened as he saw me sitting, dutifully waiting, in his grandmother's chair. His head cocked to the side as his eyes narrowed.

"For a minute there, I thought you'd left before I gave you permission. For a minute there, I thought you had *defied* me, Myshka . . . For a minute there, I thought you'd lost your fucking mind."

Standing, I switched on a smile. I strolled over to stand before him and ran my finger slowly down his chest.

"Never, baby," I purred to appease him. "I'd never defy you. I never have and I never will."

Alik wrapped his arms round my waist and pulled me to his damp chest, the impact robbing me of my breath. He held me in place by the back of my head.

"You're gonna make the perfect wife, Kisa. I've been wanting you in my bed, sleeping beside me, for too fucking long. I hate sending you back to your father every night, not being able to fuck you for hours, tying you to the bed, making you scream, making you bow down to my every command . . . fuck you until you can't walk. Been wanting to fully own you, to possess you, to release you from the Pakhan's grip and have you under my complete control . . . for *too* fucking long."

"Soon, baby," I soothed.

Alik loosened his grip on my hair, his harsh blue eyes losing their anger for the briefest of moments.

"Yeah," he replied. Slapping me hard on the ass, he pressed a bruising, owning kiss to my swollen lips. Alik swiftly broke away and, walking back to his bedroom, shouted over his shoulder, "Serge is downstairs. He'll take you to church." I relaxed but stiffened when he ordered, "Only after you change. Don't you dare go out looking like that. I'll seriously lose my fucking shit if you do!"

"I won't. I love you, baby. Always," I blurted. This stopped Alik in his tracks.

He turned, jerked his chin, a flicker of a smirk curling his upper lip, and he said, "Myshka, I love you too."

My shoulders sagged with relief at his show of affection. I calmed. It was during these tender moments that I glimpsed the small amount of humanity in Alik. These were the moments I cherished. Even as children, Alik was uptight, always angry, always wanting to inflict pain on others; he frequently did on other kids. His papa had raised him to be this way. I understood it; it was how Brava men *had* to be raised. But years of fighting and killing in The Dungeon had hardened him to the point where the kinder side of his personality grew weaker and weaker, the dark steadily and surely blotting out any light that remained. In this Bratva life, and with what Alik did for a living, it was essential he be this way. However, I wished his softer side would linger a little longer.

It was stupid of me and, to others, inexplicable. But I loved Alik in my own way, well, as much as my shredded heart would allow. I wanted him to have peace. He was so tormented . . . so dark inside that I just wanted to help ease that.

Lost in Alik's light, beautiful smile, my heart soared, floating on a loving hope that I would see some good in him, that I'd finally got through to him, but my reverie soon dissipated when, as always, his brief moment of gentleness was overwhelmed by harshness.

Alik's insane desire to possess me came to the fore as he warned, "Anyone even looks at you tonight or even speaks to you, you tell me. And act appropriately. Don't speak to men . . . only Father Kruschev. Don't want my woman looking like a whore."

I nodded dutifully. His eyes narrowed as they drank in my body. "Wear something that covers you, *all* of you. I don't wanna have to kill some fucker for staring at your tits. You've got to think about these things, Myshka. When you're my wife, when I own you completely, there'll be no mistakes. I'll whip you into shape soon enough. You'll be an example to all the Bratva wives."

"Okay, baby," I whispered in trepidation.

Alik ran his teeth over his bottom lip, eyes leaden, his cock hardening and bulging under his towel.

"Get out of here, Kisa, before I fuck you against that wall and make your papa even more pissed at me for being late."

With this dismissal, I turned on my heel and fled down the stairs into the waiting black Lincoln Navigator. Serge, the driver and my papa's most trusted *Byki*, bodyguard, glanced back at me in the rearview mirror and politely asked, "Where to, Miss Volkova?"

I loved Serge. He was like an uncle to me. He'd been driving me everywhere and protecting me my whole life. He'd never married or had any children. I think he regarded me as his daughter in some way. I could tell him anything and he'd never tell another soul. He was an old man now, in his seventies, but I knew he would be with my papa until he died.

"Home to change, then church, please," I replied.

Serge stared at me for a fraction too long in the rearview mirror. I could tell he was concerned. Of course he wouldn't dare say it aloud, but I knew he disliked Alik and that I was worried about my duty, my fate, to be Alik's wife. His silent fear for me seemed to grow every day.

Stowing his concern, Serge pulled out into the always bustling traffic of Brooklyn. I watched the bright lights glare through the darkened window.

At least for tonight, at church, I would taste a few hours of much-coveted freedom.

2

KISA

"Kisa, you're distributing the care packages on the street tonight, okay?"

I smiled enthusiastically at Father Kruschev, but inside, my stomach rolled. I hated distributing the food on the streets, preferring to serve it from the safety of the truck. It was too humid outside. I hated walking down the dark alleys and narrow streets of Brooklyn—they were clogged with the homeless, not all of whom had good intentions.

The food truck halted, and I moved next to Pavel, a graying, short, fat man from our church.

"Looks like we're buddying up tonight, Pav."

Pavel's pale, crinkled face smiled at me warmly. "The Lord will provide you with his gratitude, Kisa. You are doing *His* work after all. You are doing a *good* thing. An *honorable* thing. It is good for you."

I fought the urge to roll my eyes and tell him my life was so fucked up that I didn't think the Lord gave a damn about me. Instead, I nodded in fake agreement. Pavel had emphasized the words "good" and "honorable" because of my papa. The word "good" and Kirill "The Silencer" Volkov didn't normally feature in the same sentence. Pavel had been around a very long time and witnessed, many times, the destruction the Pakhan and the Bratva had wrought upon their enemies.

But as much as people feared my papa, I loved him. I always wanted the best for him. I made sure I attended church and gave alms because: (a) my papa ordered me to do so, to appease Father Kruschev—my papa was eternally worried about the brutality of my family's business and its effect on our souls. And (b) if there *was* a God, I needed to rack up some good deeds on behalf of my family, to bargain with on our respective judgment days. By my reckoning, as it stood right now, our scales were heavily imbalanced on the side of bad, and we were all completely damned and looking at a long stretch in the flames of hell.

Call me optimistic, but I was hoping these small weekly acts of charity would bring us all one step closer to not being completely unsaveable and labeled "evil sinners" for eternity. Plus, I actually enjoyed helping the needy. Not only did it give me a break from the twenty-four-seven surveillance by my papa's thugs, or Alik's ever-watchful eye, but it also served to remind me that, although I was trapped in a life I didn't want, I never went without food, I lived in the best of houses, I wore the best of clothes . . . I was blessed in this life of material needs, and I felt good helping change someone else's life.

"Okay, we're ready to begin," Father Kruschev called out.

All of us volunteers unbuckled our seatbelts. Sighing, I zipped up my ill fitting unshapely thin turtleneck and loose jeans.

I stood and headed to the small kitchenette at the back of the truck. Father Kruschev handed me my first round of care packages and smiled at me in thanks.

"Stick to your group tonight, Kisa. Dangerous people come out when this kind of heat hits the city."

Returning a comprehending smile, I turned and stepped off the truck into another boiling summer's night.

The first truck had already pulled in and my best friend, Talia, made her way toward me. She was Ivan Tolstoi's—the third boss in the Bratva—only daughter. I watched her walk my way, all tall with blond hair and bright brown eyes. I had to smile at her four-inch heels. Even distributing cold cuts and blankets to the homeless was an excuse for her to wear her knee-high leather Gucci boots.

"Kisa! I thought you were giving tonight a miss to go out with Alik? Or has he let you off his short leash for a while?"

I shrugged off Talia's pissy comment, trying to act all nonchalant. "He had business to attend to with our papas, so *I* decided to come here tonight. Father Kruschev asked me at church on Sunday if I could help." I gestured to the care package in my hands. "So here I am."

Talia's eyes softened and she pulled me into her chest, careful not to crush my bundle of food and blankets. I winced as her shoulder pressed against the large bruise on my arm from last week when I'd displeased Alik at a business function. I'd been talking to a male business associate of his father's "too long," and he'd warned me of his "displeasure" with his vise-like grip and hushed, harsh words in my ear, but I held back my reaction and accepted the pain. I would never question Alik; my life wasn't worth the strife.

When Talia pulled back, she eyed me skeptically and asked, "Are you okay with that, Kisa? You always seem a little distant when we talk of Alik. Wedding jitters? Or is it something more?" Her brown eyes dropped to scan my outfit. "And what the fuck are you wearing? It's like an oven out here and you're dressed for the snow!"

I threw on my six thousand-dollar veneered smile and batted my hand in front of my face. "I'm cold, so I wrapped up. I think I might be getting flu or something. Giving charity isn't a damn fashion parade, by the way, Talia. And I'm fine, just sad not to be spending the night with Alik. Instead, here I'm again." I rolled my eyes. "For my family's sins . . ."

Not once did Talia's eyes leave mine, but eventually, she let it go and linked arms with me. "For all the sins of our families! Well, let's get this done so we can hit a bar and get drunk! Father Kruschev has put me in another team. He knows we talk too much and neglect our duties if we're together. So move fast and meet me back here soon. I need alcohol!"

"We'll see," I replied, knowing I would be making my excuses to bow out of Talia's invitation. Alik would go berserk if he thought I was hitting the bars. He would think I was picking up men. And with Talia, of all people. Alik hated her, thought her a slut for actually living a normal life. He also hated who her brother was to me, and he hated that she kept his memory alive. The last thing my papa and the Bratva needed was for Alik to flip and kill someone else. Once Alik's temper switched into gear, there was no stopping his inner killer from raging forth. My father was fast running out of favors within New York's judicial system to keep him from being locked up.

Pavel waved me over and, giving Talia a kiss, I quickened my step toward the band of volunteers and began trying to save some lost souls.

• • •

"God bless you, child . . . God bless you . . . You always take such good care of me."

I smiled at the old man as he delved into his care package, immediately eating the ham sandwich that was tightly wrapped in saran wrap. He had been here at this spot for years. Well, I corrected myself, at least the three years I'd been serving with the church. Pav said this old man had probably been living on these streets for at least three decades. He always hid down here in this small alley, like a scared mouse afraid to leave his hole. I'd snuck away from my group against orders, but I couldn't leave him without his food parcel. Something about this old man spurred me on to save him. He always looked so . . . broken, so sad.

I could relate.

"Kisa? Kisa, where are you?" A distant voice attracted my attention. I instantly recognized it as that of Pavel.

Glancing down to check on the old man, I smiled when I noted he was wrapped up in warm blankets and buried under a mass of boxes hiding him from view.

"Kisa?" Rolling my eyes, I groaned when Talia's frantic voice joined that of Pavel.

Great.

Glancing toward the growing gathering of volunteers at the end of the long alleyway, I started to jog their way, when suddenly, a scruffy, bearded man ghosted out of the darkness, tripping me to the cool, wet ground with a deliberately outstretched foot.

With no time to scream, I hit the ground, my palms scraping against rough asphalt. Suddenly, my attacker's weight pressed down on my back as he tried to snatch my purse. He stank of alcohol and stale body odor. I fought back a retch. I didn't recognize him as one of the homeless who frequented this alley. And he had absolutely no idea whose daughter he was fucking with!

"No! Get off me! *Help!*" I tried to scream, but the man's weight on my back stole my voice from sounding out in the empty alley. The volunteers hadn't seen me here, being attacked, too far out of sight in the darkness to witness the crime.

My attacker kept yanking on my arm, making me see spots. I tried to free my arm from its place underneath my stomach, to release my purse, but it was trapped.

Then I abruptly stilled as I felt a sharp blade caress the side of my neck.

"Hand over your purse, bitch, or I'll cut your fucking throat," the low-toned voice ordered, but I couldn't free my arm. Fear spread through my whole being.

The blade pressed farther into my neck, and I closed my eyes, expecting the worst. Suddenly, I heard a deep roar and my attacker was hauled off me, his strangled protest muting mid-wail as a crunching sound echoed around the towering walls of the alley.

Frantically crawling forward to escape the noise, I scrambled to my knees and flipped over on to my ass . . . and immediately stopped breathing at the scene before me.

My attacker was pinned against the wall as a huge hooded man pounded his face and stomach with clenched fists. I couldn't take my eyes away. The hooded man was relentless, each punch delivered with precision, his chest heaving in excitement and his feet rocking from side to side as he relished the outlet for his aggression. He was enjoying the fight . . . He was getting off on violence . . .

I recognized the signs from watching Alik rip apart his victims in the cage.

Crawling to the wall of the alley, I used the damp brick to stumble to my unsteady feet and whipped my head to the hooded man . . . who now had his hands on my attacker's jaw.

As I realized what he was about to do, I lurched forward and shouted, "No!" But with a sharp jerk of his large hands, a loud snap ricocheted off the walls. My attacker's lifeless body dropped to the ground at my feet—neck broken.

I stared at the unmoving body. Death didn't usually faze me. I'd seen many dead bodies in my lifetime, more than most undertakers see in their whole careers, but the ease with which the hooded man killed filled me with fear and dread. It was obvious he had killed before; no first-timer was that smooth in the kill.

My eyes drifted up to the hooded killer, who was eerily still. He faced his victim, fists clenched at his sides, his packed chest rhythmically rising and falling under the sweatshirt that clung to his heavily muscled torso.

He was close to me. So close that I could feel the heat radiating in waves from his body. My breathing was labored and I wanted to get the hell out of here. But I couldn't move, caught in hypnotic rapture as I stared at the strange man who loomed menacingly before me.

He took a step forward, my body bracing for attack, then he took another step closer. My back hit the wall as I drew back in fear, and the hooded man took one final step until he was almost flush against my chest.

My eyes were wide as I stared at his dark form and my breath came slow at the close proximity. The hooded man never moved, just stood still before me like a statue.

He was huge; wide and tall. Only the bottom half of his face was in view—his full lips, his stubbled strong jaw . . . the bare top of his wide chest, demonic-looking tattoos covering his beautifully defined high pecs.

His head tilted up and more of his face hove into view. My heart began to pound harder as I waited to see his face, but the material from his hood hung low, shielding his eyes.

I watched as the man's teeth ran over his bottom lip. Mustering a modicum of bravery and clearly defying all of Alik's rules, I cautiously edged forward and blurted, "You . . . you saved me."

My hands were shaking, my legs and voice, weak, and as dangerous as this man seemed, his body too tense and rigid, my fear waned. It seemed, as we stood here toe to toe, he wanted to study me, be closer to me.

The hooded man's jaw tightened and his head tilted to the side, as if contemplating what I'd said. I couldn't take my eyes off him, his aura animalistic, feral, yet it somehow . . . *wasn't*. I couldn't explain it.

As I drew slowly closer, his scent drifted on the warm wind. It was intoxicating, meadow fresh, like he'd been outdoors for months, like the scent of the first snowfall settling on the cold grass in Central Park. It cut through the stench of the dirty alley like a knife through butter, sending shivers down my spine.

"Do . . . do you have a name?" I asked, my voice gaining some strength.

The hooded man's built frame suddenly straightened, like a jolt of electricity had just ripped through his body. For the first time I heard his heavy breathing in the quiet alley. He was breathless, sucking in air like he'd taken a hit to the chest. He was breathless at my question.

He took a step back, then another, and another until he moved beside the attacker on the ground. I edged forward, drawing his attention, but he never lifted his hood.

His head was always downcast. He wouldn't show his eyes.

The hooded man bent and flipped my attacker's corpse with his foot. He kicked the body into a dark corner of the alley like he was kicking away an empty beer can. Then he started to back away.

My heart sank and I pushed out my hand, signaling him to stop. "No! Please, I just want to thank you for saving me. That man . . . I think he was going to kill me. You saved my life . . ."

But my words had no effect. The hooded man backed off, his fists clenched once more. Then he sprinted away down the opposite side of the alley.

"*Wait!*" I shrilled, but all I could see was his dark garb disappearing into the shadows.

A cold hand suddenly gripped mine. I screamed out in shock, spinning around to see Talia, her face pale and her brown eyes wide.

"Kisa . . . what the hell just happened?" she whispered, her voice urgent.

Then the shock of the attack I'd resisted, delayed with staring at the hooded man, instantly surged through my body and tears dripped from my eyes.

"I . . . I was attacked . . ." I cried and Talia wrapped me in her arms.

"Shit! Who was that man running away?"

"I don't know. But he saved my life." I pulled back and looked at Kisa. "He k-killed that man to save my life."

"Shit!" Talia hissed again. "I'll call one of papa's men to dispose of the body."

That stopped my tears. "They can't tell my papa or Alik. They'll go insane if they knew I'd broken away from the group to go on my own."

Talia stared at me like I was crazy, but reluctantly nodded her head. "It's okay. I know someone who'll keep this quiet. I won't tell them you had anything to do with it."

"Thank you," I said in relief.

Talia stroked my messed up hair. "Can you walk? Are you okay?"

"Just shaken up," I replied. "I'll be fine, Tal. I just don't want papa or Alik to know about it."

Within seconds, Talia was pulling me down the alley and away from the kill scene.

Casting one final glance in the direction the man had sped off, I let Talia lead me back to the truck, all thoughts of the murdered man on the alley floor out of mind.

Father Kruschev watched me approach, quietly shaking his head in reprimand.

Stepping onto the truck, the waiting volunteers clearly pissed at my tardiness, I slumped into a vacant window seat, my forehead hitting the hot glass.

Talia sat beside me and gripped my hand in silent support, but I kept staring out of the window as the truck slowly rolled into the road.

My attention fell lazily upon the rows and rows of homeless men and women hunkering down in their makeshift shelters for the night. I shuddered at the thought of what just happened, the gravity of the attack, of the kill starting to hit home.

My heart filled with sympathy for the homeless and their unfortunate situation. Then, out of the corner of my eye, I caught sight of a large, no, a *huge* dark figure sitting at the end of the rundown street. A huge dark figure sporting a gray sweatshirt with the hood pulled over his face, sitting with his legs crossed, head downcast. A huge, dark male figure clutching a big glass jar in his hands. My palms spread on the window as we rolled by. My eyes urged him to look up so I could see his face. A passerby walked past him and causally dropped money into his jar.

I froze in realization.

The man who saved me . . . the man who had just saved my life was . . . *homeless?*

The man who fought like an animal freed from a cage, a killer . . . was begging for money in the street?

I owed my life to a mysterious homeless man on the street.

A homeless man who fought like a killer.

3

818

One month ago . . .
Guns firing.

    Crashes.

    Screaming.

    Gunshot after gunshot and the tumult of shouting pounded through the stone ceiling as I paced the small area of my dank cell. Above me was a stampede, the thunder of hundreds of feet; prisoners were on the loose. And here I was trapped in this fucking cell!

    I need to get out. I must get out! I screamed inside my head as I ran my hand over the metal bars keeping me trapped inside.

    Charging the door of my cell, my right shoulder slammed into the metal. It didn't even shake. Wrapping my hands tightly around the bars over the "window," I scanned the dimly lit hallway, its flickering dull bulbs swinging back and forth from all the heavy movement upstairs. This level of the prison, the *Gulag* as it was known amongst the inmates, was reserved for us champions, the most prized of the death fighters. The fucking killers, the murderers, the monsters they'd created to want nothing but to feel rage and spill blood. We were jailed in the bowels of this shithole, no chance of escape. Our cells were too far apart to ever see another fighter except when we were training.

    My breathing became ragged. Bellowing in frustration, I pulled on the steel bars, my arm joints creaking with the enormous pressure I put them under. My bulging, drug-created muscles corded with the effort. I roared out a final yell when they refused to budge.

The shot they'd just given me was making my skin crawl and was evoking the need to fight. I was scheduled to fight later tonight. I felt rage, nothing but rage.

I needed to kill. It was the only way to stop the rage.

The first shot had been fired about thirty minutes ago, I guessed. I didn't know; time had no meaning in the Gulag.

I could hear the other fighters shouting, screaming that they'd been released, could hear the screech of cell doors being wrenched open, the screams of men dying.

I was fucking incensed.

I wanted blood.

And I needed to fight!

My blood boiled under my flesh, fiery, searing, preparing me for a fight to the death. To do what I did best—maim, slaughter . . . kill.

Roaring out, I released the cell bars and once again began pacing the cell. My eyes, even in the dark, focused on the wall and the name engraved in the stone. *Alik Durov.* Underneath was an address. *Brooklyn, New York.* Below that, a motive. *Revenge.* Lastly, there was a clear instruction. *Kill.*

I had no memory of writing it down, no memory of my life before this place. Didn't know if I ever had a life outside of these stone walls. My brain had shut down, blocking out anything but the need to kill, erasing any knowledge of who I was, where I was from, and why I was in this fucking shithole. But one thing was certain. *I* had written that name, that address, that motive, and that instruction. When I stared at those jagged letters carved permanently on the wall in my line of sight, anger consumed every cell in my body and I knew, without a doubt, I had to do what the inscription commanded.

But I had to get out of this place first.

The sound of the hallway door slamming open echoed off the walls. I rushed to the bars to see what the fuck was happening. My skin was itching with the need to break free, to join the fight . . . to get my revenge.

The clinking of cell doors opening made my heart race faster. My knuckles cracked with the intensity of my grip on the bars.

"Get me the fuck out!" I growled as I heard heavy footsteps approach my cell. My cheek pressed hard on cold metal as I stretched to see who was coming, my hands rocking the cell door until blood began to ooze from the constantly splitting skin on my fingers.

"Go! Go!" a male voice ordered a prisoner, and I heard a man running away. "They've been overpowered. Head for the east gate."

They've been overpowered. Hearing these words spoken out loud, I lost it. Wildfire pulsed through my veins. Running to the back of my cell, I charged the door, my shoulder dislocating with the force.

Seizing my right hand, I popped my shoulder back in place. "GET ME THE FUCK OUT!" I bellowed, my voice sounding as sharp as razors.

The light above my cell flickered off, plunging me into darkness, but it didn't matter. I could hear everything, I'd learned to embrace the dark. Thudding on the stone floor made its way toward me. My roaring and bellowing increased.

Suddenly, the footsteps stopped and I could hear the sound of heavy breathing outside my cell.

"Get. Me. The. Fuck. Out," I warned. I caught a nervous flicker of movement to my right.

Two men.

Two men were pussying out of facing me head on.

"It's him," one of them whispered as my jaw ticked in annoyance. "It's 818."

"I won't tell you again. Get me the fuck out, or when I find you, I'll snap your spines," I threatened in a low voice, as the bars creaked louder with the pulsating power of my anger.

The men still didn't move. I could smell their fear and it just fucked me off even more.

"Get him out!" a voice ordered from behind and, suddenly, the familiar face of 362 came into view—my greatest rival but the man I spoke to and respected most.

362 grabbed a key and unlocked my door, his broad chest bare, black sweatpants covering his legs and his long black hair hanging down his back. He swung the door open and met me toe to toe at the entrance.

His brown eyes bored into mine as my chest pumped with adrenaline. Then he smirked and slapped me on the arm, laughing. Shaking my head, I sized up the two men who blocked my way and then I smiled. I could kill the two weak fuckers in seconds. Snap their necks before they could fucking blink.

The smell of piss filled my nostrils as the two men stood frozen, wide eyes fixed on me. Then the tension of the moment was shattered when a gunshot rang out from upstairs.

362 backed up. "We'll go out through the east gate. The guards have been overpowered, but they'll send more soon. We're the last to be freed. No fucker dared come down here apart from those two. They had no idea it was for you and me."

362 set off at a sprint back up the stairwell, leaving me stunned at the entrance of my cell. I looked down at the invisible line that separated me from the hallway and, when I looked down, my hands were shaking.

My hands were *shaking* . . .

I'd never left my cell of my own accord before. I'd never been beyond this room unless to fight, be tortured, or train.

I ran my hand over the mass of scars from being tortured along my body, still feeling the pain that had been inflicted when I'd tried to remember my past. The metal rods the guards would use to shock me, the ones that made you feel like you were dying until you lost consciousness. The pain that felt like fire raging through my body every time I tried to remember anything from my life before this place.

Hearing shouts and what sounded like a brawl upstairs, I clenched my fists and ran back into my cell, ripping my spiked knuckledusters off their hook on the wall.

Bending down to the tub of dirt I kept on the floor, I dipped in my two fingers and ran the dark, almost black, mud under each of my eyes. I'd always hid my eyes. I didn't know why, it was just something I'd always done. The guards liked it, thought it made me look more vicious, so they collected the dirt for me. They said it made me look more animal than man in the cage.

Slipping on my weapons of choice, I ran my fingers over the carved writing on the wall and recited my mantra.

Alik Durov.
Brooklyn, New York.
Revenge.
Kill.

Hearing the familiar sound of the guards' heavy footsteps on the stairwell, I threw the hood of my sweatshirt over my head, rolled up the sleeves to free my knuckledusters, and gritting my teeth with single-minded intent, ran full force at the three guards coming my way.

Years of life in the cage, fighting to the death for sick fuckers' entertainment ensured my strikes were quick and effective. I was a reigning champion. I was the sure bet . . . I was a machine . . . I was death.

My spiked fist punctured the chest of the first guard, his heart and lungs sliced open, guaranteeing a swift death. A blow to the head of the second guard saw him drop lifeless to the ground. The third guard turned on his heels when he recognized me. He should. This fucker had beat me, tortured me. It was his time to feel pain.

He'd run just four steps when I gripped his shoulders, wrapped my foot around his calves, and bent him backward until his spine snapped in two. Dropping his corpse, I pounded up seven flights of stairs, not even out of breath.

Revenge.
Kill.
Revenge.
Maim.
Alik Durov.
Brooklyn, New York.
Kill.

They were the only thoughts occupying my mind as I navigated my way through the narrow hallways, dodging bodies under my feet, following the rush of fighters of all ages . . . even scared little kids, freshly brought into this hell.

I pushed people out of the way heading to the outside, my lungs burning as they coped with the unfamiliar sensation of fresh air. I stumbled as the freezing night breeze whipped the skin on my face and oxygen filled my raw lungs.

Fresh air.

I hadn't been outside for . . . I didn't know how long. *Years,* I thought. Years trapped in a cell without a glimpse of daylight, breathing in stagnant air, a mixture of dampness, mildew, and blood . . . .

And death.

Death had a unique smell, a unique taste. I had breathed it in day and night, tasted it for so long that I found it difficult to breathe in the clean freshness of the outdoors.

Seeing the other fighters run free and out of the east gate, a guard sprawled on the floor caught my eye, a stab wound to his stomach. 362 was backing away with bloodlust in his eyes, his bloodied sai in his hand—his choice of weapon in our Gulag cage.

362 watched me approach. "We're free, 818!" he shouted, his face lit with excitement and his words seemed to echo in my ears, my mind not allowing me to believe it.

"Wh-what now?" I asked, looking around the yard filled with dead bodies, the ground drowning with blood, the Gulag's sirens wailing and prisoners running for the safety of the nearby forests.

362 dropped his tense shoulders and moved before me. "This is it, 818. It's what we've been waiting so long for. What we've survived for." His eyes brightened and he said, "It's time for us to seek our revenge."

R-E-V-E-N-G-E . . . I spelled out each letter in my head, feeling the anger take hold of me. My mind suddenly caught up with my heart telling me my chance had finally come. After years of killing and becoming the monster the guards had wanted me to be, I was going to get my revenge.

"Where are you going?" I asked 362.

"West," he answered darkly. "My retribution lies in the west."

362 had been the one to make me write Durov's name on my cell wall, I didn't remember him doing that, but he told me he had when I first arrived. He too had a name on his wall. Those inscriptions drove us. They gave us a past when there wasn't one left in our heads. They gave us a reason to live.

We stood there, matching each other's stares, when 362 pressed his hand onto my arm, gripping my bicep tightly.

"Go kill the one that condemned you, 818. You're ready. You've been ready for this day for far too long."

Mirroring his action, my hand hit his arm. "You too."

362 dropped his hand but looked up to say, "Hopefully we'll meet again, 818. If not, get back the life you lost and I'll see you in the next."

With a nod of his head, he turned on his heel and sprinted out of the large metal gate. Dropping down to the guard scum, I fisted his shirt, my anger flaring when I saw recognition flash across his face.

He need be scared. I was going to gut the fucker for keeping me in this hell, for hurting me when I was a kid, for doing *things* to me when I was a kid . . .

"Don't . . . don't hurt me!" he cried, and my lip curled in disgust.

Shaking his puny body until his teeth chattered, I demanded, "Which way to New York?"

The guard paled and my fists tightened, threatening to choke him. "Which direction?"

The guard's mouth opened and closed, but he couldn't breathe through my grip. I loosened my hold just enough to let the asshole speak. "East. New York is east."

The sound of trucks approaching in the distance prompted me to lean down and ask, "And where the fuck are we?"

The guard started to lose consciousness, and by the pool of blood on the floor, gushing from his stomach, I knew it was only a matter of seconds until he passed.

"Fucking answer me!" I snarled. "Where the hell are we?"

"Al-Alaska," he replied.

I threw him to the ground, done with the bastard now that I'd gotten what I needed. The trucks neared the Gulag and I knew I had only a few minutes to leave before more guards arrived and locked this place down.

Alik Durov.

Brooklyn, New York.

Revenge.

Kill.

Reminded of my purpose, I rose to my feet when the guard laughed and my eyes shot straight to him.

"We . . . we made you who you are . . ." he whispered, blood now dripping from his mouth. "*We* made you strong . . . unrivaled . . . a champion . . ." He trailed off, coughing and spluttering, choking on his own blood.

I saw red.

Incensed at his words, I raised both fists, the sharpened spikes of my knuckledusters facing down, and with a rage-fueled roar, I pushed the spikes straight into his chest. The guard's mouth dropped open as he released a silent scream, and pushing down all of my muscled weight into his chest, I snarled in his face and slowly twisted the spikes of my knuckledusters. Victory surged through my body as his eyes bulged and, fighting for breath, he gagged for the last time. I witnessed the life leave his eyes, nothing remaining but the unseeing stare of death.

Panting with the victory of the kill—what I was trained to do, all I was created to do, all they had trained me to do—I slowly rose to my feet, then set off at a sprint.

Within minutes, I broke through a line of trees into a dense forest, heading east.

And I wouldn't stop until I reached my destination. I wouldn't stop until I killed a certain . . .

Alik Durov.

Brooklyn, New York.

Revenge.

Kill.

4

818

After a month of sneaking on fishing boats to the mainland, stealing food, and hitching a ride on cross-country freight trains, I arrived in New York City.

I wasn't prepared for what awaited me: bright lights, a bustling city packed with ever-moving tides of people—completely the opposite of all I'd ever known. Yet strangely, it all felt familiar and comfortable—the stink of thick smog, the vapors of tobacco and liquor, and the sounds of fast cars with their horns blaring.

Stumbling into a back alleyway on the edge of Brooklyn, a searing pain shot through my head. I pressed down hard on both temples. Disjointed images were zapping through my head, a group of kids playing, a small group of older men kissing three boys on their heads, proudly smiling as they were introduced to a large gathering of people. My head felt like it was going to explode and that conditioned feeling of fire running through my veins engulfed me as memories tried to push through. For a month now I'd had no shots, no drugs the guards pumped me full of daily to keep me big, to keep me strong, to keep me angry, and more and more unfamiliar images were filling my head.

The visions dissolved as quickly as they came and I found myself huddled against a hard, damp wall with sweat drenching my skin. Then the numbness I'd felt my whole fighting life settled back into place.

I ran the name and address through my mind. Within seconds, I was jogging down unfamiliar streets, somehow knowing exactly where to go. My feet were carrying me forward to an area with large brownstones, expensive cars, and well-dressed people.

As I entered one particular street, a sense of excitement coursed through my body. Quickly, I searched the numbers of the houses . . . until I found myself outside a block of luxurious apartments. Somehow I was certain it was the address I wanted.

Security guards paced menacingly in front of the glass-walled entrance. I slunk back into the mouth of a nearby alley, melding with the shadows, eyes fixed on the door.

I waited for hours, hours spent skulking around the building, scoping out a way in. But it was impenetrable, far too protected. Then when dawn broke, a large dark-haired man with a buzz cut, looking as though he was in his mid-twenties, walked out of the building, strutting his built frame like he owned the fucking world. Every hair on the back of my neck pricked, followed by rage igniting in my stomach.

It only took one glance to know I was looking at Alik Durov, the cunt I was going to kill. Everything about him from his Slavic face and closely shaven head to his built body screamed wealth and arrogance— I detested the fucker on sight. I would take pleasure in making this kill. I'd draw it out to intensify the bastard's pain.

A few seconds later, a large black car pulled up in front of the building. The dick, Durov, stepped in the driver's side and took off down the street. Like lightning, I took off at a sprint, hugging the still-darkened edge of the pathway. I tried to keep up with the car, but I knew even at my fastest pace I couldn't track the car.

Two blocks down, the car was held up in heavy traffic. Crossing the busy road, horns blared at me, but I had a single-minded purpose—to confront this asshole alone, somewhere.

The car turned right and I followed it three blocks down to a deserted parking lot, a deserted parking lot next to a large warehouse, a warehouse that Durov parked in front of, and slowly he got out.

Reaching into my pockets, I slid on my prized bladed knuckledusters and clenched my fists, enjoying their cold touch on my skin. I stared at Durov's back, imagining where I would sink the spikes—his skull so I could watch his blood spurt like a geyser, the top of his neck, circling around his body to witness the life leave his eyes, his kidneys so

I could watch his body die slowly, internal organs shutting down one by one, or straight into his heart, quick, effective, mortal.

Moving stealthily round the lot's perimeter, I made my approach, stopping only to swipe dirt below my eyes, leaving the choice of killing blow to my instincts. Suddenly, a side door flew open, an older, hard-faced man stepping through.

"Durov! Get your ass in here. You're late!"

Durov.

It *was* Alik Durov.

My target . . . my *kill*.

Durov laughed at the man and, within seconds, he was in the building. Pissed at the missed opportunity, I checked around to make sure I wasn't being watched. Then I jogged across the warm asphalt, making sure my hood covered my head and hid my face. Something about this whole scenario felt too much like I'd been here before. Like I hadn't spent my life trapped in the Gulag hell, killing for survival, piercing flesh and taking lives. *No*, something, some twist of my gut told me Brooklyn, New York, meant something to me, like some sense of my past was clawing its way out from under my skin.

Circling the warehouse, I found a small window. Ducking down to the ground, my chest to a patch of dirt, I peered inside and my blood began pumping at the sight.

A training gym . . . and Durov walked up to a bag and began throwing punches.

He was training to fight.

Fight.

I was made to fight.

It's all I knew how to do.

My eyes flared, anticipation running through my veins. I knew this setup. I'd lived this for years and years. And the cage . . . every link of metal, every spring of the floorboard, every inch of razor wire was my home. Every stain of blood on that white surface had made me the man—the *monster*—I was today. But what really made my heart race was the row of weapons lined on the wall. The chains, daggers, and blades told me all I needed to know: the fights in this place were to the *death*.

This *was* a death match ring.

It called to everything I had become—a stone-cold killer, a fighter—and by the look of things, Alik Durov was also a fighter to the death.

As my nostrils flared, my hands began to shake with the rush, the adrenaline, with the plan of revenge forming in my mind. I would join this fight ring, I would slaughter this cunt, and I wouldn't lose. Never had.

Rising to my feet, I walked through the entrance, the smell of sweat and blood filling my nose. It calmed me right down.

"Who the fuck are you and what do you want?" My attention snapped to a short, squat man sitting at a small desk. He had pulled out a gun and aimed it right at my forehead. I kept my hood low, shielding my eyes. I would never meet another's eyes. Something deep inside never let me.

His eyes widened in fear when I stepped forward, the gun not fazing me. "I want to fight. Want in the cage. I want to kill," I growled in a deep, rumbling voice. I saw the man sizing me up, pissing himself—I wasn't surprised. I was tall, built like a fucking tank, tattooed, scarred . . . fucking dead inside.

I had nothing to lose. I feared nothing, not even death. Death would be a welcome end to the life I'd lived. But before my end, I would be taking down one Alik Durov with me . . . and I wanted to finally know why.

"You got a sponsor?"

I said nothing, and the asswipe took my silence for a no.

Standing up, he kept the gun aimed at my head. He took out a cell and called someone. I recognized the device; the guards were always yapping on the fucking things, depriving me of sleep. Someone obviously answered and a sharp grunt sounded through the speaker.

"Yiv? You're needed out front."

He snapped the phone shut, but I never once moved. I wanted this fucker intimidated enough to let me in. I needed to fight. I needed to kill.

"What the fuck's wrong at this motherfucking hour?" a graveled, gruff accent complained, and then a big middle-aged guy came into view.

As soon as he saw me, his eyes narrowed and he folded his bulky arms across his chest. "Who the hell are you?" he snapped.

"Your fucking cage's wet dream and your fighters' worst nightmare," I replied icily, bringing my fists to my chest and cracked my knuckles. The sound of each crack echoed off the bare walls.

The dick holding the gun and this Yiv glanced to each other. Yiv pushed the gun from the guy's hand and stepped forward.

"You fought in a cage before?"

"Yes."

His lip curled. "This ain't no pissant MMA or WWE ring, you get that? Stakes are higher. Prices are paid with blood . . . with pieces of flesh. This is The Dungeon."

My silence encouraged him to step forward, sizing me up. "You Russian?"

His question caught me off guard. I didn't fucking know. My number was 818. I was raised in the Gulag. I was trained to kill. I had slaughtered over six hundred opponents. This was all there was to me. No history, no name, no family.

Just numbness.

The guy said something to me, only this time it was in another language. "I said are you fucking Russian?"

He'd spoken a different language than the guards, but somehow I understood it. He was speaking Russian? How the fuck did I know Russian?

Without thinking, I replied yes in the same language, and the guy's face lit up.

"You haven't got a sponsor, which means you'd be a buy-in."

"What have I got to do?" I asked, the strange language pouring from my lips. My body tensed with the fact that I might get a way into this hellhole, this fucking heaven on Earth to me.

"You need to pay. That's the only way in. We got a trainer that's just lost a fighter, but it's going to cost you."

"How much?" I asked. Yiv jerked his thumb at the guy who handed me a slip of paper with a number written down.

As Yiv was walking away, he shouted, "You get that cash, you're in. Training has already started for the rest of the men. The Dungeon begins in two weeks. It's a three night ultimate battle to the death. The survivors fight in the final. You win, you win big. You have until then to get it together."

The Dungeon.

Two weeks.

Revenge.

Alik Durov.

Kill.

I was going to do anything to get that cash.

Slamming the doors open, I fisted the paper in my hands, secured it in my pocket, and tried to think of what to do next. Then I saw a bunch of men sleeping on the street, hats out in front of them, begging money from passersby.

In a split second, I headed in that direction, grabbing a candle jar off some house's tree. Tipping the candle to the ground, leaving it in my wake, I found a spot on the street, sat down, pulled my hood farther over my head, and placed my jar on the ground.

Two weeks.

I had two weeks to get the cash.

And I'd do anything to get in that cage and slice open Durov's chest.

5

KISA

"Are you okay, miss?" Serge asked as he drove me through the awakening streets of Brooklyn toward the docks.

I pulled my gaze from outside the window and nodded my head, offering Serge an appeasing smile.

"It's just a hard day. That's all."

Serge's expression turned sympathetic in the rearview mirror. "Luka Tolstoi's birthday," he said, and I momentarily lost my breath just hearing those words out loud.

I stared down at my fidgeting fingers and nodded my head. It always pained me to think of Luka. Twenty-six years ago, the three Bratva bosses were all married and each had a son. Luka was born first, then Alik only a few months later. My brother Rodion and I followed a year later—we were twins. And finally, a year after that, Talia was born, Luka's sister.

We all grew up together, the heirs of the New York Russian underground. We played together, spent days together in school, or hid together in secret when a threat to our *mafiya* was made by a rival. It was during these years that I became obsessed with Luka Tolstoi. He, my brother Rodion, and Alik were tight, the three male heirs to the Bratva rule. Rodion was destined to lead, Alik was second to him and Luka the third and final heir.

Luka and I shared something special. From toddlers, we were best friends. Then as the years passed, I knew I had fallen in love with him.

I may have only been a child, but I loved him completely. Heart-crushing love.

Mama always said the stars aligned when we were born, that God made us a match. From the first time we saw each other, Luka took me in his arms and swore his protection over me to my mother. Mama used to say she caught him staring into my crib only hours after I was born. Then when she asked what he was doing, he asked her if he could have me. My mama joked and told him it would be my choice when I was old enough to crawl, and from the minute I *was* old enough to crawl, my mama told me I only ever crawled to one boy . . . Luka Tolstoi.

I'd agreed to let him have me. After all, God had created us to match.

Luka had a kind smile and the most beautiful dark-brown eyes. But it was Luka's upper left iris smudged with a small splash of blue that made our mothers think we were destined to be. Mama said God placed a piece of my eye within his so we would always know we shared one soul. Luka was my protector. I adored the way he always held me close, making me feel safe, especially from Alik.

Alik was jealous that Luka had my heart.

When the three boys became teenagers, it all went to shit. In one fateful night, I lost Rodion and my Luka, leaving Alik the sole heir. That was when he immediately staked his claim on me.

Still now, at twenty-five, I missed Luka as if he'd just died yesterday. The pain was still as raw as the day I'd been told he was gone forever. A part of me just never believed that he did what he was accused of. I just couldn't think him responsible for killing my brother.

"Keep your head up, miss, and the day will pass by just like any other," Serge said sagely. Laying my head against the leather, I closed my eyes.

I was sick of so much loss . . . so much death.

Ten minutes later, after a silent journey, I entered the gym, my black-skirted business suit firmly in place, and headed to my office. I passed by the busy room of shirtless men training, punching bags, and lifting weights. I searched the room. A certain pair of light-blue possessive eyes locked onto mine and a slow, determined smile curled on a familiar set of lips.

Yiv, Alik's trainer, was pushing him hard at a renegade, his every muscle in his tight, packed body straining with the technique. Throwing the fifty-pound dumbbells to the ground, the thud echoing around the gym, pulling fighters from their programs, Alik's eyes flared with need and he thundered toward me—no, *stalked* toward me until I'd backed up into my office. Dropping the fighters' personal files on the table, Alik stormed into the office, slamming the door and closed the blinds.

"Myshka," Alik growled in a graveled, craving voice as his hungry gaze ate me up. His flushed skin glistened with the sweat from the intensity of his workout, his thigh muscles protruding under his shorts. "Fucking missed you last night, Myshka. Don't like sleeping alone."

My stomach churned with apprehension. I was always fearful of Alik when he was in one of *these* moods. He was always possessive, that was just how he was, but pumped by the workout's fueling of his inner violence and his veins filled with The Dungeon's fighters' daily cocktail of creatine, protein shakes, and testosterone pills, Alik wanted to fuck me, own me . . . and do so as rough and as hard as possible.

Alik's huge frame moved forward and cowed me. His hand reached out and in a second, he'd ripped the buttons from my jacket and hitched up my skirt, my ass now balanced on the lip of the table.

"Why do you look so sad, Myshka?" Alik asked coldly as my hands began to shake. Every year. Every year on this day I would endure one of his "hard fucks." He knew I was sad that it was Luka's birthday, and the jealous rage rooted in every fiber of his being always manifested on *this* day.

"Alik, baby. Please. I'm not sad." I tried to soothe, but I felt his cock harden and rub up against my pussy.

Alik's fingers dipped into my panties and began circling my clit as his other hand yanked off my bra, his mouth immediately sucking on my breast, only removing it to hiss, "You're a fucking liar. You're thinking of that murdering cunt." His lip curled in disgust and he bit into my breast, causing me to cry out in pain. He smiled and said, "Don't worry. I'll fuck the sadness out of you. I'll remind you who you belong to."

He became this aggressive whenever we'd been apart, even if it was only for several hours, but on *this* day, I had to lie back and take whatever punishment he deemed fit.

Alik's teeth again bit on my nipple. Then he wrenched his mouth away. "I go insane when you're not near me, when I'm not all you're thinking of. I go insane wondering what you're doing, which fucker is watching you, picturing your pussy, him fucking this sweet cunt."

Alik rammed his fingers into my channel, causing me to throw my head back and release a long strangled moan. His hard cock was suddenly free from his shorts. Taking my wrists, he pushed me flat on the table and slammed inside me with a guttural groan. He began pounding into me, teeth bared in pleasure, eyes burning with aggression.

Lifting his left hand while strumming my clit with his other, he grabbed my face and hovered above me. "You didn't call me last night, Myshka. You fucked up. Did some fucker look at you last night? Did you talk to anyone? I couldn't stop thinking about you out on the streets last night, men getting hard for what's mine. You forgetting you got a man at home, a man that owns every fit piece of this body?"

My heart flipped as I pictured the man who had defended me. The large homeless man clutching a jar, the man I had dreamed about last night, the one I couldn't get out of my head. The man I'd fallen asleep thinking of . . . forgetting to call Alik in the process—a grave mistake on my part.

Alik's gaze hardened and his eyes narrowed in suspicion. He could sense my lie. He knew, but no, how could he know? I had to reassure him, to assuage his concerns. Had to make him think it was all about him. Just him and me . . . no Luka and definitely no hooded rescuer.

"No, baby," I whispered, my eyes rolling back as pressure from my approaching orgasm built between my legs. "Only you. Only ever you. I belong to you. You'll have me forever soon." My voice was frantic as I begged, strived to think of anything that would calm his jealous rage.

A crazed but satisfied hiss slipped through his lips, his thrusts picking up speed. "I own you, Kisa. There'll never be anyone else for you but me. I fucking own these tits." He squeezed on the plump flesh, ripping a cry from my throat. "I own this ass." He continued as he slipped his hand under my ass and pushed his finger inside. I gripped his shoulders and dug my fingernails in deep at the unwanted sensation. Alik suddenly stilled and squeezed his hand tighter on my cheeks until the pain made tears well from my eyes. "And this cunt, this tight, wet cunt . . . Who owns it, Myshka? Who. Owns. It?"

I stilled, all actions suspended by this threat-laden question. Alik's dick lay in wait at my entrance. His fingers built an almost unbearable pressure on my jaw, his unwavering stare boring, until I said, "You, Alik. You own it."

His stern expression softened, allowing the softer Alik a brief moment of play before he slammed into my pussy, his finger searching my clit, unrelenting in its movement. My legs stiffened, my back arched, and I came, my channel choking Alik's cock. I hated that he knew how to make my body react to his touch. I didn't want such pleasure when he was like this, but I knew fighting the inevitable was pointless.

Alik's thrusts became furious and he gripped my thighs so tightly that it would definitely leave a bruise. "Fuck, Myshka . . . FUCK!" he called out and spilled into me. His eyes were crazed with possession . . . with inert possession.

Alik pressed a consuming kiss to my quivering lips, then abruptly pulled out of me, righting his training shorts as if nothing had happened.

"Get dressed. Our fathers will be here soon," Alik ordered coldly. Panicking, I jumped from the table, pulled on my skirt, and fastened my shirt just as a loud double knock sounded on the door.

My father. I knew that distinctive double knock.

Alik smirked and dropped down to casually drape onto a chair as I flustered, straightening my long brown hair. A couple of seconds later, the door opened and my father walked through, followed by Abram Durov—Alik's father. Ivan Tolstoi—Talia and Luka's father—came through last. He was the quietest out of the group, kept to himself. I always thought it was because of the shame he carried over Luka. For his son to kill the Pakhan's son, then for him to die too, was like a sentence in itself. Ivan was the finance man, the one who handled the mob's money. He had little to do with The Dungeon. He handled the books from his home office along with Talia, attended the matches through duty. But he rarely came to the gym, never really took an interest in the fighters. In fact, I was surprised he had even showed today.

Alik stood and greeted each of the infamous Bratva bosses with a triple kiss. Then my father's—Kirill "The Silencer" Volkov—gaze fell on me and a wide smile spread on his lips.

"Kisa!" he greeted. Smiling at the happy face of my father, I walked around the table and he pulled me to his chest.

"Papa," I greeted in reply, then moved to greet Abram and finally Ivan, whose hug always squeezed me just that little bit too hard and lasted just that second too long. I had always loved Ivan like a father. He was a kind man, the conscience, the calm of the Red bosses; Luka had been just the same in nature.

But Abram, no, there was always something off about the man. He brought violence to the Bratva. He forgave no one; he ensured dirty deeds got done. Alik was pissed most of the time due to his inability to do anything right to please his father. We were all aware that Alik's anger came from the violence meted out by Abram to Alik from when he was a kid.

"Please, sit, papas," I said, gesturing to the chairs. All of the Bratva—my family—took their seats as I moved behind my desk to take mine. Alik pulled his chair next to me.

"So," my father said as he turned to me, "how are we looking for this season?"

Alik smirked. He ran his hand up my back to rest his grip on the back of my neck. It was a possessive move, a move to assert his dominance, all to show his worth to the Bratva.

"Good, Papa. All the trainers have fighters, except—"

"Who do you fucking think?" Alik interrupted me and laughed. Abram, Alik's father, smiled in response as Alik added, "The fucking Georgian Albatross! Lost another of his guys in the first warm-up fight. Fucker got his throat slit by Sav's man at the start of the first round. I'm telling you, the prick's cursed. Five seasons of first-round losses. No fucker will fight for him this year."

"He must have a fighter," Ivan said calmly. "The Dungeon must have all the scheduled fights. We have too much riding on this year for Viktor to fuck it up. Biggest income we've ever had. We're only getting bigger and bigger, which means better fighters, more fighters."

"We'll work it out," I said. Ivan and my papa gave me wide smiles. Papa leaned forward and patted my hand. "You have this place running like a well-oiled ship, Kisa. I know you'll get it done."

A knock sounded on the door and Yiv, our head trainer, entered. Although Alik's personal trainer, he was responsible for all the new fighters who came through The Dungeon's door.

"Yiv, we were discussing the Albatross," Abram said smugly. Yiv ran a tired hand down his face.

"Yeah. He already lost this year's man and his sponsor's pulled out. Fucking lot of money too," Yiv explained.

"We got any replacement prospects?" Ivan asked, all business. The Dungeon, the Bratva's underground gambling ring, was their principle source of income. They had several sources, mainly drug running and arms dealing, but this place was the cash cow. There was too much at stake to mess up. The Dungeon ran all year round, low-level fighters, more dirty street fights than anything else, but for three nights each year, The Dungeon held its championship—it was three nights of nothing but death, money, and only one winner.

Yiv shook his head, then stopped and said, "We had a guy drop in this morning. Said he wanted to fight in the cage. Big fucker too. Russian. Seemed fucking insane."

Papa turned his head to face Yiv. "How did he know we were here? Not an undercover Fed, is he?"

Yiv shrugged and paled slightly at my papa's pissed-off tone. "No idea. But that guy looked soulless, dead inside. My gut tells me he just wanted to kill some fucks for fun."

"And?" Abram pushed. "Did you trial him or do we have to bring someone in from outside? We're running out of time."

Yiv edged closer to the door. "Told him he'd have to buy in. He left, but I'm pretty sure he'll be back. Something in his dead voice told me he needed in that cage. Probably some serial killer who wants to shed blood without being locked away."

"Like all us Dungeon fighters, you mean?" Alik joked, causing all the men in the room to laugh, well—all except Ivan. My blood ran cold. Alik was a straight-up killer; he wasn't lying. And if he didn't have this underground life as an outlet, I was pretty sure he would still need to kill. It was the part of him I feared most. The part of Alik that needed to take another person's life for him to keep sane.

Papa stood, as did Ivan and Abram. Papa turned to Alik. "You're needed tonight again. We got business with the Chinese. Need to smooth some shit out after you gutted one of their soldiers for staring wrong at my girl."

All the blood drained from my face, and I turned to face Alik. "You killed someone for just *looking* at me?"

Alik shrugged as if he'd done nothing wrong. "Caught him watching you from across the street when we went to dinner. Remembered his face. When I saw him at the deal last week, decided I wanted to see his intestines on the ground at his feet."

I closed my eyes and tried to breathe slowly through my nose, stopping the nausea climbing up my throat. When I opened them again, Alik was staring happily at his hand on the nape of my neck, not a care in the world.

"I'm busy tonight," Alik said to my father, but I couldn't stop feeling sick.

Alik had zero remorse.

He had no sense of right and wrong, no moral compass or conscience. He terrified me at times.

My father's fist slammed down on the desk. "You *will* be there tonight. You *do not* disrespect the orders of your Pakhan! You may be a champion fighter, Alik, the most lethal one we've got, but cross me and I'll fucking gut you."

Papa seldom showed anger. If he did, those at the receiving end didn't live to regret it. Alik was in a unique position. He was the only surviving heir of the Bratva. He *had* to keep breathing.

Alik tensed at my father's wrath. "I need to see Kisa tonight. I *need* it!"

My papa's eyes narrowed. The room fell silent. "You're coming, Alik. That's final."

Alik's hand suddenly gripped my neck, and I almost whimpered at the pain his hold brought. "Then she stays at my place tonight," he demanded.

I closed my eyes. Again, I tried to breathe slowly through my nose in a monumental effort to stay calm. Papa would *not* allow it, could *not* allow it. Alik would flip and I would end up beneath Alik on this desk— again—until he'd worked off his rage.

Papa's eyes flared and his mouth tightened into a thin line. "You're not married *yet*, Alik. She stays at *my* home. You won't make a whore out of a Volkov!"

Alik began to shake with rage. I placed a hand on his thigh, trying to cool him down. But when he jumped from his seat, fists flexing and face reddening with anger, I knew he'd blown all his fuses.

"I'm fucking through with it," Alik yelled. "We've been engaged for two years and it's about fucking time she lives with me! You've made us wait too long!"

My father's silent response told me how pissed he'd become at Alik's display of disrespect. Abram lunged forward before my papa had a chance to, and with cupped hand, struck Alik on the lip, drawing blood.

"Enough! Show some fucking respect, boy, or I'll do more than cut your fucking lip," Abram hissed, embarrassed by his son's outburst.

Alik gritted his teeth, saying nothing in response. He would never say anything back to his father. Alik was his father's puppet.

I stood, legs shaking, and cleared my throat. Alik glowered at me. Flashing Papa an appeasing glance, I stepped up to Alik and, taking a tissue from my desk, pressed it to his lips. He didn't flinch when I pressed the tissue to his cut, but his crazy possessive eyes bored holes into mine.

"Go with our fathers tonight, Alik. I'll be fine alone."

Alik pushed away my hand and fisted my hair. "What will you do . . . *alone*?"

Lowering my eyes, ignoring his suspicion, I shrugged. "Go to church."

Alik's hand twisted my hair, but I didn't raise my eyes. He knew the reason I was going. After all these years, it was amazing how my child-hood connection with Luka drove Alik to insanity.

"Alik! She's going to church. You'll come with us and take care of this family. It's your duty," Abram commanded.

Alik grunted in anger, pressed a rough kiss to my head, and abruptly left the room. I heard the men follow him out the door to check on their fighters. When I looked up, Ivan hovered at the exit, watching me with a sympathetic gaze.

"Talia and my wife will also be at church tonight, Kisa. They'll be happy to see you there."

I nodded and offered a small smile. "I hoped they would be, Papa Ivan. I'll . . . I'll be happy to see them too . . . I'm glad you came in today.

I love to see you too . . . I . . ." I trailed off, my throat clogging with emotion.

For a moment, I saw raw pain reflected in his eyes, but he left without another word, and I slumped down on the seat behind my desk.

First things first, I had to organize the fighters and make sure The Dungeon's business was done. Then I would take myself to church and mourn the boy I was supposed to hate . . . but could never find it in my heart to do so.

6

KISA

Serge dropped me off outside our Russian Orthodox Church. I stepped out into the stuffy night, black headdress and long-sleeved, calf-length skirted dress firmly in place as orthodox tradition demands. I quickly ran up the steps and went through the large doors, entering to the sound of the choir singing hymns from their rehearsal room upstairs. The large church was dark, a dark challenged only by the soft glow of candlelight. As always, when I entered this place, I glanced up to the paintings on the ceiling, images of the saints, of Mary holding Jesus.

A hand pressed gently on my shoulder. Looking to my left, Father Kruschev's kind smile greeted me.

"Father," I greeted and pressed a kiss to the back of his hand.

"Are you joining us on the food trucks tonight, child? We are a volunteer down and I could use your service," he asked hopefully.

My heart began pounding at the thought of my defender sitting on the street, holding that jar. Before I had time to consider the consequences of my actions, my head nodded in agreement.

"Excellent," Father Kruschev said, gesturing for me to light a candle. I walked past and he added, "It pleases me to see you so dedicated to helping the needy, Kisa. It will purify your soul."

I offered a tight smile but scurried away as fast as I could. I wasn't trying to save my soul tonight or trying to help the needy. I was serving my own selfish desire, a desire—no, a pressing *need* to see that man again, to see his face, to ask who he was . . . why he was on the street.

Taking a long candle, I lit the wick with that of another and offered a silent prayer to my Luka. May he forever rest in peace.

Moving to the end of the pew, I crossed my chest to the crucifix hanging somberly on the wall. Clasping my hands, I closed my eyes.

Feeling as though my chest would crack, I was transported to the past . . .

Twelve years ago . . .

The New York summer was stifling, the humidity too much to bear. I lay on a towel as the sun blazed down on Brighton Beach. We always came here for the summer. The Bratva kings descended on this little slice of Russian heaven from our houses in downtown Brooklyn. Papa and his "associates" would spend the summer months "discussing and taking care of business" while the kids and mothers would spend it lazing on the sand and eating ice cream.

I liked summer. It was a time I could get away from our rigid life in Brooklyn, a time that "the heirs" wouldn't be called away to learn their craft, a time when Rodion, Luka, and Alik could relax . . . a time when I could hang out with Luka all day long.

Closing my eyes, I smiled at that thought as I soaked up the rays in my secluded spot. Suddenly, a dark shadow fell over me, bringing a brief moment of coolness to my scalding skin.

Cracking my eyes open, hand shielding the sun, my stomach sank when I saw Alik smiling down at me, his board shorts hanging low on his hips.

I didn't say anything, just balanced on my elbows as he slumped down beside me on the towel, his thigh rubbing against mine.

Alik's always harsh narrow eyes surveyed my body, and I no longer felt the warmth of the sun. Shivers ran down my spine as Alik's finger gently trailed down my arm. His nostrils flared, and I froze in fear. Alik always made me feel this uneasy. His eyes tracked me wherever I walked. He would beat up any boy who so much as looked my way. He threatened them and told them I was *his* girl . . . Well, all except one. The one who truly *was* mine, the one whose eyes showed a piece of my soul.

"What're you doing, Myshka?" Alik asked. I swallowed at his pet name for me—*his little mouse.* He'd called me that for years, for as long as I could remember anyway.

I glanced around to see who was nearby, but no one was in sight. Alik's hand suddenly wrapped around the back of my neck, and I gasped in shock.

"I said," Alik pronounced in an angry voice through gritted teeth, "what're you doing? Don't ignore me. I *don't like* to be ignored."

I caught sight of Alik cracking the fingers on his right hand. I also glimpsed a large black-and-blue bruise on his thigh, hidden under his shorts. My gaze snapped to him in surprise. What had happened to him? It looked terrible.

Alik noticed what I was looking at. He quickly covered his bruise, jaw clenching in anger. Alik turned away his head momentarily, and I internally cursed. It must have been his papa. I knew he hurt Alik. I heard his screams coming from his room as we visited his house growing up, then witnessed Alik's bruises, limps, and occasional broken bones after "meeting" with his papa when he'd done something wrong.

Alik was never anything but angry, never anything but hateful . . . except toward me. Something changed in him when I was around. He was never calm, but a softness crossed his eyes when he looked at me.

"I . . . I was laying out in the sun," I said softly, and the iron grip he had on my neck loosened, but he didn't let go. Alik was fourteen, but his incredible strength was more like that of a full-grown man.

Alik dropped his hand. "I'm going to lay with you." I didn't dare question him, so I offered him a timid smile and rested down on the towel.

I lay motionless, then jumped when I felt Alik begin tracing the edges of my bikini top. "Alik, what are you doing?" I asked, trying to bat away his hand.

Alik's hand caught my hand in a grip. "Get off, Myshka. I'm touching you."

"But—"

"Shut up! You'll do as I say," Alik snarled. I did as told, too terrified to fight him off when he commenced tracing the triangle edges of my bra. "So pretty," Alik murmured as tears built in my eyes.

My hands began to shake, yet I just closed my eyes and let Alik touch me, feeling his lips press onto my stomach. I wanted to cry for help, but I couldn't. As stupid as it sounded, I often felt sorry for Alik. I didn't want him to be beaten any more by his father. My complaining would do just that. Physically, I couldn't fight off Alik and I certainly didn't want to anger him further, so I let it happen. After all, it wouldn't be the first time.

"Mmm . . ." Alik moaned as he lapped at my skin, his finger trailing down to the edge of my bikini bottoms. Alik's finger ran along the edge of the material, stealing all my breath from my lungs.

"Alik, don't, please—" I managed to say, but I was interrupted when a voice hissed, "What the hell are you doing, Alik!"

In sheer relief, I looked up and found Luka Tolstoi towering above us, a furious expression on his handsome face.

"Fuck off, Tolstoi!" Alik hissed as he gripped my wrists tighter. Luka's eyes bulged at the action. When I whimpered out loud, Luka gripped Alik by the hair, dragging him to his feet. Luka hit Alik square on the face. Alik stumbled back, bringing up his fingers to his burst lip. He smiled coldly at Luka—a disturbing bloodied smile.

Luka leaned down and pulled me up beside him, protecting me from Alik's view.

"Go," he ordered. I turned to run away, casting a backward glance to see Alik watch me flee. He had an angry expression on his face.

I didn't stick around to see them fight. This happened a lot. Alik would try to take advantage of me, and Luka would be my champion. They would fight, Alik would take a beating off his father, or worse, my father, then life would continue as normal for a few days—until Alik did it again.

I ran until I reached my favorite cove. No one ever came down here. I slumped down against the rock where I always sat, always sat with Luka.

Entranced by the waves crashing on the shore, I didn't hear Luka approach. I jumped as I looked up to see him watching me as he leaned against a rock.

"Luka!" I said breathlessly. "You scared me!"

Luka sighed and ran his hand down his face, moving around the rock to sit beside me on the sand. We said nothing at first, Luka also too focused on the crashing of waves on the sand.

His fingers brushed against my fingers. Then they wrapped around my hand, which he lifted to his lips. My heart fluttered like a humming-bird's wings.

Turning to me, Luka pushed a loose strand of my brown hair behind my ear, then pulled me in close to wrap his free arm around my neck. I relaxed against his warm body and wrapped my arm round his toned waist. He had grown so much lately. He was getting so big and so hand-some that my heart could barely take it.

Luka sighed loudly, his warm breath blowing in my hair. "You have to keep away from Alik, Kisa. He's obsessed with you and he's danger-ous." I tensed in Luka's arms and felt him pull me closer still. "I shouldn't be telling you this, but Alik's papa is training him to be a fighter, an enforcer. He's hard on him, and I can see Alik becoming addicted to the violence. He loves it, Kisa. Stay away from him."

Squeezing Luka tighter, I replied, "I was laying out in the sun. Talia went shopping with your mama. You and Rodion went for lunch with Papa. I didn't think I was in any danger. Alik just has a crush on me. He wouldn't hurt me."

Sighing, Luka pressed a kiss to my head, and I slumped farther against his warm body.

"I don't like him. I can't stand the way he looks at you," Luka said coldly.

Slowly leaning back, I looked into Luka's brown eyes, the left with a smudge of blue in the iris, making them so beautifully unique.

"How does he look at me?" I asked tentatively.

"Like he owns you. Like you belong to him. When you're around, he doesn't focus on anyone else but you."

"And why does that bother you?" I asked shyly, trying hard to swal-low the nervous lump in my throat.

Luka's beautiful gaze met mine and his lips parted with a brief ex-hale. "Because you belong to me, Kisa. You always have." Luka's face thawed and he pointed at my eye, then his left. "You're a part of me, remember? God put a piece of you within me so when we were born, everyone would know we matched."

My skin felt on fire, but I knew it had nothing to do with the burning temperature of the afternoon sun. It had to do with Luka. Luka and that tale his mama and my mama would always tell us.

I loved him. I'd always loved him. I would always love him. Luka, *my* Luka. I was only thirteen, he was only fourteen, but he was so much more than my best friend . . . He was my whole world.

"Luka . . ." I whispered, my soul melting at his words. And his lip hooked into a smirk.

"*Kisa . . .*" he imitated. Then his gaze fell to my lips and my heart raced to an almost impossible speed. "I want to kiss you now," Luka said, all humor dropping from his beautiful face.

"But I've . . . I've never been kissed before . . ." I said, a blush forming on my sun-kissed cheeks.

Luka tilted his head and gave me a crooked smile. "Me neither."

My eyes widened and relief melted in my chest. "You haven't?" I asked in shock.

"Who else would I have kissed?"

I shrugged. "I don't know? You have a lot of girls at church following you around."

Luka laughed and shook his head. Squeezing my shoulders, he leaned down and rasped, "But none of them are *you*." Luka pointed to his eye again. "We match. Why would I want anyone else? Nobody else is you. Long brown hair, blue eyes and tanned skinned beautiful you."

Dipping my eyes, I pushed my toes into the sand, loving the soft feel of the hot grains beneath my feet. When I lifted my long lashes, I met Luka's eyes and whispered, "Okay . . ."

Luka tensed and regarded me so seriously that my stomach began doing flips. His hand released mine and he gently cupped my cheek, hand slightly trembling. "You ready?" he said, licking his lips.

Swallowing my nerves as he moved to only an inch from my mouth, I confessed, "I hope I don't mess this up."

"Not possible," Luka said as he leaned all the way forward and pressed his lips against mine. Everything seemed to go quiet around us and my eyes closed of their own accord. Luka's lips were so soft and, like the pieces of a puzzle, fit perfectly against mine. There was no movement of tongues, no frantic caressing of lips, just two innocent young mouths feeling one another's intimate touch for the first time.

Finally pulling away, Luka wore an expression of shock, making my heart thump too slow. But when his swollen mouth pulled into a happy, besotted grin, I knew mine reflected his own.

Luka's heavy arm pulled me down to curl into his chest, and I stared out at the glistening water in perfect contentment.

"Like I said . . . we match," Luka confirmed—I think to himself. I knew right then and there that I'd given my soul to this boy . . . I knew there'd never be anyone else that ever came close.

"Kisa?" a heavily accented female voice called out from my right. Sitting back in the wooden pew, wiping away the tears from my sacred childhood memory, Mama Tolstoi came into view. She too had dressed in all black—the traditional color of mourning. Not a day had gone by in twelve years that Luka's mama hadn't worn black.

Rising to my feet, I smiled at Mama Tolstoi and embraced her. "How are you, Mama?"

Her brown eyes—the same eyes as Luka's—stared off to look upon Christ on the cross, and she shrugged. "Today is a very hard day, my girl."

My stomach fell and I nodded my head, unable to speak through the threat of tears. Talia joined us at the pew, and I saw her eyes rimmed with red. She could barely meet my gaze. Today was our mutual nightmare.

"He would have been twenty-six today," Mama Tolstoi added. The tears that had been a threat to me finally trickled slowly down my face.

Mama Tolstoi reached out and grabbed my hand. "You two would have been married and perhaps I would have been a grandmama by now." Her eyes gazed over and she added, "He would have loved you your whole life. You would have looked so beautiful on your wedding day and my Luka would have looked so handsome in a tux. Your mama would have smiled down from heaven on that day, Kisa. Her heart would have been so full at the two of you committing to one another under God's eyes."

The picture Mama Tolstoi conjured up might as well have been a dagger to my heart. She squeezed my hands to gain my attention after I had to look away, too upset by what she'd said.

I stared into her tense brown eyes when she gripped my hands tightly and said, "He wouldn't do it, Kisa. He wouldn't have killed your Rodion. My boy, your fated love, would not have taken his best friend's life. He was wronged. Deep down you know this."

Bowing my head, the tears came thick and fast. I believed her words, but I still remembered Rodion's eyes glazed with the new presence of death, Alik stabbed and in hospital.

"Mama, come," Talia said, interrupting her mama's plea for her lost son. Talia moved around her to press a kiss to my cheek. Wrapping her arm around her mama's shoulders, Talia led her out of the church, leaving me alone in the expansively ornate room, all the eyes of the saints staring down at me, balefully watching my despair.

"Kisa?" Father Kruschev said, and I cast my gaze to the back of the room. "Are you still good to join us on the truck?"

Breathing a sigh of relief that Father Kruschev had found something for me to do, I made my way to the back of the church. I turned one more time to look to the altar and whispered, "May God bless your soul, Luka . . . I love you, lyubov moya, *my love* . . . I know I was made for you too . . . We matched . . . you were part of my heart . . ."

7

KISA

"Kisa, you stay in the truck. You were out on the streets last night. Stay in the safety of the truck tonight," Father Kruschev said as I unbuckled my belt and panic flowed through me.

"If it's okay, Father, I prefer to be outside. I need fresh air."

Father Kruschev gave me a sympathetic smile. He believed it was because of Luka's birthday. I confess in part it was, but I couldn't lie to myself. I had to admit that I wanted to see that man again—my defender.

Who was homeless . . .

I closed my eyes and shook myself. I was losing my damn mind!

Zipping up the leather jacket I had brought over my black dress, I stepped out onto the street. It was hot, but without the jacket, Alik would think I was showing too much skin.

Pavel cast me a weary smile. "Back with us tonight, Kisa?"

I shrugged and helped one of the other volunteers load the care packages onto the street. When everyone was set, I scooped up my packages and headed east to where I'd spotted the man sitting on the street.

Passing three homeless people, two men, one woman, I made quick work of dispensing the care packages and turned the corner to the next block, praying I would see the man hunkered down.

Taking a deep breath, I turned onto the street and, in the farthest, darkest corner, saw a large shadow and a jar of glass glinting from the nearby streetlamp.

My heart began to race like I'd run the damn New York Marathon, and checking there was no sign of danger in my vicinity, I moved silently across the street to stand right in front of the man, his dark-gray sweatshirt in place, hood pulled low over his eyes, his body as still as stone. The jar in his hands had coins and random notes in it but it was only filled halfway to the top.

Like last night, I was immediately struck by him. This time his static position allowed me to really assess his frame. He was big. Maybe two hundred and twenty pounds, athletic looking, slightly bulkier than Alik. His black training pants were covered in dirt, and on closer inspection, I noticed his hands were covered in rough, broken skin, dried blood clearly etched into the flesh.

"Hel . . . hello?" I managed to ask, my voice shaking like a leaf in a storm.

He didn't move. He looked like he was barely breathing.

I willed him to look up. I wished him to push back the thick gray material of his hood and look up at me. I had to put a face to the actions of last night. Something in my gut pushed me to make a connection, to get a name . . . a visual, *something.*

But he did nothing.

Glancing over my shoulder, I took in the quiet street and I slowly bent down, warily watching the man the whole time. He didn't flinch. For a time, I wondered if he was deaf. Any noise I made didn't seem to register.

"Excuse me? Are you okay?" I said, holding my breath as I waited for him to look up and reply.

Nothing.

I inched closer. "I'm with the church. You saved me last night. Do you remember? Do you need anything? More food, blankets? Would you please talk to me?"

Still nothing.

Absolutely nothing.

His gray sweatshirt was zipped up, hiding what I guessed was a broad chest. His shoulders were huge, his traps visible through the thick material. His legs were crossed as he clutched the open-topped Mason jar resting on the ground.

My heart beat furiously, my palms sweated, and I found myself reaching out to pull back the hood.

The material slid back like I was unwrapping a Christmas gift. No, it wasn't that safe. I'd observed this man in action. He killed a man without remorse. Reaching out to him would be like putting my hand in a wild animal's cage. I had no idea if he was a threat to me or not.

A cropping of messy sandy-colored hair emerged, followed by the most beautiful chiseled face I'd ever seen. A broad forehead, defined European cheeks, a strong jaw, perfectly full lips, and stubble covering his golden skin.

The man's eyes remained downcast as though he hadn't even felt the material of his hood being pushed back off his head. The only indication that he'd noticed me at all was the slight tightening of his fingers on that jar he was holding.

My breathing quickened and all I could do was stare. I was struck mute and still by his looks, his unkempt raw and rugged looks. My stomach was tightening, my hands began to shake, and my pussy began throbbing.

He was perfect—wild, rough, stern—absolute heart-stirring perfection.

"Do . . . do you need anything?" I asked again through a clogged throat, my voice barely a whisper. "Please, talk to me," I begged, feeling all hope drain from my limbs. "I want to thank you for saving me."

Again, there was no response, and I realized I wasn't going to get anything from this man. I studied his sharply featured face. He looked to be in his mid-twenties, but with dirt and dried blood covering his face, in reality, he could have been older.

I found myself desperate to know his story. Why was he here? Who was he? But his silence pushed me away. I sucked warm air into my lungs in an attempt to calm down. I didn't know why this was so important to me. But I *had* to know why he was collecting money. What was it for? Did he really need help?

I kneeled there for minutes just listening to his deep breathing. Then I sighed and placed the care package of food and blankets at his feet.

"I . . . I'd better go," I announced and slowly got to my feet. I was about to turn around when the man cleared his throat, and I froze.

"*Mnny,*" was all I heard, his gruff, deep voice unintelligible.

I turned to face him. His head was still downcast.

"What?" I asked urgently and bent down until my knees hit the ground, praying he would speak again.

His fingers gripped the jar and he tilted it up in my direction. "Money," he growled.

I visibly shook at the deep timbre of his feral-sounding voice. It was primal, animalistic. I slapped a hand on my chest as I fought to breathe. I dipped my eyes to try and meet his, but his chin lowered until it almost touched his defined, ripped chest. He could sense I was trying to make eye contact, yet he wouldn't let me see him.

Filling my lungs with the humid night air, feeling their ache, I asked, "Money? You need money?"

A grunt told me I had it right, and I bent down farther. "How much?"

Nothing happened for several seconds, before one of his rough hands let go of the jar and he reached into his pocket, pulling out a tattered piece of paper. He held it out for me to take. I reached out for the scrap. When my finger brushed his warm finger, a current like a bolt of electricity shot through my body. I almost leapt back at the sensation. He must have felt it too as no sooner had our fingers touched than he pulled his hand back and tucked it into his pocket.

With trembling hands, I unfolded the crinkled paper and my eyes saw a number: ten thousand.

My eyes locked on the man whose full lips were pursed.

"Ten grand?" I whispered, yet he said nothing. "Ten grand?" I said louder, betraying my disbelief. "What do you need that kind of money for?"

His free hand clenched slowly into a fist and the split skin began to seep with droplets of blood. I was gripped by fear as I watched the droplets fall to the sun-parched ground.

"*Revenge,*" he snarled.

I startled at the severity of his tone, at his rough voice, his voice that caused sparks to ignite deep in my stomach.

"Revenge?" I whispered in confusion, fighting to keep the nerves from *my* voice.

His clenched hand slackened and once again resumed its place on the jar.

"Revenge . . . revenge on the man who lied."

I slowly stood, not knowing what to do, not knowing whether it was right to fund his . . . *revenge*. I wanted to push him for more, but he was back to being a statue. I looked down at the money in the jar. He had about fifty dollars, if that. He was never going to raise that kind of money out here on the streets.

It was hopeless. What he was doing was hopeless.

I ran my hand through my hair and almost laughed. What the hell was I doing? And was I seriously contemplating giving him ten grand? For *revenge?* Up to now, the very thought should have sent me running for the hills, but I was a princess of the Bratva, the only daughter of the Pakhan. Revenge put food on my family's table; it ensured we all lived to see another day. Revenge was my family's M.O., my family's legacy.

And ten grand was nothing to Kirill Volkov's family.

I could get this amount tonight from the safe at the gym. No one but me knew the cash was there. Hell, no one would miss it. It was the gym's Christmas donation to the church. But I was in two minds. It was charity and it was earmarked for the church; however, I was now pretty convinced that giving the money to a single man hell bent on revenge, though not the Lord's original idea of alms, was charity enough. This mysterious man had saved my life. He killed *my* attacker to save *my* life.

It was blood money, payment for a sin against the flesh. What was ten thousand dollars compared to that?

Crouching down, I placed the piece of paper on top of his jar and promised, "I'll be back later tonight."

Turning on my heel, I jogged back to the truck and, from my cell, called Serge to pick me up. Ten minutes later, he arrived and I made my excuses to Father Kruschev.

I jumped in the backseat of the car and Serge turned his body to face me, worry etched on his face. "Miss Kisa, what's wrong? Has something happened?"

Shaking my head, I asked, "Serge, I need a favor. Please, can you take me to the gym, then back here?" I looked up at him through my lashes, the guilt of this request playing heavy on my heart. "But don't tell Papa or Alik."

Serge stared at me and his gray eyes narrowed slightly. "Are you in trouble, Miss?"

I shook my head.

"Is this going against something you were ordered not to do?" Serge pushed further.

"No," I whispered. "It's something I *want* to do for someone . . . something to pay back a debt. But Alik wouldn't be happy. He'd think I would have betrayed his orders."

Serge blew out a long breath but, dropping his head, turned around and buckled his seatbelt. "I hope you're not lying to me, Miss Volkova," he said, and I exhaled a pent-up breath.

"I'm not, Serge. I *swear.*"

Serge gave a curt nod and silently pulled out onto the street. A while later, we arrived at the gym. Serge guarded me as I slipped inside and ran to my office. I quickly opened the safe hidden in the wall, pulled out the cash, and stuffed it into my purse.

After locking my office door, Serge looked at me with suspicion in his eyes, but I brushed past him without saying a word. Dutifully, he followed me outside into the car.

In another twenty minutes, we pulled back in front of the street where the food truck had stopped, only this time everywhere was deserted. The church truck was gone for the night and most of the homeless were asleep under their blankets.

I went to open the door, clutching my purse, when Serge opened his door and stepped out onto the sidewalk.

"Serge? What are you doing?" I asked in panic.

Serge folded his old but still beefy arms over his chest, his black suit looking too tight. "Miss Volkova, I might have agreed to escort you to the gym and back here, even though it wasn't on Mr. Volkov's or Alik's approved list, but there is no way I'm letting you walk around these streets alone at this time of night."

I stepped forward, a pleading look upon my face. "Please, Serge. I need to give a homeless man here some money and I must do it alone."

Serge shook his head in exasperation and stormed forward, gently gripping my bicep in his hand. "Kisa, what the hell is going on?"

I dropped my eyes. "I . . . I . . ." I blew out a sharp breath and met Serge's eyes. "Serge, I was attacked last night while doing the church's work. I was in an alley, alone, where I was told not to go, handing out a care package to one of the regulars, when some guy tried to steal my purse and put a blade to my throat. He . . . he was going to kill me."

Serge turned a deathly shade of white, eyes searching all around us. "Who? Who the fuck attacked a Volkov? I'll kill him!"

"No!" I hissed and shook Serge's arm. "That's what I'm trying to say. Another homeless man came to my defense. Hell, Serge, he ended up killing my attacker. I . . . I owe him, and he needs money. I want to help him in return for saving me."

"Fucking hell, Kisa!" Serge groaned. I could hear how pissed he was from his tight accented voice. "Why the hell didn't you tell your father when you got home?"

"I couldn't, Serge. Alik would've found out. He wouldn't understand that the man saved me. He would think there was more to it. He'd kill the man who saved my life, out of jealousy. You know he forbids me to speak to men." I paused and let that hang in the air. "You know this, Serge. You know what he's like."

Serge checked that the area was clear. "Let's go. You have ten minutes."

I took off in the direction of where the man had been sitting. Turning the corner, I was relieved to see he hadn't moved. His hood was firmly pulled down and his hand was still wrapped around the Mason jar.

"There," I whispered to Serge. His eyes followed the direction in which my finger pointed . . . and he reared back in shock when he laid eyes on the beggar's large frame.

"*That* man? Christ, Kisa!" he asked.

Without giving him an answer, I trotted over the street, motioning for Serge to hang back a bit. He did so, reluctantly.

Cautiously approaching the man, I let my heels click on the asphalt so he would hear my approach. I kneeled down before him and, exactly as before, saw his hands tense. It was as if he were expecting to be struck . . . or he was gearing himself up to fight.

"It's okay . . . It's me, again . . . from before," I said and rolled my eyes at how stupid I sounded. It was pathetic.

I was pathetic doing this!

The man didn't say anything, not that I'd expected him to. So I opened my purse and began pulling out the cash, pushing it into his jar.

I started when I saw his head lift slightly, watching me fill his jar to the brim. In a flash, he reached out and grabbed a tight hold on my hand. I didn't react, afraid Serge would come running. Feeling flushed at the touch of his rough hand, I slotted the last of the money into the jar and picked up the sound of his heavy breathing.

"It's all there, everything you need," I said quietly. Suddenly, the sound of a gunshot rang out in the distance. It made me jump and whip my head around to look at Serge.

"Shit! Stay here!" Serge ordered and took off around the corner to check it out, his Beretta pulled from his jacket and now firmly in his hand.

My attention moved to the man again, whose hand had released mine. He was screwing the top onto the jar whilst rising to his feet. As soon as he was upright, I stood before him and tried to gaze up into his eyes. His head dipped again and I wanted to scream out in frustration.

Tucking the jar under his arm, he backed away. I knew he was about to take off and disappear into the night. But in a moment of desperation, I reached out and grabbed his sweatshirt sleeve, pulling him to a stop. He wrenched his arm back and strode forward, causing me to stumble back in fear. My back slammed against the slick wall and I heard a low, threatening grumble emerge from his mouth, making it clear that I shouldn't have touched him. For a fleeting moment, I feared he would strike me.

Holding my hands out for protection, his broad chest slammed into my palms, all hard, defined muscles beneath his shirt as he pushed forward, my hands beginning to shake. I could feel his thumping heartbeat against my palm—he was jacked up, fuming on the spot. Every part of me filled with fear, made worse by a street light above us which flickered on and off, illuminating his gritted teeth.

"Wait! I'm sorry," I said quickly. The man's body froze. "I . . . I only wanted to see your face . . . before you left. I wanted to see the man who saved me."

The dark hood tilted slowly to the side, and the heavy rise and fall of his chest seemed to increase. He didn't want me to see his eyes. That only made me more curious. Keeping the jar tucked under his left arm, he stopped pushing against my hands. Taking the chance while I could, I cautiously reached up and torpidly pulled back his hood.

My eyes were trained on his face as it came into view—that strong jaw, that unruly sandy-blond hair, his dark stubbled cheeks, high cheek-bones, and . . .

I waited with bated breath for his dipped head to rise and finally meet my eyes. He did so with painstaking slowness, long, dark lashes downcast, like he was fighting against his instincts, like gravity was keeping his eyes pulled down. Until, with nostrils flaring and his breath blowing hard, he lost the battle to keep his anonymity and his eyelids lifted to reveal the dark irises underneath and his hard gaze suddenly bored into my eyes . . .

Then everything stopped—time, the ability to breathe . . . my whole entire world.

Choking on a gasp, my hand flew to my mouth and my legs collapsed beneath me. In a New York minute, my ass hit the hard ground and cold shivers tracked down my spine.

The man's face was blank as he towered over me, knowing I had been felled by his stare. He was raw, stern, and he was glaring at me like a killer before he rips apart his victim, a predator before he devours his prey. There was no emotion in his expression, no compassion for me now sitting on the sidewalk, no thanks for a generous donation. He was as cold as an arctic winter . . . but he was a beautiful monster, and he had no idea why I despaired.

Hearing the kicking of a can down the far side of the nearby alley, the man pulled up his hood, his *disguise* and, in a flash, sprinted away into the darkness.

I failed to pull oxygen into my lungs, wheezing as I tried. *Those eyes* . . . those eyes were imprinted into my brain, they were soldered onto my soul. My voice was stolen by the shock of what I'd just seen.

Brown eyes . . . a pair of rich chocolate-brown eyes, the left iris smudged with a flash of blue . . . the exact blue from my eyes . . . just like . . .

No . . . how could it be?

He died . . . *He* had died over twelve years ago.

That man was a monster, a killer, devoid of emotion, with little ability to communicate. Luka . . . Luka was my best friend, my love, a Bratva boy . . . He died . . .

But . . . But . . . ?

"Kisa!" Serge's voice cut through my panic. Suddenly appearing before me, his arms instantly scooped me off the floor. "What the hell?" he spat out before carrying me back to the car, placing me in the backseat. "Shit!"

He asked me several times what was wrong, but I didn't know what to say, what to believe . . . My mind kept replaying what I had just witnessed.

Brown eyes . . . rich chocolate-brown eyes, the left iris smudged with a flash of blue . . . the same color of my eyes.

"Kisa!" Serge called from the driver's seat as he fired up the car. "What happened? Were you harmed?"

I shook my head in response to his increasingly frantic questions, all the time gripping my seatbelt with fisted, trembling hands.

"Fuck! Then what?" Serge pushed. "Where did the man go? Why are you crying? Shaking?"

I met Serge's eyes with my vacant stare, still too busy replaying the scene in my head to really *see* him. It couldn't be Luka . . . It was impossible . . . He was dead . . .

My heart exploded like a cannon. Serge slammed his heavy fist down on the steering wheel and threatened, "Kisa! You tell me what's wrong or I'm telling your father that you took money from the gym and handed it out on the street to a homeless man like it was fucking Christmas!"

Silence filled the Lincoln. I took a deep breath, wrapped my arms around my waist, and I whispered, "I . . . I think I've just seen a ghost . . ."

8
818

"So are you ready to kill or are you ready to be killed?"

As I sat on the bench in the back room, the cries of hundreds of men shouting their bets beyond the door made my hands shake with nerves. 362 sat in front of me, smiling with a shit-eating grin as he wrapped his hand in a well-soiled white sports bandage.

This guy had been on my ass since I'd arrived a month ago. He was three years older than me, one of the best fighters in his division here at the Gulag, yet he immediately saw me as a threat. Three years his junior, I still matched his size. For a few weeks, the warden took me to a gym, made me train in fight techniques, telling me I would have my first match soon. Every day, I would wake, train, eat, and sleep. I had a routine, but my dreams were plagued with the boy I'd seen in the ring. The one with the dead look in his eyes, his opponent's guts on the canvas. I knew it would be me soon, forced to kill or be killed.

362 stared me down waiting for my answer.

"I'm going to kill whoever the fuck gets in that ring with me," I promised. 362's smile just grew wider at my pissed-off tone. I focused my attention on the white tiled floor, psyching myself up for all that I'd worked for. My legs bounced as the noise from the cage grew louder, and I knew the current fight was coming to a close. My skin was twitching from the shot I'd been getting everyday. My muscles were growing, aching all the time. I was sweating constantly and I was agitated twenty-four-seven, the littlest thing pissing me off.

"You'll become addicted, you know," 362 said, and my eyes slammed to his, fiery rage racing through my veins. His long black hair ran down his back, and he jerked his chin in the direction of the door that led to the cage. "Out there, all the men betting on your strength, on your will to survive. You'll become addicted. You'll live for the kill . . . live to see the life force drain from your opponents' eyes. In that cage we're both Gods and monsters."

My mouth tightened and all my muscles tensed. "Never," I spat back, my voice sounding deeper, rougher.

362 simply laughed.

"This is your first fight. You have no idea how it's going to feel," he taunted.

Fists clenching, I said flatly, "I'm going to do what I need to do to get out of here. That's it. I'm not like you. I won't like it."

362 jumped to his feet and approached me. I stood, the concrete cold beneath my feet, and we met face to face. I was Russian; some Georgian piece of shit wasn't going to best me.

"Not like me?" 362 quizzed. I clenched my jaw and glared into his fucking dead eyes. He smirked, then stepped farther forward until his feet touched mine. "You're gonna end up exactly like me. You're gonna die inside. You're gonna spill so much blood that it's all you'll see. At first, you'll hate it, but with each kill, you're gonna need it more and more, like some fucking drug. You're gonna change. Who you are now will no longer exist. You'll forget who you were. You'll forget anyone you ever loved." 362's lip hooked into a dry smirk, but then his face went blank. "I've been here years." His head tilted forward until his mouth was at my ear, but I held my ground. "And I have no fucking idea who I was before I was brought to this hell. And in time, neither will you."

My breath came in hard pants, but then 362 moved back. Before I'd even seen him raise an arm, he ploughed his fist into my stomach, my legs buckling as I fell to the ground.

"Enjoy your first fight . . . I've seen your opponent. You shouldn't die tonight, as long as you keep your eyes alert and you don't pussy out."

Spit landed on my cheek as I lifted myself off the ground and stumbled onto my feet. A sudden boom of raucous cheering erupted from the cage. My heart began to race. The gun in the basement sounded.

The current fight had ended.

One fighter had died.

The other now knew what it was like to kill.

And it was now my turn.

Footsteps sounded down the hallway outside, bolts unlatched, and the steel door flew open, a guard appearing before me.

"Out," he ordered.

Glancing to the back booth in the locker room, I caught sight of 362 practicing with a sai, his bladed choice of weapon. The thin blade twirled around his fingers as he watched me pass, his face betraying no emotion.

The guard smirked as I strode toward him and held out my hand for him to cuff. My stomach tensed as he looked at me; my skin crawled in disgust.

Once my wrists were bound, the guard dragged me into the dank hallway, pulling me down a set of steep stairs until the door opened and I entered the mob of men surrounding the cage.

My breathing echoed in my ears as I approached the octagonal metal cage where the Gulag's warden waited. Some posts around the outside of the cage were manned by guards taking the spectators' money.

The guard at my back pushed me forward. Then he undid my handcuffs. The warden gripped me by the neck and threw me toward a table full of weapons.

"Chose," he demanded.

Nervously, I looked at what was on offer: blades, axes, sai, chains . . . and at the end, a bladed pair of silver knuckledusters.

"Choose!" The warden sneered. "We don't have all fucking day!"

Reaching forward, I grabbed hold of the spiked knuckledusters, sliding them onto my damp hands, the feeling of steel against my skin so strange.

The guard behind gripped my arm and, turning me around to face the crowd, pointed to the number they'd tattooed on my chest—818. Dozens of eyes focused on me, and money began to change hands.

The guard made me stand for ages, like an animal on show. I surveyed the unfamiliar faces of the crowd, heart thundering in my chest, palms sweating, and the fear of imminent death almost paralyzing my legs. A firing gun sounded and, abruptly, the guard shoved me up some steps and into the claustrophobic octagon. A boy about my age clutched an axe; he was being pushed into the octagon from the opposite side.

My eyes were glued to his. He was about my height, but he was thinner. He too wore only black shorts, the number 591 tattooed across his chest.

As he stumbled into the cage, piss ran down his legs. I could see by the shaking of an axe in his right hand that he was terrified.

The cage doors slammed shut. The warden stood outside and banged on the cage wall, the sound sounding like thunder. "Only one of you comes out alive. No fucking around. No rounds. No breaks. Just kill."

My eyes widened as I took in his words, but I knew this was what I was here for. I had to kill this boy in order to survive.

The boy looked across at me; by the way he stood, I knew he couldn't fight. But my papa had taught me from a young age how to take care of myself. I knew how to fight. I knew how to inflict pain . . . I knew how to kill.

A gun sounded, and the joint erupted. Men were hammering the cage like hungry animals; they shouted things I couldn't make out.

The warden bellowed for the fight to begin and adrenaline filled my muscles. My opponent stood frozen on the spot, his eyes roving the sick crowd in fear.

My pulse beat fast, the dull thumping deafening in my ears, drowning out the roar of the spectators.

"Move!" the warden screamed. He'd lost his shit. Our two guards stood at the doors behind us, rifles aimed straight at our heads. Self-preservation took hold; I moved to the center of the ring, my opponent receiving a hit on the head by his guard. The boy stumbled forward, crashing into my chest. The volume of the crowd dramatically rose as our bodies collided. Taking advantage of my stronger stance, I punched out my right hand and hit the boy square on his jaw. Blood showered the boy's face. Dazed, the boy fell back, hitting the floor. Seeing my chance, I straddled his waist and struck him again on the face. Surprise registered on the boy's face as blow after blow rained down on him. Teeth tumbled to the ground and his flesh tore under the spiked edges of my knuckledusters.

"Please . . . " the boy whispered, his quiet voice sounding like a foghorn in the middle of the insanity beyond the cage, "Don't kill me . . . I don't want to die . . . I'm scared . . . "

My gut twisted upon hearing his plea and my shoulders sagged. I was exhausted and out of breath. Glancing around the dimly lit dingy room, my eyes drank in the howling, bloodthirsty crowd, and my stomach recoiled in disgust. Grown men. Grown men cheering for kids to shred each other, to tear each other to death.

Wiping a bead of sweat from my brow with the back of my bandaged hand, I rolled off the whimpering 591 and staggered to my feet. The guards raised their guns at my movement. I hit the cage's metal mesh, which groaned as if it were in pain.

"What are you doing, boy?" one of the guards asked. Everything seemed to slow down, my pulse throbbing too slow.

The warden circled the cage until his angry face was inches from mine on the other side of the metal. "Get back and finish him!"

Nausea built in my throat as I looked at my guard's hard face. He had to be in his fifties and he was built like a tank. The barrel of his gun was aimed squarely at my forehead. "You have five seconds to get back over there and kill that pussy, or I'll shoot you both."

I heard a similar threat being issued from the opposite side of the cage. Hearing a loud scream, I turned just in time to see 591 charging at me with his axe raised high. Though shocked at this move, I dodged out of the way and dove to the ground—just in time to see 591 crash into the metal of the cage, axe slamming hard against the steel links.

He whipped around to confront me, eyes crazed, the whiteness of gritted teeth shining through his bloodied mouth. 591 panted like a rabid animal. I knew then what had to be done.

My fight response kicked in, sending a surge of energy through my whole body. As 591 charged me, I dropped and wrapped a leg around his calf. 591 lost his balance. As he fell to the ground, without pause, I jumped on his back. I raised my knuckledusters, spiked blades pointing down, and with a fast punch and a deafening roar, lodged the blades into the bottom of his skull. Immediately, 591's body slackened beneath me.

A gun fired and the crowd roared as blood began gushing from 591's wound onto the concrete floor. Shocked, I couldn't move. Staring down, I saw that my bladed weapon was still embedded in his skull. I pulled the blades out, and vomit spilled from my mouth as chunks of bone and flesh came away with them.

A hand roughly gripped my neck, hauling me to my feet. A heavily booted foot pushed 591; his corpse rolled over. 591's lifeless eyes stared up at me, tearing at my guilty heart. I'd killed. I'd taken a person's life.

Staggering forward aided by a push on my back, I was once again dragged through the crowd of men, this time exchanging cash. My guard flung me on the floor of the locker room at the back of the basement.

The steel door creaked when slammed shut. I worked on taking long, deep breaths as I struggled with the pit of pain in my stomach. A pair of bare feet came into view. When I looked up, 362 towered over me, stretching his muscles and gripping his favored sai with both hands.

"Block it out," he ordered.

Reluctantly, I raised my head and sat back on my heels, closing my eyes at the sight of blood spattered on my skin. When I opened them again, 362's attention was fixed on the steel door, but he threw a glance my way and added, "You have to block out the kill. Block out anything that stops you from surviving."

I shook my head slowly, clenched my fists, and retched when a piece of bone fell from the knuckleduster and clattered to the ground.

"Block it all out. Survive. Take the beatings. Take the shots. Take the torture, the electric shocks to make you forget your past. Let them turn you. Let them fuck with your head. Let them turn you into a monster. Let them turn you feral." 362 paused and added, "And anything else the guards want to throw your way when they enter your cell in the middle of the night. That's the only way to make it through the Gulag. The only way to stay alive."

The steel door burst open again. Rolling his neck, 362 spun on his heel and gripped his favorite black sai tighter. A cloud of darkness suddenly masked his face. It was a blank, dangerous expression that made shivers run down my spine. 362 strode into the hallway, no cuffs on his wrists, no guard forcing him into the cage. I stared numbly at the door. Then I heard the crowd burst into cheers. They loved him. Those fucked-up men loved 362.

Dragging myself to my feet, I stepped up to the grimy mirror in the stinking box of a bathroom that reeked of shit and piss, just like the rest of this fucking hellhole. I wiped the glass, a bloodied streak from my sopping bandages leaving its mark.

As I stared at my reflection, I couldn't find the boy I'd always seen. Instead, I thought of my parents, but their images were distorted, so I couldn't picture their faces. Panic ran through my bones as I tried to remember their features. But it was no use. My memory wouldn't let me. Next, I thought of—, of him, my friend lying on the ground, his life taken by a dagger to the heart. But I couldn't picture his face. I couldn't even vaguely remember what he looked like. Hands gripping the sides of my head, I squeezed my eyes shut, memories steadily slipping from my mind.

The drugs. The drugs were making me forget. They were fucking with my mind. I was remembering less and less, day by day.

"No!" I screamed. Punching out, I smashed the edge of the mirror, a shard of glass shattering on concrete. I couldn't see them! I couldn't picture their faces!

Concentrating hard, I tried to picture her . . . my solnyshko . . . but she appeared blurred. All I could remember was a featureless face crying and colorless eyes staring at me in disappointment. The sight of it made my insides twist in fear . . . And then I saw him. The one who put me in here. The liar. He had no face, nothing to recall but his name now scrolling across my mind—Alik Durov. He was the reason I was here in this shithole. I clung to that name, even as everything else drained from my memory.

It was like doors slammed shut, their entryways forever sealed. My brain started shutting out my past, shutting out everyone from my past, shutting out emotion, shutting out any feeling of guilt for killing 591.

"Block it all out. Survive," *I told myself.*

362's order ran through my mind, muscles tensing as the boy in the mirror steadily filled with numbness. The boy in the mirror quickly became 818 from the Gulag: location unknown.

I blocked it all out. I took the beatings, the drugs, the torture . . . and every-thing else they threw at me.

I did everything I was ordered to do.

And I survived.

Gulping in the sticky Brooklyn air, I jerked awake, body drenched with sweat as I slept behind a dumpster, still gripping tightly to the jar of cash clutched to my chest.

My dream ran through my mind, head pounding with the images. Unzipping my sweatshirt, I ran my fingers over my chest and traced the tattooed numbers. *818.* My eyes squeezed shut. I saw the kid still look-ing into the mirror.

A pain ripped through my skull as I tried to remember, the drugs now slowly wearing off.

ARGH!

Revenge, I thought. *Forget the motherfucking dream and get your revenge.* Zipping up my sweatshirt, I glanced up at a dark but lightening sky.

It was morning.

Jumping to my feet, I stepped from behind the dumpster, cracking my stiff neck and focused on the dockside gym. A light was on inside, cars entering the underground parking garage to the side of the building.

Blood searing in my veins, I pulled my hood over my head, pounded over the asphalt and pushed open the doors. The weak dick from before was behind his desk. He shit himself again, pulling the same gun on me *again.* I stormed to the desk without even flinching.

The barrel of the gun pressed against my chest as I slammed the jar of cash on the wood. The dick's eyes shot down to the jar, then back up to me. Sliding off the stool his fat ass was perched on, he banged on a side door.

"Yiv!"

My eyes bored, my jaw tensed, and my palms still clutched the jar.

The side door suddenly flew open. Yiv walked through, a pissed scowl aimed at the guy behind the desk.

"What?" Yiv spat, then saw me standing at the desk. His expression changed on a dime, and he hesitated for a minute before he asked, "You got the money?"

I pushed the jar out in front of me and gave him a single nod. Yiv stepped forward and, without counting the cash, pushed the jar at the other guy. "Take it to the boss' office."

The guy disappeared, and Yiv lifted the counter. He flicked his chin, signaling me to come through. I followed behind Yiv, savoring the sound of the punching of bags being hit and the grunts of men in training. My skin prickled with the need to train—a driving need to get back to building my body into the honed weapon it had become, to maintain my focus and kill.

The steel of my bladed knuckledusters weighed that bit heavier in my pocket, reminding me of the task I had to perform, of the fights I had yet to win.

Yiv led me to a room filled with about a dozen men, but my eyes sought out only one . . . and there he was, dead center, his packed body training on the salmon ladder. His fists were wrapped around a metal bar and he used his upper body strength to climb up the rungs as effectively as anyone I'd seen.

I made sure my hood was pushed low over my head.

"You get a trainer, you get the use of the gym all day, and you turn up whenever the fuck we tell you to. You eat here, take whatever the hell we want to pump you with and you don't complain," Yiv said, leading me to a back room.

He glanced back at me, seeing my attention on Durov, and smirked, pointing his way. "That's my fighter, Alik 'The Butcher' Durov. He's the one everybody wants to beat. Five time champion. The guy is a fucking king in that cage. That mean bastard will never die."

My nostrils flared with rage as Durov dropped to the floor. Taking out a dagger, he turned to a dead pig hanging upside down on a hook from the rafters. It only took a few perfectly precise strikes for Durov to slice the pig in half. He stood back, chest heaving, eyes lit with that addictive fire of violence, his blade dripping blood at his feet.

That bastard will *die*, I thought.

As if sensing my fury, my hatred for the man I'd vowed to destroy, Durov's psychotic stare tried to meet mine, but my hood covered my eyes. His eyes narrowed as he stared me down.

A hand grabbing my shoulder made me react. I gripped the wrist with my right hand, spun around, and slammed the attacker against the wall, his arm almost breaking as I wrenched it up his back.

"Hey! It's Yiv!" a muffled voice said. It was the trainer, so I let go and stepped back. Yiv turned and ran his eyes up and down my body. Shaking his arm, he declared, "You're quick. Good. You'll need to be quick here in The Dungeon."

I didn't give a response, and Yiv carried on down the hallway. Still feeling Durov's eyes on me, I glanced back and he was resting his arms on the ladder, watching me.

Watch me, I thought. *See the man who is going to slaughter you.*

Yiv led me to a back room where a drunken man was lounging in a seat, clutching a bottle of vodka in one hand. Yiv cursed and kicked the sleeping drunk's leg. "Get the fuck up!"

The drunk snorted and woke, his bleary eyes immediately landing on me. "What?" he asked in a heavy accented voice.

Yiv reached forward and yanked him to his feet, the half-empty bottle of vodka smashing on the floor. Yiv turned to me, the drunk's unfocused eyes meeting mine, and Yiv pointed to the trainer. "Viktor, you got a fighter."

The trainer—Viktor—seemed to hear this. Brushing aside Yiv, Viktor stood right in front of me. My lip curled as the older man gripped my muscled arms, walking around me to check I was in good shape.

Viktor's eyes narrowed. "Your name?"

I stared blankly at the floor. "I have no name."

Yiv backed away to the exit door and I could hear his fucking condescending laugh. "You have a week and half of training until the contest. You report here every morning and don't leave until we say you can. You signed up for this. We now own you. You belong to The Dungeon. You leave, we kill you. You talk of this place, we kill you."

"Understood," I replied.

Yiv laughed again and looked at Viktor, then at me. "He's never had a fighter make it past round one."

Zipping open my sweatshirt, keeping my eyes down low, I saw Yiv's smile drop from my peripheral vision as he drank in my ripped, scarred, and tattooed body.

"He's never had a fighter like me before. I bring death."

Yiv, for a brief moment, looked worried, then immediately walked out the door. Hearing Viktor snort behind me, I swerved, fisted his shirt, and rammed him against the wall. His face reddened as he tried to say something.

"What—"

"You listen to me and you listen good. I don't fucking need you. I'll win this alone. I'll kill Durov alone."

Viktor's eyes suddenly lit up. "You want Durov?"

"It's the only reason I'm here," I growled.

Viktor tried to smile but I dropped him to the floor. Reaching into my sweatshirt pockets, I pulled out my knuckledusters and pushed them on my fingers; I immediately calmed. These weapons were a part of me.

Viktor rolled to his feet, his eyes huge as he stared at my chest, the color draining from his cheeks. "Wh-what did you s-say your n-name was?" he stuttered. Shrugging off my sweatshirt, I kept my eyes down and spotted a shelf filled with supplies. Walking across the room, I picked up the jar named "Eye Black," dipped my fingers into the grease and smeared the black under my eyes.

Stretching out my arms, feeling the familiar exercises loosening my limbs, I repeated, "I have no name."

"No name? What has anyone ever called you?" Viktor asked from behind me.

818, I thought, but I dared not say the number out loud. Catching my reflection in mirrors lined against the wall, I saw the tattoo forcibly etched on my back by the guards. Dropping to the floor, I started with a few reps of push-ups.

When Viktor's feet came into view, I paused briefly to say, "Raze. The only name I've ever been called is *Raze*. Because I'd *raze* any fucker that got in my way."

9

KISA

"Have you paid off the Feds? Are the high rollers on board for all three nights?" I asked Talia through my cell as I got out of the backseat of the car and headed inside the training gym to my office.

"Yes and yes. Everything's arranged." She bristled. Talia was efficient and equally as competent as me at arranging fight nights. "We're still a fighter down. How are we doing with that?"

I pinched my nose as I slumped behind my desk. "I'm on it today. Yiv mentioned a buy-in, some mysterious big psycho who came in showing an interest, so I'm going to try and follow up on that."

Talia helped Ivan with the finances, the sponsors and the men that chased up any outstanding debts. She never attended the fights. After losing her brother years ago, she couldn't bear to be around violence and death.

"Good," Talia said in relief. "Now that's all done with, how are you feeling after the other night? You seemed quiet last night at church, too quiet I thought."

My stomach tightened at her words and I sighed, tracing the knots of wood on my desktop with my fingertip. "I'm fine, Talia. You know why I was quiet. You were too. That date . . . it's too hard . . . ." I paused, then added, "I feel like my heart breaks more and more each year. People say that time heals, but it's bull. Time just makes me miss him more, and that ache in my stomach that's been here for years just grows stronger."

Talia's heavy sigh echoed on the phone. "I know. I hate that day every year. Mama never stops crying and Papa never helps; he hides away in his office. It's always such a fucking mess, and they all look to me to fix it somehow, like I can change what he did. Like I can bring him back from the dead."

"Yeah," I said, not knowing what else to say.

Only silence from the other end of the phone came through.

"You okay, Tal?" I asked.

I could have sworn I heard a sniff, a slip of emotion from my normally ice-cold friend, but Talia's brightened voice soon came through the line. "Always okay, Kisa, always. You know me. I have thick Russian skin. So," she said, shifting the conversation, as if those words had never been spoken between us. "Seen any more of your homeless defender? I know you went with Father Kruschev again last night." Talia's voice was hushed, like she was hiding our discussion from anyone who might be listening.

I crooked my head around, making sure the door was closed to the busy gym. Then Talia picked up on my silence.

"What's happened?" she asked, a hint of excitement entering her voice. "I know that pause of silence by now, Kisa!"

Taking a deep breath, I blurted, "I saw him, again, last night."

"Kisa!" Talia reprimanded. "You didn't! If Alik finds out . . . fuck, he'll go crazy!"

I squeezed my eyes in panic and blurted, "And I gave him ten grand . . . "

I was positive a tumbleweed rolled through the office during Talia's silence on the other side of our conversation.

"Talia?" I called, unsure if she'd hung up.

"Kisa . . . what the hell's going on?"

"He saved my life. And he told me he needed ten grand. It's nothing to us, Talia. You know that. So I gave him the cash."

"You just gave it? No questions?" Talia asked, incredulous. "It was probably for drugs!" she proclaimed.

A chill ran through my body, balking at her attitude. "No—"

"No? You mean you know what he wanted it for?" she interjected.

"He said it was for . . ." I swallowed, knowing how damn dark it would sound.

"What?" she pushed.

I took a deep breath and said, "Revenge . . . " I let that word hang in the air. Even at a distance, I could feel Talia's worry, her concern for my safety and possibly my sanity.

"Revenge?" she said quietly. "On who, for fuck's sake?"

"I don't know," I whispered, feeling foolish. "But I . . ."

"But you what?"

"I believed him. I felt he needed it. There is just something about the guy that called to me. I can't explain it. I feel . . . drawn to him . . ."

"Kisa! What is it with you and this guy? You're acting insane!"

How could I explain? How can anyone ever explain the inexplicable?

The image of the hood pulling back and the reveal of his eyes had replayed endlessly through my mind. My mouth opened to tell Talia that he had the same eyes as . . .

But I stopped myself. I couldn't talk about Talia's dead brother. I couldn't tell her this man had the same eyes . . . eyes that matched mine. I'd even looked up the condition early this morning when I couldn't sleep—Heterochromia. It was a common eye condition. But *his* eyes were the exact color of *Luka's*, the placement of the condition, that smudge of my blue on the upper left iris . . .

Christ! Maybe I *was* going insane! The pressures of living this life causing me to breakdown.

"Kisa?" Talia's voice was lighter now. "Is this about marrying Alik? Are you acting this way because the plans are starting to turn into reality? Are you sure you want this?"

A nervous laugh bubbled up my throat as Talia trailed off, and strangely, tears sprang to my eyes. "I have no choice, Talia. You know it's true. It's the perfect marriage, one my father and all the Bratva are making sure happens. It's just . . ."

"What?" Talia asked.

A salty teardrop trickled down my cheek. I wiped it away, chastising myself. "I always dreamed I'd marry . . ."

"Luka," Talia responded in sympathy.

"I know. I'm stupid. I'm twenty-five and acting like a child."

"No," Talia said softly, "you simply have a broken heart. Sometimes they never heal. But . . ."

I sucked on my bottom lip to stop from sobbing out loud. "What?" I whispered.

"Sometimes when a heart breaks, it starts to let in the light."

"Tal." I cried quietly, this time allowing my tears to flow.

"Look, Kisa, I know how you felt about my brother." She hiccupped a sob and added, "And he loved you too. It was like you were only in each other's world. No one else existed. It was strange for being so young."

My heart plummeted again.

"But I have to let it go. I have to marry Alik. That's what you're saying, right?"

"No! I mean, yes. I mean . . ." Talia cleared her throat. "You've got to move on, for your own happiness, but it's no secret I don't like Alik. He's way too possessive of you, Kisa. He . . . he scares me. I'm afraid, for *you*."

My body tensed, feeling the urge to defend Alik, to protect him. "But he needs me, Tal. He wouldn't cope if he didn't have me. Imagine what he'd be capable of if I wasn't around to calm him down."

"You know how fucked up that sounds, don't you?" Talia replied in dismay.

"But it doesn't make it any less true. This is all I've known for so long. I don't know how to be without him anymore."

Talia sighed. "Okay, Kisa. You're old enough to make up your own mind."

I nodded even though she couldn't see me.

"Right, well, I've got to get more work done. The Chechens are attending this season. That means big money, Kisa, which means there can be no fuck-ups. Keep me updated on the new fighter. We're cutting it close. Papa's concerned."

"I will. Speak later, Tal."

I hung up the phone and leaned back in my chair. A knock sounded on my door. "Come in!" I shouted, and Yiv poked his head round the door.

"Miss Volkova, we got the buy-in. He's training with Viktor now."

A huge feeling of relief washed through my body, and I grabbed my pen. "Thank God! Have we got a name?"

Yiv shrugged. "Viktor said he calls himself *Raze*."

My eyes darted up from the Post-It note, and I frowned at Yiv. "Raze?"

"Said he didn't have a name. Just called himself Raze." Yiv opened the door. "He's in the weights now if you want to talk to him."

I nodded my head and added him to the roster at the lowest level. Newbies, unless approved by my father, did the early fights, the fights for less money. And it wasn't uncommon for fighters to have no names; sometimes they preferred to use an alias. The only people insane enough to fight to the death were murders, serial killers, those repaying a debt to their sponsors, or the truly messed up. I was sure Alik crossed into a few of these categories . . . which was a disturbing thought all in itself.

Feeling I needed a walk, I decided to go check out this new fighter. Opening the door, I walked through the small, private weight rooms where the fighters were training. I was proud of the quality of this year's contestants. The men were more ruthless and brutal than any we'd been able to secure in recent years.

The Dungeon's Championship reputation grew year by year in the dark world of underground gambling rings. The Dungeon had more prestige than ever, which equaled more money. The fact that my father's Byki were here day and night until the gym closed, lining the gym walls in their masses and packing AK rifles, said everything about the mental state of this year's crop of fighters. Papa didn't want any more pre-fights breaking out, no more early deaths—which did happen each year. And he definitely didn't want me endangered, which looking at what some of the contestants had done in their pasts, well, it was a real possibility.

Keeping my head down from the lustful glares of the fighters, I headed to the back room where the newbie was training. Hearing the distinct sound of grunts and the metal to metal of weights clanging, I entered the door and was greeted with the domineering sight of a large man's back, a back full of scars and burns, red marks and raised white skin. He had a huge tattoo across his bulking shoulder blades, which read, "RAZE."

The new fighter was lifting weights, his ripped and cut muscles tensing and flexing. He was in great condition. A perfect addition to The Dungeon.

Viktor noticed me walk in. He moved from in front of the fighter, counting his reps on a clipboard, to greet me. "Miss Volkova," Viktor said, coming to stand next to me as I kept watching this Raze.

The fighter didn't stop lifting, and I didn't stop staring. I tried to open my mouth to say something to Viktor—about the fighter's progress, his stats, if he'd be any good in the cage, what he'd chosen as his weapon—but I was struck dumb watching him lift such impossible weight with a fierce intensity. My thighs tightened as I felt moisture pool between my legs.

I cleared my throat and ran my hand over my forehead. I had no idea what was coming over me lately, but lusting after another man was not . . . *normal*. I was turning into a whore.

Viktor nudged me and held out the clipboard for me to read. As I ran my eyes over Raze's statistics, they bulged. I snapped my gaze to Viktor, who raised his eyebrows and nodded his head. The only other fighter we had who worked as hard was . . . Alik.

I surveyed the tattoos and scars, which were all over this man's back. I flinched at some of the images: laughing evil clowns, what can only be described as satanic and demonic lettering spelling the word "RAZE." His tattooed name alone told me the type of man this was—lethal, unforgiving, a born killer. But it was the tattoos beneath that had me entranced: what looked to be hundreds and hundreds of tally marks littering the bottom of his back, then continuing around his sides and, I guessed, over his stomach too.

I swallowed hard when I speculated what those tally marks represented. Deaths. They were counts of the people he'd killed.

A strange feeling crept into my stomach as I thought about it for the first time. This was somebody who could rival Alik. Alik was so strong and infallible in the cage. I'd never thought about him losing a match; the possibility never even crossed my mind. But this guy, at least on paper, he really could be a genuine contender.

I had to tell Papa. Raze didn't belong in the lower ranks. If he could fight as well as he could lift, he should be a headliner. It would help if we could get an idea about his past, the story behind his name.

"Raze?" Viktor called as I made notes on my pad, and I heard a dumbbell clatter to the floor. "You need to meet Miss Kisa Volkova. She runs things around here, for her father. He runs the whole show."

Raze turned to face me; it felt as if a northern wind had gusted in. He pulled my attention. Scribbling the last note on the paper, I looked up to see a ripped and cut muscled man standing panting, salty sweat dripping to the floor. His eyes were downcast, Eye Black smudged underneath each one to disguise his eyes. But like a spell, a will for him to lift his gaze, his head lifted and I found myself staring into a pair of brown eyes, the left iris smudged with a hint of blue . . . my blue, the color from my eyes . . .

"Y-you?" I whispered as I drank in this man. It was him. *Him!* All six-four, two twenty pounds of him. Tanned skin covered in scars, marks, and sadistic tattoos. I saw the recognition flash across his eyes, but in a second, his stare was numb again, like he was blocking me out, like he was blocking everything out, except the rage he kept hidden. I grew breathless as his packed abs and pecs tensed under my scrutiny, his bulging thighs clenched at my attention, and his traps danced as his jaw tightened the more I stared.

And his face? Finally, I could study his face in the light, and my God . . . he was beautiful. Without meaning to, my lips parted in want and a silent hiss slipped out. Raze's stern face was covered in dark stubble, three large scars marring his weathered skin, one down his cheek, one angled down his forehead, and one slashed under his left eye. But they didn't make him any less handsome. *No*, Raze couldn't be described as *handsome*. Rough, raw, dark, dangerous, intimidating . . . the opposite of handsome. But I couldn't tear my gaze from him regardless.

And then those brown eyes with a hint of blue bored so fervently on my chest, a chest panting a shade too hard, betraying the effect he was having on my traitorous body. My nipples became erect, far too sensitive against the material of my camisole. The brush of the fabric sent jolts of pleasure to my clit, and I had to fight the urge to drop my hand to my pussy, from palming the flesh of my breasts.

And then one thought broke through the trance, through the hellish spell I'd found myself under. I had given him ten grand. He was the buy-in. I had given him the money to get his revenge . . . and he'd bought into my Dungeon.

"Viktor, leave us alone," I ordered rather too harshly, my demand met with silence.

I stared at Raze and he stared back, the tension palpable between us. "Viktor, leave," I commanded again.

"Miss Kisa—"

"Viktor! Leave!" I shouted. I heard Viktor sigh and exit the training room, slamming the door.

My heart pounded like a drum in my chest, so hard I feared Raze could hear it in the few feet between us. His sheer size was intimidating, his cold stare bone chilling, and I had to fight the urge to think of Luka.

But this man was *not* Luka.

Steeling my nerves, I asked, "Why are you here?"

Raze's eyes flared and his lips tightened, but no answer was forthcoming.

Anger infused my blood and I stepped closer, watching his muscled chest tense, and I snapped, "Why?"

A growl ripped from his throat and he closed in on me until I smelled that fresh snow smell of his skin mixed with the scent of his workout.

I gasped as Raze's large frame loomed over me, causing me to stumble back until my shoulders hit the wall. I darted my gaze up to meet his and held my breath.

His brown eyes darkened as he stared down at me and his face flushed red.

"Raze—"

"Revenge." The ropes and veins in his traps bulged in tune with his reply.

"On who?" I whispered, watching a small bead of sweat running from the bottom of his throat down his chest, before fluttering my eyes up to refocus on his mouth. His lips were full, his cupid's bow defined.

Raze's palm slapped on the wall above me, caging me in, and his head lowered even farther, my breasts heaving at the proximity. He inhaled deeply, drinking in my scent. His face flushed and, for a moment his eyes closed, a frown pulling on his forehead.

Raze began shaking, his muscles twitching, and I could see a storm brewing in his acrimonious expression as his eyes snapped back open.

"On the man who lied. On the man who wronged me. Condemned me. And turned me into *this*!" He reared back, slapping his chest. Raze walked to the punching bag and slammed his fist into it so hard that the heavy chain from the ceiling groaned. Raze set to a short pace, back and forth, back and forth, and I remained still against the wall, just watching him.

"What? What has he turned you into?" I asked cautiously and immediately regretted the question when Raze seemed to exude resentment. Shivers raced down my spine.

Raze stopped dead and ran his bandaged hands down his face. His attention immediately shot to me, and he said, "This killer. This monster who needs blood, needs to kill, maim, slaughter."

My hands were now shaking, gaze fixed on the tally marks. Raze obviously caught my stare. Moving to the bench, he picked up a steel knuckleduster, well used if its look was anything to go by, yet the spiked sharp blades glinted in the florescent light. A whimper escaped my mouth.

Raze stalked over my way, slipping the knuckleduster on his hand, and set me in his sights. Fear froze me to the spot. I tried to swallow back a cry. Raze didn't stop until he was almost on top of me, his hands fisted at his sides, the right clad in steel lifting to run over his abs, his abs covered in uneven, straggly inked tallies.

"My kills," he announced coldly, his voice sounding like he'd swallowed broken glass. The fear I harbored deep inside intensified. I focused on his mouth, his face, and saw nothing but rage. It was as though any emotion but hatred had been cast out. No humanity was evident in his stare . . . but those eyes . . . those eyes!

"Over six hundred," Raze suddenly added, dragging me back to the here-and-now. I followed the trail of his hand and realized what he'd just said.

"Six hundred?" I gasped.

Raze's lip hooked into a humorless smirk. His spiked hand fisted, and I heard his knuckles crack as he leaned in. "*Over.*"

Raze's feet edged forward again, and he held out the spike and brought it toward my cheek. I couldn't breathe as the metal drifted closer to my skin, only then to witness Raze drag it down his bare chest and abs to a tally comprising three marks.

Slamming the spike into his skin, blood instantly pooled, and he dragged it down to make a messy, uneven line. All the time, he didn't remove his brown eyes from mine. I wanted to cry. I wanted to stop him from harming himself. I wanted to gaze into those eyes and pretend I was here with Luka. My kind, beautiful Luka, brown eyes with a blue smudge that matched mine.

But this man, this *Raze*, was fucked up. *Too* fucked up.

He wasn't my Luka, no matter how hard I wished he was.

Releasing the spike from his torso, Raze directed his hand my way, and I flinched, bringing up my hand, which clutched my pad and pen, to defend my face. The pen was ripped from my grasp. Raze placed the plastic between his teeth and snapped it in half, spitting shattered pieces to the floor. Ink began to drip on his skin. Guiding the broken pen to the new gash, Raze stabbed it along the cut and rubbed the ink into the open wound.

"Raze!" I shrilled. I fought the urge to knock the pen from his hands. But Raze soon released it from his grip and, lowering his mouth to my ear, said, "Another kill . . . *your* kill, the one I killed for *you*."

As I choked back my shock, Raze backed away. He threw his knuckleduster back to the bench, and resuming a vacant concentration, he lifted the dumbbells and continued his routine.

Slapping my chest, I worked on breathing. What the hell had just happened? Who *was* this man?

Gripping my notebook, just as I was about to leave, a burning question spilled from my lips. "Who exactly is it you want revenge on?"

Raze paused, only for moment, and without facing me, uttered, "Durov. Alik Durov from Brooklyn, New York. Revenge. *Kill.*"

Icicles ran down my spine as he hissed out that name like he was spitting out poison, and I ran out of the room, ignoring Viktor who was leaning against the wall just outside, and slammed the door of my office. Turning the key in the lock, I made sure no one could come in.

Reaching into my desk, I grabbed my cell and called Talia . . . which went straight to voicemail.

When the beep sounded, I hushed out, "Talia! Call me back. It's urgent. I need to talk."

Slamming my cell closed, I sat behind my desk, mind starting to replay what had just happened. Raze was disturbed. Cold. Unfeeling . . .

And I was insanely and irrevocably attracted to him. His fresh snow smell, his rugged and raw face, his ripped and cut body . . . the muscles, the tattoos . . . the way he growled when he talked, but . . .

It was the eyes. I was losing my mind over those eyes.

And he wanted revenge on my fiancé. Knowing Alik, it could be for any number of things. Alik had built up an army of enemies over the years.

What if he killed Alik? What if this year Alik lost?

I waited for the sorrow, the pain, but I only felt numb.

"For fuck's sake, Kisa!" I reprimanded myself, feeling turned on from thinking about Raze, of impossibilities.

Yet still I found myself wrenching open my desk's top drawer. Digging under the files, my hand found a cold edge of metal. Making sure the blinds were closed, I pulled out the old tarnished frame and stared at the picture inside, running my hands over the glass.

The picture was perfect: two children, one girl, one boy, one summer beach. The boy's arm draped over the girl's shoulder as they smiled for a close-up. Her eyes were light blue, his eyes the richest of brown, but the left iris was smudged with the girl's light blue.

They matched.

God made them this way so they would recognize themselves as meant for one another when they were born, so they would always find each other no matter where they were on Earth.

I looked up and stared at the door, picturing those same eyes on a killer in another room in my gym . . . Raze? Luka? A warm feeling washed over me at the possibility. But no, surely it was . . .

Impossible?

It was *impossible* . . . right?

My cell phone rang. Talia!

Flipping the cell open, I sighed and said, "Talia . . . I think I fucked up."

10

RAZE

My muscles ached with the weight of the dumbbells, adrenaline still pumping through my veins.

One . . .

Those eyes.

Two . . .

That smile.

Three . . .

That face.

Four . . .

Those tits.

Five—

Throwing the heavy dumbbells to the floor, I stomped to the bench, slipped on my knuckledusters, and walked to the leather-bound post. I worked at my strikes, that fucking euphoric feeling of the spikes slicing into the post taking over.

I visualized a torso, a face, the fucking smug-ass face of Alik Durov, but that woman, the boss of *The Dungeon,* her scent wrapped around me, tugging at my attempt to concentrate. Finally, I stopped, and leaned on the post. I shook my head as flashes of images raced through my mind. Sand, hot weather, my lips touching someone else's. But I couldn't make out faces, couldn't remember . . . Fuck, I didn't want to remember!

I had one goal. One chance to kill Durov, on my terms, in my arena.

Stepping back, I raised my fists, but Volkova's face was there again, in my mind, not moving from my fucking mind. My cock hardened. I was being driven insane with the need to come.

That woman.

Since I'd seen her getting attacked, I'd had to act. I'd had to save her. An instinct, a gut feeling forced me to snap that cunt's neck.

And she ran this ring? She fucking *ran* this death ring!

I groaned. Those nipples, those firm tits pushing against her top. Throwing my head back, I squeezed my eyes shut. I'd never had a woman. Never sank into a woman's hole. Never kissed a woman's lips. But *her* lips, I wanted wrapped around my cock.

Fight. Focus on the fucking fight! I kept telling myself, but my cock was throbbing, aching. The new tattoo, the sign of my recent kill, pulsed. I'd killed for her. Spilt blood for her . . . a stranger, an unknown.

A frustrated roar built up in my throat. Drawing back my fist, I plunged it into the post, which rocked at the force of my blow. Leather ripped and the wood beneath splintered.

Ripping off my knuckledusters, I stormed into the bathroom and locked myself in a stall. I leaned against the wall and ripped down my shorts. Grabbing my hard cock, I started pumping hard, gasping at the sensation.

I closed my eyes. Volkova's face was there, her pink lips parted, her blue eyes watching me, her nipples hardening, her thighs clenching and heat rising on her fucking beautiful face.

I growled as I worked myself harder, hips swaying back and forth as I pictured bending her over, ripping off her panties, and sinking my rock-hard dick into her ass. It was warm and wet and choked my dick like a vise.

I huffed out a breath at the building heat climbing up my dick. My balls tightened and, slamming a clenched hand against the wall of the stall, I came hard, chest sweating, breath panting fast.

I opened my eyes, steadied myself, and wiped my hot cum from my hand. I left the stall and noticed Viktor hovering near the punching bag, a curious look on his face.

Walking to the bench press, I straddled the bench and lay back, gripping the barbell. Viktor cleared his throat.

Ignoring the shitbag, I hefted the bar and heavy weights from the stand to begin my reps.

Someone, probably Yiv, knocked on the door and ordered, "Raze, out here now."

Placing the weight back on to the stand, I rose to my feet and walked out into the wider gym, my gaze narrowed and to the ground. There I saw fighters all itching to draw blood, like feral animals being held back on a leash, coaches standing by, watching on.

Then my blood ran cold as Durov pushed through the crowd, his narrowed eyes trained on me.

I stood my ground, fighting an overwhelming urge to rush forward and break his neck. But I wanted his death to be drawn out, real slow, humiliating. Durov clicked his neck from side to side. I had no memory yet of how he'd lied, how he'd condemned me to the Gulag, but I didn't give a fuck. I would remember in time. Every fiber of my being told me this prick must die.

Alik's strut stopped just in front of me, his bare feet coming into view. I kept my chin down as I studied his every move from my peripheral vision. He was built for death match fighting. But so was fucking I.

"*Raze* is it?" he asked, and I could hear a smirk pull on his thin lips.

I kept staring at the ground, my silence causing him to step forward. "What's the matter, can't look at the champion? The man who can kill all the shits in this competition?" I didn't react, though my blood boiled inside. "Get in the fucking cage," Alik then ordered. One of the trainers opened the steel door to the octagon and, without hesitation, I stepped inside.

I stood in the center and braced for an opponent. Alik flicked his chin in the direction of a dark fighter to his right, a fighter twice my size, but this didn't faze me.

"Get in with him."

The fighter's coach pointed to the door, and I stayed still, my eyes remaining locked on the ground, even as I felt the fighter's presence fill the cage.

"The Turk, champion of the Chinese underground," Alik said. "Let's see what you got. First man to knock out wins."

I clenched my hands into fists just as the Turk charged, his large, heavy feet bouncing the floor of the cage. I tilted my head to face him, unmoving, watching his slow movements with tight eyes, my gaze zoning in on his weak and untrained attack.

The Turk charged me and lifted his fist to strike. Ducking, I jabbed his kidney, then struck his jaw before he'd even had a chance to react. Turning around, I slowly walked away, eyes again fixed on the ground, as I heard the Turk hit the floor—unconscious.

The other fighters grew restless, a mob of psychos shouting, eager to take me on. I looked up, sure Alik couldn't see my eyes under the black grease from here.

Alik's eyes flared with rage. He turned to a blond-haired fighter and screamed, "You're next."

The blond entered the cage as the Turk's trainer dragged out his knocked-out ass. The blond gave me no time to prepare. He ran at me full force. As he was about to tackle me, I quickly spun away. Gripping his neck, I used his momentum to slam his thick skull into the rigid metal of the cage. Then I forced him back to ram his nose into my knee. The guy slumped to the floor, a pool of blood already forming.

Standing straight, I wiped the blood from my hands on my torso. I caught a glimpse of Durov seething on the spot. I saw his gaze shoot to the left. I followed his line of sight and my gaze fell on Volkova, who had stepped out of her office. Her face, betraying shock, took in the scene. Then her huge blue eyes met mine, once again locked into the pull that was pulsing between us.

Movement from the side brought my attention back to Durov, who was sprinting toward the cage. My muscles rippled as I braced for his attack. Suddenly, a loud clapping from the back of the room stopped Durov in his tracks.

A gray-haired man stepped forward. He wore a long black coat and a suit, his excited eyes not once straying from me. Durov paled when the man stepped forward. He stared at me, teeth gritted in frustration, chest veins dancing under his flesh.

He wanted me dead too.

Fucking perfect.

"Alik, don't you dare think of getting into that cage," the man said, then looked at Volkova, and my blood began pumping. "Kisa, come," he ordered.

Kisa . . .

Kisa bowed her flushed face and walked over and stood beside him.

"The buy-in?" he asked, his cold eyes drinking in my still form. His eyes narrowed as he focused on the number—818—tattooed across my chest. I dropped my chin, avoiding eye contact.

"Y-yes," Kisa stuttered.

Durov roared and punched the nearest wall, evidently losing his shit. The man didn't even flinch, too busy forming a smile on his sharp face. This guy exuded power; he had to be the one in charge, the boss, the Pakhan Viktor had fucking talked about nonstop. The most powerful man in New York, ruthless, not to be fucked with.

"He goes on the headline roster," he ordered Kisa. She nodded in agreement.

"Like fuck he does!" Alik boomed out as he faced up to the Pakhan, his torso tight with strain. A nervous hush settled on the gym as Alik fumed on the spot. As quick as a flash, the Pakhan gripped Alik's face in his hands and pushed him back against the mesh wall of the cage. Alik smashed into the metal, which clinked and groaned at the force of impact.

"You will show me some fucking respect or you will force me to lift my hand and drill it into your skull." The Pakhan didn't raise his voice, keeping cool and calm.

I'd always found the silent ones to be the most dangerous opponents.

"Do. You. Understand? This is my cage, my business, and you will fucking learn to obey me."

Alik nodded and the Pakhan stepped back. He adjusted his coat as if nothing had happened, his blue eyes fixed on me.

"Get down here," he demanded.

I pushed open the cage's steel door and walked over to him. His eyes assessed my every step until I stood before him, head dropped low. The Pakhan circled me, his hands testing my muscles like I was a slab of meat, and he nodded his approval.

"I liked what I saw in the cage. You'll headline, and you'll make me a lot of money." He turned to three huge men who surrounded him, but not before he bent down to kiss Kisa. "We'll speak later."

"Yes, Papa," she said obediently. He then shot a dark look at Durov, who had yet to move from his position by the cage.

Within seconds, the Pakhan swept out of the gym, and Yiv shouted for everyone to get back to training. But I could smell Kisa again, her sweet scent filling my nose and hardening my dick. She hadn't moved either, her blue eyes watching mine. I could feel their heat. Her heat. Her pull on me. I flickered my eyes to her for just a second.

"Don't you fucking look at her again or I'll carve out your eyes from your skull!" Durov threatened as he brushed past me.

Durov stopped at Kisa's side and gripped her neck, Kisa crying out at his move. Every cord of muscle stiffened as he wrenched her to his chest, twisting her hair and jerking her head back as he took her mouth in his, tears of fear dropping from her eyes.

An image of a young girl being held down, crying, wandered through my mind, and a boy throwing a punch at another, protecting her, followed, but it evaporated when Alik pulled back from Kisa's mouth and he dragged her to the office by her hair, Kisa apologizing to him every step of the way until the office door shut.

My stomach clenched as a jealous rage took hold. I had to use all of my willpower not to storm into the office and rip Durov off Kisa's lips. Unable to take my stare off the office door, I heard Kisa shout out as she was slammed against the glass window, the blinds parting enough to see Durov ripping down his shorts, him licking the palm of his hand, cupping between her legs. As Durov's eyes met mine, a crazed possession shone, and he rammed his cock into Kisa, gripping her cheeks, just like the Pakhan had done to him.

I handled the venomous hate, which infused my body, but only just. Something within me snapped. The image of the young kid punching another began to feel all too real. I stepped forward, intending to rip off Durov's fucking head, when a hand landed on my arm and stopped me in my tracks.

Looking up from the stubby fingers wrapped around my wrist, I saw Viktor's scared face looking at me.

Wrenching his hand from my skin, I shoved him back until he stumbled. I towered over him and ordered, "Don't ever fucking touch me again!"

Viktor held out his palms in submission and, shifting from foot to foot, nervously signaled for me to follow him into our private training room. Without casting a glance back at the office, I followed Viktor, pacing the space of the training room as he closed the door.

"I'm going to tell you something important before you get yourself killed. Alik Durov is the heir to the Bratva, and Kisa Volkova is his fiancée, the only daughter of the Pakhan."

Viktor's words only stoked my rage. Durov owned Kisa. She was *his*. I didn't like hearing that. Fuck, I felt murdering crazy on hearing that fact.

I wanted her. I had no reason to, had no idea who the woman was, why I was drawn to her . . . why she was fucking up my training, but I wanted her.

I wanted Durov's cock out of her with a fierce intensity. I was fucking beyond insane at the thought, the brief glimpse, of that cunt fucking her. Her ass belonged to me; there could be no other explanation. Her sweet scent, her beautiful face . . . her blue eyes called for me to protect her.

A searing, white-hot pain sliced through my head, causing my eyes to slam shut. As I tried to breathe through the pounding headache, its intensity forced me to one knee.

You have to keep away from Alik. He's obsessed with you and he's dangerous.
Sand.
Sun.
One boy.
One girl.
Feelings.
Strange feelings gripped my gut, making me feel, piercing the numbness.
Memories . . . ?
"Raze! RAZE! Can you fucking hear me?"

Blinking hard, my vision slowly returned and I gasped. Viktor had dropped to one knee in front of me. "You okay, son?"

Breathing steadily through the now diminishing ache, I sucked in a deep breath and hissed, "I'm not your fucking son!"

"Look," Viktor, whispered in exasperation, "stay away from Kisa.

Stay away from Durov until you meet him in the cage. You don't fuck with the Volkov Bratva. All that surrounds them is death."

Exhaling slowly, I stated, "I *am* death."

I looked to Viktor from the corner of my eye and he paled. Then his gaze dropped to the number on my chest. My pecs tightened as if the ink were burning my skin. My head tilted to the side as I watched Viktor swallow.

"What?" I snapped and grabbed Viktor's shirt.

"Where did you come from?" he asked, a nervy edge to his voice.

"Far away," I said, remembering the place the guard had told me the Gulag was based.

Beads of sweat ran down Viktor's head and he lowered his eyes. My lip curled at this pathetic weak man who I'd been saddled with, and I got to my feet. In minutes, I was in front of the mirror, power pressing, as Viktor cracked open a bottle of vodka behind me, slumped into a chair, and drank himself to sleep. With every press of the two hundred fifty pound weight, I heard Kisa crying as Durov fucked her, saw Durov smirk as he ploughed into her, licking his palm for me to see.

Hours later, when everyone had left the gym and the lights were turned off, I crept from where I had hidden in the bathroom and hunkered down on a training mat in my private training room. This gym would now be my home, until Durov was dead.

As I shut my eyes, Kisa's face came into view, and a young boy's voice started to echo through my mind . . .

You have to keep away from Alik, Kisa. He's obsessed with you and he's dangerous . . .

My eyes snapped open and a fractured image fixed itself in place.

Kisa? The boy in the memory had said *Kisa*.

11

KISA

The Dungeon was full. Men, thirsty to gamble for high stakes, leaked into the tunnel leading to the dank underground warehouse on the docks of Brooklyn. This place was well hidden from the public, normal everyday people who like to think that nothing sinister was happening under their noses. People who believed organized fights to the death were fiction, fantasy played out on TV. They were happy in their ignorance of my reality.

But the people here, now, they were criminals, the dregs of society. I came here every day of every week, but the next three nights were what The Dungeon was about—the prime fighters, the men who put on a show and died. They gave their all, they spilled blood, and they drew their very last breath in this place.

The Dungeon was what we Bratva were best known for. This was the biggest gambling ring on the East Coast.

As the Byki lined the outskirts of the basement, keeping control, the cage was center stage. I stayed in the back rooms, hearing the thudding of feet on the ancient stone floor. The excitement for spilled blood, for death, charged the air.

The Red kings, my father and Ivan, were in their private booth at the back, hidden from view but able to oversee their enterprise and watch their money rolling in. Abram would be with Alik. He always hovered close, pushing him, goading him, then watched his puppet from beside the cage.

There were eight fights tonight, the latter ones involving Raze, then Alik. They were both fighting strong, headline fighters. I fully expected both of them to win, but here in The Dungeon, nothing was a safe bet. Alik was experienced and full of confidence, and Raze? Well, Raze was a complete unknown, but the place was buzzing with the anticipation of seeing him fight. Papa had told Ivan of his skill in the cage, and Ivan had built up the hype.

Raze had trained all week, my father becoming a fixture at the gym to watch him. He was fast becoming Papa's favorite. That fact only served to made Alik even more furious, more unstable, more possessive, and Abram wasn't happy about his son's newly arrived competition either.

And me? I had become completely obsessed with Raze. I watched him train through the blinds of my office window when Alik wasn't in the gym to catch me. My body set on fire simply at the sight of his bare torso bending and flexing as he lifted weights or sparred in the cage or ran on the treadmill. My heart pounded and I often became lightheaded, such was the draw I had toward this man.

My every thought was overcome by him. Raze was always the first one in the gym and the very last to leave at night. It was as if he *didn't* even leave. He had one focus: becoming the best fighter we had. And making things worse still, he stared at me when no one was looking. The men talked about Raze. About how he never looked anyone in the eye. About how fiercely he trained. But when I passed by, when I had to speak to the coaches, he watched me with those brown-smudged-blue eyes, tracking my every move, like he only *saw* me. His muscles tensed solid when I was near. His nostrils would flare as he inhaled my scent. But he never spoke. Never communicated. Just watched . . .

Always watched me, prompting goose bumps to spread like wildfire on my skin, evoking familiar nervous/excited stirrings in my stomach that I hadn't felt since I was in my early teens.

"Five minutes," I abruptly called as I rapped on the first fighter's door. The coach yelled back that he heard me, and I walked down the hallway toward Alik's room. He needed me there before every fight. Said if he didn't have me close, he would lose his mind, couldn't focus and couldn't win. Said he needed to know where I was so he could keep me safe. Truth was, he couldn't stand seeing me around other men and the Dungeon was full of them. It was just easier to give in and do as he said rather than have him stressed, which might affect his upcoming fight.

He needed me. It was that simple.

As I neared Alik's door, a flash of movement caught my eye. I spotted Viktor leaving Raze's room up ahead, and I ground to a sudden halt. Raze would be in there, alone. It was his first fight, and I wanted him to be okay. A heart-wrenching twist of my gut almost brought me to my knees when I thought of him losing tonight. A pain so severe it left me breathless.

Why was I so attracted to him? I didn't know him. Nothing about him made any sense to me. He was wild and untamed, severe and animalistic. I knew he wasn't Luka, couldn't be *my* Luka, but a feeling deep inside told me to keep pushing to find out.

Of course it was irrational. Of course it was stupid. Of course it was impossible. But when your heart's so deeply involved, logic flies straight out the window.

I glanced at my watch and noted I was early; Alik wouldn't be expecting me for five more minutes.

Five minutes.

I could have five minutes with Raze.

Making sure he was prepared for tonight. At least this was the lie I told myself to excuse my erratic and dangerous behavior.

I hadn't seen Raze yet today and my chest ached because of it. Viktor brought him here to the gym. Alik had me jailed in his bedroom all day, fucking me over and over and over. One time he fucked me so hard my thighs were bruised and my throat was sore from crying.

Alik made me bleed. He rammed into me so hard that he made me bleed . . .

"You want to fuck him, Kisa? You think he's better than me, just like your papa does? You want to fuck that cunt Raze?" Alik had asked, pushing inside me so roughly that tears of pain splashed down my cheeks.

"No," I'd cried. *"Baby, no. You're seeing things. Imaging things that aren't true."*

Alik's mouth dropped to my ear and his fingers dug into my cheeks, forcing me to meet his rage-filled eyes.

"He watches you, did you know that? Doesn't meet anyone else's eyes like the fucking coward he is, but he watches you. Do you watch him too? Do you think you can fuck him and leave me?" he roared. He bit into my shoulder as I shook my head, trying to say no.

Alik thrust inside me in a frenzy, and I let more silent tears fall.

"You won't ever be free of me, Kisa. I own you. Every inch of you! You're with me until the end."

Shuddering at the memory, still feeling the soreness between my legs, I acted on instinct and followed my heart instead of my head. I marched forward to Raze's door. A nervous hand reached out to grip the doorknob, and sneaking one more glance at the empty hallway, I opened the door and bolted inside, shutting the door as I did so.

Closing my eyes, back pressed against the wood, I exhaled in relief that Alik hadn't caught me. Then I sensed a dark, dominant presence . . .

Raze.

My eyelids fluttered open to find myself faced with that now familiar broad, tattooed scarred chest and torso of ragged tattooed tallies. A musky smell assaulted my nostrils, prompting my pussy to contract in need.

I followed the tanned, scarred skin north, over thick pecs, impossibly high traps, up over a square jaw, and up to a pair of burning brown eyes.

He was wired for the fight.

Pumped with adrenaline.

"Raze . . ." I whispered, but my words stuck in my throat as he leaned in close, his nose almost touching the delicate skin between my shoulder and neck. Raze raised his arms above my head. Then he inhaled, long and slow. My eyes shuddered closed and my palms met with Raze's hot skin, my fingers drawing lazy circles around his nipples, feeling a hot bolt zing all the way down to the apex of my thighs.

He was smelling me, a deep rumbling growling in his chest as he inhaled my floral perfume. The attention he was giving me was almost primitive . . . Neolithic. It was like Raze had been stripped bare of any manners, ripped from the Stone Age and stripped of any boundaries.

And I'd never been so captivated, so mesmerized by anyone in all my life.

Raze's warm nose moved to the side, his warm breath ghosting over my face. The tip of his nose traced the shell of my ear before his full lips dragged over my lobe. Shivers of pleasure ran down my spine and into every cell in my body.

I had never felt this before. Never felt this overwhelming lust, this consuming level of instant attraction . . . this raw and insatiable need to be with a man. It was dangerous. It was haunting. It was forbidden. And although it was wrong, it felt so perfectly right.

Fanning my loose, long brown hair with his sharp exhale, Raze rasped, "You don't belong in here. Why are you here?"

Like a bucket of ice water had been thrown over my head, I pulled back so quickly that the back of my skull hit the wooden door. Raze pulled back, but only an inch, refusing to give me any room to breathe. He loitered in my personal space, unnerving me beyond belief.

His dark gaze was cold, only made more severe by the Eye Black smeared below his eyes, though there was fire in his pupils as he stared me down. He wasn't unaffected by me. Maybe . . . just maybe he felt this powerful strange connection to me too.

"I . . . I came to see if you were ready for your first fight," I said nervously.

A small twitch of his cheek and the slight narrowing of his eyes told me my question was unwelcome.

"Always. I'm always ready. Always ready to *kill*."

I summoned the courage to stare into his eyes. I knew it was impossible, but those eyes were so, so familiar, like I'd known them all my life. My mind became filled with confusion, with hope, with doubt, with the overpowering necessity to learn more about this man.

"Tell me your real name?" I blurted out.

Raze's face instantly blanked, all feeling seeping from his features. He stepped back, and I immediately felt his loss, felt cold without the burning heat from his body.

Moving from the door, I asked, "Raze, please. It's been haunting me. It's stupid . . . but I need to know your name. You remind me . . . I just feel like I know you—"

Raze's head snapped up and he said, "Eight one eight."

My attention dropped to the large tattoo on his chest. Confused, I traced the numbers with my eyes . . . *818*.

"Eight one eight?" I questioned under my breath, but Raze clearly heard my subtle whisper and strode toward me.

Gripping my hands, he selected my forefinger. My blue eyes fixed on his brown eyes, and he began to outline his large 818 tattoo with our joined hands. I lost my breath, heart beating like a drum, as if it were trying to break free and meld with his.

The air around us was electric, all my synapses firing like bullets. The ambient noise from the first fight slipped into silence as my flesh met his. Raze's gaze became glassy, like he'd drifted off to another world. Then he leaned in and his nose was back in my hair, inhaling my scent, his stubbled cheek scratching my throat.

Hands still on his chest, my breasts heaved in need. "Raze . . ." I murmured, feeling on fire with lust, going out of my mind due to my ever-wayward hormones. I didn't understand this pull. I didn't understand why my wanting Raze was so strong, so very strong. So strong I could barely resist him.

Raze inhaled deeply and said, "All I can think of when I take in your scent is sand . . . and sun . . . and sea . . ." He shook his head and his face twisted up in disbelief, a momentary hint of vulnerability in his expression. "But I've never seen a beach, never felt sand beneath my feet or smelled the sea . . ." His eyebrows pulled down.

Every fiber of my body froze. All the air escaped my lungs. A suffocating tension built in my chest as I watched Raze's face run rapidly through a gamut of emotions. I stood stock-still.

Was that hope or disbelief settling in my heart?

Impossible.

Impossible.

Impossible, I tried to tell myself, but . . .

Sand and sun and sea . . . Luka, me . . . Brighton Beach . . . God! The beach, the beach, the salty air, the scent of sand . . . It always reminded me of Luka. He always told me it reminded him of me . . . of our cove, of our first kiss . . .

My knees began to shake and I stumbled back, only to reach up and grip Raze's cheeks, his huge body turning to stone as I looked into those familiar hypnotic chocolate eyes.

"What? Why? Why did you say that? To *me*?"

Raze's eyes narrowed and he jerked back his head, my hands slipping from his face like leaves drifting from the trees in the fall. That same cold demeanor once again commandeered his face, the chill he always wore, any trace of vulnerability snubbed out. Raze began to pace the holding room floor like a wild animal locked in a cage, like a wild cat in captivity. His frame seemed to occupy the entire space of the room and I could feel his confusion, his agitation crackling the air around us.

His eyes repeatedly squeezed shut and his head twitched like he was fighting something in his head. His neck muscles corded with the strain, or was it pain?

Lord! He looked like he was in pain.

"I'm not here for you, for memories I don't want. I'm here for revenge!" he growled, his softer side gone, the frightening icy killer back in place. "I'm 818 and I'm here for my revenge. On the man who lied. On the man who made me into *this*."

The heels of his hands pushed into his eyes and he shook his head. His hands dropped only to make fists at his sides. Then he blasted out a frustrated bellow.

My head was spinning.

Why did he think of the beach? Why were his eyes exactly the same as *his*? Why did he smell sand, sun and sea when he was around me?

Without thinking it through, I leapt forward and held Raze's rough face in my hands. I searched his sharp features for any sign of recognition, but under the thick dark stubble of his cheeks and his scarred and weathered face, I could find none.

"How old are you?" I asked, holding my breath.

Raze stilled, eyebrows furrowed, like his mind was shrouded in a thick fog. "I . . . I don't know." My heart cried out at the lost look on his face. His gaze looked panicked, even afraid?

He reminded me of a little boy in that brief moment. Right then, my heart cracked, and I wanted to give him comfort. Me, a woman, wanting to give comfort to this hulking brute of a killer. But what if he was Luka? What if the impossible became possible? Luka's body was never returned to his family, to be identified, to be buried . . .

My heart started to race faster as all kinds of possibilities circled around in my head. And when Raze's head tilted to the side in confusion and he pursed his full lips, my frantic heart nearly exploded . . .

"Luka, leave me alone!" I said, folding my arms across my chest, and Luka laughed behind me, his arms wrapping around my shoulders from behind.

"Don't be like that, Kisa. Me and Rodion were just joking around."

"You and my brother were picking on me! When you two are together, you're a nightmare!"

Luka spun me around in his arms, his stunning, beautiful eyes concentrating on mine. His smile faded, his head tilted to the side in that adorable way, and his full lips pursed. "Forgive me, solnyshko?"

I loved it when his head tilted to the side and his full lips pursed. He only ever did it when he was sorry or immensely confused. It made him look so beautiful. My heart melted when he looked at me that way.

Sighing in defeat, I rose on tiptoes and pressed my mouth to his. "I forgive you, Luka. I'll always forgive you . . ."

The door flew open, ripping me from my childhood reminiscence. I instantly dropped my hands like Raze's skin had become a naked flame. Viktor's shocked gaze met mine as he witnessed our intimate encounter. I immediately leapt back and quickly righted my hair.

"Miss Volkova?" Viktor asked. Rushing past our resident Georgian trainer, I burst into the hallway, just as Alik's door flew open and my furious fiancé stepped through.

My body stiffened with fear. Alik's possessive eyes quickly sought mine. I was irrationally worried what he would see in my expression, the realization that Raze *could* be *my* Luka. Alik hated Luka. It suddenly occurred to me that he showed no emotion when Rodion or Luka died. I knew it was because he was pleased that he now had me to himself, that Luka no longer stood in the way of getting what he wanted to possess.

Alik's lips tightened and the bone of his jaw clicked with anger as he walked to where I stood, his heavy hands grabbing my biceps. He pulled me to his damp chest.

"Where the fuck have you been?" he snarled, the hand on my left bicep inevitably moving upward to clutch the back of my neck.

"I . . . I was working," I said quickly. To evade his suspicion, I flattened my uneasy palm on his cheek. "But I'm here now, baby," I soothed as I felt his grip slacken and his deep exhale of relief. "I'm here to help you win this fight."

Alik pressed his clammy forehead to mine and he forced me into the holding room he always used here at The Dungeon. Once the door was closed, he forced me against the wall, his hands roaming over my body. I noticed bottle after bottle of creatine, steroids, and testosterone pills.

As his finger plunged into my channel, I closed my eyes and let myself drift away on a ship of memories . . . Alik's free hand hitched up my dress and he began fucking me against the door.

I pictured a beach. Sand. Sun and the sea . . . and I pictured my Luka kissing my lips . . . my Luka looking at me with head tilted to the side and his full lips pursed. Then I pictured Raze's hard face. Raze, with whom I was becoming more than obsessed. I pictured what Luka's face would look like older, stubbled, and with scars, worn down by hardships thrown in his path . . . and a part of me excitedly but foolishly hoped my Luka could be the fighter in the other room . . .

That Luka could be Raze . . .

12

RAZE

"What the fuck was *that*?" Viktor hissed as I stood in the center of the room, my head spinning from flashbacks . . . *A hot sunny beach, a boy and girl kissing . . . a girl pissed at a boy but forgiving him with a smile.*

Kisa's question about my name and age stabbed at my brain. But nothing, nothing came through; no answers emerged to answer the questions she had asked. I'd always been numb. I'd learned to only ever be a fighter of the Gulag who had a burning need for revenge. I'd learned to never give any thought to my name. I'd learned to never think about my age, where I'd come from. I'd learned to always accept I just . . . was . . .

Fuck!

"Raze!" Viktor snapped. For the first time, the booming of his familiar accent made me freeze.

I stared into the drunk's eyes and stomped forward until I towered above him. My head tilted to the side as I studied his face. Viktor was well built, tall, and, if his accent was anything to go by . . .

The tattooed 818 on my chest felt like it was burning, and I said, "You're not Russian. Everyone here is Russian, but you . . . you sound different."

Viktor paled and glanced to my tattoo, then again to my face. He shook his head and answered, "No. I'm not Russian."

Stepping even closer, smelling the burn of alcohol on his breath, my teeth ground together and I demanded, "Where are you from? And don't lie."

Viktor swallowed hard, a defeated expression veiling his face. "Georgia."

"You speak like *them*," I growled, thinking of the guards, the guards of the Gulag who would beat me, belittle me, dismantle me piece by piece . . . come into my cell at night . . .

Viktor slumped to the chair behind him. "That's because I *was* one of *them*," he whispered. I burned with rage. A storm, a fucking hurricane of violence built up inside me.

"You were a guard?" I hissed through clenched teeth, my neck aching from the tightness of my muscles.

"Not a guard, a transporter. But I attended the fights in the Gulags, even helped train some of the fighters."

"*Gulags?*" I repeated, shock in my voice. "There's more than one?"

Viktor nodded and sighed. "There are many. Places where souls are forgotten, places where young men disappear from the face of the earth, places where they become nothing more than fighting monsters."

"And me?" I asked through gritted teeth. "Do you know me?"

Viktor shook his head. "No, not personally. I've never seen you fight. But that tattoo on your chest comes from one and only one gambling ring: Georgian. Your tattoo tells me you came from a Georgian Gulag. I knew it the instant I saw you. You have the same dead look in your eyes all the inmates have. The look that remains after they've had their humanity ripped out of them."

"I'm from Alaska. My Gulag was in Alaska," I pushed.

Viktor looked up at me and said, "I went there only once. I took the fighters where they needed to go, delivered the fighters to the Gulag's door. I had no choice until I'd paid my family's debt. Then they took me on as a trainer. I spent years training fighters for the Gulag's cage until I was bought by the Pakhan and came to train fighters full time here in New York, for the Bratva."

My eyes narrowed. "You were successful in the Gulag? Your fighters won?"

Viktor nodded. "I was. They did. My fighters were undefeated until I was brought here. I'd have been killed if I failed."

"And had you heard of me? *818 . . . Raze?* The guards called me

Raze because I would raze down anyone in my path. The warden forced me to have the tattoo on my back, for the spectators."

Viktor stared just that second too long, telling me everything I needed to know.

"Everybody in the Gulag had heard of Raze." His eyes dropped and he pointed to my chest. "Of . . . you. Everyone believed you were the meanest son of a bitch out of all the death cages."

Reaching down, I hauled him to his feet, his drunken eyes losing focus. I didn't give a shit what he'd done in his past. He could train champions. All I needed was for him to get me to the final . . . against Durov.

"Then you'll train me. You'll train me to kill Durov."

Viktor glanced away, a strange look on his face. "I can't create any more death. I can't deal with how many kids I turned over to those sick fucks. Can't deal with how many kids I got killed, training teens to be monsters. I'm fucking broken because of it."

I shook him and his neck lolled back. Then I made him meet my eyes again.

"I don't give a shit about your conscience. There's no pussying out of this life. We kill. And you'll add one more death to your bloodied hands: Durov's. I won't stop until he's bleeding out from his throat. I won't stop until he breathes his last breath, knowing it was me who sent him to hell. Then you can go and drink until your liver rots. I couldn't give a fuck. But you *will* train me. You *will* make me win."

"Why? Why is Durov so important? What's his history with you, if you've been in the Gulag all your life?"

Viktor's face wore a strange expression. Was he holding something back? But he looked away and the expression was gone. "Not that I'm complaining. The asshole is evil. The way he treats Kisa is disgusting. But why the hell is it so important to you to kill him?"

My mind clouded over; it always did when I thought too hard about revenge on Durov. Somehow Durov's name was there in my conscience, a beacon shining red, telling me he had to die. "I don't know why or how he did it. All I have is the need for revenge on Alik Durov. But I do know he took everything from me. I can feel it. I sense it. I just know he has to die. And I have to win. Nothing else matters to me but that."

Viktor's chin dropped, and as I released him to the ground, he ran his hand down his face. "Okay. I'll train you. But you're the last one. Fuck, maybe you'll be my redemption. Finally righting what I've helped make wrong all those years."

I didn't care what the fuck he was talking about, what demons he fought. He was just a drunken fool. But I was going to defeat Durov if it was the last thing I ever did. And Viktor was going to get me there.

A hard knock sounded on the door, and a voice called, "Raze! You're up!"

Viktor squared his shoulders as I slipped on my knuckledusters, rolling my neck to loosen up my muscles. I breathed in Kisa's lingering scent, and it gave me the strength, the adrenaline kick to awaken my muscles.

Viktor opened the door and we went outside, storming down the tunnel like a fucking tornado coming to raze anything in its path. I could hear the sound of stamping feet echoing off the cold walls. The tunnel was dark, but soon a light appeared, showing me the mouth of The Dungeon. The Dungeon that would help me carry out my vengeance.

Viktor glanced back at me as we approached. "Your opponent is new, unskilled, the Chechen Viper. He's a sadistic murderer picked up by the Chechens to fight in exchange for keeping him from the Feds. Viper uses a bladed chain, so stay low, strike his torso, his vital organs, when he withdraws to swing the chain. Aim for a quick kill. No showboating. Make it quick and simple. Shock and awe, stun the crowd. Make the other fighters fear your efficiency. You do that, it's a less-than-a-minute match. You'll have shooed yourself in as the one to beat. The Bratva's new star and a potential opponent for Durov. You only have a couple of fights to win to get to the final. Keep that in mind because Durov will *always* make the final."

I drank in what Viktor said, taking note, locking the information down. I cracked my knuckles and cracked my neck, prepping for the fight. A nervous excitement surged through my legs and stomach, causing me to bounce on my toes, readying me for the addictive feel of fist hitting flesh, for getting in the ring and spilling blood. My pulse thumped as I visualized the first hit, the spray of my opponent's blood on my chest, the crack of his bone under my feet. I would take down this animal, slaughter him and cut him up like meat.

Viktor slapped his hand on my face and my bulging eyes met his. "You're Raze. You're death. Let's fucking *RAZE HELL!*"

Growling through my teeth, my pumped-up traps tensed, and with a determined focus, I stormed down the walkway to the cage, running up the steps and into the arena. The animal I was sent to kill paced the other side. I knew with one look this fucker killed for kicks, scraped off the street, no training in fighting to the death.

The telltale signs of his fucked-up mind were there: the twitching of the neck, the smug smirk on his mouth, the jumping of his muscles. His body needed to kill, needed to feel the rush that only comes with stopping someone's heart. But this cage was *my* motherfucking domain, all I'd ever known. What this sadistic fuck, who probably killed women and kids by the boatload, didn't know was I had killed bastards much more fucked up than him.

I killed because I had to. *I* had no other choice. I was already dead, no more than a number—stripped of morals, stripped of freedom, and stripped of life. I was an animal conditioned to inflict pain without remorse. And you couldn't kill someone who had no soul.

The door to the cage slammed shut, trapping us inside, the bolt sliding into place. The red mist I used to defeat opponents infused my body. The monster I harbored deep inside was freed.

The Chechen Viper wrapped the chain around his fist, the triple spiked ball swinging in circles at the bottom.

He smiled at me, his teeth gleaming gold. I paced my side of the cage, waiting for the gun to fire so I could end this fucker's life. A few seconds later, a member of the Bratva walked to the side of the cage. I didn't lose focus on the Viper, my target. I never take my eyes off the walking dead.

The gun fired.

The crowd erupted, screaming at the top of their lungs. The Viper leapt forward, swinging his favorite chain above his head. As Viktor had predicted, the Viper showed a lack of skill as he hurried to get in the first blow. I ducked as the spiked ball traveled over my head. Using his raised arm to my advantage, I swung my right fist, piercing my blades deep into Viper's kidney. Then with my left fist, I quickly pierced a lung. I kept walking forward, not looking behind. I watched the mouths of the

crowd drop open and eyes widen at my speed. Then I heard the sweetest sound of all. The sick fucker I had to slaughter dropped to the floor;
my blows had brought him to his knees.

Turning my head, bladed fists clenched by my sides, as expected, I
saw my opponent on his knees, head bent, chain at his side. Leaping to
stand in front of him, I jerked the chain from his hand, planted my foot
on his chest, and kicked him until he fell on his back, blood pouring
from his wounds as he gargled for breath. As his dulling eyes looked up
at me, I swung his chain and ploughed the spiked end straight into his
face, sending him to hell with his own weapon. His face was gone, no
longer visible, not even to the devil.

As his skull crushed in, the spectators went wild and the victory
gun sounded. Dropping the chain to the bloody ground, I released a victorious roar and paced around the ring, dragging my knuckledusters
along the metal links, waiting for the door to open. When I was halfway
around, something made me look up, some magnetic pull. I never looked
up, never showed my eyes to anyone but the man I was about to kill. But
this time, I couldn't resist. High up in a box way above the crowd, Kisa's
face came into focus. Her palms were pressed against the protective glass.
Her face was awash with relief, a small smile flickered on her lips, and
happy tears shone in her blue eyes.

I could barely drag my eyes off her. But when the cage door opened,
I stormed out, too much aggression still coursing through my body to
stay still, too much hatred for the sick fucks in the crowd to accept their
fake fucking adulation.

A pathway cleared as I stormed through the crowd. Like prey flees
from a predator, instinct told them to move, to get far away from danger. Viktor dropped in step by my side. As I approached the mouth of the
tunnel leading back to the waiting room, Durov stepped in my way, a
pissed look on his face. His fight was next, once the cage had been washed
down. Without stopping, I knocked him out of the way with my shoulder, and a laugh came out of his fucking mouth.

I kept walking, needing to burn off my excess aggression, when he
taunted, "So you know, 818, I can still taste her dripping pussy in my
mouth. I just fucked her hard, *real* hard."

As if a leash had been jerked on a collar around my neck, I came to a dead stop. A burning fire coiled in my gut, a protective surge taking grip as I thought of Kisa. Inhaling deep, I tried to calm my anger, but it didn't work. Nothing fucking worked. That woman was crashing through my defenses, breaking down walls I didn't want to come down.

Viktor moved in front of me, out of Alik's view, and advised, "Move. Don't give him the satisfaction."

I nodded my head, but I couldn't stop my rage, when pain blinded me and a memory hit me hard . . .

"Get the fuck off her, Durov," the boy ordered.

Durov's expression turned to stone.

"She's mine. She belongs to me!"

"She doesn't want you." The boy stepped closer and, dropping his voice, said, "Durov, she's mine, and I'll kill you if you touch her again."

Durov smiled a cold, unnerving smile. "I'll get her some day, and there'll be nothing you can do about it. I couldn't leave her alone in that bikini. I had to touch her. I want to fuck her."

Without thinking, the boy drew back his fist and, fueled with rage, sent it straight into Durov's psychotic face, the sheer force of it knocking him to the ground.

"You're insane! You're fucking sick in the head!"

Durov smiled, as if not feeling the blow. "Maybe, but she's going to be mine. I want her. I need her. She calms me, and I'll do anything to own her and have her all to myself and fucking away from you . . ."

The image flash caught me off guard. As I turned my head to look back at Durov through hooded lids, I saw that same cold expression on his face . . . same as the memory. I'd had a memory of a teenage Durov . . .

Durov smiled that same psychotic smile. "I own her, fucker. Always have. You go near her, or if I find you looking at her again, I'll kill you."

Shaking, on the threshold of losing control of my anger, I whispered to Viktor, "Get me to the gym. I need to train, work off this rage, or I'm going to kill him, here and now!"

Viktor didn't question my demand. I followed him down the tunnel, away from that fucking dead man walking, Durov. I smirked knowing his days were numbered and I would soon be spitting on his cold corpse.

Then my mind drifted to Kisa and the look of relief on her face, palms pressed against the glass. That small warm smile pulling on her lips, those tears of relief in her eyes. And for the first time in . . . *forever*, something besides rage ached in my chest.

It was a foreign and strange feeling, but as I thought of Kisa's face, it felt familiar.

It felt . . . right.

13

KISA

"You should've seen him, Talia. He destroyed the Chechen in seconds. It was unbelievable. It was all anyone could talk about."

"And Alik?" Talia asked, and I sighed. "He was as cruel and as dynamic as always. He fought the Turk. He toyed with him for what felt like an age, gutting him piece by piece with his dagger. The crowd loved it, Abram smiling at his son proudly at the side of the cage, but I couldn't watch. It was too much. I hate it when he kills them so slowly, so violently."

Talia was silent, then said, "But you could watch Raze kill someone?"

Staring at the photo of me and Luka as kids, clutched in my hands, I squinted my eyes, studying his face, his beautiful face.

"Kisa?"

"Yes," I whispered. "I could watch him. He didn't toy with his opponent, even though I'd heard he was a sick murderer from the streets and probably deserved it. He didn't drag out the kill. He didn't hang around the cage, jogging laps for the glory of the crowd. He left the cage and then, when I went to the holding rooms to see if he was okay, he and Viktor had already left the building. I don't even know where he stays. I suppose he's staying with Viktor. He's so reclusive, private."

Seconds went by before Talia said, "You've completely fallen for him, haven't you?"

I opened my mouth to argue, but I shut it again, declining to lie to my best friend. I wanted to tell Talia what I'd been thinking about Raze, that he had close similarities to Luka. That I had dreamed he *was* Luka, come back from wherever he'd disappeared to, from the dead. But I knew I couldn't voice these words without proof. This was his sister. She'd already mourned for him, held her family together when he left . . . died.

"I've fallen for Raze," I admitted and heard Talia sigh in trepidation.

"Be careful, Kisa. You're skating on thin ice. You can't fall for anyone outside of the Bratva, outside of this family," Talia sternly warned.

Of course I knew she was really warning me about what Alik would do if he suspected anything was up.

"I will," I replied, my cell beginning to beep as yet another call tried to come through.

"Tal, I've got to go. I've got another call . . . It's Alik," I said, suddenly feeling drained.

"Well, you'd better answer him. He already hates me. I don't want to give him more ammunition. Speak soon," Talia promised, and I pressed the button to hear music blaring through the speaker.

"Alik?" I shouted, holding the phone away from my ear.

"Myshka?" Alik shouted over the music. "Just calling to check you were home and in bed."

My stomach tensed and anger made me seethe. Alik wasn't checking for my safety. He was making sure I was back in *my* version of the cage— obeying his rules, accepting his control of me—while he went out to play, dipping his wick in anything with a wet pussy.

"I'm home. I'm going to bed," I replied tersely.

"Good. Don't leave," he ordered harshly. I closed my eyes, trying to rein in my ire, when a female voice enticed Alik to go to a back room with her.

"Where are you, Alik?" I asked with feigned politeness.

Stony silence greeted me until the music faded and the sound of a door closing came through the speaker.

"I'm out. It doesn't fucking matter where," Alik said darkly. "I'm doing Bratva business. I'm here with associates."

"You're at The Triangle?" I guessed. The titty club the Bratva owned, that his father managed. After Alik fought, he had to fuck.

Normally, it was me who had to suffer against the wall at the back of The Dungeon, but this time we finished late because Alik had drawn out his kill. Papa ordered me straight home, courtesy of Serge, and of course, he wouldn't let me stay at Alik's place overnight, not until we were married, so Alik took his cock to the sluts. I knew with these women, he really let his true colors show. I'd heard that some ended up in such a state that they'd been hospitalized. Talia had heard rumors that some of the women he fucked, once they'd disappeared into a private room with my fiancé, were never heard from or seen again.

As screwed up as it sounded, I was glad he took out his sick fantasies on them and not me. Yet strangely, I knew as messed up as Alik was, he would never hurt me . . . not unless I tried to break free of him. My life was safer with him if I acted the role of the perfect Bratva wife. What hurt most was my father was so proud of me for taking that honorable mantle.

"Shut the fuck up, Myshka. I'm out, working off the fight. Your papa took your wet cunt from me or you'd be screaming under me right now. Even though his wrinkled dick is here in the club with me, getting sucked off by hookers your age. You know I need to fuck, but these sluts are never you, baby, never my Myshka. They're just whores, nothing but cum bags. I think of you the whole time I'm inside them, picturing you squirming beneath me, scratching my back. How's that? That make you feel better? You just sit tight at home and I'll see you tomorrow. And as long as you stay inside, we don't have problems. Yes?"

"Yes," I whispered in reply, feeling sick to my stomach.

"I love you, Myshka," Alik said, his harsh tone thawing a few degrees.

"I love you too," I replied. It was rote, sounding more like a Stepford Wife than a loving fiancée besotted with her true love.

The cell went dead, and I leapt from my bed, hand to my forehead as despair swept through me. I hated this damn life, trapped in a cage by Papa and Alik's psychotic obsession. I was twenty-five, for Christ's sake, yet I was locked away like some virginal fifteen-year-old.

At times I hated my life.

The Byki would be downstairs, protecting the Pakhan's stronghold, in reality stopping me from leaving the front door, but I just had to get out. I needed fresh air. And I'd never disobeyed rules, so even contemplating sneaking out was causing me to break into cold sweats.

Grabbing my jacket from my closet, I swung it on and headed to my window. Carefully opening it, I crept onto the fire escape. Tiptoeing down the metal stairs, I jumped onto the sidewalk. Checking that I hadn't been seen, I began walking in the shadows, occasionally glancing up at the night sky, picturing Raze's eyes meeting mine as he won the fight, my relief of his victory evident on my face.

He had looked for me. He'd found me in the sea of gambling men.

Lord! I couldn't get him from my head! I was going crazy wondering if this mysterious homeless man could be my Luka.

The sound of a car pulling up beside me made me turn. Headlights flared and blinded me. I jumped back, suddenly fearful of who might be after me. Then Serge's familiar face came into view, his window open and his light eyes boring into mine.

"Serge!" I said, out of breath and in shock.

"Miss Volkova, what are doing out of the house? You know it's not allowed." Serge reprimanded me, and then all I felt was pissed off.

"Serge, I needed fresh air. My fiancé and my papa are out at a titty bar. Alik's probably screwing a long line of whores while I'm trapped inside my bedroom like a naughty child. He told me not to move or I'd piss him off, and *that's not how a good wife of a Bratva boss should act.* So I needed some fresh air, okay? I'm twenty-five, I run a multimillion-dollar gambling ring made up of murderers and psychos, and I just wanted to take a damn walk on my own for once in my life!"

Serge's face softened as I panted, my breath lost through exertion, and pulling the car to a stop, he got out of the driver's door.

"You can't be out here, Kisa. It's too dangerous. Too many men wanting revenge on your papa, Alik, Abram, Ivan . . . Hell, take your pick! I know you feel trapped. I'm not stupid. I've been with you since you were little, but I can't disobey orders or they'll kill *me.*"

Dropping my head, feeling guilty at my tirade, I insisted, "I'm not going back yet, Serge. I'm suffocating under their rules. I'm drowning . . ." Tears filled my eyes and I tried in vain to blink them away, but I found myself whispering, "I'm miserable."

Serge sighed and stepped forward, pulling me into his chest for a hug. "Then I'll drive you somewhere. That way I'll know you're safe and you can still have some freedom."

Tipping my head back at the bright moon, I then looked to Serge. "Fine, thank you. Please take me to the gym. I may as well get some work done if I can't sleep."

Serge's face relaxed and he opened the rear door for me, nodding his approval. He slipped back into the driver's seat, and we raced through the streets of Brooklyn. I smiled at the groups of women stumbling from bars with their friends, not a care in the world, and the couples wrapped around each other's waists, high off being together, enjoying each other's company—probably heading back home to make love.

I was happy for those people, but what I felt was crushing disappointment. It would never be me. I would never be allowed out with friends. I would never, could never, have a loving relationship with Alik. Jealous possession isn't love. I knew that much. He would always control me. I was becoming so desperate to escape my fate that I was imagining a homeless fighter being the only boy I'd ever loved.

I would be a prisoner until I died . . . the life of a Bratva queen.

Deciding to close my eyes to any other sight that would cause me pain, I rested my head back on the seat and zoned out until we arrived at the gym.

As I opened the back passenger door, Serge tried to follow me inside to the gym.

"No, Serge, please. I want to be alone," I pleaded.

Serge stopped in his tracks.

"Miss Volkova, you know I can't leave you. It is forbidden."

"I know. Can you please just wait out here until I'm ready to go home? Please . . . I need some time alone."

Serge stared at me, and my stomach rolled, thinking he was going to say no, when on a sigh he shook his head. "I'll wait in the car. If you need me, call," he said, getting back into the cab and waving his cell to show me he was keeping it close by. Giving him a thankful smile, I unlocked the side door and entered the sparse and empty warehouse-turned-gym, switching on only minimum lights. I headed for my place of solitude, my office.

As I approached the office door, I noticed a muted glow coming from under one of the training room doors at the back of the gym. I frowned. Nobody was meant to be here. The gym had been locked and secured once all the fighters had gone to The Dungeon earlier in the day.

Someone was here.

Feeling a sense of fear run down my spine, I hurried to my office safe and, checking over my shoulder, opened a heavy door to pull out my Beretta. Papa insisted I could access one of these bad boys wherever I went—all over our house and at several secret locations here at work.

My breathing was shallow as fear took hold. I walked slowly and silently toward the back room that emitted the light. Rather too preoccupied with steadying my shaking limbs, I took little note of where I was and whose training room it was.

Standing at the door, I steeled my nerves and took in a deep breath before placing my hand on the doorknob and slowly turning it. The door creaked open.

Bringing my gun up higher, I edged through the doorway. The first thing I noticed was a mat on the floor and a thick blanket forming what looked to be a makeshift bed.

Someone was sleeping here?

Who—?

Taking me off guard, a hand slapped across my mouth. I tried to scream as I was quickly disarmed and held in an unyielding grip. Warm breath ghosted past my ears and a pit of dread opened in my stomach.

I could feel a heart pounding in the attacker's chest pressed to my back. All I could think was that my father wouldn't cope if I died too. He'd lost my brother, my mother, and I was now sure I was going to die here too, until my attacker rasped out, "Stop struggling."

All the hairs on the back of my neck stood up and every muscle froze, obeying his command.

"Good," he growled. "Don't scream and I'll remove my hand."

I nodded awkwardly, still trapped in his grip. As I tried to relax my muscles, his hand gradually pulled away from my mouth. His large body stepped back from being flush to my back.

Unsure if my feet would work, I started to turn, hearing deep breathing behind me. The dull glow from the adjoining bathroom was the only light in the dim room, the man's shadow darkening the old whitewash wall.

Holding my breath, I whipped myself around and immediately gasped when I found Raze glaring at me. Dressed only in black boxer briefs, his large muscled, ripped body tensed as he watched me with those hypnotic brown eyes.

"Raze?" I whispered, legs now feeling like Jell-O.

Raze watched me and his nostrils flared, his cheeks flushing as heat rose up his face. "Kisa . . ." he rasped out, almost like he was in pain.

As my name tumbled from his lips, my stomach tingled, my breasts ached, and moisture pooled between my legs. Raze had switched on every part of my body, as if it were on fire.

Edging closer, feeling the waves of heat from his body, his fresh scent hit me, and a whimper escaped my lips. A rumble sounded in Raze's chest. My need to touch him, to feel him, grew to an impossibly high level. By the clenching of his fists at his sides, the gritting of his teeth, and those hungry eyes, I knew he wanted me too . . . desperately.

"Raze . . ." I whispered as my toes met his and, unconsciously, my finger lifted to run down his stubbled cheek. There wasn't a scratch on his body from the fight tonight. "Why are you here?"

Raze's eyes closed at my touch. Looking down, I saw him harden beneath his black boxers, the material straining with his size. My hand continued to travel down, shivers wracking Raze's skin at my touch, his full lips parting to let a slow hiss of breath slip from his mouth.

At this moment, I wasn't thinking of Alik, my father, my duty as a Volkova, or even the consequence of touching Raze like this. The need to break free from my suffocating life was driving me forward, making me reckless in my choices.

All I could think was how beautiful Raze was. How strong and fearless, how feral, how raw. He was untamed. He had no social grace, was devoid of knowledge about how to be a regular person. He was curt and aggressive, but his expressive eyes, when they looked at me, made me feel safe, made me see there was someone else in there . . . someone my soul matched. Gave me faith that he wasn't the monster he seemed.

"I sleep here," he answered eventually. His body remained as still as a statue as I continued to marvel at his muscles, drinking in his demonic tattoos, wondering why he had such evil images permanently etched on his skin.

My finger stopped its exploration and my eyes looked up to his. "You're staying *here*?"

"I have nowhere else to go," he replied gruffly. And with that, pain sliced through my chest as if my heart had split in two.

Raze dipped his head to escape my sympathetic gaze.

I lifted my finger and tipped up his chin. I stayed silent until his eyes looked to mine, and I asked, "Where have you come from?"

Emotion leaked from his expression and he whispered, "Hell."

My attention was drawn to the demons on his chest, the number, then his tallies . . . and finally to the newest addition scraped onto his skin—his kill from tonight.

The air seemed to pulse around us as some unexplainable force pulled us together. Raze's neck tensed, every vein and threaded cord protruding. He was physically holding himself back from me.

I was fighting the attraction, tensing my thighs as I squirmed, trying to alleviate the pressure building at my core. But when my palms landed on Raze's chest, his hot skin almost scalding my palms, he leaned in, his nose tucking into the crook of my neck.

I moaned as he inhaled and growled, "I want you."

Three words. Three simple words became my undoing. Spoken roughly, dominantly, yet it sounded like poetry to my soul.

Without giving me time to think, Raze gripped my arms and drove me backward until my ass hit the wall. He was panting into my neck. Releasing a hungry groan, my hands grasped his messy sandy hair, and I tipped back my head, giving him more access. As his bulging thigh slipped between my legs, his stiff cock brushed against my throbbing clit.

"Raze!" I cried out as pleasure took hold, and I pulled on the thick strands of his hair.

Raze let out a sound like the snarl of a wild animal. He reared back his head, his unsure brown eyes looking into my blue, and he asked nervously, "Can I have you?"

My heart beat so fast at the severity of want on his face that I thought I would pass out, or my heat would shatter me into a million pieces.

Raze squeezed his eyes shut as his arms wrapped around me, holding me so close, like he was scared I would try to run away.

"Can I have you? I want to have you . . . I *need* to have you," he
whispered, his deep voice guttural and rough, tense like a taut rope about
to snap.

Letting any lingering worries flee my mind, I threw my arms around
his perfectly sculpted shoulders and, brushing my mouth past his ear,
whispered, "You can have me, Raze. You can have all of me."

Raze stilled, long seconds ticking by, but then I felt the slow, wet
lick of his tongue along the side of my neck, and he sprang into motion.

His arms released me. Suddenly, my shirt was ripped apart at the
seams, the buttons spraying on the ground. Raze's face was determined,
and he was lost in his lust.

My breasts were hard under my bra, aching to be touched. Focusing
his brown eyes on my heaving chest, Raze ripped my bra apart, bare
breasts exposed, and his mouth immediately latched onto a hard, raised
nipple. His tongue furiously licked at my flesh and my eyes rolled back at
the sensation. I almost came just at the feel of his hot mouth on my skin.

"Raze . . ." I murmured, clutching his muscles in my hands, becoming more and more turned on by the rough and scarred skin under my
palms.

Untamed and savage growls ripped from Raze's throat. His hands
lowered and split apart my pants. The material tearing in two, he threw
them to the ground. I stood there only in my string black thong, arms
still gripping Raze's bulking biceps. Raze stepped back and his wide
eyes drank me in from head to toe, his cock now so hard it nearly ripped
through his boxers. Still transfixed at my exposed breasts, Raze dipped
his hand into his boxers and began sliding it up and down his dick in
what had to be the best torture on Earth.

"Raze . . . I need you. Let me have you too," I moaned as I palmed
my breasts, pinching my nipples as I watched this usually controlled man
come slowly undone.

Grumbling something I couldn't make out, Raze wrenched down his
boxers, his long, thick cock coming into view. I almost passed out at how
strong and wild he appeared, about to take me . . . or in his words, *have me.*

"Raze, please," I begged one more time, and this time something within him snapped. Lurching forward, Raze's hands went straight to my thong, his legs bent, and he snapped the thin piece of string from my body. I was now totally bare.

His calloused hands smoothed up my thighs, over my hips, my waist, before moving in to cup my breasts. I watched his eyes ignite with need, and I slipped my right hand down his stacked abs and wrapped it around the wide girth of his cock. Raze threw back his head and hissed as his fingers pinched my nipple, and I slowly began to stroke my hand up and down, loving watching him fall apart.

Raze's left hand slapped against the wall behind me, his hips rocking back and forth with the movement of my hand. His eyes were closed, his mouth gaping; he looked breathtaking, and I found myself begging, "Kiss me."

Raze abruptly stilled and his eyes snapped open, the smudge of blue seeming to shine like the clearest sea against the dark canvas of the brown.

My eyebrows furrowed at his strange reaction, and he jerked back a few steps, my naked body now feeling cold.

"Raze?" I questioned, and he started pacing the floor before me, his face torn and panicked.

"Raze?" I pushed again, and his eyes slid to mine, then away again. I felt our connection slipping. I had no idea what I'd done.

Feeling a chill settle over my naked skin, I turned to cover my breasts with my hands, when Raze released a pained groan and came at me again, his chest and hips pinning me against the wall and his large palms on my cheeks. His eyes were focused on my lips, and he was panting hard, but my heart fell when I saw nervousness in his eyes.

My hands cupped his cheeks and Raze looked to me. "Raze?" I asked. "Have you ever kissed anyone before?"

A wash of uncertainty and then perhaps embarrassment engulfed his face. "I . . . I don't know," he said quietly. "I don't remember."

Tears pricked my eyes. What the hell had happened to him? And where the hell had he come from?

"It's okay," I said and began leaning in. Raze stiffening at the action. He was like a statue as my lips hovered just an inch from his, and I whispered, "Can I have you?" My heart beat frantically.

Raze's shoulders relaxed, and I used the opportunity to press my lips against his. My heart instantly swelled and a sense of souls merging filled me so much it was almost unbearable.

Raze's hands on my cheeks, at first unmoving, tightened their grip, and his lips slowly began working against mine. That was all it took. One touch, one kiss, and something within him snapped and his mouth possessed mine, his tongue spearing into my mouth, controlling mine.

Feeling a wetness between my thighs, I moaned and began grinding against his thigh, then shifted over until his cock was flush against my pussy. I tried to rip my lips from his mouth, but Raze's seemed fused to mine. He wouldn't let go. He owned me with the kiss, having me, *completely* having me.

My hand ran down between us and I cupped his balls, massaging them in the palm of my hand. Raze let out a roar into my mouth, and his hips started thrusting into my hand, his cock sliding along the drenched folds of my pussy.

Managing to pull my mouth away, I demanded, "Fuck me, Raze . . . Fuck me."

And that was all it took. In seconds, Raze had flipped me around and bent me over the nearby bench, my cheek pressed to the hard wood. I didn't even think about protection. As stupid of me as this was, I really didn't care. I was on the pill, and at this moment, it was enough.

Something in my gut told me to just trust him.

I felt his fingers on the cheeks of my ass, but he'd trapped me in place, and I whimpered at his strong touch. Then his fingers were suddenly running down the crack of my ass, and every part of me tensed.

"Raze!" I called in alarm as his finger pushed into the tight hole, and I tried to get up. His firm hand held me in place and panic replaced passion as I fought back against this unwelcome intrusion. The finger soon pulled out, but when I looked back and saw him fist his cock and head for the same place, I began fighting to lift off the bench as the tip pressed flush against the one place I didn't want him to go.

"Raze! Stop!" I ordered.

Raze's jaw clenched and his eyes fixed on mine.

"Not there!" I begged, witnessing his eyebrows pull down in confusion. My fear this time was replaced with sadness when I realized he didn't understand why I was protesting.

Fighting back the rising lump in my throat, I said, "Lower." I saw Raze look down at my pussy, and confusion clouded his face. "Lower, fuck me in the other hole." I guided, a devastating truth becoming evident in my mind.

Raze . . . where the hell have you come from?

"I don't understand," Raze rasped, his face and tensed body racked with confusion.

Leaning back, I took his dick in my hand and slid him along my pussy. When he was at the entrance and his thick thighs rested against the back of mine, I said, "Now push in. Fuck me here."

Raze's gaze focused back on his breaching cock. Reaching out to grip my hips, he began pushing forward, the tip slipping into my entrance. Then he suddenly stilled, and I relaxed, cherishing the sensation, just in time for Raze to dig his fingers into my hips to an almost agonizing grip and surge forward, slamming into my channel until he was fully rooted to the hilt.

"Raze!" I screamed out as he roared, and I could feel his hands physically shaking as his chest met my back and he panted hot breath into my hair.

"Fuck," he groaned, and his hips began rocking back and forth, his dick so wide it scraped against my G-spot, my eyes closing as I savored the feel of him within me. I could feel him everywhere: within my body, in my heart . . . in my soul.

"Kisa . . ." Raze groaned as his hand brushed my hair from my back and his warm lips pressed to the skin on the nape of my neck, making me shiver. His lips dragged down my spine, making me moan uncontrollably, and then his tongue began to lap at my damp skin.

"I remember this," he said as his hips became more demanding, his cock plunging farther within me, all sense floating from my mind.

"I remember something. It felt so good. It *feels* so good . . . with you . . . only with you . . ."

Tears misted my eyes, and I pictured my first time . . . with Luka. We were too young, too inexperienced, but that memory was my world.

I felt like I was making love to Luka again. Everything about the way he was cherishing me, made me think of Luka.

Feeling Raze begin to build to orgasm, I wanted to go with him. Needed to find release at the same time. Reaching behind me, I took his hand and brought it around my waist and placed his fingers on my clit.

"Circle your fingers here. I want to come with you. Stroke my clit and make us come together," I instructed.

Raze rumbled a groan as my clenching channel wrapped around his cock, spurring my orgasm further.

Raze's length seemed to grow bigger as he thrust inside me faster, the man savage and fierce in his lovemaking, wild and primitive, focusing only on our pleasure.

That burst of delicious tension began burning at the bottom on my spine and surges of heat spread to my clit. I felt Raze's thighs tighten against my legs as his fingers became frenzied, as his thrusts became stronger, longer, harder, and rougher.

"Kisa," he hushed out as the sweating skin of his torso slapped at my back. I opened my mouth to respond, but I couldn't speak. When he pounded into me one last time, stilling and bellowing out as he came, I tipped over the edge with him, indescribable pleasure making me see lights.

Raze's arms wrapped tight around my stomach as his knees hit the floor, causing him to sit back, taking me with him. I sat in his lap, his sated cock still jerking inside me.

As the minutes passed in silence, his breathing settled, and I stroked along his toned forearms, treasuring the closeness, treasuring the most meaningful sex of my life.

As my fingertips danced on his arm, a low rumble sounded in his chest, and I smiled. He liked my touch. Raze then moved his legs, and standing, keeping me locked in his arms, he carried me to his makeshift bed and laid us down. He kept me secure in the strong hold of his arms; he couldn't bear to let me go. As possessive as this move was, I loved every second of it. I'd never felt more complete than I did in his embrace, locked to his chest.

Lifting his rough and scarred hand, I pressed my lips to the skin, enjoying his warmth on my back.

Hearing a staggered sigh slip from Raze's mouth, I tensed and then my world splintered into sorrow when he whispered, "I . . . I didn't know it was like that." His deep, husky voice was filled with shame, embarrassment. Unable to stand the ache in my heart, I turned in his arms and the desolate look in his eyes cut me as deep as any dagger could.

He lowered his gaze, and my heart beat more rapidly as I stroked my fingertips over his cheek. "Tell me what happened to you . . . please. I want to know."

Raze's face turned to stone as I watched him war with different emotions. Then he shook his head, his brown eyes darkening. "I . . . I was in the Gulag."

Slowly sitting up on my elbow, I stroked back the messy strands from Raze's head as his forefinger landed on my breast and began circling the nipple, his tongue sliding along his lips.

"Gulag?" I questioned, trying to stay focused. "Isn't that some kind of old Russian prison from the war?"

Raze nodded and his finger began to shake. "It was a prison. We named it the Gulag because of its shitty conditions. One where they keep you caged until they force you to fight to the death."

Anger contorted his beautifully masculine face, and I leaned forward to press a kiss onto his lips. The shaking immediately stopped and a moan caught in his throat.

Pulling back, his pupils dilated, he stole my breath. He looked so much like Luka at that moment I found it difficult to deal with the possibility.

Because if Raze *was* my Luka, I was about to hear what had happened to him all those years ago when we all believed he had died. When we were told he had been burned . . . When he had been torn from my life, without explanation, cutting my soul in half.

"Why were you there?"

Raze's eyebrows furrowed, and I could see he was fighting to remember. When a black look came across his face, his mouth tightened and he said, "I don't remember. I don't remember anything but death, violence, pain and . . ."

My breathing came short when I thought of how he was going to take me. He was going to . . .

Shuffling closer to Raze, until we touched skin to skin, I threaded my fingers through his hair and asked, "Why were you going to take me from behind . . . like that? Did . . . did . . . ?" I stopped talking, unable to ask the obvious question. There had to be an explanation, but I wasn't sure I was ready to hear it.

Raze's brown eyes widened and he dipped his chin, hiding his head from view. He was such an enigmatic hulk of man, but at that question, his face clouded over like a storm. His position became fetal.

"Raze . . ." I said, choking on a sudden rush of sadness as he slowly lifted his head.

"I remember the first time one of them came into my cell. He was big, and I'd just been beaten with a bat. I couldn't move, but I watched him walk toward me, untying his belt and pulling down his zipper. I remember being pushed onto my stomach. Then I remember pain. Pain like nothing I'd felt before. Then all I can remember is blocking everything out. Blocking those cunts out every time they came into my cell, until I was too big for them to control, too big and dangerous for them to fuck."

Without him knowing, his hand had gripped mine and he was squeezing it like I was giving him strength to continue, like he was drawing the courage and the strength from me to talk about these horrific rapes. I could barely see through the torrent of tears falling down my cheeks, trying to think of ways to make everything better for him.

"Raze, oh my God," I cried and pressed my forehead to his, devastated this had been part of his life in the Gulag.

He said nothing in response, but his grip on my hand didn't loosen. I guessed it was the first time in years he had been comforted. Of course, I had heard of conditions in Russian-owned underground prisons, but what I'd heard didn't compare to what Raze had revealed.

"How old were you?" I asked, peppering kisses down his cold, stubbled cheeks.

Raze clenched my hair in his hands and said, "I . . . I don't know. It's hard to know my age. None of us ever had birthdays."

Regaining some composure, not wishing to drown him with my suspicions, I continued. "And they made you fight? To the death? As a child?"

Raze nodded his head once, gaze blanking out, taking him off somewhere else. "Yes. They ran a gambling ring. Just like this one."

Nausea built in my stomach as he compared The Dungeon to the Gulag. At least I had the comfort of knowing we didn't imprison and serially abuse kids, forcing them to fight until the death.

"Raze, I don't know what to say. I'm devastated for you," I said, feeling inadequate—no, pathetic.

Raze gripped the back of my head and pulled me down and timidly kissed me. I was immediately lost to his familiar kiss.

Raze broke away and stared at me. "There was a breakout. Some fighters got free and murdered the night guards. There were always less guards at nighttime. The rest of the prisoners rioted and started fleeing."

"How did you get free?"

Raze's lip hooked into a smirk. "362."

"362?" I questioned, confused.

"362. Another fighter, the only one I ever spoke to." The tone of his voice had changed.

"He was your friend," I surmised.

Raze's half smile reverted to an impassive expression.

"Friend?" he asked as if he were savoring the sound of the word on his tongue.

My heart bruised just that little bit more. He had no idea what a friend was.

"Yes, your friend. You spoke with him, spent time with him. Confided in him . . . Liked him?"

"I trained with him. He helped me adjust to life in the Gulag. Taught me how to block things out. We would never fight. We were the Gulag's two best fighters. When the riot happened, he freed me. Most of the others would never have dared approach me. They were too scared of me. But not him."

A smile pulled on my lips, and I asked, "And where is he now? Did you come together to New York?"

He shook his head. "I don't know where he went. West somewhere. We all just ran."

Raze stared and stared at me. I assumed I'd pushed too far for one night. Color had drained from his cheeks and his body sagged. Feeling warmth spread in my chest at his devoted attention, I pressed a kiss to his forehead.

Raze's expression softened. His finger landed on my neck and traveled down to my breast. I closed my eyes, once again cherishing his touch.

"I want to touch you," he said. His finger stopped and he looked into my eyes.

Taking my hand, I brushed my finger over his left eye, the one with that smudge of blue.

Biting my lip, I mustered the courage to ask, "Have you noticed that your left eye has a smudge of blue amongst the brown?"

Raze studied me, and his hand lifted to touch his eye, his eyebrows pulled down. I held my breath, waiting for what he had to say. And then hope bloomed within me when his head tilted to the side in confusion and his full lips pursed.

"We match," he rasped out and narrowed his eyes, observing the color of my eyes. "Your blue is the same color in my left eye."

My bottom lip trembled. I could no longer hold back the sob choking my throat. Raze would have no idea why I was crying. How could he know that saying those two words—"we match"—could, in tandem, inspire such high hopes and such deep sorrow within me.

This was Luka. This *had to be* Luka. Of this I was becoming more and more convinced. It no longer felt like an obsessive fancy, some stupid teenage, love-struck hope that this damaged and raw man was created just for me. I believed more and more that this was real, veritable, tangible, a soul-colliding connection from God.

This man, this tortured and scary hulk of a man seemed to be my match. Mama seemed to have been right all along; even lost, it looked like we had found our way back to one another. But if this was my Luka, he was broken. Had no memory. I dared not push too fast, too far, for fear of scaring him away.

Taking his hand still resting near my eye, I pulled down the palm and laid a kiss to its center. "We match," I whispered back. Raze's lips stretched into a smile. That smile, the brief flicker of happiness on his face was my undoing.

My God, he *was* beautiful.

Shifting Raze's hand down to my breast, his expression morphed from happiness to lust. His fingers squeezed my flesh and I closed my eyes and moaned.

"I like touching you," Raze murmured.

Then I placed my hand on Raze's shoulder and pushed him onto his back. He let me control the situation, and I knew it was because of his inexperience. It made the moment that bit more special to me. He trusted me enough to let me lead the way. I straddled his hips and immediately I felt his cock harden and push against my ass.

Our gazes locked and electricity arced between us. Raze's hips began lifting, searching for my entrance. Leaning forward, I placed my hands on his chest and slowly impaled myself on his length. Not once did I tear my eyes away from his face; I drank in every wave of pleasure as it rushed across.

As I moaned and took him fully inside, I started to gently move up and down. Raze closed his eyes, his hands holding my hips.

"Open your eyes," I whispered, but Raze shook his head, his forehead wrinkling in concentration.

My eyebrows furrowed in confusion, a twinge of insecurity rippling through me, until Raze gasped and said, "I'm closing my eyes so I can feel being inside you." He placed his hand over his heart and rasped out, "I've seen too many bad things with these eyes. This, I will feel in my heart."

Water fell from my eyes at his beautiful but heartbreaking words, and resting my breasts on his chest, I placed soft kisses on his neck as I worked my hips faster. More rumbling growls of pleasure sounded from his throat.

Raze's hand slipped around my waist to my back, and my breath came faster as I felt myself building to orgasm, his satisfied grunts telling me he was nearly there too. Licking and nipping at his throat, I journeyed my lips to his mouth, and Raze immediately met me kiss for kiss, our tongues wet, hot and dueling, as shivers ran up and down my spine. I came so quickly and so powerfully that I pulled my mouth from Raze's and cried out in pleasure.

Raze's long groan soon joined mine and I felt his warmth flood my womb, his hands holding down my hips to extract every moment of pleasure.

Fighting to catch my breath, I lay contentedly in Raze's arms.

"Kisa . . ." he whispered, rolling my name on his tongue, and I froze, praying he would say something else. *I know you. I remember you. You're the girl I was designed to love, my God-given match, my solnyshko.* But he didn't. Instead, he inhaled a deep breath and said, "Why do I feel like I've known you all my life?"

And at that moment I knew . . .

My beating heart exploded like a supernova of light. I savored this moment and a smile tugged on my mouth. He might not remember specifics, but deep down in his tragically damaged mind, in the mind blocking out his past to protect him from the present, my Luka . . . my Raze . . . He knew me. He felt that connection that always kept us close.

"Kisa-Anna," he murmured as he raked his fingers hypnotically through my hair.

I sucked in a sharp breath, and Raze clearly felt it, felt my shocked reaction. His hands stopped dead.

Lifting my head, I stared at him through blurred eyes and asked, "Why did you call me Kisa-Anna?"

Raze opened his mouth to speak but slowly closed it again. "I don't . . ." His eyes squinted closed and he ran his hand over his head as though he was hit with a migraine.

"Raze?" I asked.

He blinked, then blinked again. "I don't know why I called you that . . . but I think . . . I think that's your name. It feels right."

Nodding through my tears, I said, "Yes. It does feel right."

I laid my head on Raze's chest and closed my eyes, relishing his touch while I could. But I knew I had to go, and after I didn't know how long spent in his arms, I reluctantly tore myself from his body, looking down to see his face . . . a face that appeared . . . hurt?

"I can't have you, can I?" he asked, devastation in his voice.

"I . . . I . . . It's complicated," I stammered and began scooping up my ruined clothes, trying to dress as best I could with the tattered bits of material, praying that my long summer jacket would cover me.

"It's because of Durov, isn't it?" he pushed, the feral, untamed side reasserting itself.

"He's a dangerous man, Raze."

Raze got to his feet and gripped my wrist, preventing me from pulling up my pants. "So am I."

"I know, Raze. I know. But you don't understand. We're engaged. There's expectations," I explained, but I continued to dress. Mixed emotions and thoughts clouded my mind. Questions welled up. Could I explain all I knew to Raze? Did I dare tell him about his connection to the Bratva? How could I make him remember what happened to my brother, if he did kill him? And how could I ever get out from under Alik's controlling hand?

"But *I* want you. Will you come back again tomorrow? I need you. I want to touch you again. I can't bear to think of you with him."

Dressed as best as I could manage, Raze's fingers linked through mine, and when I looked up, he was staring at me in deep concentration, his eyes darting from side to side, like he was trying to remember something. I was mush the moment his head tilted to the side and his lips pursed.

This was *definitely* my Luka.

I had to figure something out.

"I'll be back here tomorrow after dark," I told him. Raze's tense shoulders sagged in relief. "But tomorrow when you train, you can't let on to Alik that we've been together. He can't find out."

Raze tensed again. "He doesn't faze me."

I touched his cheek and said, "I know. But we really need to keep this quiet."

Raze blew an annoyed breath through his nostrils, but he nodded in agreement. Balancing on tiptoes, I pressed a kiss to his full lips, once more admiring his naked ripped body. Reluctantly, I backed out of the room, keeping his gaze until I closed the door on the lost love of my life.

My head was spinning, my stomach filled with both fear and excitement.

Exiting the gym, I caught Serge's questioning glance as I slipped into the car, but I ignored it, still feeling the aftereffects of Raze inside me.

I smiled to myself.

Kisa-Anna . . . Only Luka ever called me that name.

I had found my love again.

I just had to make him remember who I was to him . . . before the Gulag changed him. Before he'd been ripped from my life.

14
RAZE

"Come with me," the boy encouraged the girl, sneaking into her bedroom on the ground floor of her father's mansion. He checked that none of the Byki were near enough to catch him.

"Where are we going?" the girl asked sleepily. Crawling out of her bed and throwing on a sweatshirt over her pink tank and short set, she accepted the boy's outstretched hand. He was hanging out of the window. He was dressed all in black, like a thief. The girl couldn't help but laugh.

The boy tilted his head to one side, pursed his lips, and asked, "What are you laughing at, solnyshko?"

"You," she teased but took his hand anyway as she melted under his smile. Her bedroom door creaked open. The boy and girl froze in panic and the girl's brother staggered into the room.

"What's all the noise, Kisa?" her brother asked, wiping the sleep from his eyes before lowering his hand and fixing his gaze on the couple sneaking out the window. He wasn't surprised to see the guilty faces of his twin sister and his best friend. The brother rolled his eyes and shook his head.

"Where the hell are you taking Kisa at this time of night?"

The boy looked to his best friend and shrugged. "Out? For fresh air? Any of them work?"

"At one in the morning?"

The boy shrugged again. Then the brother crossed his arms over his chest and lifted his eyebrow. The boy came into the room and faced the brother. "Rodion, come on, man! Don't be an asshole! I want to spend time with Kisa away from our fathers."

Rodion pointed at Kisa. "That's my sister you're trying to corrupt!"

"And my girlfriend," the boy shot back. "I'd never do anything to hurt her. You know it. I'm going to marry her one day."

"Please, Rodion, we'll owe you," Kisa pleaded from behind the cover of the boy's protective stance. Rodion stared at his sister, then the boy, then back again. Then her brother shook his head.

"Fine, go! I need to sleep."

He began walking out of the room, dismissing them with a wave, but looked back and said, "Don't get her pregnant, or Papa will cut off your balls. She's thirteen and she isn't your wife yet."

The boy rolled his eyes at his best friend, but Kisa's face flushed bright red and she threw a pen from her desk at her brother. He laughed playfully in reply.

Rodion left the room, and the boy knew he'd cover for them. He then turned back to the girl, taking her hand and leading her out of the open window.

"Where are we going?" she whispered as he led her down toward the beach.

Once they were out of sight of the house, he draped one arm around her shoulders and pulled her close to his side. "Our cove. Where else, solnyshko?"

Kisa wrapped an arm round his waist. Within a few minutes, they were at the closed-off cove, and the boy led them to their favorite spot. Taking off his sweatshirt, he spread it on the sand and, sitting down, he gently pulled Kisa to sit between his legs and wrapped his arms around her waist.

The boy and his Kisa watched the rolling waves in silence, the bright moon huge against the dark water. Kisa dreamily looked up at the boy and smiled. They were alone on a beach and it was perfect.

Kisa's blue eyes were misty as she looked at the boy. He knew right then how much she loved him. She was so beautiful to him. He didn't have a single memory that she wasn't in. Even from young kids, she was always with him, and he'd always kept her close, protecting her, cherishing her. He couldn't see anyone but her. Even then, at fourteen, no other girls enticed him to look their way. He loved this girl. He knew she was it for him, a gut instinct telling him so. Together, he believed they were perfect.

They were from the same criminal life. The boy knew as the years passed and their duties came into play, she would support him and never question his

line of work or choices as the Bratva called upon him to lead the Russian underground in New York.

Kisa wasn't fazed by death and danger.

The boy smiled to himself and thought of the tale his mama always told him
as he was growing up. That God created them to match, in every possible way,
the smudge of blue in his left eye perfectly mirroring the girl's blue.

Dipping his head, the boy pressed his lips against hers. Kisa moaned into his
mouth, her hand lifting to slip around the back of his neck.

The kiss became deeper. He broke away to shift her down on the sand, and
he crawled on top of her, feeling her warm body beneath his.

It didn't take them long to lose control, and the boy broke from Kisa's mouth
on a gasp. Her lips were swollen. Her hands gripped his neck and she tried to pull
him back down.

"Kisa-Anna," he said and pressed a kiss to the side of her neck. "We have
to stop. I can't . . . We can't . . . I need to stop . . . We need to stop."

Kisa's blue eyes dipped. She turned her head to the side, staring at the moon.
The boy dropped his head to her shoulder, trying to get himself under control,
breathing through the tingling in his stomach.

She placed her hands on his cheeks, pushed until he lifted his head and stared
into her eyes. "Please," she whispered, "I want to do this with you."

The boy's eyes widened and his heart beat faster in his chest. "Kisa, are . . .
are you sure?"

Kisa nodded shyly. "Can I have you?" she asked.

Feeling like his heart exploded in his chest, the boy said, "Yes," and he
pressed his lips back to hers.

Later that night, Kisa lay in the boy's warm arms, and he couldn't stop himself from kissing her face. "I love you, Kisa," he confessed. She turned to him and
dipped her eyes, overcome by shyness.

"I love you too. I'm glad you were my first."

"And last," the boy promised. He wrapped her tightly in his arms. Both
were naked under the modest cover of his sweatshirt.

"I can't imagine ever sharing this with anyone else . . . ever," Kisa said,
and she sighed.

He couldn't have agreed more.

They were young and in love . . .

But the boy knew, without a shadow of a doubt, that she was the one and only girl meant for him.

They were meant for each other.

Fighting to catch my breath, my eyes shot open and I stared at the steel rafters above. I was drenched in sweat. My mind scrambled and fogged from this dream, a dream that felt all so real.

A girl.

A boy.

A beach.

Kissing . . .

Wait!

Kisa was in it, just a teenager, fucking some boy on a beach. I waited for a surge of jealousy, a wave of anger to sweep through my body at the thought of anyone else touching her, but it didn't come . . .

The boy in it reminded me of someone. But I couldn't think . . . it was someone I couldn't place. Didn't recognize.

He was happy.

He loved Kisa.

And Kisa, as always, looked beautiful. Smiling at the boy and telling him she loved him too.

I breathed heavily through my nostrils, my heart pounding as if she were saying those words to me. My chest began to ache and my hands began to shake.

But she didn't tell me. She told some boy on a beach that she loved him . . . not me, not Raze, the monster, the killer . . .

It made me think about what my life had been like before the Gulag. What *I* was like at that age?

I didn't know anything about where I came from. I didn't know anything about my family. So many events since I'd arrived in Brooklyn had confused me. Flashes of dreams. Glimpses of images. Were they real memories fighting their way into my conscious mind?

My dreams were so real that I woke up with a clear recollection of every detail. I couldn't remember ever having such dreams before meeting Kisa, and she was in every single one.

She felt so real to me, important.

Or maybe I was so desperate for her that I needed to imagine some connection. So desperate to actually have someone give a shit about me that I wanted to mean something to her too.

Then anger and rage burned in my chest as I pictured her with Durov. Kisa was *mine*. I felt she was *mine*. I knew she belonged to me. I wanted her. I wanted her to be mine, not shared with that psychopathic cunt.

Durov was an unfeeling, murdering bastard. I'd seen that look in his eyes, in so many fighters' eyes. And the way he looked at Kisa, I knew it wouldn't be long until he killed her too. He'd snap or she'd step out of line, and rather than lose her, he'd kill her to make sure she would never leave him.

Something told me it wasn't the first time I had protected her from him. Then a gaping hole opened in my gut when I thought of him marrying her, that it was because of me that he made her his possession . . . that somehow I'd failed her.

I had to kill him. It was the only way I could save her from him. I wanted to puncture his black heart in the cage.

Squeezing my eyes shut, I tried to remember something, *anything*, from my past. But that same old pain sliced through my head and, in frustration, I slowly opened them again. I rubbed my hand over my nose, remembering the dream. I could smell the sea and feel the sand the boy and Kisa had lain on. I'd been there, but I couldn't connect the memory to anything real.

And in the dream, Kisa had a brother . . . a brother who loved her, and the boy was his best friend. I'd never heard Kisa mention a brother before. He wasn't a fighter. I'd never seen him around the gym.

Shit! Maybe it was just a fucking messed-up dream after all.

The sound of the main door opening made me jump to my feet. I threw on my training shorts, pushing aside the mat and thin blanket that still smelled of Kisa. My mind immediately raced to last night.

Kisa. My Kisa-Anna . . . under me, wet and hot and screaming my name.

I'd loved fucking her, loved being inside her, stroking her brown hair and kissing her face. I wanted her to be all mine, to have her belong to me. Never before had I had anyone who cared for me. But I wanted her now . . . only her, and smelling her scent on that blanket spurred me on to kill Durov.

But the memory of last night with Kisa-Anna riding me like she did brought a sick feeling to my stomach. It made me face something I'd never before confronted.

The Gulag, the guards . . . what they'd done to me for years, taking me like they did . . .

I didn't know there was any other way to be fucked. And I'd almost taken Kisa that way. It would have hurt her. I could still taste her panic in my mouth.

Storming to the punching bag, I slammed my fist into the hard worn leather and tried to pound out my shame, my guilt . . . my fucking embarrassment. I could have hurt her. I couldn't bear the thought.

I was so wrapped up in releasing my fury that I didn't see Viktor come through the door, until he stood before me.

Then all I saw was a red mist.

Launching myself at my trainer, I fisted his shirt in my hands and pushed him away from me until his back thumped into the wall. Viktor's eyes betrayed his shock, and his face turned a deep shade of red.

"Did you do it too, you sick fuck?" I asked tightly, snarling as my blood boiled.

"Do what?" Viktor choked out.

Leaning in, I growled menacingly, "Fuck little boys in the Gulag. Did you pin them down and fuck them too?"

Viktor's red face paled and he shook his head. "No . . ."

"LIAR!" I boomed out, lifting him up to quickly slam his back against the wall.

"No . . ." Viktor gasped, and seeing his eyes bulge, I let him go and stepped back. I began to pace as Viktor slumped to the floor, rubbing at his throat.

"Raze, I swear, I never did that . . . I would never do that."

I looked at him in disgust. "But you knew about it? Knew they fucked little boys?"

Viktor dropped his head. If anything, he seemed to crumple as he slumped even farther. "Yes."

"And you did nothing to stop it?"

"What could I do? I've been paying off my family's debt since I was a teen. First for the Georgians, now for the Russians. My papa was a gambler and fucked us all over. I was the lowest of the low. I had no power in those places. I'm not the mob. I'm a grunt, disposable."

I ran at Viktor, getting a kick out of his loud whimper as I approached, and punched the mirror above his head, shattering the glass, which rained down on his head.

"Yeah? No power? Neither did I when I was forced to take guard cock up my ass!"

I stilled as those words slipped out of my mouth, and cold shivers skittered down my spine. I had no idea that what the guards did was wrong. In fact, I'd never thought anything that happened in the Gulag was wrong. It was life. It was what happened day in and day out. Why did I suddenly know it was wrong? Why was something inside me suddenly telling me I'd been raped?

Fuck! I'm feeling too much lately, unable to block it all out. I have to keep it blocked out. I need to kill. To fight. To get my revenge.

My head throbbed, a sharp pain pierced my skull, and a familiar scene abruptly played in my mind. It was of the very first guard that I met, the first one who fucked me, beat me, trained me. It wasn't of his rape or his baseball bat that he beat me with; it was being pushed down the stairs to the Gulag basement to show me my future, to show me two young boys in a cage, one slicing open the stomach of the other.

"Welcome to hell, boy."

I closed my eyes, heart pounding, temples throbbing, and tried to cling to the memory.

My eyes snapped open and I stumbled back in shock. That was me . . . That boy was *me*. I'd been taken from somewhere. My home? I couldn't remember, but I did remember that I'd been knocked out and tied up. We traveled for what seemed like days. Then I woke up in a cell, and I was immediately forced down to the basement.

I saw spots in front of my eyes, and then I felt a hand slap my cheek.

"Raze. Snap out of it, son. *Raze!*"

Blinking furiously, my vision cleared, and Viktor was in front of me, his face . . . concerned? Worried?

I wanted to push him off me, but I still couldn't move. I was paralyzed.

Viktor sat up and stared at me. Holding out his palms, he said, "Raze, listen to me. I've seen it with hundreds of fighters who've left the gulags, or any of the other underground prison death match rings the mafiyas have. They're everywhere, son. Hundreds of fucked-up kids like you, only knowing how to kill, not feel. They pumped you full of so much shit and tortured you for years, they conditioned you to not remember anything but the need to kill. You've blocked out your past to cope with what they made you do. Then, when you get out and the drugs leave you, triggers fuck with your mind, you start getting memories and remembering things from your past. And you can't handle it."

My eyebrows pulled down, but my legs and arms still wouldn't move. Viktor cleared his throat and moved forward, lifting his hand slowly, finally placing it on my shoulder.

"Just let the memories in. Don't fight them. Don't push yourself to remember. If something's familiar, let it play out. Best way or you'll end up killing yourself."

A feeling of dread settled in my stomach. "I don't know if I want to remember. I came here for one thing and one thing only: revenge. I didn't come here for memories." I dropped my head, staring at the tattooed tallies of my kills, my number 818, and said, "What if I don't like who I was . . . ? What if it sends me over the edge?"

Viktor slumped to his ass and ran his hand down his face. "Isn't it better than the cold monster you became in the Gulag? That you are in The Dungeon's cage? And after you kill Durov, what then? Where do you go then? Another death match ring? There's hundreds over the country. You could keep killing, making money until you're slaughtered . . ." Viktor took a deep breath. "Or you could live, son. You could *live* . . . get back your life."

I shook my head. I hadn't thought that far ahead. I only ever had one goal: kill Durov.

"I can help you to defeat Durov, but you need to help yourself, to remember your past. Right now you're an animal, a machine that can only kill. But you were more, you *are* more than that."

My eyes were trained on the ground as my head felt numb, too numb to think, but then a question from Viktor's mouth tore right through that haze.

"Why Durov, Raze? *Why* Durov?"

My chest tightened and my hands began to shake as a broken memory pushed through to my mind.

Three boys. Three boys by the falls. On a family vacation. Two of them best friends. The third had a knife. The third stabbed one of the others . . . Then . . . then what?

Energy filled my limbs again as I grew frustrated with the memory not showing me what I needed to know. Why Durov? Who were the boys? Who was stabbed? Was I there? Was I one of the boys?

I wanted to know why that was. I wanted to know what I made myself forget, at least forget everything but the name of the cunt I had to kill.

Alik Durov.

Brooklyn, New York.

Revenge.

Kill.

Sounds of fighters beginning to train filtered into my training room. Viktor got to his feet and held out his hand.

"Get up, Raze. Train. And stop letting your past hold you back. Instead, use it to fuel you. This is your chance to take back your life. Get your revenge! Then get back your life!" Viktor glanced to the door, then back to me again. "Then you can get the girl. When Durov's gone, you get the girl."

My anger faded as I thought of Kisa. She was my balm, my calm. My Kisa-Anna.

I held Viktor's gaze for a while, just breathing, centering my focus, coiling the fire inside, then gave him a curt nod. The guy was just as fucked up as me. I could see it in his eyes. But he understood me. I didn't like him, but he understood me. No one else could.

As I got to my feet, Viktor waved for me to follow him into the main area of the gym to use the ropes. As I entered the training space, the main doors opened from the underground parking and Durov walked in . . . his hand gripping *my* Kisa's neck. Her expression was blank and her eyes unfocused.

I physically shook upon seeing her under that bastard's control.

Viktor stayed close. "Ignore it. Control your anger. Kill first, live later. Then get the girl."

I tried to curb my rage by taking hold of the ropes and lifting them to Viktor's counts, but Alik stopped dead center in the gym, directly in my line of sight, and crushed his lips on Kisa's. The hardest battle I'd ever had to fight was stopping myself from charging the prick and ripping my woman from his arms.

Kisa let it happen, but her body was stiff and unmoving. Anyone with eyes could see how frightened he had made her, but then that's what he probably wanted, her too afraid to leave him. I wanted to decapitate him with a blunt knife. But she'd told me to act normal, to not give us away, so I was fucking acting normal.

Dipping my nose to my shoulder, I inhaled deep and could still smell her on my skin, her hands gripping my shoulders as she came. That scent kept me from killing Durov. I held on to the fact that she would see me tonight after the fight . . . and by the end of tomorrow night, he would be dead and she would be mine.

Durov let Kisa go, and she scurried off to her office without looking back. She looked beautiful in her black suit and her long brown hair tied back.

Then Alik was suddenly in my face, Yiv stepping behind him, ready for him to train. I kept my head low.

"Heard you're against Goliath tonight." I could see his face split into a shit-eating grin from my peripheral vision. "He's a last-minute buy-in by my father. You know, to give the crowd a real show. Really test what you're made of."

His eyes dropped to my workout regime that I hadn't stopped while he shot off his stupid mouth. He laughed. "Looks like you'll be slaughtered tonight, Raze. That fucker's going to kill you. Can't say I'm fucking sorry." He leaned in and whispered, "And when I win, I'll drag Kisa back to the holding room and fuck her up the ass. She hates it, tries to fight me . . . but it only gets me harder."

Fighting the explosion of rage inside, I let his comment go over my head and kept my focus, but I felt Viktor's panic beside me. I wasn't fazed by this fight tonight. I'd never been afraid in the cage. It was *my* domain, *my* home.

Durov moved out of sight, and I glanced to Kisa's office, only to be driven further in my workout when I saw her peering through the blinds, watching me.

Intent refueled my muscles, and I didn't give a fuck who this Goliath was. I was going to *raze* him the fuck down.

Just one more tally tattoo to add to my torso and one less person in the way of having Kisa as mine.

15

RAZE

The stamping of hundreds of feet shook the structure of the holding room walls in The Dungeon's basement as Durov's fight took place. I was skipping rope, warming up my body for my fight, when a huge cheer made me look to the door. I skipped harder, waiting for Viktor to come and tell me who'd won.

I didn't have to wait long.

Minutes later, Viktor walked through, his eyes down. "Durov won," was all he said, but by the green tint to his face, I could see that Durov had done more than kill. He'd toyed and played with his opponent, again. Probably sliced him apart with his dagger, but in a way that kept him breathing until the last strike.

Durov was "The Butcher" after all.

Viktor walked to the basin at the edge of the room and threw water on his face, then came to stand in front of me. "I got a look at Goliath. Got some stats."

I kept my eyes on Viktor, but didn't stop my warm-up.

"He's Georgian, new this season to the underground. But he's never lost a match. He's ruthless, has minimum weaknesses. Has about twenty pounds on you and about four inches in height."

I formed a picture of Goliath in my mind, visualizing bringing him down.

"Weapon?" I asked.

"A black sai," Viktor replied.

I stopped skipping.

Freezing, I asked, "Is he Gulag?"

Viktor nodded. "Yeah. Saw one of the trainers from one of the West Coast gulags. He's one of their prize fighters. They've taken him on the road. Entering him in the underground contests around the country." Viktor handed me a water bottle and gestured for me to drink. "You're going to have to be smart with this one, Raze. He's quick. Undefeated. So are you. But by tonight, one of you will be dead."

A knock rapped on the door, and the familiar words, "You're up!" were shouted through the wood.

I took off my sweatshirt and slipped on my bladed knuckledusters, smeared under my eyes with Eye Black, letting the hot rage fill my muscles as I prepared for the fight ahead.

I heard the noise of the crowd grow louder, telling me Goliath had stepped into the cage. Viktor opened the door and led me out into the dim hallway. I glimpsed Durov in his holding room, an older man slapping him on his blood-covered chest, congratulating him. He looked like him. I just knew the cunt was his father. He looked just as fucking evil as Durov.

The hallway was dank, filled with the stench of death and trails of blood from previous fighters. I could hear my breathing in my ears, even over the roar of the crowd, and then I heard something else . . . the calling of my name.

"Raze!"

I looked to the side at the opening to another hallway. Kisa stood in the shadows. Viktor stopped dead and raised his eyebrow. Ignoring him, I rushed to the side and immediately lifted Kisa in my arms and pushed her back to the wall.

Kisa's blue eyes hooded as my chest pressed against hers, and I leaned forward to run my nose down her cheek. "Kisa . . ." I murmured as Kisa's hands played with my hair.

Her palms slipped down to my cheeks, and pulling my mouth to hers, she pressed her lips to mine. Growling into her wet mouth, I pushed my tongue inside until it met with hers. Kisa's tits hardened against my bare skin.

Her hands pressed harder on my cheeks and she ripped her mouth away, panting. Her fingers stroked at my cheeks and my cock hardened, my hips thrusting against hers.

"Raze . . . I had to see you," she whispered.

My nostrils flared as I smelled her scent, wanting to have it on my tongue.

"I want you," I said, and I saw tears fill her eyes. I didn't know what was wrong. All I could do was stare at her in confusion.

Kisa's expression suddenly changed and she smiled at me, running her fingertip down my neck. "I love it when you do that—tilt your head to the side, I mean."

My brows furrowed, not understanding what she meant, but I ignored it to ask, "Why are you crying?"

Kisa wrapped her arms around my neck and tucked her nose. "I've just got you back when I thought it was impossible and you don't even know it yet."

I felt even more confused. Then I pulled her back to face me, and, through her tears, she whispered, "I've seen who you're fighting."

I tensed. "So?"

"He's huge, Raze. I asked around about him, and he's never lost a match. He always gets his kill."

"So do I," I said tightly, not enjoying her lack of faith in my skill. I was a killer. Undefeated.

"I know, but . . ." She swallowed, staring into my eyes, leaning in to kiss the left one. "I'm terrified of losing you tonight. Abram had him brought in from under my nose. He's scared, Raze. I know it's because you could truly beat Alik in the final."

My heart turned to steel as her words kindled my determination to beat Goliath. To fuck over Alik and his father.

Pressing my forehead to hers, I promised. "I'll win."

A sob escaped her mouth, but I caught it as I pressed my lips to hers.

"Please," she spoke against my mouth. "I have so much to tell you. So much I want you to know. You need to survive."

"I'll win, *Kisa-Anna*," I rasped again, feeling her fear for me pulsing through her slim body. But what she didn't know was I thrived on fear. It pushed me further.

I wouldn't lose . . . not when I had Kisa in my mind and her life to save from Durov.

"You'll win," Kisa said with a relieved sigh.

A cough sounded behind us.

Viktor stepped closer, shock etched on his face, and said, "Raze, we've got to go. You're needed in the cage."

I pressed another kiss to Kisa's lips, took her finger and ran it down my stomach. "There'll be another tally here tonight . . . and then I'll have you again. When you come to me."

Kisa tried to smile, but I could see the nerves racking her body. I stepped back into the hallway and pounded down toward the tunnel, right into the crowd, men moving back to let me through. I had the cage in my sight, filled with bloodlust and the need to kill. I saw my opponent already circling the ring but paid no mind to him. My only concern was for Kisa . . . surviving for Kisa. Surviving to protect and care for Kisa.

I ran up the steps and got to the steel door.

"Let me in!" I bellowed, banging on the door. A guard came up behind me and released the lock, and I immediately bounded into the cage, clenching my fists.

Then I looked up . . .

And my stomach dropped.

362?

362 was tattooed on Goliath's chest.

As the door slammed shut, my opponent looked up. I saw the recognition flash across his face. He stilled. I stilled. And the gun fired a shot, telling us the match had begun.

Neither of us moved, too busy staring at one another.

He was your friend . . . Kisa's words from last night ran through my mind.

"Friend?"

"Yes, your friend. You spoke with him, spent time with him. Confided in him . . . Liked him?"

"I trained with him. He helped me adjust to life in the Gulag. Taught me how to block things out. We would never fight. We were the Gulag's two best fighters. When the riot happened, he came down and freed me."

My heart beat faster than ever as I stared at 362 . . . Goliath? Kisa said he'd been my friend, and looking at him right now, sai in hand, for the first time ever in the cage, I couldn't force my legs to move.

I couldn't bring myself to fight . . .

"818, come. We'll do weights," 362 called from the other side of the gym. I cautiously joined him at the bench press and stood behind to spot him as he lay on the bench.

"You'll train with me. You've got what it takes to survive. Training with those sniffling fucks you were brought in with will get you killed. They're weak. Scared . . . They don't belong in the cage."

"You're not afraid of fighting against me?" I asked.

362 smirked. "I'm older. It won't happen. And when you get older too, if you become a champion like me, they'll never pit us against each other. They'd lose too much money if they did."

I nodded and spotted his first press. "Then I'll train with you."

362 smirked and began lifting his weights as though they weighed nothing. "Stick with me, kid, and together we'll get out of this hell alive."

"Why me?" I asked.

362 stopped and looked up at me. "Because I can see you didn't do what you were brought in here for. It's all over your face, in your eyes. You're innocent, like me, but you're strong, can fight, can survive . . . like me. Most kids here will die within the first few weeks, if not, by the end of their first year. But us, we'll survive."

"You want to get out for revenge on the one that put you here," I said knowingly, because I felt exactly the same way.

"I do. And I'm going to have that day, as will you. Train with me, spar with me, and we'll both get our revenge."

362 got back to his weights, and we trained together for years, until we became the champions he envisaged.

We survived to get our revenge.

But now my revenge was blocked by my friend, my Gulag brother.

362 walked to the center of the cage, and my legs carried me forward too. My fists clenched, pointing the blades forward just in case he struck, but I could see in 362's dark eyes that he wasn't going to attack.

When we were face to face, his chest rose and fell rapidly, and he cursed under his breath. His face was pained, contorted.

"818," he said quietly.

"362," I said in return.

He lowered his head.

"This is your revenge? This is your path to the man who lied, who condemned you, who made you into one of us?"

I nodded. "And you?" I asked, beginning to hear the upheaval from the crowd, unease that we hadn't started fighting.

"They caught me two hours away from the Gulag. I ran, but they caught me again. They've made me fight for them. Travel around the country, making me fight to the death. Then last night, I was sent here. To end the fighter who just stepped in the ring with me. I was told to make you suffer. To make it slow."

I froze. "Durov," I snarled.

362 narrowed his eyes. "The one who sent you to the Gulag?"

I didn't reply. Hadn't remembered the details yet, but Durov was responsible somehow.

Guards began to surround the cage, rifles at the ready. 362 moved closer still. "If I win tonight, I am to be freed. I will *finally* get my revenge."

Closing my eyes, I understood what he was saying. We both wanted revenge. And only one of us was stepping out of this cage alive.

I opened my eyes, and 362 held out his hand. His face, for a brief moment, showed regret, and during that moment, I let slip a hint of compassion for my . . . friend.

Taking his hand in mine, I nodded and said, "I am grateful for your friendship."

362 smirked. He always smirked. "Promise me this. If you are victorious tonight, you will get your revenge . . . for the both of us."

I squeezed his hand and said, "Only if you make the same promise."

362 dipped his head in acknowledgement. Our hands separated; all feeling, all compassion, fell away and supercharged adrenaline took hold.

We stepped back. The guards relaxed. Only one rifle was raised again, to fire the shot signaling the restart of the fight.

I knew this fighter, how he moved, how he thought, his weak areas, his strengths. But he also knew me. For the first time ever, I felt a pang of fear. This man could beat me. As we began to circle each other, I knew by the look on 362's face he was thinking the same.

362 suddenly lurched forward and struck my arm with his sai, the blade slicing into my skin. But he didn't get away unscathed, for as he withdrew his sai, I pierced him with a glancing blow to his thigh. 362 stumbled back as it sliced nearly to the muscle.

I felt blood running down my arm. 362 suddenly charged at me, dragging us both to the ground. The crowd went insane, their fists banging on the metal links of the fence. 362 and I grappled on the floor, both struggling for dominance, both evenly matched.

But 362 was bigger and he managed to pin me down. His face tensed and his expression cooled as his sai came down toward my face. The crowd volume increased to fever pitch.

I tried to push back, but 362's strength was unrivaled and his size unmatched. Every one of my muscles strained. I could feel my veins throbbing in my neck and temple, but the sai came ever closer to my throat. This would be a kill. 362 would pierce my throat and I'd be dead.

My head tipped back as I pushed harder still against 362's downward moving arms. I caught sight of Viktor on the side of the cage, screaming for me to live, to get my revenge.

But beyond Viktor, and at the entrance to the hallway, was my Kisa . . . and Durov stood behind her, pinning her against his chest, forcing her to watch me fight as tears filled her eyes. Durov watched me with a sneer on his psychotic face. It was all I needed to completely fuel my defense.

Kisa tried to turn her head as I felt the tip of the sai press against my skin, but Durov grabbed her cheek in his hands and wrenched her unwilling attention back to me, his tight mouth barking something in her ear.

Her blue eyes filled with terror as she watched me. And like an overtaut cord pulled too tight, I snapped. Roaring out in frustration, I rolled my hips, knocked 362's sai from his hand, and flipped him on his back.

I saw nothing but red as I straddled his waist and speared a first bladed fist into his neck. Felt nothing but rage as my second bladed fist skewered his temple. Felt nothing but single-minded determination to slaughter Durov as I lifted both fists and, pointing them straight down, plunged them into 362's chest, the wheeze of his dying breaths assaulting my ears, wrenching me from my anger.

362 was bleeding like a river, my skin coated with his blood. His eyes shone at me. I noted approval in his stare as my hands fell to my sides, an ache constricting my chest.

"Revenge . . ." 362 uttered, choking on blood washing back down his throat. "Make him pay . . ." Then 362 was gone, his chest stilling. The crowd erupted. But all I could do was stare at 362 lying dead on the floor of the cage. I couldn't move my arms and legs, a sharp pain dead center of my chest.

The steel door opened and Viktor ran in. He crouched before me. "Raze. Son, we need to move."

I looked up at Viktor, then down at 362 beneath me. "I knew him," I said, my voice breaking.

Viktor nodded and laid his hand on my shoulder. "I know, son. I knew it the minute I saw his tattoo and your reaction as you stepped into the cage."

"He was my . . . friend," I managed to blurt out, the term unfamiliar and bittersweet on my lips.

Viktor gripped my bicep and helped me to my feet. "We have to go, son."

Viktor and I walked straight out of the cage and down through the crowd. Hands slapped at my back in congratulations, I kept my eyes low and I started to move faster until I was in the hallway. Then I found myself sprinting into my holding room. Once inside, I went straight to the bathroom and puked into the toilet, my body breaking out in cold sweats.

Viktor was at the door, cursing under his breath. I didn't know what the fuck was happening to me.

I slumped to the ground, seeing smears of blood on the grimy floor tiles. Viktor wet two washrags and pressed one on my arm and the other on my throat.

I didn't flinch. "You need stitches, son. That sai got you good in places."

"Then do it," I said numbly.

I'd never ever felt this . . . this . . . *ache* before. This pain . . . this guilt? Was it guilt? I'd always blocked out the kills. Those men I'd faced were just animals for the slaughter, and I was the man that brought death. There was no over thinking. Just instinct and duty to the Gulag carrying me forward.

But this time . . . I felt everything: remorse, shame, devastation . . . I felt like death. *I* felt dead inside too.

"Where are you living, son?" Viktor asked as he pulled out a needle and thread from the metal cabinet above the basin. He began to patch up my arm. I didn't feel the needle piercing my skin. Didn't feel the thread pulling together my split flesh.

"At the gym."

Viktor paused and shook his head. "Damn, son. Just . . . damn."

After my cut was stitched, Viktor forced me to shower and took me back to the gym. When he'd gone, I closed my eyes as I lay on my thin mat. All I could see was blood, blood everywhere. And 362 staring up at me as life drained from his eyes.

I'd never felt remorse, regret, but right now, I was drowning in it.

16

KISA

"Why am I taking you to the gym again, Kisa?" Serge asked as I met him on the sidewalk shortly after Alik dropped me off at my papa's house. Papa was already out entertaining the Georgian mob that had brought Goliath tonight and Alik was en route to join them, so I knew I would have all night free.

It was always like this when the championship was on. The mob bosses had to get business in all avenues done. But tonight just seemed different, my stomach swirling with nerves like something bad was going to happen. I knew it was a combination of both Alik's strange mood and Raze's strange reaction after he won his fight tonight.

Alik had been furious that Raze had won. So furious that he hadn't even used my body post-match as was his usual M.O. He'd just dropped me off at home and coldly ordered me inside.

Alik was fearful. I'd never seen him fearful before. But him seeing Raze beating Goliath tonight with such incredible skill and strength had taken him to a state I'd never seen from him before: introverted, quiet, pensive.

It scared me more than his aggression. I didn't know what to make of a non-expressive Alik. Of a distant and non-possessive Alik.

But right now, I tried to push all thoughts of Alik from my head. I needed to see Raze. Alik had forced me to watch his fight, trying to assert his dominance over me. And, my God, Raze had nearly died. But something was wrong with him afterward. He didn't look pleased by his win. He couldn't get up, like he was shell-shocked, staring down at Go-liath with a devastated expression. Viktor had to lift him from his knees to get him out of the cage, support him as he walked down the hallway. And worse, I couldn't go to him. Instead, I had to go with Alik.

I resented Alik for that. For once, I completely resented him.

I looked to Serge, Raze's cutting face prominent in my mind. "Please, Serge . . ." I begged, and he stood stoic in front of me before opening the back door of the Lincoln and gestured for me to go inside. I slipped into the backseat and Serge got behind the wheel.

He turned around. "Kisa? What's going on? You sneaking out like this is putting us both in danger. I'm not doing it unless you start giving me some answers."

I dropped my eyes to the sidewalk outside and warred with what to do. I looked to Serge again and my eyes filled with tears.

"Kisa, are you in trouble?" he asked, but I shook my head. "Are you . . . have you been seeing someone else? Behind Mr. Durov's back? Are you meeting him at the gym?"

"It's not like that, Serge." I sniffled and wiped the tears from my eyes. "It's more than just 'seeing' someone."

Serge's face paled. "Kisa! You *are* seeing someone else? Do you have a death wish? Mr. Durov will kill you both if he finds out. That man is unstable at the best of times, but about you? He's beyond insane." His gaze fell but then focused back on me. "Who is it?"

"You wouldn't believe me if I told you. I can barely believe it myself."

"Kisa, you're not making sense."

My stomach rolled with the words I was about to say, the secret I was about to confess. Serge sat farther forward, and I whispered, "You *won't believe me* if I tell you."

"Try me," he said curtly.

"It's . . . it's . . . Luka . . ."

Serge stared and stared at me like I was a moron. "Luka?" he asked. "Luka Tolstoi?"

"Yes," I replied in a barely audible voice and clutched the purse on my lap. It was filled with photos and mementos from our childhood. Tonight I was going to try and make him remember. Tonight I wanted him to remember me . . . us . . . *everything.*

I just wanted my Luka back . . . at least I wanted as much of him back as was left. I'd have any part of Luka at all, I'd take any tiny scrap of him that remained.

"You're being unfaithful with Luka Tolstoi?" Serge said dryly, confusion lacing his Russian accented voice.

I nodded, and he stared at me like I'd gone insane. "Kisa, Mr. Tolstoi died years ago in an accident. His body burned to death. What's really going on? Who are you trying to protect?"

"Raze—"

"The new fighter?" Serge interrupted. "What the hell has he got to do with Luka?"

"He *is* Luka, Serge. Raze *is* Luka."

"Kisa, I don't know what—"

"He got sent away to an underground prison after Rodion was killed, off the grid, and he was forced to become a fighter. A death match fighter, Serge. I know it sounds unbelievable, but it happened. He has no memory of who he is, where he's from, or who we all are to him. He was tortured and abused. He's like an animal, just fighting and surviving, no humanity, but the fleeting glimpses I get when he looks at me . . ." I swallowed hard and said, "When he's with me . . ."

"Kisa, this is all—"

"His eyes are the same as Luka's, brown with a smudge of blue in his left iris. His mannerisms are the same. He tilts his head and purses his lips, his *full* lips that are the exact same shape . . . And he has these dreams, vivid dreams. They're memories, Serge, not just dreams. I'm sure of it. Being back in Brooklyn, he's remembering more and more. It's Luka. He's come back to me." I looked up into Serge's shocked eyes and said, "And he needs my help. I've got to make him remember. I need to know what happened all those years ago. We all do. There's just so much pain. So many unanswered questions that have been swept under the rug."

Serge sat in silence, and I knew he didn't believe me. I didn't care, because I knew the truth, and it was up to me to save Raze. It was up to me to make him realize his feet had found their way home.

"Just take me to the gym, Serge. And please wait because I need you to drive us to Brighton Beach later on."

Serge went to argue, but I turned my head and leaned against the window, ending the discussion.

I entered the gym and headed to Raze's training room. The whole place was mostly in darkness, but for a single light hanging from the ceiling. Raze sat against the far wall, his head hanging low and his torso covered with black and red. His legs were stretched out in front of him. I'd never seen someone who'd just won a match look so defeated.

"Raze?" I said in panic and rushed over to him.

Dropping to my knees, I grabbed a nearby towel and pressed it against a long fresh tally mark on his torso, twice as long, twice as deep, and twice as aggressive as his other kill tattoos.

"Raze, what have you done?" I asked and tried to look into his lowered eyes. He didn't speak, didn't even flinch when I applied pressure to his sliced torso. He sat gripping a broken pen and bloodied razor blade in his hands.

As I checked the rest of his ripped and scarred body, I noticed a huge stitched-up slash on his arm and stitches along the bottom of his throat.

I remembered the exact moment in the match when he'd gotten them—the moment I thought he was going to be taken from me. Having that happen only made me more desperate to teach him about who he was. He was to fight Alik tomorrow night, the two of them having progressed to the final, and tomorrow night, I would be losing one of the only two men that had ever meant something to me. But I knew who I wanted, who I'd only ever wanted, and right now, he was lying down on this hard floor like his world had just been torn apart.

Luka needed to come back to me. Finally, after all these years in captivity, he needed to be freed. He needed to know he was loved.

"Raze, please look at me," I ordered in a gentle voice, fighting back tears, and Raze slowly lifted his head. His eyes were rimmed with red and he had the most haunting, devastating expression on his face. My heart lurched at the sight. I reached out and laid my hand on his cheek.

"Lyubov moya, what's all this? Was it the fight tonight? Was it because you were hurt? Because it was a close match?"

I caught Raze's hand lift from his side, and the razor blade fell to the floor. His rough, bloodied palm laid on the back of mine still on his cheek, and I froze.

"I killed my only friend," Raze rasped out, and his fingers wrapped around mine. His grip was so tight . . . so telling of his internal emotional turmoil.

My breathing caught in my throat and my thoughts immediately went to Rodion. Did he remember? Did he remember that night? Was he talking of my brother? Had he remembered his past?

My hand began to shake with the gravity of what this could mean.

"What friend? What are you talking about, lyubov moya?" I asked, trying to keep the quivering nerves from my voice.

Raze's gaze took on a blank stare, and he replied, "362."

I blinked at his answer and immediately thought back to our conversation last night. "362? From the Gulag?"

Raze nodded slowly and his hold on my hand tightened. "Goliath . . . "

Suddenly, everything made sense. It wasn't Rodion's death he was remembering; it was the man tonight, the Georgian Goliath. "The man you killed tonight was—"

"My friend."

My bottom lip trembled upon seeing this strong, untamed, and harsh man reduced to a hulking body of muscle filled with nothing but guilt and remorse.

"Raze . . . I'm so sorry," I soothed.

"He was recaptured when we escaped, by the Georgian mob. He told me if he'd won tonight, they were granting him his freedom. And once free, he could get his revenge on the people that sent him to the Gulag. After all those years surviving, teaching *me* how to survive . . . He was innocent. He deserved that revenge, but . . . "

Raze's eyelids fluttered, and I leaned in to press a kiss to his forehead, his cheek, and to the back of his hand fixed upon mine. "But what?"

"But so am I . . . " he whispered, and my blood cooled to ice in my veins.

"You are what?" I pushed.

His eyes widened as something in his mind clearly hit home and his torso tensed as though in shock. "I'm innocent," he whispered, clearly unable to speak louder. "Kisa . . . I'm innocent. I didn't do what I was imprisoned for. I didn't do what I was accused of." Raze's hand now fully encompassed mine, and he looked down at our clasped fingers. "You're shaking, Kisa-Anna. Why are you shaking?"

A sob escaped my throat and I released my hold on the towel to plant it over my mouth. The tears of relief poured from my eyes. He hadn't done it. Luka hadn't killed my brother. He was innocent. I always knew he was innocent.

"Kisa? I don't understand why you're crying." Raze's head tilted to the side and I dived to his chest, breathing in the heady scent that was all him, not caring if my clothes became soiled by blood and ink.

Raze's strong and comforting arms wrapped around my back and he kept me close. "*Shh*, solnyshko," he whispered, and my crying stopped and I lifted my head and stared into his eyes.

"Solnyshko?" I questioned, and Raze looked up in thought before glancing back down at me.

"It means 'little sun,'" Raze said matter-of-fact. "In Russian, I think." Then his forehead creased and his eyebrows pulled down as if he didn't understand why he knew that piece of information.

"You called me 'my love,'" he suddenly said, watching me, studying me like I was a problem he was trying to solve. I nodded and fought to keep my bottom lip from quivering. "*Lyubov moya*," he said, repeating the words slowly, sounding out each syllable before his eyes widened. "It means 'my love' in Russian. You called me 'your love.'"

"I did . . . lyubov moya" I replied and pulled out of his embrace. I caught his stuttered, shocked inhale, but just let him sit thinking of my old term of endearment for him.

Quickly wiping my eyes, I then ran my finger around his new tattoo. "Why is this so much longer than the rest? So much more pronounced than the others? You've really damaged your skin."

"Because 362's death was honorable where the others weren't. He died proudly. He died like a fighter should." Raze ran his fingertips over his scar and added, "He died before gaining his revenge. He was cheated out of retribution on those that wronged him. But he never gave up until the end. His recognition on my skin needs to stand out because he, as a fighter and a friend, stood out in my life."

My heart shredded hearing him speak, and I realized no matter how far I delved into my imagination, into my worst nightmare, I would never fully understand what he went through in the Gulag. He was a child. A child forced to be a killer, and amongst that hell, he'd found someone to care for . . . and he'd just been forced to kill his friend in cold blood.

Sorrow made me feel sick to my stomach. I couldn't help but be grateful that 362 was dead and I still had my Raze.

"I thought . . . I thought for a moment he was going to kill you . . ." I trailed off, my voice catching in my throat at the thought of losing my soul mate twice in my life. No heart could sustain that.

"He was winning," Raze confessed.

I gasped, and Raze leaned forward and ran his fingertips down my neck. "But then I saw Durov forcing you to watch me die and it fueled me. Gave me the strength to fight back and overpower my friend." Raze's gaze dropped to my lips, and he murmured, "I have to protect you, Kisa-Anna. I believe I was made to protect you." His face screwed up like he was trying really hard to remember something, and he added, "I had to protect you from Durov . . . *again*."

My heartbeat drowned out the noise of the air conditioner whirring in the main gym. "*Again?*" I questioned, and his eyes crinkled with confusion.

"Yes. I think . . . I think I've protected you from him before . . . " Taking my hand, Raze pulled me forward, searching my face up close, and asked, "Have I? Have I protected you from him before?"

I nodded, nerves stealing my voice.

Raze swallowed, his Adam's apple bobbing, and he croaked out, "Did I . . . ? Did I know you before?"

Stifling a threatening sob with the back of my hand, I cried, "Yes. Yes, you did. You knew me very well."

Raze's bare muscled chest began to rise and fall and lines framed his scrunched-up eyes. He was trying to remember, but by his held breath and frustrated exhales, I knew he couldn't. Something was blocking him, preventing him from fully embracing who he was before.

Releasing myself from Raze's hold, I reached into my purse and pulled out the old silver frame of two young children smiling for the camera and handed it to Raze, who looked down curiously at the picture.

He was like a caveman seeing the world's treasures for the first time, unsure what to make of the strange world he had been suddenly thrust into.

I watched his face with fascination as his brown eyes studied the children. He pulled the frame closer to his eyes and scrutinized the snapshot while my heart fluttered as fast as a hummingbird's wings.

His thumb ran across the girl's face and he looked up, watching my face with the same intense attention.

"I've seen this girl in my dreams."

"Yes," I whispered, and he lowered his eyes again and reared back his head.

"And this boy too. I know him too."

"Yes," was all I could say in response, praying to God he gave Raze the gift of memory. That he remembered who both of those children were, and when he did, he still wanted me . . . and in some deep, hidden part of him, realized he loved me just as much as I'd always loved him.

"This girl . . . " Raze said and lowered the picture frame and crawled toward me, his sculpted shoulders rolling at the movement, his packed abs flexing. Once before me, Raze pointed at my eyes, his head tilting to the side. His mouth hovered just before mine and his warm, enticing breath made me close my eyes.

"No!" he ordered, and my eyes snapped open on a gasp. Raze brought the frame forward and placed it next to my face. A knowing expression washed over his sharp, assessing handsome features. "You . . . you are the girl in this picture."

I felt tears trickling down my cheeks and I nodded, unable to speak, and he sat back, staring at me as though he were seeing me for the first time. "You're the girl from my dreams . . . "

"Yes, Raze, yes," I answered excitedly.

He exhaled a long breath like he'd just run a marathon, and he slumped back against the wall again, clutching the frame to his chest, just staring at me.

I held his gaze, willing him to remember more, but when a single tear ran down his stubbled cheek, it took everything I had not to fall apart.

I lurched forward and threw myself into his arms. "Lyubov moya! Please . . . no," I whispered and wrapped my arms around his neck and straddled his hips, feeling his heart thundering in his chest against mine. "It's okay. We'll get you to remember who you are. You'll remember everything in time. I promise."

His body shook and his nose tucked into the crook between my shoulder and neck, and he hugged me back, so tight it was a struggle to breathe.

We were silent, quietly sitting and comforting one another, when he asked, "Am I . . . am I this boy in the picture? The one holding you?"

I stilled and so very slowly pulled back to face him. Raze's eyes had darkened, glittering with questions, and when our gazes collided, I replied, "Yes. I think you *are* the boy in that picture. At first I didn't know, but now I'm sure. It's *you* . . . "

Raze didn't show any reaction, but his hand abruptly cupped my cheek and his head tilted to the side. We stayed that way for minutes and minutes, until his lips parted and a rush of breath poured through, and he whispered, "My Kisa-Anna . . . my solnyshko . . . God put a piece of your blue eyes in mine so we would always know we matched . . . "

Like a dam breaking, relieved excitement washed through me like a river amidst a hurricane, and I sobbed and cried, "Luka . . . my Luka . . ." before pressing my lips against this man's, tasting the essence of the boy I had been created and destined to love. Loving the lost man I now held in my arms.

Raze froze against my mouth, and I broke away to see his eyes shining, looking lost. "*Luka?*" he questioned, only for his eyes to widen, and he sucked in a sharp breath. "Luka . . . I was called Luka . . . My name was Luka?"

"Yes." I smiled and peppered kisses all over his face.

His hands clenched the thick strands of my brown hair. "Kisa-Anna, *my* Kisa-Anna," he kept murmuring over and over, and I was sure I would never tire of my name pouring from his perfect full lips.

"Yes! Yes, Luka. I'm yours! I was made for you."

We stayed clutched in each other's arms for what could have been an age, when I eventually pulled back, gave him a long sweet kiss, and said, "Would you come somewhere with me? I want to take you somewhere . . . somewhere special."

Raze tilted his head to the side but, without question, replied, "Anywhere. I . . . trust you."

He trusted me . . .

Rising to my feet, I took Raze's hand, led him into the bathroom and, wetting a rag, cleaned the area around his new tattoo and laid gauze over his new scars.

Raze slipped on a sweatshirt and sweatpants. I couldn't help but smile when I realized it was that same gray hooded sweatshirt that I had first seen him in, and I held out my hand.

Raze lifted the hood over his head—I assumed it was instinctive for him to hide as we were going outside—and came forward and cautiously took my outstretched hand. I wrapped my fingers in his and squeezed.

Raze's brown eyes caught mine from under his hood, and without a word, I led him outside, his huge frame dwarfing mine.

As we slipped out the back door, I spotted the awaiting Lincoln, and Serge jumped out of the car, his tall broad body tense like he was prepping for trouble.

Raze pulled me to a stop and pushed me behind him as if Serge were going to be a threat. I jerked on his hand and Raze growled, "Stay back."

I pushed my way around Raze and pushed on his solid chest with my hand until his eyes dropped to mine. "He's a friend, Raze. Like 362 was to you. He's my friend." I cast a glance back at Serge and knew Serge could hear everything I said out in this quiet parking lot, but I knew I could trust him. "You used to know him too. He used to be like an uncle to you."

Raze's head tipped to the side, and I could see his eyes squint under the shadow of his hood as he stared at Serge. I lifted my hand, laid it on his cheek and whispered, "Let yourself remember, Luka."

Raze's eyes slammed to mine at the mention of his old name, and as he glanced up at Serge again, I saw the moment the memory fixed in place. His tense muscles relaxed and a labored breath exhaled from his mouth.

"Serge," he hushed out quietly. "Serge." Raze rolled the name around on his tongue, and as I glanced back to Serge, his face was pale and he looked to me in shock. I knew he'd started to believe me.

Taking Raze's hand once more, I walked him over to Serge, who couldn't take his eyes off my fighter, my long lost love.

"Serge," I greeted, and Raze froze, his head dipped down, and his hood covered his entire face.

Serge was silent.

Looking up at Raze, I said, "Raze, pull back your hood."

Raze didn't move for a few long seconds, but he eventually lifted his hand and drew back his hood, his downcast eyes slowly lifting and fixed on Serge.

Serge's eyes were assessing as he studied Raze up close.

"Sergei?" Raze said, and Serge blanched further at the use of his full first name. He looked at me in disbelief, just as Raze said, "I . . . I *remember* you." Raze gripped my hand and pressed it to his lips, the action almost making me drop to my knees in happiness.

"You would drive me and Kisa to school . . . and to the beach?"

"Yes," Serge replied, and I heard the clogging of his throat and saw the tears build in his eyes. "Christ! It *is* you! You look different, but . . . yes, it's you."

"I told you I'd found him. That he'd come back to us," I said, and Serge shook his head, astounded.

"We thought you were dead. We were told you'd died in an accident."

I felt Raze stiffen and I panicked. I'd never talked about the murder or his apparent death. I'd never told him of his family, of Talia, of Ivan, of his mother, who still to this day could not move past the loss of her son. Raze had never mentioned any memory of his family, so I didn't want to push. I couldn't bear losing him again if it all became too much and he ran.

"What accident? What death?" Raze asked tightly, and I could see the pain etching his face. It was like it physically pained him to remember his life before becoming a fighter.

Serge's eyebrows pulled down, and I subtly shook my head, telling him without words to go no further.

Lifting to my tiptoes, I pressed my lips to Raze's and asked, "Would you go somewhere with me now? Serge will drive us there."

Raze pulled back and, without hesitation, answered, "Yes."

Serge made himself busy by opening the back doors of the Lincoln, and we climbed inside.

Raze was tense as he sat in the car and I stroked at his arm. "Are you okay, lyubov moya?"

Raze cleared his throat and shifted on the seat. Placing his hand on my knee, he squeezed. "Cars make me nervous. I . . . I haven't been in many, and I don't like not being in control."

Picking up his heavy arm, I laid it over my shoulder and cuddled into his waist. Raze's thumb stroked at my arm, and I sighed. I'd never felt like this. Even as a child, and infatuated with Luka to the level I was, I wasn't old enough to understand that your feelings can deepen even further with age. I didn't know believing you had lost your soul mate and then having them re-enter your life made the word "relief" too simple of an emotion, because the reality of having your heart fixed back together was too indescribable for words.

Looking up, I saw Serge casting the odd glimpse at the two of us, and a happy expression filled his face. He'd always loved Luka, and in truth, he'd always hated Alik. I knew that by the way he now looked at me safe in Raze's arms. It filled him with happiness. I knew he worried what my life would be like with Alik. And tomorrow night, my true love and my fiancé would fight to the death. I almost couldn't breathe at that thought of that fact, so I chose to block it from my mind and focus on being joined with the other half of my soul right now, right this second. Just living in the moment.

Raze pulled me closer to his side and ran his nose amongst my hair. "We used to sit like this, didn't we? You under the protection of my arm, safe."

I smiled against his abs. "Always."

"I think I remember that."

"Good, lyubov moya. That's really good."

17

RAZE

As soon as the car door opened, the familiar smell of the sea hit my nostrils, causing flashbacks to assault my guarded mind.

A boy.

A girl.

The beach.

A late summer's night.

Kissing . . . Something more . . . something big . . . something life changing . . . something that made my chest ache . . . something that just felt right.

Kisa took a red plaid blanket in her hands, yanking me from the memory as Serge opened the door.

"I want to show you somewhere, Raze," she said, and I got out of the car. I closed my eyes as I heard the sound of the sea waves, as I smelled the salt in the air.

A calm washed over my body as the sea waves crashed against the shore. Hearing people's voices in the distance, laughing and having a good time, somehow made me feel at home, for the first time ever. I tried to let myself enjoy this. I had never enjoyed . . . *anything*; too concerned with fighting, killing, training . . . revenge to ever let myself just be.

Tipping my head back, I sucked in a deep breath and let the muggy night air fill my lungs, only exhaling when Kisa took my hand in hers and began pulling me to the warm sand.

"I'll wait for you here," Serge shouted from behind us, and I glanced back to see him getting back into the car. He threw me a smile as he shut the door, and I gave him a curt nod in return.

Kisa and I didn't talk as our feet hit the sand. We didn't talk as she led me along the shore's edge, only stopping so I could remove my sneakers. As soon as the grainy sand hit my bare feet, I sighed and stared out at the dark water, the moon hanging low and bright.

It made me think of the dream, the one where the boy had been making love to Kisa on the beach. My eyes darted down to Kisa staring out at the ocean too, and my heart slammed in my chest, so loud and hard I was sure she would hear it. But she just kept looking out into the night, and I just kept . . . remembering.

I was remembering . . .

They were young, very young, when they'd been together, but it had meant so much. They were nervous, too nervous, but when the boy was inside her, her pussy so tight and wet, it stole his breath.

She'd been so nervous as the boy took her on the sand, making her his, something switching inside of him as they came together, like the final piece of their souls had fixed in place and all that was left was them as one.

"It's my favorite place on Earth," Kisa whispered, suddenly breaking through the quiet of the night, and I stepped to the side until I was behind her, draping my arms around her shoulders and resting my chin on her head.

"You come here a lot?" I asked, seeing large boats in the distance, sailing across the horizon.

Kisa tensed up, then said quietly, "I haven't been here in twelve years."

I frowned in confusion, but before I could question why, she turned in my arms and took my hand. "It's this way."

Following her lead, I asked, "What is?"

Kisa's beautiful face suddenly looked happy and she leaned into my side, her scent hitting my nose, keeping me calm. I didn't like being out in public. I didn't like open spaces. I'd been caged up too long, so long that freedom and open areas made me feel uneasy.

"Our cove."

We walked for a while before we climbed over some rocks and, hidden away from sight, was a small blocked-off patch of sand. Kisa sniffed beside me. "It hasn't changed at all," she whispered and jumped off the rock down onto the sand.

Looking back, her blue eyes were bright, her long black dress clung to her fucking beautiful hourglass curves, and her long brown hair blew in the light sticky wind.

"Kisa-Anna . . . " I rasped out and went to jump down too, but suddenly I came to a stop as something big came back to me . . . something I think I'd known since the night I'd saved her. I just didn't know how to actually *feel*, how to let it in, until now.

My eyes widened as I stared at my woman. "I had her . . . " I said under my breath and only to myself, memories of *us* together flooding my mind. "I had her. She was mine . . . " I repeated, as I thought of us on this beach, in this cove, in Serge's car, on the pier.

I stretched up my neck and glanced over the rocks to see a long pier shining with lights, and my heart boomed like a crash of thunder in a thunderstorm.

Kisa laid out the blanket on a patch of sand nearest the rocks, and I leapt down beside her. Within seconds, I had lifted her into my arms. Her surprised blue eyes met mine as her hands gripped onto my biceps.

My eyes bored into hers, and I said breathlessly, "I had you. I had you since the day you were born. I asked your mama for you and she said yes."

Kisa's face filled with a gamut of emotions: happiness, sorrow, and . . . hope? I didn't know, but she nodded and her eyes misted over, moisture threatening to fall.

Dropping to my knees, the memories so strong I couldn't stand any longer, I laid Kisa on the blanket and hovered over her. Warmth filled my chest like the sun had moved its home inside of me. I'd only ever felt cold before. The cell was cold. Killing was cold . . . I was always cold, but right now, I was warm . . . I felt alive. No longer dead inside.

I gazed into her eyes and saw only happiness in her stare.

"Raze . . . " she murmured, stroking through the strands of my hair, but I couldn't speak.

We'd always been together. Her and me, from birth, we were always together.

Urging Kisa's hand from my hair, I threaded my fingers through hers and studied her slim fingers, the nails painted pink, through my cut and scarred hands, marks from years of fighting, my knuckledusters marring the skin . . .

As we sat on the sofa, Kisa pulled out a book to read, and I watched her eyes racing along the sentences, an excited smile on her lips.

"How long do you think our fathers will be in there?" I asked, wanting her to look at me, to pay me attention, not the damn book.

Kisa glanced at me over the page and shrugged. "Don't know. Papa always takes a long time when he's doing business."

I nodded but never took my eyes from her face. Kisa dropped her head and blushed. I was nine now, she was eight, and I couldn't stop staring at her face every time I saw her. She was so pretty.

Kisa began reading again, and I shuffled closer to her until our arms brushed. She glanced sideward at me and started chewing on her lip.

I tried to sit back against the couch, but I couldn't stop watching Kisa-Anna. My hand started to twitch and I wanted to reach out and touch her. She was my best friend, and best friends should touch, I thought.

Without thinking it through, I reached out and took her hand in mine, wrapping our fingers around each other's.

Kisa gasped and said, "Luka, what are you doing?"

I shrugged. "Holding your hand."

"Why?" Kisa whispered, staring at my thumb stroking her skin. She was so soft.

"Because I have to," I answered honestly, and she seemed to stop breathing for several minutes before exhaling, her long eyelashes fluttering when she looked at me.

"Okay," she whispered, and something warm spread in my chest and down to my stomach. "I . . . I like it."

I smiled and Kisa blushed again. "Me too. I'm going to hold your hand all the time now. I'm never going to let go."

"I don't ever want you to," she said shyly, and I pulled her to rest back against the couch, her side tucked next to mine, our hands still fused together.

"Read to me," I said and closed my eyes.

Kisa took a deep breath and started her story from the beginning.

"They were always meant to be together, one boy and one girl, two hearts split into two, sent to far-off lands on their own. For God wanted to see if true love could be tested. He wanted to see if two halves of one soul could find each other again, even against the odds. Years would pass, they would both be hurt, they would both be sad, but one day, when they least expected it, they would stumble into each other's paths. The question is: would they recognize each other's soul? Would they find their way back to love . . . ?"

"We would hold hands," I said, my vision snapping back into focus, almost like I had no control of the memories rushing into my mind like a waterfall. "You would read to me. I would hold your hand and you would read to me."

Kisa nodded frantically and tears slipped out of the sides of her eyes onto the blanket. Her left hand raked through my hair, and my eyes squeezed shut, more images almost drowning me . . .

"I love your hair, Luka . . . It looks like gold and feels like silk," Kisa's young self had said as I lay on the grass in a park.

"Mmm . . . don't stop. I love it when you play with my hair."

I gasped at the images in my head, and concentrated on feeling her hand in mine. "You would stroke my hair in the park," I said, my voice increasing in both volume and speed as more memories came racing back.

"Yes." Kisa sobbed, her bottom lip trembling, but her blue eyes shone like she wanted more and more. "Yes, I would."

"Kisa, quickly, follow me. Father Kruschev isn't looking!" I took Kisa's hand and we ran out of the church onto the steps, where I pulled Kisa to my lap and pulled her in for a kiss.

"Mmm . . . Luka." Kisa moaned and gripped the collar of my shirt.

"I fucking hate church, it's boring," I whispered against her mouth, and Kisa pulled away, laughing at my confession.

"You can't say that! God is watching!" Kisa hissed, and I tucked my head into her neck, just breathing her in.

"Nah, he's already given me you. He obviously loves me enough to give me a free pass to sneak out of the service and kiss my girl."

Kisa pulled me to face her, and I could see how much I meant to her in that one look. "Luka . . ." She trailed off and pushed her lips against mine. "Then he loves me enough too, because he knew I could only ever want you."

"Church," I choked out, my straining arms holding me above Kisa, now beginning to shake. "Us on the steps."

"Yes! Yes, Raze! More, please remember more," Kisa begged, and I closed my eyes again . . .

"Luka . . ." Kisa whispered, and I couldn't help but smile.

"Kisa," I said back, then looked at her wet lips. I blurted, "I want to kiss you now."

"But I've . . . I've never been kissed before," Kisa said, blushing, and I lost my breath at how beautiful she was, giving her a smile.

"Me neither."

Shock spread on her face. "You haven't?"

"Who else would I have kissed?" I said, pissed that she'd think any other girl would ever matter to me.

She shrugged. "I don't know. You have a lot of girls at church following you around."

I laughed and shook my head. Squeezing her shoulders, I leaned down and rasped, "But none of them are you." I pointed to my left eye, the one that had a smudge of blue in the iris. "We match. Why would I want anyone else? There was only one girl made for me."

"We kissed," I recollected and looking down, ran my hand through the sand. "Here," I said in shock. "We had our first kiss here, on this spot."

Kisa's happy laugh mixed with her crying and she pulled me to her lips, her mouth wet and salty with her tears. Her hands were tight in my hair, and I cupped her face, not wanting to let her go, as her thighs wrapped around my waist.

Retracting her lips an inch from mine, she asked, "What else, Raze? What else did we do here? Can you . . . can you remember? Please . . . let yourself remember . . ."

•   •   •

Dipping my head, I pressed my lips against hers and she moaned into my mouth, her hand lifting to slip around the back of my neck.

The kiss grew deeper, and I broke away to shift Kisa down to the sand. I crawled on top of her, feeling her warm body underneath mine.

It didn't take long to lose control, and I broke from Kisa's mouth on a gasp. Her lips were swollen and her hands gripped my neck, trying to pull me back down.

"Kisa-Anna," I said and pressed a kiss to the side of her neck. "We have to stop. I can't . . . We can't . . . I need to stop . . ."

Her blue eyes dropped and she turned her head to the side, staring at the moon. I lowered my head to her shoulder, trying to get myself under control, breathing through the tingling in my stomach.

Kisa's hands rested on my cheeks and she pushed on my face until I lifted my head and stared into her eyes. "Luka," she whispered, "I want to do this with you."

My eyes widened and my heart beat hard in my chest. "Kisa, are . . . are you sure?"

Kisa nodded shyly. "Can I have you?" she asked.

Feeling like my heart exploded in my chest, I said, "Yes," and I pressed my lips back to hers.

Later that night, Kisa lay in my warm arms, and I couldn't stop myself from kissing her face. "I love you, Kisa," I confessed, and she turned to me and dipped her eyes, overcome with a sudden rush of shyness.

"I love you too. I'm glad you were my first."

"And last," I promised and wrapped her tighter in my arms, both naked under the modest cover of my sweatshirt.

"I can't imagine ever sharing this with anyone else . . . ever . . ." Kisa said on a sigh.

I couldn't have agreed more.

A pained groan slipped from my mouth and my stomach clenched, my cock hardening as Kisa lay underneath me, her nipples beginning to poke through her dress. I lowered my mouth and licked along the bud over the material, my hips grinding against her hot pussy as she arched under my touch.

"Raze . . ." Kisa murmured, and I reached for the bottom of her dress and pulled it up her legs to her waist. Her panties were small and black, and a possessive growl fled my lips as I bent forward and licked along their seams, inhaling that musky smell that I was addicted to.

The need to taste her took control of me and in seconds, Kisa's panties were scattered on the sand behind us. Her cunt came into view, only a small patch of hair on her mound and her lips drenched wet.

Reaching out, I ran my fingertip down her slit, and Kisa's hips bucked and, closing her eyes, she released a long moan. Sitting up, I ripped off my sweatshirt, suddenly too hot. Kisa watched my every move, her blue eyes shining with need.

My cock throbbed, a steel pole, but when Kisa let her legs drop apart even farther and she palmed her tits, I leaned forward and, running my lips over the inside of her thigh, followed my instinct and swiped along her slit with my tongue.

As soon as the salty taste filled my mouth, I needed more. I began lapping, drinking her in. Kisa's hands ripped at the strands of my hair. This only made me lose it more. Using my strength, I placed my hands on her inner thighs and pushed them apart as far as they would go, opening her wide to take her however I wanted.

Kisa's hand slipped from my grasp and landed on her pussy, and I watched with held breath as she touched herself. Pre-cum dripped from the tip of my cock and my balls ached with the need to mark my woman, to have her again . . . but this time knowing who we were to each other, who she was to me.

Kisa's fingers began stroking at her swollen clit, and my nostrils flared watching her mouth drop open and her tongue lick along her bottom lip.

"Touch me, here, Raze. Lick me. Suck me here on my clit. Make me come in your mouth."

My heart pounded so hard at her words that I thought it would rip from my chest. I leaned forward, lowering my mouth, knocking her hand out of the way so I could do as she asked.

It was the first time I'd ever tasted pussy. Her scent drove me forward. Using my thumbs to spread her lips, I circled the tip of my tongue over her clit. Kisa moaned and jerked as soon as it made contact. My tongue became frenzied, licking her clit over and over, and Kisa's legs began to shake, her nails clawing at my bare shoulders.

"Raze . . . lyubov moya . . . that feels . . . that feels . . . Ahh!"

Kisa screamed as my lips wrapped around her clit, sucking and my finger pushed inside her dripping hole, pumping back and forth.

My senses were going crazy. The musk of her pussy, the taste of her juices, the wet feel of her channel, and the noises slipping from her mouth. Sucking even harder and pushing a second finger inside her, Kisa stiffened and, digging her nails into my skin so hard I knew she'd drawn blood, Kisa came hard, screaming into the quiet night. Slowing my movements and removing my fingers from her slit, I traced over her lips with my tongue as Kisa panted and began stroking at my hair.

Lifting my head, I crawled over Kisa's spent, beautiful body and I took in her hooded eyes and flushed face.

She stared into my eyes and ran the back of her hand down my cheek. "Did you remember, lyubov moya? Do you remember anything else?"

Closing my eyes, licking along my lips, I opened them again, only to nod and reach down, freeing my cock from my sweatpants. I was so fucking hard, and I needed to be inside Kisa. Needed to hear her call my name.

Crawling back over her body, I pulled the straps of her dress off her shoulders, her tits coming into view, her pink nipples hard and waiting for my mouth. Bending down, I sucked the right into my mouth, palming the flesh in my hand, only to reluctantly release it to do the same to the left.

"Lyubov moya, I need you inside me," Kisa moaned, moving her hand to wrap around my cock and began stroking it back and forth. Lurching back onto my heels, I threw my head back and hissed through my teeth. My balls were tight as she worked me over and over, but when I felt a wet lick lap at the tip of my cock, my eyes snapped open and every muscle in my body tensed.

A low growl rumbled in my chest as I looked down to see Kisa on all fours, her tight ass in the air and her full lips wrapped around my dick.

"Kisa . . ." I groaned, my voice low and graveled. "Fuck, that feels good . . ."

Kisa moaned, her back arched, and she moved her head forward, taking as much of my dick into her hot mouth as she could, the tip hitting the back of her throat. Warmth started building at my knees and traveled up my thighs, and I knew if Kisa kept eating at my dick, I was going to come.

Squeezing my eyes shut, I fought back the need to have my woman swallowing my cum and managed to push her head away, her full lips red and glistening and those blue eyes bright as she looked up at me with the most beautiful expression on her face.

Unable to speak, I pushed her back until she was flat on the blanket, and I closed my eyes, clearly seeing myself in this position years ago, feeling nervous and inexperienced but felt so connected to Kisa below me that my arms were shaking as I entered her, as I broke through her virginity.

"Baby, look at me. Keep those eyes open as you make love to me. There's no more bad, only good between us," Kisa whispered, and I did as she asked, using my arm strength to hover over her small trim body and my thighs to push between her legs until the tip of my cock hit her hot slit.

Kisa's hands stroked over every inch of my back, my taut arms, my neck, traps, and through my hair. Her touch almost undid me, and as I looked down at her, everything seemed to slot into place. This was my woman, my Kisa-Anna, the other half of my soul.

Lowering myself until I was propped on my elbows, I ran my nose up her cheek inhaling her scent and moved down into her hair, my mouth stopping at her ear.

"I remember taking you here on this beach. I remember it being our first time. We were kids, maybe teens? I don't know. But I sneaked you out of your house and brought you here, to our cove. We kissed, and it turned into more . . . Then you asked if you could have me . . ." Kisa's face was drowning in tears, and I tipped my head to the side, wiping her cheeks with my hand. "And I said yes."

"Raze," she cried, and her breath hitched.

Feeling like something wasn't right, I froze.

Kisa's expression changed from happy to worried. "Raze? What's wrong?"

As she spoke my name, I knew that was it.

Raze . . . Raze, Raze, Raze . . .

Kisa's hand raked through my hair. "Raze," she murmured again, and I suddenly gripped her wrists, keeping her still, her blue eyes widening in shock. "Raze, what—"

"No!" I said through gritted teeth. "Don't call me that!"

Kisa's face lost color. "Why?"

Why?

Why?

"Be-because it's not my name. I'm not prisoner 818. I'm not . . . I'm not Raze . . ." My chest constricted like I couldn't breathe, and I let go of Kisa's wrist to rub at my sternum.

"Ra—" Kisa stopped herself and stilled my hand with her own, then brought it to her lips to kiss. "Why were you called that?"

I stared toward the sea and my eyes lost focus, too lost in the memory. "The better I got at fighting"—I huffed a humorless laugh—"at *killing,* I couldn't be stopped. I just got better and better, and the bigger and faster the opponent they brought to face me, the more vicious I became. With the blades on my knuckledusters, I'm unstoppable. The guards joked that I'd *raze* my opponents. Word spread and then the warden forced the tattoo on my back to please the crowd, who would chant it as I entered the cage."

I blinked until my vision slipped back in place. Then I looked to my Kisa again. "So hearing that word doesn't sound right from your lips. You don't treat me like the guards did, like those men did."

"No, and I never will . . . You've been wronged, but no more, baby."

Folding my arms above Kisa's head, keeping her close, I said, "I want you to call me by my name . . . my *real* name."

Kisa's expression finally changed from worry to understanding, and with tears once again filling her eyes, she nodded.

"You . . . you want me to call you . . . *Luka,*" she whispered knowingly, and hearing that name slip from her lips as I held her in my arms just about undid me.

My cock hardened even more, but it wasn't enough.

"Say it again," I demanded roughly, and Kisa swallowed hard, her legs widening, her thighs tightening around my waist, and she drew my cock in toward her pussy.

As my tip pushed through the entrance, Kisa's hands wrapped around my neck and she lowered my ear to her mouth. Both of us groaning, I sank in my dick inch by inch.

Kisa stilled me with a squeeze of her thighs. Her warm breath blew past my ear. "Luka," she moaned, "make love to me . . . my Luka."

Like a door had been opened, I roared out loud and used all my strength to push forward, slamming into Kisa until I filled her completely, until she screamed my name. *Luka.* Until she screamed it over and over again.

Luka, Luka, Luka . . .

This time as I made her mine, there was no thinking, just feeling. For the first time ever I was actually *feeling* things. My throat choking with the *amount* of things I was feeling. I'd blocked out everything for so long, been numb for so long, that I didn't know how to deal with it, so I focused on being inside my woman, on the moans and whimpers pouring from her mouth as I pressed against her swollen clit, as my cock brushed against that spot inside her that made her go crazy.

Her hard nipples brushed against my damp chest, and every time I pushed forward, Kisa gasped at the friction, at the feeling of my dick filling her, telling her who she belonged to.

"Luka, my Luka," she moaned into my ear, and every syllable from her mouth drove me further and further, made my hips thrust faster and faster. "You came back to me . . ."

"Kisa," I said in a tight voice, feeling my balls tighten almost to the point of pain. "I'm going to come, solnyshko . . ."

Her fingernails dug into my shoulders and her breathing stuttered. "Close . . . so close, Luka . . . Fuck me harder . . . harder, Luka, harder!"

With every bit of strength I had and with all the power I could draw into my thighs, I rammed forward, my skin slapping against Kisa's pussy, the sound of us joined together like this pushing me over the edge.

My dick swelled, my mouth gaped, and hearing Kisa shrill out her orgasm, I reached forward and sank my hands in the warm sand beneath Kisa's head and filled her with my cum as her cunt strangled my dick.

My forehead fell on Kisa's mussed up hair.

I was catching my breath, minute by minute, trying to cope with this new beat to my heart, when Kisa whispered, "I love you, Luka. In all these years without you, I never stopped."

Every fiber of my body froze.

"Love?" I asked, frowning. "What . . . what is that?"

Kisa's thighs loosened around my waist and she pushed on my chest until I looked into her eyes. "Love, lyubov moya. You don't remember what that is?" Her voice sounded sad, like I'd hurt her somehow.

I didn't want to hurt her. The thought of hurting her, hurt *me*.

I dropped my head in embarrassment. "No . . . I don't really understand what it means. I've heard of the word, but it has no meaning to me."

Kisa reached back and took my hand, bringing it to lie over her chest, her heart thudding against my palm. My heart started thudding too.

"Love is an emotion, Luka. It's shared between two people. Two people who can't stop thinking about each other. Two people who think of each other every single day, every second, day and night. Two people who want to spend the rest of their lives together." She paused to press her lips to mine, then pulled back. "Two people who make love, just like we did now, and know their souls belong to each other, and *only* each other."

A tear ran down Kisa's cheek, and leaning forward, I kissed it. Pulling back, I tilted my head to the side to stare at Kisa's beautiful face.

"Then I . . . then I love you?"

Kisa stayed still for a moment, then surprised me by wrapping her arms around my neck and burying her face in my chest. "I hope you do, Luka. I pray you still love me too." And I felt the wetness from her eyes on my skin.

I clutched her to my chest and rolled us to the side so I could stare at her face. I didn't think I'd ever get sick of her face. Kisa sniffed but fought to pull a nervous smile on her face.

I laid my head on my bicep and pointed to my chest. "So this . . . *ache* I've had in my chest since I saw you is . . . love? When I see you in my dreams, and want you, it is because I love you?"

"Luka . . . Is that true?" she whispered, hope in her quiet voice.

I nodded, and she hooked her forefinger around mine. I looked at our fingers joined together and, for some reason, couldn't look away.

"I have always loved you, Luka, and always dreamed you'd come back to me. I knew it was impossible, but I always prayed you, some-how, miraculously would."

"My . . ." I cleared my throat, trying to put into words what was stuck there.

Kisa held her breath and our entwined fingers tightened.

"My . . . Something within me, here," I pointed to my heart. "Here." I pointed to my stomach. "And here." I pointed to my mind. "Tells me I should have you. That you should belong to me. That you *do* belong to me, and that I belong to you."

"And there," Kisa said, pointing to my eye.

"Here?" I said, pointing at my eye too.

Kisa nodded and smiled. "That smudge of blue in your eye, says you always have."

My pulse began to race and for once, my blood felt like it was pumping through my veins, not lying stagnant, finally bringing me back to life.

"Why, Kisa?" I asked. "Why is it like this between us?"

Kisa dipped her eyes, not saying anything for a while, but then she smiled shyly and murmured, "*Whatever our souls are made of—*"

"*His and mine are the same.*" I finished off, the words coming from some locked-away memory in my mind. My eyebrows pulled down, and I watched happiness flood Kisa's face. "What . . . what is that? Why do I know it?"

"It's *Wuthering Heights*, a book I used to read to you before you were taken away. It's a line from that, one my mama used to say applied to us. We used to like it."

"Where is your mama?"

Kisa sighed a shaky sigh and her eyes glistened. "She died, Luka. She died when I was fifteen."

Death. It was everywhere.

Neither of us said anything for a while, but as the night drew on, I pulled Kisa to my chest. "Kisa?" I said.

"Mmm?" she murmured sleepily against my chest.

"I will kill Durov tomorrow night."

Kisa stiffened, and I held my breath. She never talked about how she felt about him, just told me he couldn't live without her and he needed her. But I needed her too, and the difference between Alik and me was that she needed *me* by her side, keeping her safe.

"I know," Kisa finally whispered back, but I could hear the pain in her voice. A flashback from when I was a kid suddenly came to me, and my body jerked upright, Kisa falling to the sand.

I gripped my temples as the memory came quick, the pain piercing my skull almost too strong to endure . . .

"You killed him, Alik!" I shouted, covered in my best friend's blood as Rodion turned cold in my arms.

Alik held out the knife he'd stabbed him with, his eyes were wild and a crazy smile spread on his lips.

"No, Luka, I didn't kill him." I watched as Alik drove the knife into his own stomach and he dropped to the floor. "You did! You argued. You fought, and you pulled out a knife and killed him."

"What . . . what the fuck are you talking about? You're insane!" I shouted, but Alik was already screaming for help.

"He's gone," Alik said, looking to me and gripped his stomach. His blood poured out as he pointed to Rodion's body. "The Volkov heir's no more. I did just what my papa commanded. Now, one day, I'll be the Pakhan. Rodion was too weak to lead, too nice. Me, I was born to be ruthless, to kill anyone in my way."

My blood turned to ice when I heard he'd killed Rodion for power. His father had ordered him dead so his son would be next in line.

Jesus Christ!

"And me?" I whispered, numbly. "Why the fuck are you setting me up?"

Footsteps approached and our fathers' voices called our names. Alik shouted back, flopping back onto the ground, but not before he smiled at me and said, "Because I needed someone to blame and I want what you have."

I shook my head in confusion. "What—"

"She was always meant for me, not you. I need her. She's the only one who calms me down. She's the only one who stops the voices in my head that tell me to hurt people. And her being obsessed with you is getting in the way of making her mine."

I stumbled back as what he said registered in my mind.

Kisa.

He killed Rodion for power and was framing me for . . . Kisa? Before I knew it, I was on top of him, ignoring the blood pouring from his stomach, punching at his face.

"You won't hurt her, you sick fuck! You'll leave her alone! You're insane! You should be locked up!"

Alik smiled at me as I beat his face, like he wasn't feeling the blows. I stilled in shock and he slipped the dagger in my hand.

A man came bursting through the trees, and seeing his son dead on the ground, he dropped to his knees. All I could do was watch as he tried to bring him back to life, then scream into the air when the CPR didn't work.

Another man came through next.

The men saw me on Alik, my fists coated with blood, my mouth tight with anger. I got to my feet and stumbled back until my ass hit the ground. My legs wouldn't move as I took in the scene. I couldn't speak. I couldn't speak to explain . . . my best friend was dead.

One of the men rushed forward and ran to Alik on the ground, then I noticed the men's eyes slam to me, then to my side.

Turning my head slowly, I glanced down at what they were all staring at and saw the bloodied dagger under my splayed hand.

I opened my mouth to try and explain what happened, but just as I did, Rodion's papa got to his feet, blood covering his coat, the move pulling my attention.

"Luka, what have you done?"

"Luka! Luka!" Kisa's panicked voice cut into the night. "Breathe, breathe . . . You're not breathing. Try and calm down."

I focused on Kisa's face, on her hand stroking back my hair. Finally able to move, I lifted my hand and took hers in mine.

"What is it, lyubov moya? What did you remember?" Kisa asked, and I could hear the nerves in her voice. "You're scaring me."

"D-Durov," I stuttered out. "Durov killed Rodion, stabbed himself, then pinned all the blame on me."

18

RAZE

Kisa's hand began shaking as she held mine, and I saw her face pale, the reality of that fact hitting home just as the dam of my blocked-out past broke and memories came flooding out, blindsiding me.

"Rodion," I whispered, feeling like I'd just taken a punch to the kidney. "Rodion was my best friend, wasn't he? We were like brothers. Yes? Is that—"

I watched tears fall from Kisa's eyes. My eyes grew wider as I pictured Rodion's features: light-brown hair, blue eyes. I dreamed of him sometimes. He was the boy in my dreams. His features had always been blurred, and I was unable to ever make out his identity. But now I could picture him with crystal clarity. I knew him. I—

Shit . . .

I looked at Kisa again. She was slumped over, her back shaking with the force of her tears. And then in my mind, I saw her and Rodion together: at church, at the beach, round a table, by their father's side . . .

Lifting my hand and pressing it on her back, I swallowed hard. "He . . . Rodion was your brother, wasn't he? Fuck, Kisa, Rodion was your blood."

A sob slipped from Kisa's mouth and she slumped onto the sand. Crawling forward, I covered Kisa with my body and wrapped my arms around her waist. She leaned into my arms and cried harder, her hands reaching out to grip onto my thighs while I tried to breathe through the memories of my past hitting me with the force of a truck.

"Kisa," I murmured. "Durov killed him . . . He killed him . . ."

Another loud sob ripped from her throat and she began shaking. Pushing herself upright with her hands on my thighs, Kisa lifted her head. Her beautiful face was red and wet with her tears.

"No! I always thought his death must have been an accident. A misunderstanding. Some other explanation. I-I—" Reaching out, she gripped my biceps, desperation in her expression. "Why? Why did Alik kill him? What had Rodion ever done to him? I don't understand! They were friends!"

I squeezed my eyes shut, holding my breath like I could force the memory.

"Please remember. Please remember," Kisa begged.

The Volkov heir's no more. I did what my papa commanded.

Dragging in a gasp, I looked at Kisa and suddenly saw a man's face in my head. He was tall, dark, older, a fucking evil glint in his eyes. *Just like the guards*, I thought. He had that sadistic, controlling look in his eyes that the guards always wore.

"His papa," I said, and Kisa could only blink. "His papa told him to take out the heir . . . so he would be next in line. So he could lead when he was old enough."

"No," Kisa said, shaking her head. "No! Abram wouldn't do that. He loved Rodion!"

"Alik stabbed Rodion because his father told him to. That's what Alik said!"

The shaking of Kisa's head grew faster. "No, no, no, no!" She staggered to her feet and wrapped her arms around her waist. Her feet suddenly stopped in the sand, and she asked, "And Alik? Wh-why did Alik stab himself and blame you? Why take you from me too?"

Every muscle in me froze and my heart thundered in my chest. Kisa saw my reaction and her arms dropped to her sides. "What?" she asked, her voice laced with dread, fear . . . anxiousness.

Feeling a sudden rush of protectiveness, I lurched forward and crushed my mouth against hers, Kisa moaning in surprise. Her hands slammed to my hard pecs, but her mouth moved against mine like she couldn't resist what we had, the spark that was between us.

Pulling back, breathless, I pressed my forehead against hers, gripping tightly onto her neck.

"Luka . . . please . . . tell me," Kisa begged, her voice barely a whisper.

Inhaling a ragged breath, I closed my eyes and answered honestly, "Because of you." I opened my eyes, and Kisa backed away, her gaze searching mine. She was shaking her head, tears spilling down her cheeks. "He needed someone to blame and he wanted you, Kisa-Anna. He wanted you away from me."

"No!" Kisa turned her back to me and held on to a nearby rock. Her head shook back and forth, and all I could do was to stand there watching her, every muscle tensed with the unknown . . . the unknown of how to be with her . . . how to make her feel better.

I stood there like a mute and watched her fall apart. But when a pained scream ripped from her throat and she fell to her knees, my feet seemed to move of their own accord, and I dropped behind her, wrapping my arms around her slight body.

"He's . . . he's troubled. He's always been troubled with voices in his head. Urges to hurt people. He needed me, even then, he needed me to stop the urges," she whispered. "He's always been so possessive of me. But I never thought . . . I couldn't have imagined . . ." Kisa's breath hitched and she began turning in my arms. I froze, unsure of what she was doing, when she crawled on my lap and laid her head on my shoulder. I fought to breathe quietly, her actions making something within me warm, like her touch her closeness thawing the thick ice in my blood.

Kisa's bloodshot eyes traced the graphic demons I had tattooed on my chest—a gift from the guards who wanted me to look evil to the Gulag crowd—and her breath blew against my neck, sending shivers down my spine.

"I can't . . . I can't take that he blamed it on you, my beautiful Luka, my best friend, my soul's other half . . . because of me . . . because he *wanted* me . . ."

She sucked in a shuddering breath and her hand dropped to trace round my stomach. "That he would injure himself so . . . so . . . brutally to create such an impressive lie against you."

I closed my eyes, trying hard not to lose grip of my rage at the thought of Durov and what he had done.

But that was shot to hell when Kisa said, "He never even let me grieve your death. He just swooped in and took me for his own. I was only thirteen. But I was his. My father didn't complain, he was lost, and then a couple of years later my mama died of a heart attack—the pain of losing my brother was too much for her to bear. Papa's only child was now with the only heir—it was the perfect outcome from such a horrific situation. And I was so numbed by grief of losing everyone I loved, that I never fought him. In fact, I was glad someone was there for me."

Kisa lifted her head and pressed three kisses on my rigid jaw. "I had lost you . . . I didn't care much about anything after that . . . until you saved me in the alley and my heart began to beat again." She sucked in a breath. "I hadn't even realized it'd stopped."

Not knowing how to respond, I gripped her tighter.

"Luka?" she asked. I grunted a reply. "Where did you go? What happened?"

I narrowed my eyes and concentrated on my past. "Your father took me to his office, along with Alik's." My eyebrows pulled down, my head aching. "Someone begged for my life. Another man was in the room with us, I think, but I can't make out his face."

Kisa stiffened in my arms. "You don't know who that man is? What he looks like?"

The man was older and maybe had light hair, but that was all I could see. I tried to keep going while I still had this memory in my mind. I was afraid if I focused too much on the man trying to spare my life, the whole memory would come tumbling down.

"He pleaded with your father to not kill me, but Durov's papa wanted me dead. I . . ." My heart started pumping hard and I could feel my blood rushing through my veins. "I remember feeling fear, but I couldn't open my mouth. Durov's father was so angry that he intimidated me . . . He stole my voice with his glare. Gestured to me that he would kill me if I spoke. I was mute with shock. The man who tried to defend me started arguing with him, and . . . and guns were pulled."

I squeezed my eyes shut and shook my head, parts of the memory becoming grainy. "The next thing I knew, your father told me there would be no cops involved in my crime, in my murder of Rodion, but that I was going to be sent to the motherland, to Russia to a contact he had there. He told me I would be punished. He told me I would be in a prison for kids, doing manual labor on a farm deep in the Russian countryside . . . He told me I would never come back to Brooklyn."

Kisa came closer, almost melding herself into my chest like she wanted to crawl into my skin. "My God, Luka . . . I remember them taking you away. I was taken home . . . and all I remember is being numb as I lay in my bed."

Kisa looked up at me and placed her palm upon my skin. "What happened next? Because . . . because after you left, and I didn't know where they had taken you, we were told you were dead."

The smell of smoke burned my nose. The sounds of screeching tires skidding to a stop. There was a bus . . .

"I was in a bus. It was cool outside. Night. I remember not being able to see through the glass because the windows were so steamed up. There were four, maybe five of us being taken away somewhere. Nobody talked. We all sat separately. But I could feel that we were all scared. We were all young . . . teens? Some could've been even younger. Some had been sold by their families to work on the farms."

I stared off at the lights on the pier, almost feeling drained by how much I had remembered tonight. But the lights blurred and I could suddenly see something else in my mind. The lights . . . the screeching of tires . . .

"The bus was run off the road," I blurted, my voice speaking aloud a memory it was currently processing. "Headlights from a van blinded us on a dark road. There was a loud bang and the driver of the bus swerved and we rolled into a ditch.

"We were all screaming, but the driver wasn't moving. I remember climbing over the seats, hearing the other boys moan from their injuries, and crawled to the driver. But when I got to him, I could see blood. I could see a hole in his head . . . a hole I knew he didn't get from the accident."

I pressed the heels of my hands into my eyes, the pain of such memories coming too strong.

"Luka?" Kisa whispered and began rubbing at my back. "Don't . . . ."

don't push yourself too much. It's okay, lyubov moya. It's okay. Don't rush yourself. This is all too much for you to go through in such a short space of time."

Anger boiled in my stomach, and I began to shake violently, my inner rage almost too much to cope with.

"No," I snapped curtly, my voice sounding deadly even to me. Kisa jumped and I heard her hold her breath at my sudden change in mood. "I need . . . to remember," I forced out.

"Luka?" Kisa asked and slowly began backing off my lap. "You need to calm down. You're turning red. Your skin is scalding!"

Tipping back my head, I roared toward the night sky, releasing all the confusion, the rage, and the frustration that had been bombarding me over the last few days.

"Luka!" Kisa cried, and I could hear her sniffing, sobbing as she moved from my lap and scurried backwards into the rocks.

"The driver had been shot, and men stormed the bus . . . Georgians . . . Georgians stormed the bus." I began rocking on my knees as the scene played out. "They beat us, forced us into the back of the bus . . ." I sucked in a long, stuttered breath and looked to Kisa, who was now dressed and pressed against the rocks as though she were facing a monster.

She was. I was a fucking cold, sick monster. This was what they had made me . . . what they'd been ordered to do to me by . . .

"They knew my name," I spat out. "Those men . . . they asked for me by my name." I blinked, but the memory of my full name didn't come. "Luka," I said and hit the side of my head with my fist. "Luka . . . Luka . . . ARGH!"

I couldn't remember my last name!

"Tolstoi," a soft voice uttered against the breeze. "Luka Jakob Tolstoi . . . that was your full name. That *is* your full name."

Shoulders sagging, I tilted my head to the side as I witnessed the expression on Kisa's face transform from fear to sadness.

Feeling my legs shake, I fell forward on all fours, my hands fisting into the sand.

"Luka!" Kisa shrilled, and I heard her drop beside me, her hand tentatively resting on my back.

"They had been sent for me," I rasped, all energy seeping from my body into the sand beneath me. "Fuck . . . I can still feel it. Like a fuck-ing dagger, Kisa, a dagger."

"How?" Kisa asked cautiously, her fingers running down my spine. "Why were they sent for you? How did you know?"

"Luka Tolstoi. You're coming with us," the man with the gun said.

"Where? Where am I going?" I asked, but I got no answer.

"To fucking hell, boy. You're going off the grid. Someone's paid us a shit-load of money to make you disappear." The guy pointed to the other boys being dragged out of the bus. "You all are."

"Why?" I asked. "Who ordered this?"

He smiled and shrugged. "You fucked with the wrong family, boy."

All I felt was dread at his words. "Durov? It was Durov?"

The man looked taken aback, but then he laughed. "Well, at least you'll know who's to blame for what lies ahead. Abram made sure you'll never ever return to Brooklyn."

Lurching to a sitting position, I stared at Kisa. "Abram . . . Abram Durov . . ."

"What? What else do you remember?"

"He organized for the Georgians to intercept the bus. He emptied it and burned the bus. They filled it with dead teens from the Gulag so there was burned bodies. But it was Abram. He ordered me taken."

Kisa's eyes shone, but her face was calmer now, numb. "He needed to protect Alik," she said, nodding. "He needed you gone so no one would know Alik killed Rodion."

My teeth gritted together and I lowered my head, taking a long, deep breath. "They never expected me to survive. They thought I'd be killed in the cage."

We were both silent for a while, but then Kisa stood and held out her hand. I looked up into her eyes and saw only strength. "But you did, Luka. You *did* survive. And . . ." She took a breath and straightened her shoulders. Resolve had settled within her. I could see it in her face. "We need to get you back to the gym. You have a fight to win tomorrow."

I watched my Kisa-Anna, and the anger I had fled my body.

I had to win this fight.

I had to reclaim my life or forever live in the dark.

Slipping my hand in Kisa's and seeing her eyes shine with tears, I got to my feet and pulled her into my chest. Her gaze met mine, and I raked back her long brown hair with my fingers.

Her eyes closed. "You have to win the fight, Luka. Justice must be served. It is the way we live. Blood for blood. You have to do it for you, for us . . . but I want you to win for Rodion. He should be avenged."

Leaning down, I pressed my forehead to hers, just *being* for a minute. I finally pulled away, picked up my clothes and put them on. Zipping up my sweater, I pulled up the hood and finally faced my Kisa. She was staring at the ground, but she looked up and a sad smile pulled on her lips.

I strode toward her and tugged her into my chest, once again inhaling her scent. "Will you still want me after I kill Durov?"

Kisa froze, but her head began to nod against my chest. "Yes, lyubov moya," she said almost silently. "I have been with Alik for so long. He needed me to live, couldn't stand being without me."

Kisa pulled back from my chest but didn't look up. Her hands played with the string on my sweater. "I've always known he was . . . different, dangerous. Always known he wasn't like everybody else . . . but I put up with it because, well, he was all I'd ever known for so long, and I knew he'd kill me if I tried to leave. He wouldn't survive without me next to him. He'd unravel, he become too dark, too unrestrained." Kisa sucked in a deep breath as my heart ached at the tone of her voice. "But I didn't know he'd taken you from me, taken my brother from me. I'd asked him about that day so much in the beginning and he swore to me that you had killed Rodion. Now everything I've ever believed has just come crashing down."

"And your father? What will he do?" I asked, feeling a wave of possessiveness over Kisa. Jealous that Durov had had her all these years. That he'd made her believe he needed her so much she could never be with anyone else.

She was mine. Not his. Never his . . . MINE!

Kisa glanced away, seeming lost in her head. "When Papa finds out what Alik did to his son, his heir, his pride and joy, and then finds out who you are, that you are innocent, he'll want Alik dead too."

"He will?" I asked in confusion.

Kisa faced me and her head tilted to the side. "Luka . . . do you remember if you had any family here in Brooklyn? Do you know *how* you know me? *Why* we grew up together? *Why* you knew Rodion and Alik?"

My hands started to sweat and my headache grew stronger again. My eyes squeezed shut and my stomach clenched, my breath pausing in my throat.

"Luka! Luka!" Kisa prompted, and I let out a long exhale as my eyes snapped back open. Sweat beaded on my forehead and I felt as though I'd been punching a bag for three hours straight.

"Don't try and remember right now," Kisa instructed, and I focused on her eyes, on her hand that rested on my cheek. "Don't. You're tired. You've put yourself through too much tonight. The color has gone from your face."

Kisa's fingers stroked my stubbled cheek and the feeling was hypnotic. I breathed with the rhythm of her caress until my heart began to slow.

"Good, lyubov moya," Kisa soothed.

Once I had calmed, I nodded my head, telling her I was good.

Kisa's question stabbed at my mind. A family? People who . . . loved me? I couldn't even imagine it. Another stab of pain tortured my mind, but I knew I had to block it out. To block out everything but the fight against Durov.

I would finally get my revenge.

"We need to go," Kisa said reluctantly, and taking her outstretched hand, we walked back over the sand toward Serge, climbing in his awaiting car.

A while later, we arrived at the gym and I kissed Kisa on the lips.

"I'll see you tomorrow, Luka," she whispered. "I'll try and come to you before the fight."

Nodding my head curtly, I opened the door of the car but paused to look over my shoulder, thinking how beautiful Kisa truly was. "I . . ." I cleared my throat, tipped my head to the side, and said, "I . . . *love* . . . you."

The words felt strange coming from my lips, but when Kisa's eyes began filling with tears and her mouth pulled into a huge, watery smile, I knew these three words were right.

Love. A new yet somehow familiar emotion for me.

Kisa scrambled over the seat and crushed her lips against mine. As she pulled back, she whispered, "I love you too. So much. So, so much."

Nodding again, I hid the sense of warmth filling my body. It took me by surprise. I didn't know how to deal with such things.

"Tomorrow," I said, stroking my thumb across her soft face and stood.

"Tomorrow," Kisa said in reply.

Serge tipped his hat at me from the driver's door.

I backed away into the shadows of the gym, once again one with the darkness.

With each step I took to my training room, I mentally chanted the words:

Durov.

New York.

Revenge.

Kill.

Tomorrow night, I would finally get my revenge.

19

KISA

"Are you okay, miss?" Serge asked, looking back at my blank face through the rearview mirror.

I continued staring out the window, an array of emotions tearing through me like burning flames. Alik had killed my brother. Alik, the man that had controlled me and possessed me all these years, the man I'd devoted my life to serving. And he'd blamed Luka, *my* Luka, for Rodion's death . . . God! Just so he could have me?

The thought made me feel sick. Feel racked with guilt. Despair and a million other emotions.

And tomorrow night, my two loves—one pure yet broken and one so dark that I now realized I didn't know him at all—they would fight to the death.

Tomorrow night I would lose one.

I knew in my heart who I wanted—no, *needed*—to survive . . . Luka. It had always been Luka.

Alik deserved to die.

"Miss?" Serge pushed again, and I met his worried gaze. "What's happened? I know that look on your face, devastation. I've only ever seen it one time before . . . and that was when we were told Mr. Tolstoi died in that crash."

I felt the tears tracking down my face, and I sniffed and wiped at my cheeks. "Serge . . . I've just found out who killed Rodion. I . . . I . . . ." I trailed off, unable to finish my sentence, the pain too much to bear.

I noticed we had pulled up to the side of my papa's house, crawling to a stop in the shadows of the dark street, out of view.

As the car came to a stop, Serge turned in his seat. "Mr. Alik?"

My eyes widened and my pulse throbbed in my temples. "You . . . knew? All this time?"

Serge shook his head. "No, miss. I didn't. But, well, I've watched him his whole life, watched him grow from a boy to a man and something was never right with him. Like he's disturbed, deep in his soul."

I swallowed hard, listening to everything coming out of Serge's mouth. And he was right. Alik had always been different. Thriving off violence, off control, off his possession for me . . . off his kills. Kills he had to make or he would turn to the streets or the rival mobs to work off his rage. The Bratva decided five years ago that he should fight for The Dungeon during the Championship. My papa wanted him to have an outlet for his rage, one that wouldn't cause trouble with rivals, and one that would also bring in a profit.

"When the news of Rodion's death was delivered to the staff, I couldn't believe Luka would do such a thing. He was a good boy, a good *Bratva* boy: stern and hard, but not overly cold. But mainly, he was loyal to his family. *Loved* his family. His papa had brought him up well, unlike Mr. Abram. *He* had raised that boy of his to be a killer. After his mama ran off when he was a baby, he brought that boy up without any affection." Serge's eyes seemed to lose focus and he shook his head. "There's just something within his eyes . . . something that has never sat well with me." Serge shifted uncomfortably in his seat. "I remember finding him as a child, killing a cat—no, *torturing* it. He saw me watching him in horror and he smiled. He smiled at me, Kisa. I knew then that something sinister ran in that boy's blood. He enjoyed killing that cat. He liked hearing it in pain."

"Oh God, Alik!" I cried. "What's wrong with him? What lives within him to make him like that?"

Serge ran his hand over his head in distress. "And the day we were told Luka had died, Miss Kisa . . . Everybody cried. Even though they believed he had killed your twin, they mourned for him. But Alik, he was cold, calculated, and dare I say, happy? Abram displayed no reaction either. Something about that whole day just never sat well with me."

"Serge," I cried, finally submitting to the sob choking my throat. "I don't know what to do!"

Serge laid his hand on my knee. "Mr. Luka is back, Kisa. I don't know where from, and I don't need to know, that isn't my business. But I can see he's no longer the Luka that left. He's darker now, tormented. His memory is in pieces. Lord, the confusion on his face tonight when he saw me, it was vast. But not a day went by from the time you were born that boy didn't look after you, protect you. And even now, with his mind warped, with the hell I know he's been put through, he won't let Mr. Alik leave that cage tomorrow night alive. Of that I'm sure. He'll kill Mr. Alik to protect you. He has earned the right to this revenge. He has earned the right to retake his place among the Bratva and know his family and where he's from."

"He doesn't remember them, Serge. None of his family. Papa Ivan, Talia, his mama, none of them."

"He will in time. But right now, he has one goal, only one thing occupying his mind . . . to right what Mr. Alik made wrong."

"God! How the hell has it all come to this?" I said, wiping at my tears. "So much death, so much pain! All because of greed and jealousy."

Serge smiled sadly. "This mafiya life is never an easy path. There has been much death, much pain. But the Lord has brought back your love, Kisa. Despite the pain, a miracle has occurred."

My stomach swirled with dread. "But . . . what if Luka can't get past all of what happened? What happens when he remembers *everything*? Will it be too much?"

"He will have you, Kisa. You saw his soul, yet you didn't recognize his face. And he knew you, even when his memories were not there. You are his light, his guide back to this life."

"He showed me his eyes," I whispered and Serge's eyebrows furrowed. Taking a deep breath, I explained, "Since the day I met him, I've noticed that he keeps his eyes down, his hood pulled over his face as if somewhere in his subconscious he knew that his distinctive eyes could be recognizable. But he let me see them. He showed me those eyes almost immediately. And as soon as I saw them, I saw my Luka."

Serge's gray eyes glistened and he dipped his head, only to raise them again. "Then he knew you too. Even if he didn't remember you, his

soul did. That boy was always besotted with you. I'd never seen anything like you two kids. A love so fierce it was like you'd been together
for a millennium."

My heart swelled at Serge's words. I leaned forward to kiss him on
his cheek, but just as I did, the passenger door flew open and Alik climbed
inside, his eyes red raw with rage, and he placed a gun at Serge's head.

"Drive," he ordered in a terrifyingly guttural voice, and I instinctively started trembling. Fear seized my voice and any movement my
mind willed me to make.

"Alik . . . baby," I whispered, trying to sound natural, unafraid.
Alik's back stiffened.

"Shut the fuck up!" he snapped, his tone deadly, his eyes bloodshot
and red. He pushed the barrel of the gun harder against Serge's temple.

"Take us to my dockside apartment," Alik ordered, and Serge risked
a glance back in the mirror. Alik drew back his gun and butted Serge
with the barrel, leaning forward. "I said take us to my fucking dockside
apartment!"

I cried out when blood trickled down Serge's face, but he put the
car in drive and we rolled off down the streets, sticking to the shadows.

"Alik, please? What dockside apartment?" I whispered, watching
his jaw twitch and redness run up his neck. I could physically see his
anger engulf his pale skin.

"I got a dockside apartment, Kisa. Had it for years. I do what the
fuck I want there."

I gasped when I guessed what that could be. "And what's that?" I
asked fearfully.

He turned and smirked at me, but his eyes were on fire. He looked
like he hadn't slept in days. "Whatever the fuck I choose to do to keep
me from ripping people apart."

Alik watched my expression, which I knew was betraying my abject
fear. My blood ran cold. He leaned forward as the car built up speed.

"You've fucked up, Myshka. I know what's been going on, and
with who."

I sucked in a stuttered terrified breath. "Alik—"

Alik's foot kicked out and smashed against the dashboard on an incensed roar. "I said shut your fucking mouth!"

As I cowered back in my seat, Alik panted, his chest rising and fall-ing. I watched him like a hawk, his head twitching and his feet tapping with impatience. I couldn't cry, couldn't show any reaction.

I was so terrified.

I'd never been on the receiving end of this Alik before. I'd never defied him or hurt him . . . until now.

He knew about Raze and me.

And I wasn't sure I was going to come out of this alive.

The docks came into view not too far from The Dungeon, but far enough away that nobody would know Alik came here. It wasn't an apartment as such, more like a fisherman's shack that had been refur-bished.

Serge stopped the car, and for a moment, we all sat there in strained silence. Lowering the gun, Alik turned to Serge.

"Stay the fuck here."

Serge looked at me in the backseat and sadly shook his head. "I can't do that, Mr. Alik."

Alik laughed and held up his Beretta, rolling the gun in his hand. "You'll do whatever the fuck I say, old man."

Serge straightened in his seat, and I saw Alik smile. I knew that smile. That sadistic smile. And I hated that it was directed at Serge. My kind old Serge.

"No, Serge, please just do what he says," I begged.

Serge's eyes set with resolve. "I can't, Miss Kisa. I could never live with myself if I let anything happen to you. You're . . . you're like the daughter I never had."

A tear trickled down my cheek as I began to plead with him, but Alik didn't give me a chance as he aimed his gun at Serge's temple. I opened my mouth to shout out, but Serge met my eyes in the mirror and he shook his head no. He was saying goodbye.

A second later, Alik pulled the trigger. Serge slumped forward, dead, and this time I did scream.

In no time at all, Alik jumped out of the car and opened the back door. "Get the fuck out," he ordered, and heart struggling to beat de-spite the shock of Serge's violent death, I moved to the door, but Alik groaned, leaned in to grab my arm, and wrenched me forward. "Fuck-ing *move!*"

Crying out once more, Alik dragged me toward the apartment, un-locked the door, and pushed me inside.

I blinked and blinked, trying to take in the room. It was sparse, only minimal furniture—a ragged couch, a small kitchenette, and a bed. My stomach rolled when I saw the sheets were messed up, used condoms on the bedside table . . . but that wasn't what had me recoiling in shock. No. That honor was bestowed upon a clearing at the left side of the open space. A clearing covered in plastic sheets . . . plastic sheets stained with blood.

"Alik," I hushed out. "What is this place?"

I felt Alik's warm body at my back, and he gathered my hair and pushed it over my left shoulder. His mouth moved to my ear. "My sanc-tuary. Where I can be the man I am. Not the one I'm forced to be out there."

"And . . . and what man is that?" I asked, not really wanting to hear the answer.

He pressed kiss after kiss along the side of my neck, sending shivers down my spine. Every part of me was tense. I didn't understand why he wasn't screaming at me. This quieter Alik was too unnerving.

"Free," he replied, making me jump.

My eyes drifted to the unmade bed, and I felt sick. "You fuck women here?"

Alik's lips froze and in seconds I was spun round by his hard grip on my biceps and slammed against the nearest wall. His harsh stare bore into mine, cold and unfeeling.

"They're not you, Myshka. They were whores. You're my woman, my whole fucking life." Darkness clouded Alik's crazed red eyes and he leaned so far forward that the back of my head ground against the hard wall. "At least you *were*. Until you fucking betrayed me. Opened your fucking whoring legs."

Alik's voice was quiet, too quiet, the softness deceiving. His head twitched and his jaw ticked as he lifted the Beretta and ran it down my cheek. He suddenly looked broken, completely devastated.

"How could you, Myshka? How could you fuck that cunt, baby? How could you let him into what's mine?"

"Alik—" I tried to speak, but Alik moved the gun over my lips, shaking his head as his other hand wrenched up my dress and cupped roughly against my pussy.

"Shh, Myshka," he whispered. "You betrayed me. You opened your legs to that fucker Raze. You made me angry. At you, Myshka. You hurt me. The only one who can keep me calm, the only one who gets me."

I shook my head, my breath coming too fast. "No! Alik!" I protested and tentatively lifted my shaking hand to rest on his cheek. As soon as my palm met his skin, his eyes closed and he took a deep breath, his head nuzzling into my flesh.

"Baby," I whispered, needing to keep him calm while my heart thundered to the point I thought it would fail to function from over-exhaustion. "I know . . . I know what you did . . . to Rodion . . . to Luka . . ."

Alik's head stilled in my palm and his gaze darted to mine, the whites of his eyes unusually bright. Then, eyes narrowed, he said, "What the fuck are you talking about?"

Tears blurred my vision and my bottom lip quivered. "I know . . . I know it was you who killed Rodion . . . I know your papa ordered you to kill him so you could be the heir to the Pakhan."

Alik's nostrils flared and his lips set into a tight line. "Really? You found this out?" he asked, his thoughts unreadable through his indifferent tone.

Swallowing, I said, "And you framed Luka, stabbed yourself in the stomach . . . and your papa faked Luka's death." I saw the flinch in Alik's eyes, and my heart skipped a beat.

He didn't know Luka wasn't in that accident . . . My God! He believed he was dead. That meant . . .

He didn't know Raze was Luka.

He didn't know I'd been sleeping with Raze because he was Luka.

Alik quickly schooled his features. "Luka died, Kisa."

"But you killed Rodion? Put the blame on Luka?" I sniffed and wiped at the tears on my cheek. "You stabbed yourself to ensure everyone believed Luka had flipped and killed Rodion." I met his gaze and said, "All because you wanted me to yourself?"

Alik's stern expression melted and he looked at me again with that disturbingly possessive adoration, his gun-free hand lifting from my pussy to push back my hair.

"You're mine, baby. You know that. And Luka was getting in my way. He was always there, touching you . . . touching what I knew was mine."

I held my breath and squeezed my eyes shut. I felt Alik's warm breath splay across my skin, and the barrel of his gun ran down my neck to lie over my breasts.

"Rodion needed to die, Kisa. He would never have been a Pakhan. He wasn't strong enough. I am. And I knew I'd have you by my side. It has made the Bratva feared more than any other mob on the East Coast."

I dropped my arm to my side, removing my hand from his face. My brother, Luka . . . Alik had zero remorse. He was proud of what he'd done.

"You *are* insane," I whispered, my throat feeling too tight to breathe in much-needed air. "I just never let myself see it before."

Alik smiled but backed away, aiming his gun in front of him, shifting its target from my head to my heart and back again.

"Insane, baby?" Alik said coldly and stepped forward, my body filling with dread. "You haven't seen anything. Because, Myshka, until now, you've always been my little mouse. My fucking light, the beat to my heart. The only thing I could love as much as killing."

Alik stepped closer still and ran his hand up my arm, then brutally gripped my bicep, squeezing until I screamed out in pain. Alik's face was right before mine, his expression blank.

"That was until you fucking betrayed me and fucked that asshole."

My eyes widened and he nodded. "You thought people weren't going to realize you were missing? The Byki reported your empty room last night, so I followed you tonight, Myshka. Followed you right to that fuck Raze . . . and then to Brighton Beach of all places." His jaw clenched. "I fucking hate that place."

Alik's hold tightened still and tears ran down my cheeks. His face then showed every single nuance of pain and rage he felt and his mouth moved right to my ear.

"I watched you fuck him. I watched you kiss him. I watched you fucking hold him, watched you stroke his hair!"

"Alik—" I cried, but just as I did, Alik stepped back and the back of his hand smacked across my face.

Losing my footing under the force and shock, I slumped to the floor, Alik pacing in front of me, hitting at his head with the heels of his hands. "Why? *WHY?*" he screamed and whipped to face me, his head tilted to the side.

"Kisa, baby, my Myshka, why did you make me do this?" Alik's voice was gentle, apologetic, completely opposite to a moment ago. I rolled my head to face him, my cheek throbbing from the hit.

Alik bent down and stroked across my forehead with the same firm hand he hit me with. "I watched you fucking him, Kisa. You fucked another guy, and now I gotta make you pay. That pussy of yours belongs to me."

I shook my head, tears spilling down my face. "No, Alik, please . . . You don't understand."

Sighing, Alik looked away, and when he turned back, I began to speak, but Alik gripped my hair and dragged me to my feet.

"Alik!" I cried, but he didn't stop, just yanked me forward until I stood at the bottom of the large bed.

"Alik, please," I begged. "I love him! I . . . I love him."

Alik froze and pulled me forward by my hair. "Say what? You want to tell me that again?"

"I . . . I . . ." Alik fisted my hair tighter, to the point I thought it was going to rip from my head.

"Tell me again!" he ordered, and I sobbed.

But then a wash of numbness filled me and, looking Alik straight in the eyes, I declared, "I love him. He's my soul mate. I want him . . . I want him . . ."

Alik paled and reared back as if I'd physically hurt him. I could actually see the pain in his face. "Alik—"

Another strike knocked me onto the bed. I didn't scream this time, just landed on the mattress and felt the blood from my bust lip trickle down my chin.

"Your soul mate? You've only just fucking met him!" Alik roared and, beyond seething, ran his hands through his short hair, then sent a punch straight into my stomach.

I coughed and spluttered as the blow robbed me of my breath, and Alik roared again. Bending down, he had tears in his eyes. "Kisa," he said quietly, running his finger down my cheek. "I don't want to hurt you, but a good Bratva wife doesn't fuck around. You're making me do this to you. You need to be taught a lesson, Myshka. You've betrayed me, but . . ."

Alik sighed and pressed kisses all over my face. My body was curled inward, trying to find the ability to breathe.

"But I need you. *But . . .*" His body tensed again. "I can't stand the fucking thought of you with him, baby. Can't get the thought of you riding his dick from my head."

Alik tipped back his head and growled in frustration. Facing forward once more, he pushed me back onto the mattress and crawled on the bed. "I need to fuck you," he said firmly. "I need to show you who you fucking belong to."

My heart sank as he spoke those words. "No . . . please, Alik . . . Please . . ."

But he didn't listen, didn't care. Alik snapped open the fly of his jeans and pulled off his shirt. Once he was undressed, he reached for my dress. I freed my arms from around my stomach to push his hands away, but Alik took my wrists in one hand and struck me across the cheek with the other. In the aftermath, he acted as though nothing had happened.

I resisted, fought back for as long as I could, picturing my Luka in my mind. I didn't want Alik to take me and rid me of Luka's feel. I didn't want him to touch me.

He killed my brother.

He framed my Luka.

Alik leaned down, teeth bared and squeezed my wrist until I heard a crack. I was sure he had broken it. Spots danced in front of my eyes with the searing pain. He ripped away my dress, running his nose up my neck, almost tenderly, then his hand wrapped around my throat.

Tears filled Alik's eyes as he stared me down, my sight fading in and out of blackness as his grip on my throat cut off my oxygen.

"Myshka, you're mine," he said as he pushed my thighs apart and placed himself at my entrance. "I *need* you to be mine."

As he slammed his cock inside me, his hand slipped off my throat, allowing me to gasp in a breath, and his hand took tight hold of my hips. He took me roughly, bruisingly, making sure I knew he was in control . . . that he, and *only* he, possessed me.

As he drove into me faster, Alik leaned forward, my eyes unable to focus through the blows to my face, the choking of my throat, the sexual assault.

"I'm gonna kill that fucker tomorrow, Myshka. Take him out. So get him out of your mind. Then no more fucking waiting. We're marrying the day after and you'll learn your place once and for all. Do you hear me?"

My head was cast to the side, my eyes trying to focus on anything around the room. Suddenly, Alik's hand slammed down on my cheeks and he forced me to look at him. Another blow branded my cheek with pain, and he shook my head as his hips slammed into my pussy. "I said do you fucking *hear me?*"

I tried to speak, but my cheeks were numb, my lips too swollen to move. Instead, a desperate noise slipped through my lips, and Alik smiled down at me, accepting it as my submission.

"Fuck, I love you, baby," he whispered, closing his eyes and biting his lip, getting a kick out of my helplessness. "Your cunt's so fucking tight . . . so fucking mine."

He stilled, neck straining as he came, and he flopped on top of me. I lay disconnected and disorientated while Alik moved about the room as though nothing had happened, but I felt everything when he crawled over my battered body and slid into me once more.

It felt like the punishment never ended, and when Alik rolled to my side, spent, wrapping me in his arms, I let a tear fall, the salty drop stinging my open wounds, until I couldn't hold on anymore and I slipped into darkness.

A slap to my face woke me. My head pounded practically blinding me and my body ached so badly that I immediately vomited to the side of the bed. I tried to move onto my back, to open my heavy eyes, but my lids wouldn't fully function, only tiny slits of the room coming into view. I tried to move my legs but they wouldn't work. I was trying to focus, struggling to remember what had happened, when suddenly, I was flipped over onto my front, my body screaming out at the action.

Alik hovered above me. "Wake up, baby."

My eyes rolled trying to obey his command and my breathing wheezed through my heavily bruised throat.

"Good, Myshka, you're learning," he praised, his voice proud. I felt Alik push into me from behind and screamed a voiceless scream at the burning pain between my legs, the force of my cry like razor blades slicing at my throat.

Pain. All I felt was pain as I was taken again, glimpses of daylight breaking through the windows.

Daylight?

How long had I been here? Like this?

Alik pushed forward like a man possessed, his lesson for me to submit and never defy him again, not yet over. The more he thrust into me, the more I lost my vision, and as Alik bellowed my name, coming within me, he exhaled in relief and turned my head to lay a hard kiss on my lips.

I whimpered as his lips pushed against my swollen ones, and he flashed me another sweet smile before he got off the bed. I watched through aching eyes as Alik got dressed as though I wasn't lying here in agony, unable to move . . . all by his hand.

Minutes later, Alik turned to me and strode forward, kneeling at my head lying askew on the mattress. He sighed and shook his head, running his fingers through my matted hair.

"You brought this on yourself, Myshka. But now you know what'll happen if you try to fuck around on me again." Alik's eyes narrowed and he leaned closer and whispered in my ear, "Then again, if you do this again, I won't ever be able to trust you, baby. So I'd just have to fucking kill you . . . and I'd kill myself too. Then we'd be together . . . always."

My heart throbbed, and I came undone as he kissed my forehead and stood. Lifting a training bag over his shoulder, Alik looked back at me and said, "I'm gonna kill this fucker . . . slowly . . . make this bastard regret he ever fucked my woman." He laughed, clearly amused. "He had no idea who he was fucking with, did he? They call me the butcher for a reason."

I wanted to cry, to beg and to stop him from leaving, but I couldn't move . . . could barely even cry.

"When I come back after the fight, with fresh blood on my hands, we're gonna go to Vegas and get married, Myshka, once and for all. I'm tired of waiting."

With that, Alik left, locking me inside this shack.

All I could do was cry and lie still until I lost the fight and submitted to the heavy pull of sleep.

20

RAZE

"You've got this, Raze," Viktor said as I pushed up from the ground, warming up my muscles, the fight only minutes away from being called. I'd trained all day. Blocked everything out of my mind but one thing . . . to kill Durov.

I could hear the roar of the crowd; it sounded bigger than on previous nights. It was the final, the ultimate fight unto the death, The Dungeon Championship.

Raze versus The Butcher.

"He has strength and experience, but so do you. He has speed and skill, but you're more advanced. He's unrivaled with a dagger, but you're second-to-none with your spiked knuckledusters. He's insane, but Raze," Viktor stopped before me as I jumped to my feet and began sparring against the punch bag. Viktor reached out and held the bag, forcing me to look up. "But you're here for revenge. Nothing even comes close to that as a drive."

I grunted my agreement, my muscles firing up at his words. The only thing that would've made this better was Kisa. She'd said she was going to come and see me before the fight, but so far she hadn't showed up.

"Kisa?" I asked Viktor as I pummeled the leather of the bag with my taped up fists.

Viktor shrugged and shook his head. "Not here yet. She isn't even with Durov."

That made me pause. Kisa was always at the gym when we trained. She was always with Durov before a fight. Where the hell could she be?

A slap to my cheek pulled me out of it and I snarled as Viktor pulled back his hand. "Focus, Raze. This is it, this is your chance. It's life or death out there, get Kisa from your head."

"I know," I growled, his slap thrusting me back into a whole world of rage.

"Good," Viktor said, "Because there's more than just you who wants Durov gone."

I glanced up at Viktor, his milky eyes boring into mine. "He's made a lot of enemies, Raze. That crowd out there are like hungry wolves. You're the first real contender Alik's ever had. The rest he's just played with like a fucking tiger plays with food, but with you, we all know you could be the one to kill him." Viktor stepped forward and laid a hand on my shoulder. "You could kill the Bratva heir. There's more than just gamblers here tonight, son. The Chinese, The Italian Mafia and Chechens want to see if the Bratva will be left vulnerable by your win."

Confusion clouded my mind. I knew that even with Durov dead there'd still be an heir, but I couldn't picture who?

A hammer on the door told me that it was time. It was time to take Durov down.

Rolling my neck from side to side, I loosened my shoulders and walked to the bench to pick up my knuckledusters. I slid them in place, the cold metal feeling like an extended part of me.

The roaring of the crowd grew louder, my feet rocked from side to side. I closed my eyes and visualized winning. Visualized Durov beneath me, bearing the brunt of my fatal blows. Visualized the moment that his eyes lost life and his black heart stopped.

"You ready, Raze?"

I blinked my focus back to the here and now. Viktor stood in front of me.

I nodded my head.

I was more than fucking ready to end Durov's life. I was twelve years ready. This was twelve years overdue.

The steel door opened and I followed Viktor out into the dank, musty hallway. I could hear that the volume of the crowd had increased from previous matches, telling me how excited they were for this championship final. I could tell by the dust falling from the stoned walls of the hallway that more spectators were here than ever before, the stamping of their feet vibrating along the long hallway.

My skin burned with adrenaline as I rocked from side to side on the balls of my feet, dressed in my fighting black shorts, Eye Black under my eyes, my heart pumping vengeance through every vein.

Lights from The Dungeon suddenly filled the mouth of the hallway and I stilled at the entrance, just drinking in the biggest crowd I'd ever seen. The crowd, filled with criminals, gamblers and worse, all screamed in my direction. I couldn't make out what they were shouting, my focus slamming to the heavily lit cage, Durov stood dead center of the octagon, his image drowning everything else out.

Chest heaving, I could hear the echo of my breathing in my ears, feel the too-fast pounding of my heart in my chest. Every muscle in my body twitched in excitement; I trained them hard for this—every single fight I'd fought was in preparation for this moment. I rubbed my palm across my stomach, across my kill inkings.

Every single kill was in preparation for this moment.

My palm ran over last night's kill. Goliath . . . 362 . . . my *friend* . . . and my eyes closed.

Lifting my eyes to the rafters, I briefly closed them, sending a promise to 362, wherever he now may be. *I will get my revenge for you too . . . brother.*

The clinking sound of metal upon metal pulled my attention. Durov had his crazed eyes fixed on mine, pacing along the edge of the cage like a psycho, his muscled body dripping with sweat, his nostrils flaring and his dagger dragging along the sides of the cage.

My lips curled over my teeth in anger, in bloodlust for this fucker who had robbed me of my life. A hand slapped on my shoulder and glancing down to my left from the corner of my eye, Viktor was staring up at me.

"Your time has come, Raze. Take it. Seize your fate."

Taking in a deep breath, drinking in his words, my legs began pushing forward down the concrete pathway, hundreds of hands slapping on my back; but I only had one target, and right now he was cracking his neck, turning his dagger in his hands, his eyes blazing with fury.

A Byki saw my approach, opening the cage door and I dived into the ring, storming straight for Durov. Durov's eyes flared with the excitement of the charge, his corded neck bulging as he braced for my tackle.

There was no time for the firing of the gun.

No time for any introduction. This was personal, this was two enraged monsters fighting to the death.

Using my speed and larger size to my advantage, I wrapped my arms around Durov's waist and tackled him to the ground, a rush of adrenaline filling me as his back smashed on the hard cage floor. Durov's arms were iron around my back, forcing a grapple on the ground, both fighting for dominance.

Gaining the upper hand, I reared up, slamming a spiked fist into his shoulder. My blade pierced his skin, but the fucker still kept coming like I never even got in a hit. Jerking his legs, he forced me onto my back, my hand losing grip on his sweat-ridden biceps. In a flash, Alik had raised his dagger and plunged it down, but I managed to roll at the very last second, his steel blade scraping the floor.

Using my feet, I kicked him onto his back, launching my body on top of him, slamming his wrists above his head. Durov's psycho gaze met mine and I could see the hatred in his eyes . . . my memories telling me that I'd had this look off him many times before.

Alik fought with everything that he had, but my grip was too strong, his weakening shoulder shedding blood from where I'd pierced him with my blade. I stared down at Durov and squeezed at his wrists, Durov's teeth gritting so hard that I heard a loud crack coming from his molars.

Leaning forward, I spat, "I'm going to fucking kill you, Durov."

Durov held his breath, and his face turned bright red; the evidence of his rage. "I'm finally going to get my revenge."

"Your revenge?" he asked, every vein protruding from his skin. "Your motherfucking revenge?"

My jaw clenched and I leaned in closer still. Alik was watching me, trying to wrench his arms from my hold. But I wasn't letting this fucker go.

"Look at me," I ordered.

Alik's good shoulder lifted to a point that it almost popped out of its socket, but I slammed my head against his, Durov's head falling back to the floor. Durov glared at me and I knew the fucker was imagining how to murder me. But this fight wasn't going anywhere until he knew *who* he was facing, or at least, the shadow of the boy he once ruined.

"I said fucking look at me!" I screamed, Durov's eyes narrowing and searching every part of my face. "Look at every inch of my face, Alik. Do you recognize me? Do you see anyone you once knew? Anyone you completely fucked over?"

Durov's eyes were frantic as they darted from side to side, his numbing fingers tightening around his dagger.

"What the fuck are you talking about?" Durov hissed, jerking his hip, fighting to throw me off.

Lifting his wrists, I smashed his hands down to the floor again, Durov's cheek only slightly twitching at the pain. "Then let me remind you. There was you, me, and Rodion at the falls." Alik stilled in my hands, his legs stopping kicking. "We were fucking around, doing nothing when you, the fucking psycho that you are, abruptly got to your feet and pulled out your knife and fucking stabbed your friend in the heart . . ." Turning my fists inward, my blades began stabbing into Durov's wrists, the shaking of his hands showing the pain.

His eyes were fixed on mine and I could see him trying to work out how I knew all this information. My eyes flared as blood began dripping from his wrists.

"Then you stabbed yourself in the stomach," I lifted my knee and rammed it into his still-prominent scar, "And then put the blame on . . ." Alik's eyes widened as I paused and I knew he'd seen my left eye . . . the one that used to fuck him off when we were just a couple'a kids . . . the one with Kisa's smudge of blue.

I lowered my mouth and said, "Me . . . *Luka.*"

Alik's body froze then began to convulse. But it wasn't in fear, no, this bastard was convulsing in outright rage, his face contorting to show the fucking demon he was coming loose.

"See, your papa had to cover for your little fuck up. Your attack on me. Because I had the only thing in the world your insane ass wanted: Kisa. When I was heading to the Motherland, to some fucking work camp Kisa's papa ordered me to, your father organized for me to follow a different road. See, I was sent to a Georgian prison, the Gulag, we called it . . . a cover for a motherfucking death ring," I flicked my chin to the crowd, "Just like this."

Alik was as still as ice as I spoke, but I could see his pulse beating wildly on his neck.

"They pumped me with drugs, tortured me, filled me with so much shit that I didn't know who the fuck I was, beat me until I forgot anything but how to kill . . . until I came back here and knew one thing, the *only* thing that's ever occupied my mind . . . killing *you*."

I watched Alik. He watched me back, until Alik pushed at my arms, his body packing a strength like no one I'd ever fought before.

Alik's body jerked, twitched, and then he fucking went insane. "You fucked Kisa!" Alik screamed, spit flying from his mouth, his arms and legs thrashing around like the crazy son of a bitch he was. "You fucked my woman! *YOU!* I should've killed the betraying bitch when I had the chance!"

The blood drained out of my face when his words finally sunk into my mind. Every inch of me tensed and I released Durov's hands and rolling to the side, dragging him to his feet by his hair and slammed him into the walls of the cage. The crowd erupted, spectators rushing forward, slamming their hands against the metal of the cage calling for me to kill him.

Durov, the fucker, just smiled and wiped his fingers under my nose. "Smell those, *Luka*. They were just all up in that whore's pussy." His eyes lit and he said, "When I beat the shit out of her for fucking you . . ." his eyes stormed over, "When I took the bitch over and over until she couldn't fucking move, until she passed the fuck out through pain . . . for fucking *you*."

I tried to suck in a breath, but I couldn't inhale. Kisa. Fuck. What had he done?

"Yeah, fucker. I saw you last night, fucking my woman, so I taught her a fucking lesson. If I'd known it was you, *Luka fucking Tolstoi,* I'd have slit both your throats in that cove you love so fucking much."

Stepping back from the side of the cage, I clenched my fists together and Alik smiled, shrugging off his shoulders.

"So are we doing this shit, *Luka*?" he said, curling his lip like it amused him that I'd been trapped in a hell because of him for twelve damn years.

"This ends tonight."

Alik smiled.

The crowd went wild.

And we both ran straight for each other with death in our eyes, my fist plunging straight into his stomach, blades first.

21

KISA

My mouth was dry.

My tongue was like sandpaper and my lips were swollen and split.

I cracked open an eye, my eyelid like lead. I took a glance around the strange room. It was dark. My breathing was too fast when I tried to remember where I was. And then my eyes landed on a cleared space at the far side of the room. A clear space covered in plastic . . . blood residue spattered up the walls.

My mind raced.

The beach.

Raze . . . my Luka.

Him remembering.

The gym.

Serge—

Serge!

A pain-filled sob escaped my mouth when I thought back to the night before.

Alik!

No!

Alik had found out about Raze and me. He'd threatened Serge, and Serge . . . *no*, Serge died trying to protect me. *My sweet, protective Serge . . .*

Tears dripped heavily from my eyes, sorrow overwhelming me and I forced myself to push up from the bed. Every part of me ached, my dress bunched around my waist, my skin covered with blood and bruises . . . He'd beaten me half to death.

Suddenly feeling nauseous, I scurried to the edge of the bed and puked all over the floor, my head thudding like a drum.

I could barely see a thing.

An incessant ticking made me wince, the tinny pings shattering my brain. I slowly rolled my head left, only to see an old clock on a battered bedside table. I stared at the face, reading the time, knowing it meant something to me.

I tried to focus on what that was, my cheek lowering to the soiled sheets. I watched the second hand tick around, my eyelids lowering with every stroke, when, suddenly, The Dungeon flashed into my head and I stilled.

The Dungeon Championship!

My chest heaved as I stared at the time. Alik and Luka were about to fight!

Forcing myself off the mattress, working hard to breathe calmly through the pain, I managed to get to my feet. Reaching down, sobbing through the excruciating aches, I slowly fixed my dress and spotted my shoes and jacket flung haphazardly on the floor.

It was a struggle, but when I had everything on, I stumbled to the door, using my hand on the wall to guide my steps and keep myself upright.

I had no idea where I was. I knew I was near the docks, but I had no idea where.

Luckily the door unlocked from the inside. Alik obviously planned that I wouldn't be able to move through his punishment or else he would have bolted me in. But I needed to get to The Dungeon. I had no choice.

Opening the front door, the hot, salty breeze immediately smacked at my face and I cried out as it stung my wounds. Ducking my head, I kept walking forward, praying to find a phone. I walked and walked for what felt like an age, my body exhausted, the apex of my thighs burning with every single step.

That sensation almost had me crying again . . . Alik had raped me, beat me . . . My *fiancé* had nearly killed me.

All these years defending him, submitting to him, when I—when we *all*—knew Alik was disturbed . . . Alik was a psychopathic murderer. The fact that he was an heir to the great Russian Bratva could no longer disguise that truth.

And when my papa saw me like this—if Luka didn't kill him in the cage—my papa would, and I was now resolved to that.

As long as Alik lived, I would never be free.

"Miss? Miss? Are you okay?"

I lifted my head to the side to see an older man walking toward me. He looked like a fisherman or something, or a worker on the docks.

"Miss, are you okay?" he asked again. Then his face paled when he took in the sight of me. "Jesus Christ! What the hell happened to you?"

"Do you have a phone?" I asked, my voice barely audible through my severely bruised throat.

"Miss, I need to get you an ambulance!"

"No!" I argued. "Just . . . do you have a phone I can borrow?"

The man nodded and pulled out his cell, handing it over. "Miss, I don't feel right not calling you help."

"This will be my help," I said and weakly dialed Talia's number.

She picked up on the third ring.

"Hello?"

"Talia?" I said as loudly as I could manage.

"Hello? Kisa? Is that you? I can barely hear you."

"It's me," I replied. "I need you to come and get me."

She paused. "Why aren't you at the fight? It's about to start!"

"Talia, please. I need you to come and get me . . . now, please—"

"Okay. Okay. Where are you?" she asked, and I could hear her moving, keys rattling in her hand.

I turned to the man. "Where are we?"

He told me the address and I relayed it to Talia.

"Kisa, what the fuck are you doing there?"

Pressing my hand to my forehead, I said, "I'll explain everything when you get here." My stomach rolled in nerves, "I . . . I have something big to tell you. But you need to hurry."

"I'm on my way."

• • •

A while later, headlights glared on the road to the dock, the bright beams blinding. Lifting my hand to my face, I watched the man who had helped me wave Talia forward.

The car came to a stop and Talia lurched out the door and headed straight for me, her hand over her mouth.

"Kisa . . ." she whispered, and I caught her brown eyes shining, filling with tears. "What's happened to you?" she said and tried to reach out her hand, but she pulled it straight back for fear she would hurt me.

I pushed off the Sea-Can, and Talia caught me in her arms as I struggled to walk. "Alik . . . Alik did this . . . to me," I said breathlessly as I made for Talia's car.

She stopped. "Alik?" Her eyes widened. "Shit! I knew he wasn't right, but I never thought he'd ever hurt you."

"Talia, please, we have to go! I'll . . . I'll explain everything in the car."

Talia led me past the old man, and I laid my hand on his arm and said, "Thank you."

Talia helped me into the passenger seat, and I slumped back against the warm leather. It felt like paradise to my exhausted body.

In seconds, my best friend jumped into the car, and beneath the car's interior light, I watched her truly take in my injuries. I hadn't seen my reflection, but I could feel how messed up I was, how bad I must look.

"Kisa," Talia said quietly and a sob escaped her mouth. I lifted my hand to land on her knee, and as if it snapped her to action, she turned on the car and began pulling away from the docks. "I'm taking you to Dr. Chazov. Then I'm calling Papa Kirill to tell him what Alik did to you. He'll gut the fucker!"

"No!" I protested. Talia looked at me like I was crazy. "We need to go to the fight. To The Dungeon Championship."

"Kisa! Have you lost your damn mind? You're not looking good, sweetie. I'm worried you're injured internally. Your face . . . your wrist! Shit, Kisa, I think it's broken!"

"Talia, I need to go there." I looked up at my best friend and took a deep breath. "We *both* need to go there."

Talia's eyebrows pulled down in confusion. "Kisa . . . you know I can't go to those things. All that death . . . I can't . . . I've never been able to face it after Luka."

We both sat in silence until Talia asked, "Why did Alik snap? What the hell happened?"

I stared out the window as The Dungeon's warehouse came into view in the distance. "I . . . I've been sleeping with Raze."

The car swerved as Talia gasped in shock. "Kisa," she said in disbelief. "What were you thinking? You never betray your man in this life! Especially Alik!"

Tears sprang to my eyes. "Raze isn't just any man."

"He's a killer, Kisa! A killer you took off the streets and put in The Dungeon! What the fuck am I not getting here? You've known him all of a couple of weeks!"

"Talia, please. Come with me tonight and I'll explain everything."

Talia sighed and reached over to put her hand on top of mine. "Okay, sweetie. I'm just . . ." Her hands began to tremble. "You're all I have left to remind me . . . to keep my brother's memory . . ." Talia trailed off, unable to finish her sentence, and I almost fell apart. I wanted to tell her now that it was Luka that I was with, but she needed to see him herself. I needed to tell them all together.

I rolled my head to face her and flipped my palm.

Talia squeezed my hand.

"Through the back door, Tal. Take the back way so we don't have to face the crowd."

Nodding, Talia helped me walk round the back of The Dungeon. Max, my papa's head Byki, widened his eyes as he stood vigil by the door and saw us approach.

"Miss Volkova! What the hell has happened? Does Mr. Durov know this has happened to you?" he asked in shock, reaching out to help Talia take my weight.

"Max, please help me up to my papa's box," I replied, bristling when Alik was his first concern.

Alik was feared. Feared by *everyone.*

Max glanced to Talia, and she nodded her agreement. Together, they helped me through the narrow hallway, my papa's men standing back, appalled at my state.

The sudden roar of the crowd made me stumble, and I looked up to Max. "How long has the fight been on?"

"About five minutes, miss."

My heart began to pound again, and I looked up the stairs to my papa's private box. "Quickly, I need to speak with Papa." I looked to Max. "Who's in there with him?"

"Just your father and Mr. Tolstoi, miss."

I exhaled in relief, and Max and Talia helped me up the stairs. As soon as we reached the top, Talia opened the door and helped me inside.

Papa and Ivan were watching the fight, the overfilled crowd visible through the large bulletproof glass window.

"Papa?" I said quietly, and my papa looked over at me, a smile still on his face as he watched the fight. But as soon as his blue eyes fixed on mine, all happiness drained from his face. My papa shot out of his chair and ran over to me, Ivan doing the same. They ushered me to a seat, my papa's face reddened with anger.

"Who did this to you?" he asked curtly. "We need to get you to the doctor."

"She won't listen. She insisted on coming here. And . . . it was . . . *Alik*," Talia answered from beside me. "He beat her, and I had to pick her up at a shack he owns on the docks."

"ALIK!" my papa roared, rushing to his feet and glaring out the window.

I leaned forward and looked out onto the cage too. The floor was smeared with blood, Alik and Luka rolling around, grappling for dominance.

"Who's winning?" I asked, and my father glanced to the cage and then back at me.

"Kisa—"

"Who?" I pressed.

"Raze gets the upper hand more than Alik, but right now, it's anybody's fight," Ivan answered, and I pressed my hand on my head.

My heart raced with what I was about to do. "Is Abram cage side with Yiv?"

My papa looked at me like I was insane. "Yes, of course. Kisa! You need to start talking. Why did he do this to you? He's a dead man!"

Taking a deep breath, never taking my eyes off the cage, watching my Luka face Alik, and trying not to cry, I said, "I have to tell you all something."

I glanced to Talia and Ivan. "About . . . about Luka."

Ivan paled and Talia's eyes darted to her father. The pain flashed immediately across their faces. Talia then kneeled down and felt my head. "Kisa, does your head hurt? Are you confused? You're worrying me."

"No!" I snapped, but then I gripped Talia's hand. My eyes filled with tears and my heart kept time with the quick stamping of the crowd's feet below.

"Then what, Kisa?" Ivan said in a softer tone. "What of my boy?"

"He didn't do it," I blurted and immediately felt the atmosphere in the room change. I looked up at all three sets of eyes. All were looking at me like I'd gone insane.

Closing my eyes, I pictured Luka's face and said, "I need to say something. Please don't interrupt me. I need to get this out."

Ivan, Talia, and my papa nodded their heads.

"Luka didn't kill Rodion all those years ago. Alik set him up. They were at the falls. Something happened and Alik stabbed Rodion and then stabbed himself to make it look like Luka was guilty."

I caught Talia sucking in a sharp breath, but I kept my eyes shut.

"Abram had told Alik he had to kill Rodion so he would be next in line, that Rodion wasn't strong enough to lead when they were older. And Alik placed the blame on Luka because . . ." I cleared my throat and felt the pit of guilt that lay within me expand. "Because he wanted *me* to himself . . . and believed I would never choose him with Luka still around. He was right. I never would have given up Luka for anything. You all know that.

"Abram didn't plan for Alik to harm Luka. Why would he? Alik would be next in line because of where Abram stood in the Bratva, but he had to protect his son. He couldn't let you find out what Alik had done. It would jeopardize everything he'd planned . . . planned under your noses."

The room was still silent, so I continued. "When Papa sent Luka away, Abram ordered for the Georgian Mafia to intercept the transport.

They burned the bus, put bodies in place of the boys en route to Russia, and took them to Alaska instead."

"What . . . what was in Alaska?" Talia's tiny voice asked.

Trying to stop my bottom lip from quivering, I said, "An underground prison, nicknamed the Gulag, ran by the Georgians. A gambling ring just like this, where their prisoners are forced to fight to the death. They torture them, force them to take drugs, build them up to a frightening size. They make them into killers, drug them and torture them so badly that they block out their past and any memories they had before the Gulag. *Any* memories. *All* memories."

Tears flooded my cheeks and my chest grew tight.

"And what happened to my boy?" Ivan asked, and I finally opened my eyes. "Did he die? Did he die in the Gulag ring? Did my boy die?" Ivan's voice cracked, and when I cast a glance at Talia, she appeared numb with shock, her hand cool on mine.

"No," I whispered. "He became a champion, unrivaled . . . He survived, Ivan. There was an escape, and he fled, having no other memories but that of New York . . . He knew he had to come back to Brooklyn." I inhaled, watching as Luka and Alik circled one another around the cage, praying Luka would be victorious. "And his need for revenge on Alik."

My papa moved my hair back from my face. "How do you know all this, Kisa? Who told you? How can you be sure it's all true? This accusation against Abram is serious. You know it means death for his betrayal if you are correct, Kisa."

I nodded my head. "I know it's true . . . because . . ." I steeled my nerves, took a deep breath, and confessed, "Because Luka found me again. We found each other again, and he told me so himself."

Talia stood abruptly. "He's . . . he's here? In New York? My brother is back?"

I nodded.

"I don't . . . I don't believe it . . . Why didn't he come to us? Why didn't you tell us sooner?" she cried.

Another tear fell. "He doesn't remember you, Tal. He barely remembers me, just fragments of his past. He only remembered all that Alik did to him when he was with me last night. But then I dropped

Luka off at the gym. Alik had followed us." I looked to my papa. "That's why he attacked me, Papa." I dipped my eyes. "I was unfaithful to Alik with Luka, and Alik found out. He punished me. He said I betrayed him, but he has no idea it was with Luka. He doesn't even know Luka is alive, that he's back. Abram didn't tell him he never died."

My father jumped to his feet and threw his head back in anger.

Ivan stepped forward with urgency. "Kisa? Where's my boy? Where's Luka now? I need to see him!"

I got to my feet as fast as I could and pressed my non-injured hand against the glass. "He's in the cage." Ivan's eyes lit with confusion, and everybody moved to the glass. "Ivan, Luka is Raze, our newest fighter . . . and he's finally getting his revenge."

"No!" Talia cried.

My papa moved quickly, and I heard him order Max, "The minute the fight is done, no matter the outcome, you seize Abram."

"He doesn't look anything like I always pictured he would," Ivan said, and I could see water glistening in his eyes. "He's too big, scarred . . . all those tattoos. He . . . He looks like an animal in that cage, a killer."

"They hurt him, Ivan, for years in that Gulag. They hurt him. But Luka's still in there. He's still there underneath. We just have to bring him back."

Talia's sobs came thick and fast. "What if he doesn't win? What if Alik kills him for real this time?"

Ivan put his arm around Talia's shoulders. "He has to, Talia. God wouldn't be so cruel to make us lose him twice."

22

RAZE

I was sliced. I was stabbed. I was bleeding.

But so was Durov. He was sliced more. Stabbed more. Bleeding more.

Every part of my body ached with exhaustion, but Alik was lagging too. His body worse than mine, and the slash across the gut from my first strike was leaking so much blood that he wasn't going to last much longer.

"Come on!" Alik hissed at me. "Let's finish this shit." Alik's words were slurred. I stared at his face and just felt numb.

"Alik, get it the fuck together!" I glanced to the side of the cage to the man who was shouting and instantly had a flashback.

Alik's papa; Abram Durov.

My lip curled in anger and I looked across the crowd, the men chanting at me to kill Durov. They all knew I had the upper hand. They wanted me to spill blood.

And then movement from higher up caught my attention, and my gaze immediately slammed on a woman stood behind a huge glass window. She was badly beaten. I couldn't tear my eyes away from her, something making me stare . . . and then my heart fell.

Kisa.

Whipping my head to look at Alik, he had followed my gaze and his eyes bugged when he saw Kisa stood at the glass.

Without pause, I ran at Alik and swept his legs with my feet. He fell to the ground, but used the movement to stab his dagger straight into my thigh.

Roaring out in pain, I turned, flipping his body, twisted my leg around his and locked him a chokehold, his arms unable to strike.

"You did that to her?" I growled and I saw Alik smirk as I looked down. I tightened my hold, his face growing red.

"I'm going to make her pay," he threatened. "When I kill you, she'll be sorry. I'm going to break her." And that was enough to break *me*. He'd threatened my Kisa.

I was done.

Done with it all.

Using my legs to roll Alik, I straddled his waist and let the pent up aggression I'd been holding for years fill my muscles. Alik lifted his dagger and sunk the blade into my calf, but I clenched my fists and began punching at his face, the spikes from my knuckledusters slicing at his skin, mangling his features.

Screaming out in rage, I couldn't stop, fueled even further by the volume of the bloodthirsty crowd. Hands were shaking the wire of the cage, testing its strength. Abram was screaming for the fight to be stopped, but I was caught in the bloodlust. Alik's breathing slowed, his body jerked, and my fists froze in the air as I started to see him dying underneath me.

I expected relief. I expected to feel whole again . . . but seeing him breathing his last made me feel nothing . . . absolutely nothing . . .

"Do it," Alik whispered, his eyes, although losing life, still taunt-ing, still as fucking crazed as they had always been.

Glancing up to Kisa at the window, I could see tears streaming down her cheeks and I knew I had to save her. I had to protect her.

She was mine. I wanted to have her again.

I wanted to be *me* again . . .

Tightening my fists, I lifted them above my head, turned them in-ward and, on a final shout, ran my bladed fists right into his chest . . . and straight into his heart.

Alik gurgled on his own blood, his eyes blazing fire, until they stilled and glazed over . . .

Durov was dead.

Removing my fists, I slumped my shoulders, my heart racing too fast and my breath coming too hard.

The crowd exploded, the volume almost deafening. The cage began to rock and I saw the Byki pushing through the crowd, making a pathway, butting men with their guns and firing warning shots into the air.

The place was lifting, the atmosphere charged with the excitement of the crowd. I'd killed the reining champion.

A lot of money had just been lost.

And I felt none of it, just stayed staring at his corpse. The sure win had just been slaughtered.

Durov's still-warm body was bleeding out as memories flooded my mind like a torrent. Me as a child, Rodion . . . and Kisa . . . my Kisa. Always with me, stroking my hair, kissing me, reading to me . . .

Suddenly, the cage door flew open and Abram pounded in, dropping to his knees to look at his son dead on the floor, shock and pain etched all over his face. A path suddenly appeared through the crowd, another man leading the way.

Jumping off Alik's body, I got to my feet, legs apart and fists clenched bracing for the punishment for killing their number one fighter . . . the Bratva heir. I'd fight my way out of here if I had to, slaughter them all. And I'd be taking Kisa with me.

A man with long gray hair entered the cage, two Byki following behind, who ran straight to Abram and wrenched him up off the floor. Abram was too numb to fight, still staring at his slain son on the cage floor.

As he looked at his son, he appeared dead too.

The man with gray hair approached me, his eyes assessing. Every muscle tensed to strike, my head lowered and I clicked my fingers, reforming them back into fists.

The man held out his hands, placating, and confusion trembled through my body. My head tilted to the side and my eyes narrowed.

The man studied me. I was dripping in blood and fucking ready to fight anyone who got between Kisa and me, when he suddenly dropped to his knees, water spilling from his eyes.

I reared back in confusion.

"Papa!" another female cried and, unable to take her hand from her mouth, tears flooding her face, she dropped beside the man and they both looked up and stared at me.

My body grew hot and I felt sweat bead on my forehead. I couldn't stop staring at the blond girl and gray man, my chest heaving and pain building at the back of my head.

Looking around The Dungeon, I could see the Byki clearing the crowd, pushing them into the hallway, deserting the dank basement. A man standing at the back pulled my attention: Viktor. I cast him a curt nod in thanks, and with a lift of his hat, he disappeared into the crowd.

For once the man looked . . . happy?

Two people began to slowly approach the cage, and my heart fell when I saw one of them was Kisa.

"Kisa," I whispered, as her father, the Pakhan, helped her up the stairs to the cage. Kisa staggered in, her face black and blue, the sight making me shake with rage.

Tears were streaming down her face, but her eyes never left mine.

"Kisa!" I bellowed and went to move toward her, when the man on his knees pushed out his hand.

"Wait!" he called, catching my arm in his grip.

Snarling, I ripped my arm back and raised my spiked fists to strike.

"No!" Kisa cried and staggered over to me, pushing at my chest. "Stop! Please, Luka, stop!"

Pausing, I looked into Kisa's swollen eyes and she shook her head. Something inside told me to trust her and lower my fist. Ripping off my knuckledusters and casting them to the floor, I ran my finger down her cheek.

"He . . . he hurt you," I stated, my voice broken.

Kisa nuzzled into my palm, so lightly that her skin almost didn't touch my flesh. She was in pain. This caused me to feel more rage.

"It's over now, Luka," Kisa whispered and pulled me closer with one hand, her other hand clutched over her waist, her wrist seeming limp.

"He broke your wrist?"

Kisa nodded, tears streaming, but repeated. "It's over now. He's gone. I'm free . . . you're free . . ." Her voice broke and I knew it was all too much for her. But she tried to smile at me. "You did it, baby. You got your revenge."

I exhaled and instantly felt drained, but when movement from the floor caught my eyes, I wrapped my arm around Kisa and pulled her back against me in protection. My body crouched and braced for any danger.

The gray man got to his feet along with the other woman, holding out their palms and Kisa gripped my arm. "Luka. Listen to me."

My eyes darted all around the cage, assessing, taking note of who was here: Kisa's papa, Abram, the Byki, the gray man, and the woman . . . and they were all looking at me like they'd seen a ghost. Staring into my eyes. I immediately lowered my head.

Kisa moved around me and I tried to push her back.

"No, Luka. Baby, please look at me."

I hesitated, but eventually flickered my attention to her and her eyes which were glistening. She ran her hand through my hair and I instantly relaxed some. "No one here is going to hurt you." She ran a fingertip underneath my left eye. "You can look at them. They can see you. They can see the real you. You're safe."

I searched the faces of everyone in the cage again, and my eyes kept fixing on the man with gray hair and the woman with brown eyes. A pain throbbed in my temple when I looked at them. But I fought it. I took Viktor's advice and tried to let everything come to me.

"Luka, I need you to remember something," Kisa said softly. Her tone was strange, like she was preparing me for something big.

I frowned and stared into Kisa's blue eyes, my stomach tensing. "I can't," I replied. "I can't remember anything else. I've tried."

Kisa nodded in understanding, her eyes wincing at the movement. "You're hurt."

"It doesn't matter about me right now. Lyubov moya, I need you to remember."

"What? What do I need to remember?" I asked, feeling agitated, my eyes blinking as the pain in my temples grew stronger.

"You. Where you came from. Who your parents are . . . your family . . ." Kisa clutched her hand in mine and squeezed.

The gray man cleared his throat and he was staring at me again. I closed my eyes trying to break through the empty block in my mind, but all it caused was more pain.

I was done with the fucking pain!

"I don't . . . I don't remember, solnyshko!" I shouted out, when the gray man stepped forward, the blond woman openly sobbing.

"Do you . . . do you remember me, son?"

I looked to Kisa whose grip had tightened on my hand and she nodded at me in encouragement. I held onto Kisa like a lifeline and my pulse began to race.

The gray man never took his eyes from mine. And images danced in front of my eyes. My eyes widened and I searched the man's face more. It was him . . . it was him.

I was older, a teen, and I was in a car with a man. We were driving to a meeting. It was my first meeting with the Bratva—

"I was a part of the Bratva," I whispered and looked to Kisa. She nodded and pressed her broken lips to my cut up hand. Her touch calmed me down.

"Keep going, Luka. Keep going." I nodded and squeezed my eyes back shut.

I was a child. It was Christmas. There was a tree, presents. I was sitting on a couch, and a man gave me a gift. A man with brown eyes and light hair . . . a man with the gray man's face . . .

"Merry Christmas, son," the man had said.

"Thank you, papa," I had replied.

I gasped for breath and stumbled back, my back hitting the side of the cage. I stared at the gray haired man and couldn't seem to breathe.

The man stepped forward again. "Luka? Do you . . . Do you remem—"

"You're . . . my papa?" I questioned and relief spread on the man's face. He nodded his head unable to speak. "You're my papa. Ivan Tolstoi," I said again and tensed as he lifted a hand and put it on my shoulder.

"My son," he rasped out and tears fell down his face. "My Luka . . . you *have* returned to us."

My heart was beating erratically, and I found myself stepping forward as my papa took me into his arms. I froze at first, refusing to let go of Kisa, but then as more and more memories returned to me, I found myself sagging in his arms.

I was huge compared to him, but I felt like a child again, in his arms.

A sobbing over his shoulder made me look up and the blond woman was watching me and my father, an expression of happiness on her face. A picture of a young girl sat beside me at a dinner table annoyingly stabbing me with her fork in my leg played in my head. Then that Christmas scene from before deepened and I saw her sitting next to me at the tree, her arm around my waist.

My papa must have felt me freeze, for he moved back and saw me staring at the woman. Kisa's hand slipped from mine. And I walked forward and saw the woman was shivering.

"You're my sister," I stated and the woman tentatively nodded her head. "Tal . . . Tal . . ." I squeezed my eyes closed and tried to remember her name. A hand wrapped around mine and the woman said, "Talia. I'm your sister Talia."

"Talia," I said, the name sounding familiar, right, "My . . . sister."

Talia cried and threw her arms around my waist. I tensed at the contact, fighting the urge to throw her off and attack. I didn't know what to do. "You're alive," she sobbed. "I have you back. I have my brother back."

Glancing at Kisa, I could see her hugging her father. She was happy for me, her blue eyes bright.

Talia pulled back and I stumbled back toward Kisa and held out my hand. "Kisa," I said, desperately needing her close. It was all too much. My mind and body were exhausted and she was all I really knew. But as I held out my hand, the Pakhan—*Kirill* . . . his name was Kirill—took it and pulled me forward.

I braced my body again, but he said, "I never knew, Luka. I never knew . . . I believed you had killed my son and that is my sin to bear. I was so saddened that I didn't suspect Abram or Alik. Abram was my brother in this life, I would never suspect he'd do such a thing. You were innocent and paid for a crime you didn't commit."

Kirill looked at Kisa. "And my action took you from her. My wife would be spinning in her grave if she knew that I had separated the two of you unnecessarily," he dropped his head, "and gave her over to a lesser man . . . a sick man . . . a murderer."

I stared at the pakhan and could see the sincerity in his eyes.

"Papa!" Kisa cried, but Kirill held up his hand.

"It's the truth." Kirill looked over my head and in the direction of Abram and pulled out his gun. He walked to my father and handed the gun to him.

"It's your vengeance to kill him, Ivan."

My father straightened his shoulders and a cold look spread on his face. "He reached into his pocket and pulled out his gun, handing it to Kirill. "It's both our kill. He ordered for Alik to kill Rodion."

A sense of familiarity filled me. These were Bratva men. These were men that shouldn't be fucked with. This was my family . . . this was where I belonged.

My father walked to Abram, Kirill followed behind. Abram was still staring at his son dead on the floor. My father took off his coat, wearing a black suit underneath, and in one strike, backhanded Abram across the face. Abram looked like he didn't even notice it.

Kirill and my father lifted their guns. No words were spoken. And after a few tense seconds they both fired shots into Abram's chest and he slumped to the ground next to his dead son.

Kisa wrapped herself in my arms and I kissed her head, gripping her tight.

My father came toward me and asked, "Luka? Do you remember your mama?"

My heart beat wildly and my muscles tensed, but now that the key to my past was opened, a dark-haired woman's face came into view and I exhaled like I'd just ran for hours.

Kisa squeezed my waist and lifted her head. "She'll be so happy. She never gave up the belief that you were innocent. She knew you couldn't have done it. She always believed in your innocence."

Nerves suddenly racked my body and I leaned down and pressed my forehead against Kisa's. "But I'm not the Luka she knew. I'm a monster, a murderer. This version of her son isn't innocent."

"You *are* our Luka. You *are* our son," my father said sternly from beside me.

"Kisa, we need to get you home so Dr. Chazov can see you," Kirill said moving behind Kisa. "You need a cast on that wrist. You need stitches, and medication."

Kisa reluctantly nodded and put her hand on my cheek. I hadn't noticed how pale she was, how in pain. "You'll be fine, Luka. I'll come straight to your parents' house afterward. You need to see a doctor too. You're hurt, bleeding."

"No," I said aggressively. "I go with you. I see your doctor."

"Luka—"

"No! Kisa, *solnyshko*. I go with you," I bent down to whisper at her ear, "I need you with me. I only feel at home with you. I don't . . . I don't know these people like I know you. You're my now, they're still my past." I stared at her helplessly. "I can't be without you. I need you." I swallowed and fought to breathe, as I admitted, "I have fear in my heart . . . I am fearful of all of this."

Kisa's eyes saddened and I knew everyone around us had heard me. Kisa took my hand and turned to my father and Talia while I kept my head low.

"I'll go see the doctor with Luka, then we'll come to you. You'll have time to prepare mama Tolstoi."

I kept my eyes lowered like a coward. But I'd felt more in the last five minutes than I had in my whole life and it was too much.

A hand placed on my bicep and I looked up to see my father. "It's okay, Luka. Go with Kisa. Get fixed up. We'll see you soon . . . *son*."

I nodded, feeling that word settle in my heart and wrapped my hand over Kisa's shoulders, leading her from the cage. In the holding room, we didn't speak, but I could feel her watching me. I threw on my old familiar gray sweatshirt, the one I'd worn since the Gulag and followed Kisa to a back door. Keeping close to the other half of my heart and, for the first time ever, keeping my hood pulled back.

23

KISA

"Are you ready, lyubov moya?"

I turned to Luka, and he was stock still, staring at his mama and papa's brownstone with an anxious look on his face.

I squeezed his hand and Luka finally looked down at me. He blinked, then blinked again. A completely lost look covered his face.

"I don't know," he answered in a husky voice. "I'm remembering so much, but none of it is making sense. I just get flashbacks of broken memories. None of them are in order. Just glimpses of what my life used to be like."

He pointed to the brownstone that was as much a home to me as it was him. "Like this house. I remember sitting on these steps with you. I remember being in my bedroom, I think . . . with *you*." Luka moved to stand in front of me and lifted my hand, the one free of a cast, and pressed it to his chest. "Every memory I seem to have has you in it." His head was down, unable to meet my eyes.

A lump clogged my throat at how scared and lost he seemed right now. He had only a few hours ago killed the man that ruined his life. I think that goal drove him for so long that now without it, he had no idea what to do next.

The rabid killer of the cage was gone, a lost boy taking his place.

I moved forward and lifted his head with my finger under his chin. When Luka's gaze met mine, those brown eyes, the left with a smudge of my blue, my heart soared. "That's because we were never apart. Since we were kids, we were one. It has always been that way. We found a way back to each other, my love."

Luka's eyes bored into mine, a flare of possession in their glare. "And will *always* be that way," he said assertively. "I'm never losing you again."

Tears filled my eyes. "And will always be that way."

The door of his parents' home opened and Papa Ivan walked out onto the steps. I held up my hand sporting the cast, and Ivan smiled sadly at me.

Luka had frozen, his expressive eyes now showing every bit of his apprehension.

"Let's go, baby," I whispered, just for him to hear.

I pulled on Luka's hand and led him toward the house. He had showered back at my house after we had both seen Dr. Chazov, both now patched up. One of my papa's men had brought him some blue jeans and a white shirt.

He looked so stunning that I almost couldn't take it. His huge muscles tested the material of both his jeans and shirt, his defined traps pronounced and his blond hair messy in the most attractive way.

I wanted him more than ever.

Luka gripped my hand, his hold like a vise as we ascended the stairs. Ivan embraced me, then awkwardly hugged his son, and I couldn't stop the tears tumbling from my eyes.

"Your mama is desperate to see you again, son. She—" Ivan's voice broke. "She won't believe it until she has you in her arms. She's climbing the walls with excitement."

Ivan led us into the foyer, and I could feel the tension pulsing from Luka, his hand rigid in mine. With a jerk of my arm, he pulled me into his chest, almost like he was using me as a shield as we walked into the living room. Talia was sitting on a chair, bouncing her leg in nerves and chewing on her thumbnail.

Mama Tolstoi paced in front of the marble fireplace, and when she saw us enter the room, she froze and stared.

I felt Luka stiffen behind me, and when I glanced up, his eyes were clenched, his head tilted to the side, and his cut full lips were pursed.

He remembered her. I now knew what his expression looked like when a memory fixed itself in place. My chest filled with happiness. He remembered his mama.

A sob escaped Mama Tolstoi's mouth and she reached behind her to hold on to the mantel to keep upright. "Luka? Luka . . . is it you . . . ?"

Luka's hand fell from mine and he stepped round me. "M-Mama?"

Luka's mama rushed forward upon hearing him speak and she held him in her outstretched arms. "Luka. It's you . . . my son . . . my boy . . ."

"Yes." Luka exhaled, and his mama wrapped her arms around his waist, her small frame tiny next to his large, broad heavily-muscled body.

"You've come home," she cried. "You've come home to us . . . I knew you were out there. I could feel in my heart that you were still alive." She pulled back and lay her hand on his stubbled cheek, standing on her tip-toes to do so. "My son . . . my son . . ."

Feeling like I was an intruder in the room, I backed out into the hallway as mother and son were reunited and walked through to the kitchen and out into the backyard. As soon as the fresh air hit my face, I immediately felt better.

Walking to a white bench in the small yard, I slumped down and closed my eyes, drawing in a long, deep breath.

I couldn't believe everything that had happened. It all seemed so unreal. Like some dream I was about to wake up from.

Feeling the gravity of everything that had gone down of late— finding out Luka was alive, that Alik was responsible, the pain Luka had been put through over the years, and now Alik dead and Luka back in my arms—all I could do was submit to conflicted feelings of grief and joy.

Dropping my head into my hands, I just let it all go, my emotions pouring out of me through my tears.

"Kisa?"

Startled, I lifted my head, frantically wiping at my bruised face with my good hand and swallowed back my sobs. "Talia, you scared me," I said, clearing my throat as she sat beside me, her stare fixing on the night sky.

Without a word, Talia's hand reached out and held mine. I closed my eyes, just breathing in the Brooklyn summer air, when she whispered, "Thank you."

Snapping my eyes open, I looked to Talia's face that, I noticed, was changed, more relaxed. My chest tightened when I realized that for years, since Luka had "died," this was the first time she seemed truly at ease.

How had I not noticed before?

"Tal—"

"I would never have believed you if you had told me you suspected . . . Raze . . . of being my brother. I wouldn't have believed it for a second. Even if I'd seen him with my own two eyes, I wouldn't have recognized him. He's so big, so aggressive looking." Talia sniffed. "Kisa, I wouldn't have recognized my own brother."

"He's changed, Tal. He doesn't look the same," I said, trying to be a comfort. "And he would always wear a hooded sweatshirt with the hood over his eyes. I think somehow he knew that people would know him when they saw his left eye. He didn't know that though. He doesn't know much. He needs to learn life all over again." I squeezed Talia's hand. "Nobody would have recognized him."

She turned to me. "Nobody but you. You felt drawn to him, from the night he saved you in that alley. *You* pursued him and realized who he was. *You* brought him back. You never gave up. Saw through the bulk, the tattoos and scars. You *saw* it was him."

I opened my mouth to reply, but I couldn't speak, my emotions too high. So we just sat there, breathing properly for the first time in years.

"You saved him," she then whispered and holding each other's hands just that little bit tighter, I knew all our lives had changed for the better tonight.

After a while, I got up from the bench and entered the house. Mama Tolstoi was in the kitchen. As soon as I entered, her eyes fell upon my limping, beaten body.

"Kisa . . . my daughter," she said quietly, holding out her hand for me to take, before wrapping me in her arms.

"It's okay, Mama. Everything will now be okay."

She pulled me into her chest and murmured, "God put a part of my son's soul within you so when he lost his way, he would follow his feet and find his way back you. You're the other half of his soul. You're his savior . . . you're all our saviors."

Fighting back even more tears, I pulled back and pressed a kiss to her cheek. There were no words.

"Your mama will be rejoicing in heaven."

"Mama . . ." I said, fighting a lump in my throat.

"Shh . . . all is well now. No need to fill it with words or explanations. Everything is as it should be. The past is in the past. Follow the newly lit path to the future. My son has returned, the man who took him away is dead and you love him with every part of your being. What more could I ever want?"

Drinking in those words, I smiled in pure joy and asked, "Where—"

"In his old room," Mama Tolstoi interrupted.

Still smiling, I laid another kiss to her cheek and walked through the living room and up the stairs, hearing Mama Tolstoi singing for the first time in years.

Papa Ivan was in his office at his desk, and for a moment, I could almost pretend the last twelve years hadn't happened. He was on the phone and I frowned when I heard him discussing the Gulag . . . discussing number 362.

"I want to know his name, where he was from and the names of the men that put him in that place." There was a voice coming through the other end of the phone, but it stopped when Ivan slapped the desk and said, "I'll pay whatever I need to pay, money's no object, this is for my son! Find the men responsible and have them killed."

I closed my eyes for a moment and sorrow filled my stomach. Luka was getting revenge for 362, his *friend* . . . on the men that falsely accused him.

Luka wanted to do this for his only friend. It almost broke me.

Opening the door to Luka's old room, I entered to see him slumped on his old narrow bed, his head downcast. He looked huge sitting on his faded blue comforter. My stomach flipped. It was surreal seeing him now, older, in this room.

"Luka?"

Luka lifted his head and his brown eyes were shining. Shutting the door behind me, I walked to the bed. I went to sit beside him, but before I could, Luka carefully scooped me up in his large arms and sat me on his lap, tucking his head into my neck, breathing in my scent.

It made me smile how this was one trait he hadn't let go of.

I stroked his hair and pressed a long kiss to his head. "Are you okay, baby?"

He shook his head indicating "no," and I held him tighter. I couldn't imagine the turmoil he was going through right now. The shock of being back here. The shock of realizing that he wasn't alone in the world. Quite the opposite in fact.

He was loved. He was loved so damn much.

"It will all be okay, you know," I soothed.

Luka lifted his head and his brown eyes met mine. "I don't know what to do now. I've spent so long with one goal, one drive, and now it is done with." His eyebrows pulled down. "What now, solnyshko? What do I do now? What if I can't do anything else but kill?"

I cupped his cheeks and laid my forehead against his. "You learn how to live again. And I'll be there every step of the way with you."

Luka's eyes filled with tears and a single drop fell down his scarred face . . . and it was quite possibly the most heartbreaking thing I'd ever seen.

"Baby, don't cry," I said, my throat clogged. "Everything is okay. I love you, I love you so much."

Luka's eyes met mine, his long dark lashes wet and he lifted a hand to lay over mine on his cheek. "I'm free . . . I'm finally free . . . I can't . . . I can't . . ."

Heart exploding in my chest at the relief on his face, I held my soul mate as hard as I could against my chest.

Moving my mouth to his ear, I asked, "Can I have you?"

Luka stilled for a moment. Then I felt a decade's worth of pain and loss flee his body. "You can have me, solnyshko. You can have all of me. You always have, and you always will."

EPILOGUE

Six months later . . .

"Lyubov moya . . ." I moaned as Luka moved within me. I raked at his strong back, my head tilted as he kissed and nipped at my throat.

"Solnyshko," Luka groaned, his hips picking up speed, his cock like steel, swelling within me the closer we came to release.

Our breathing came quick, and my hands moved to fist his hair. Luka stretched out his arms and gripped the iron of the headboard, thrusting powerfully inside me, making me lose control.

"Baby!" I cried, feeling my orgasm approach, clenching my legs around his waist. Luka's head lifted to press his mouth to mine. Our tongues instantly clashed, wild and erratic.

"Kisa . . . Kisa . . ." Luka roared, breaking from my lips as his neck tensed, his muscles cording as he came, taking me over the edge with him.

Luka jerked inside me, then collapsed on my chest, his skin damp from hours and hours of lovemaking.

Yesterday we got married.

Finally. In our childhood church, by Father Kruschev.

I was officially Luka's wife, and there was no one happier on Earth than I was right now, right at this second.

I ran my hand through Luka's blond messy hair as he caught his breath. Lifting his head, Luka pressed a long, lazy kiss to my lips and said, "I love you, solnyshko."

Running my finger down his cheek, I replied, "I love you too."

Smiling shyly, Luka, after six months of never spending a day apart, still found his freedom impossible to get used to and he felt undeserving of my unconditional love for him.

Memories of his past in the Gulag gave him nightmares and he would wake up in cold sweats, the faces of the hundreds of men and boys he was forced to kill haunting his sleep. The nightmares got so bad, Luka refused to sleep those first nights. I couldn't stand seeing it, so I defied my papa and ignored orthodox tradition. The very next night I slept next to Luka in his childhood bed, and he never woke up once.

He needed me to sleep.

I kept his nightmares away.

We'd never spent a day apart since.

Moving his face to mine again, I ensured our eyes met and said, "I have always and will always love you, all my life."

Luka awarded me with a blinding smile and kissed down my neck, down my chest, and down to my belly, where he peppered me with kisses.

Glancing up at me with hope in his eyes, he asked, "You think you're pregnant yet?"

Laughing, I held on to his arms and pulled him back up over me. "We got married yesterday, Luka."

His face fell into a serious expression. "I want a child with you."

"I know you do, lyubov moya. And it'll happen. Nothing will take me away from you again." I ran my finger over his wedding ring. "We're married now. Together forever, remember?"

He exhaled through his nose and nodded, slumping beside me, and laid his head over my naked chest. He nuzzled his head into my breast, and I smiled, knowing what that small action meant.

I began running my fingers through Luka's messy sandy hair, loving the feel of his arms tightening around mine. He loved me stroking at his hair. Said it made him feel like the last twelve years had never happened.

It broke my heart because he *wasn't* the Luka from our childhood.

He was damaged.

Jaded.

Tormented by his past.

Permanently changed . . . but he was the man I loved now, the man who was always my protector. Now he was even more so. And although life was hard for him now, with me, he was at peace.

We were each other's peace.

"Read to me," Luka murmured, completely relaxed in my arms. Smiling, I reached out for our favorite old book that was worn and aged through years of overuse. I had never thrown it away.

Maybe I always knew I would need it again someday.

"You ready, lyubov moya?" I asked.

"Mmm . . ." he murmured in reply. "Read to me." He reached up and held my free hand in his.

I smiled.

I was so unbelievably happy as we laid here in our new bed in our new home, our new brownstone, three doors down from his parents' home.

"*They were always meant to be together, one boy and one girl, two hearts split into two, sent to far-off lands on their own. For God wanted to see if true love could be tested. He wanted to see if two halves of one soul could find each other again, even against the odds. Years would pass. They would both be hurt. They would both be sad, but one day, when they least expected it, they would stumble into each other's paths. The question is: would they recognize each other's soul? And would they find their way back to love . . . ?*"

Looking down at Luka, his eyes closing as he traced his finger over my belly, a small contented smile on his lips, I knew he was praying I was pregnant.

I was too.

"You recognized mine," he murmured sleepily, slowly opening his eyes. I stopped reading and lowered the book. "You recognized my soul when I was lost."

Tears building, I replied, "I did, baby."

"And you brought me back to you," he finished and pressed a kiss to my stomach.

I shook my head. "Now that's where you're wrong."

Luka raised his head, tilted it to the side, and pursed his lips in confusion. My heart flipped at the action and, releasing his hand, I stroked my thumb along his stubbled cheeks. Taking his hand again, I pressed it against my heart.

"I couldn't bring you back because you never ever left. Not in here." I patted my chest where my heart was.

Luka smiled and laid his head back down. Closing his eyes, he picked up my hand and placed it back in his hair, nudging me to stroke him again.

My heart melted as my fingers began to move back and forth through the silky blond strands. I picked up the book and started where I left off . . .

"Their love story began on the day she was born . . ."

RAZE PLAYLIST

The Avett Brothers—"I and Love and You"
Little Big Town—"Live Forever"
Labrinth—"Jealous"
Lana Del Ray—"Gods & Monsters"
Coldplay—"Lost"
The Script—"Superheroes"
JAY Z—"Young Forever (feat. Mr. Hudson)"
Jennifer Nettles—"This Angel"
Marina and the Diamonds—"Happy"
Eminem ft. Sia—"Guts Over Fear"
One Republic—"I Lived"
Whiskeytown—"Everything I Do"
Breaks Co-Op—"The Otherside"
Emeli Sande—"River"
Greg Holden—"The Lost Boy"
Jonny Fears—"Boyfriend"
Ellie Goulding—"How Long Will I Love You"
Adele—"Don't You Remember"
A. A. Bondy—"Killed Myself When I Was Young"
Sam Smith—"Stay with Me"

RAZE ACKNOWLEDGMENTS

Raze was a very different book for me to write. It was a lot darker than I'd attempted before, brutal and complex . . . but I loved every minute of it! And, as always, I have lots of people to thank!

Firstly, my mam and dad. Thanks for all of the support. Love you both!

To my husband, for putting up with me releasing TWO novels in December. Love you. It was crazy, but we got there!

To my fabulous beta readers: Thessa, Rebecca, Kia, Rachel, and Lynn. Your comments and advice were invaluable and you worked like the clappers to get them to me in record time!

Thessa, my lovely, thank you for manning my Facebook page and keeping me in check. Thank you for being a RAZE/Luka enthusiast and encouraging me to write this novel. Love you, missus!

Kelly and Have Book Will Read Book Blog for hosting my blog tour and just being a fabulous friend. I appreciate everything you do for me. You're priceless.

Cassie, my fantastic editor. Thank you so much!

Lysa, my wonderful web designer. I love you!

Liz, my fabulous agent. Thank you for all of your support. I'm so excited about the projects we have planned for 2015! So much to look forward to!

Gitte and Jenny from TotallyBooked Book Blog. You know how I feel about you sassy gals! Love you both to bits!!!

Neda from Sub Club Books. Love you, girl!

And a huge thank-you to all the many, many more wonderful book blogs that support me and promote my books. I adore you all.

Tracey-Lee, Thessa, and Kerri, a huge thank-you for running my street teams, Tillie's Hot Cole's and The Hangmen Harlots. Y'all kick ass! And to all of my street team members—LOVE YOU!!!

And lastly, my wonderful readers. Your support, your enthusiasm, and your love means the world to me.

Here's to 2016!!!!

Big Hugs,

Tills xx

REAP

To music, for the constant inspiration.
To Johnnyswim, for inspiring this novel.

You and I, we're fire and water . . .
We're rain and thunder . . .
—Johnnyswim "You and I"

PROLOGUE: 221

Poison.

Pain.

Burning.

Unbearable fucking burning.

Rapids of lava raced through my veins.

My skin . . . my skin was too hot . . . too tight around my flesh . . .

I panted with anger . . . so much fucking anger to keep inside . . . stabbing at my brain, driving me insane . . .

Rip someone apart, I snarled in my head, *break bones, tear flesh . . . feel wet blood on my hands.*

I paced, my heavy iron chains wrapping around my wrists and ankles. I needed to kill. I needed to get out from under these chains.

Must kill to stop the poison.

Must kill to stop the pain inside.

"You're back in New York?" a voice suddenly spoke from across the room. "The Georgians have finally made their great return?"

"We have. And it's been a long time coming. We have business to settle. Business from long ago," Master spoke, and my heart began to pound. *Listen to Master. Listen to Master's commands.*

Footsteps clicked on the cold hard floor. The man was approaching Master. I paced faster.

"With the Volkovs?" the other voice asked. "Because if it is, a lot has happened in forty years. They're untouchable. Too strong."

Master laughed. "We've returned stronger."

"Do they know you're here?"

Master paused, then replied, "They'll find out soon enough. We're not hiding from the red scum."

Master turned to me, bringing a man with him. My muscles tensed and I snarled as they came close . . . *too* close.

"What the—"

"We've mastered a new drug. Proven to secure one hundred percent obedience in any subject. No other can offer this to you, Nasar. The Italians won't have seen anything like it. Your business will surpass theirs when your girls can bend to a buyer's every whim."

Master's voice stabbed at my ears. I always heard Master, my body tensing as I waited for his command. I kept my eyes to the dark wet ground as Master ordered, never making eye contact. He told me I was a dog, a killer. He told me I was his slave.

Searing heat enveloped my flesh; the white-hot pain in my head surged through my body. Shaking, I tensed before screaming out the pain. Fury took its hold.

Every muscle in my body was twitching, itching, on fire, thirsting to deliver death. My chains rattled louder as my hands clenched into fists, imagining the slaughter of an opponent, testing the strength of the heavy cuffs around my wrists.

The feet from Master came closer still. I paced faster. My heart pumped louder. I hissed loudly through clenched teeth.

Klavs, klavs, klavs—kill, kill, kill—I needed to kill.

I inhaled a long breath as the strange man approached. I snarled and bared my teeth, warning him to stay the fuck away from me.

He stepped back. I could smell fear on the fucker.

Fear.

Fear stank. Fear reeked. I hated it. Fucking *hated* it.

Klavs, klavs, klavs . . .

The poison in my blood boiled hotter still, my veins screaming at the pain of the scalding venom. I pulled on the chains around my hands, seeking release from the torment the poison brought. Muscles tensing, neck stiffening, and back stretching, I roared a deafening roar and increased the speed of my pacing.

Back and forth . . . back and forth . . . back and forth . . .

The man's feet stepped forward and began to circle me, his sweat dropping on the cracked ground of the cellar. "You have managed to control this one? He seems feral."

Master stepped forward; he came close, my body stiffening. He slapped his hand on my arm. "221 is my prized possession, my proto-type, my *dzaghii*—my dog. He obeys anything I ask of him. *Anything.* He's had a concentrated shot of the Type A drug this morning. Type A drug creates killers on demand, Type B, perfectly obedient slaves; slaves who will do anything you want." Master's voice lit with excitement. "221, here, kills with perfect efficiency. Complete annihilation."

The feet of the man stopped, stood beside me, and I could hear his heartbeat race. "Prove it," he said quietly.

Master laughed. "You brought the men?"

"They're here," the other man replied. "Bring them in!" he shouted, a command to someone at the entrance to the cellar.

He moved to stand beside Master. "I need trustworthy men by my side. Our war with the Italians is heating up. I need men who won't ques-tion anything asked of them. Men who can't be beat in a fight. I also want my stock to be obedient. I want them open to anything a buyer wants. If this drug you've created and its subject prove to be true, we have a deal."

Master stepped away. A guard approached me and began to loosen the chains. My feet rocked from side to side as the chains dropped to the ground. Looking at my hands, I slowly clenched them into fists, the cracking of my knuckles echoing around the room.

Heavy breathing came from behind me. My lip curled . . . *weakness . . .*

"221, *t'avis mkhriv.*" Master ordered me to turn and my body swerved, head down, legs bracing in his direction.

"221, *mzad.*" Master demanded me to get ready. My chin lifted. Six men stood before me. Six men smirking, holding daggers.

As another jolt of lava swept through me, a growl rumbled in my chest.

Klavs, klavs, klavs.

"221, *t'avis mkhriv,*" Master called again. The guard thrust a pair of black sais into my hands. I never took my eyes off the men who stood before me—they were nothing but prey. I rolled my neck from side to side, legs parted, ready to attack my prey. My blood rushed faster and faster, my hands itching to slice these fuckers open.

The man with Master spoke. "These are some of the best men I have. If your dog can defeat them, we have a deal."

"How many do you want dead?" Master's voice enquired.

The man sputtered. "How many? You're telling me he will kill them *all,* if ordered?"

"He'll kill until I order him to stop."

The man moved to stand in front of me, his small dark eyes glaring into mine. I bared my teeth and snarled. He immediately stepped back.

A smile eventually pulled on his thin lips as fire lit in his eyes. "I want to see him slay every last one."

"221," Master commanded. My body tensed, my fingers gripping the sais. *"Sasaklao."*

Slaughter.

My feet lurched forward, just as the six men ran at me at once. A red mist clouded my eyes as I made the first strike, blood spattering my chest.

I sliced.

I gutted.

I culled.

I fucking slaughtered them all.

1

LUKA

The Dungeon
Season Opener
Brooklyn, New York

I blinked . . . I blinked again. It didn't fucking work. Didn't remove the images from my mind.

Reaching up, I clawed at the knot of the silk tie I'd been forced to wear and loosened it off. I couldn't fucking breathe.

Every muscle in my body was tense as I sat up in this suffocating private box, looking down on the Dungeon's cage, the wide window giving me the perfect fucking view of the two fighters ripping each other apart.

The crowd noise was deafening; screaming and clamoring for spilt blood, as the first match of the season kicked off.

No matter how hard I tried to look away, my eyes were securely locked on the two men in the cage. My heart raced, my hands curled into fists, and my jaw ached as my teeth gritted together way too hard.

With every blow the fighters delivered, my legs twitched. With every spray of blood on the concrete floor, every body smashed into the wire surrounding the cage, an envious pain sliced through my stomach.

I wanted in, I wanted to rip those fuckers apart. I wanted to feel the cold steel of my knuckledusters back on my fingers, feel my spiked blades slowly pierce my opponent's flesh, and I wanted to watch as the life leaked out of his eyes. I wanted to bring death; I wanted to rip out someone's fucking soul.

The monster within me wanted out and I was losing the battle to keep him at bay. Six months . . . six months of being away from that cage, yet every instinct I had was telling me to go back. That it was where I belonged, that I deserved to keep fighting. My nightmares were getting worse . . . more memories of my killings becoming clearer . . . the guilt, and the fucking uphill battle of trying to adjust to this godforsaken world. A world that was becoming more and more difficult to be in.

Shit! I couldn't fucking breathe!

I sat forward, raking my hands through my hair, fighting my thoughts, the urges in my head. I wanted to embrace the demons inside, but at the same time, I wanted to fucking leave this shit hole of a fight ring and not feel the coming sense of death clogging up the air. I wanted to get the fuck away from the cage. It was in a cage where I'd slaughtered over six hundred men. It was in a cage where I'd killed my only *friend*.

I winced as 362's face flashed into my mind: his grin as he met me in the gulag as a kid, teaching me how to survive, and his face as I took his life, stealing his chance at revenge on those who had condemned him to the life of a fucking monster.

I saw nothing but red as I straddled his waist and speared a bladed fist into his neck. Felt nothing but rage as my second bladed fist skewered his temple. Felt nothing but single-minded determination to slaughter Durov as I lifted both fists and, pointing them straight down, plunged them into 362's chest, the wheeze of his dying breaths assaulting my ears, wrenching me from my anger.

I'd killed him. I'd watched as his dark eyes frosted over with the coldness of death. I'd watched as the color from the fight drained from his face, and I'd listened to that final beat of his heart until there was nothing but the deafening scream of silence.

"Revenge . . . ," 362 *had uttered, choking on blood washing back down his throat.*

I'd fucking promised him my revenge on the people who sentenced him to the gulag's cells; the people I still hadn't found; the people I still hadn't killed in cold blood.

I was failing 362, my only friend. And I couldn't fucking live with it.

Jerking on my chair as the crash of memories assaulted my mind, my heartbeat drummed too fast, and the screaming rush of my blood racked through my ears. In that second of panicked movement, my eyes went to the center of the cage as a fighter gripped his weapon of choice—a jagged hunting knife—and sent it straight through the eye of his opponent, the crowd noise soaring in volume.

My father and the Pakhan got to their feet and clapped, demonstrating their superiority to the bloodthirsty crowd below. The bloodthirsty crowd who were already exchanging money and placing bets on the next fight. All of the desperate and sadistic fuckers thanking the Russian kings for this damn dungeon of death.

My father looked down at me and aggressively flicked his chin. He was ordering me to stand, to clap, to stand like a fucking regal God at the window, to show the fuckers jamming up the Dungeon that I was the Bratva *knayz,* the Russian Mafia prince. The sole heir and the one destined to take charge. We constantly had to show our strength.

But I couldn't move. This suit I was forced to wear was fucking suffocating me. This silk tie, although loose, still feeling like a damn leash tying me to this Bratva role I couldn't bear to embrace.

I tried to move, but I couldn't force myself to lift from this chair. Memories of 362 bleeding out below me were stabbing harder at my brain, stealing my fucking breath.

My eyes squeezed shut, sweat pouring down my cheeks. I was losing it, I was fucking losing my shit.

Six months of this fucking torture. Six fucking months of slowly going insane, too many painful memories and flashbacks scourging the fuck out of my brain.

I abruptly lurched to my feet, and the Pakhan darted his gaze to me. "Luka?"

The room began to spin, the walls fucking closing in on me.

My father stepped forward. "Son? What's wrong?"

But I couldn't answer them. I had to get out, needed to get the fuck out of this tiny fucking box.

Staggering to the steel door barricading us in, I used all my strength to smash it open, snapping the top hinge clean off the frame.

"Luka! Come back!" I heard my father shout as I disappeared into the dark hallway. I ignored him as I turned to race down the steep staircase that led to the packed crowd.

"Mr. Tolstoi?" one of the *byki* called as I ran past him. Heads turned as I pushed through the mass of scumbags trying to get to the side of the cage to fucking see the carnage inside. But all the fuckers moved out of my way, sensing that I'd rip them in two if they got in my fucking path.

I headed for the hallway, the familiar hallway that I'd walked down when I was Raze, the death-match fighter I'd been conditioned to be since a child. The hallways where I'd lived as a Dungeon fighter, stayed each night, only one focus in my mind: revenge on Alik Durov, my childhood friend that, along with his father, had condemned me to a life of killing.

Ignoring the trainers and fighters filling the narrow space, I staggered to the locker room I used to occupy. Smashing my shoulder into the door, it burst open and I slammed it shut, blocking out the world.

It was quiet in this room, no noise fucking with my head. This locker room made me feel safe.

Walking into the center of the room, I kicked off the leather shoes from my feet, feeling the cold from the asphalt ground. Tipping my head back, I stood in the sliver of moonlight slipping through a crack in the wall and ripped off my tie. Hands shaking, I roared when I couldn't undo the buttons of my shirt. Gripping the expensive material, I pulled hard, the shirt slicing in two, shreds drifting to the floor.

Bare on top, my chest heaved at the severity of my breathing. I tried to calm down . . . to think of my life now, away from all the gulag shit, but it wasn't any fucking use.

Walking to the wall, I slammed my palms against the cold hard stone and closed my eyes, just trying to fucking breathe. But this room made me feel like the old me. I felt like *him,* Raze. I felt like the death-match fighter 818. I felt like the Georgian gulag's bringer of death. Luka fucking Tolstoi was a stranger to me. The *knyaz* of the New York Russian Bratva was a total fucking stranger.

The same feelings of how to kill, how to position my bladed knuckledusters just right to cause the most pain, circled my mind . . . and I fucking embraced it. It was familiar . . . it felt like . . . *me.*

Suddenly, a hand gripped my shoulder. Sensing the familiarity of a gulag guard attack, years of being a "fuck thing," a punching bag for those abusive pricks taking me back to that lost kid I used to be, I turned and gripped the fucker's neck under my hand, smashing him back against the wall. A red mist fogging my eyes, I gritted my teeth and lifted the asshole off the floor.

No one would hurt me again . . . *ever.* I was stronger now, tougher. I was a built and conditioned fucking stone-cold killer.

Fingernails raked at my skin; wheezing breath filled my ears. But my hands squeezed tighter, the familiar feel of draining a life pumping me the fuck up.

The flailing cunt in my hands began to go weak and I tightened my grip, almost snapping his neck. This fucker would die. He wouldn't get to rape me no more. Wouldn't get to push me in that cage and kill another innocent kid. *I* was an innocent kid, too. This fucker would die. This fucker would die slowly, painfully, under *my* hands. They wouldn't touch me anymore. They wouldn't push me in that fucking ring anymore—

"Luka!"

Too focused on the kill, on the rush that came with feeling a pulse slow to a stuttered stop in a neck, I didn't hear the door open behind me. My mind was a damn slide show of images, fucked-up images of my kills; kids begging for their lives, guards pointing their guns in my face if I didn't finish those kids off. Pain, torture, rape, blood, so much fucking blood—

"Luka, stop!" A distant yet familiar voice broke through into my stormy mind. I shook my head.

"Luka, put him down." The voice was soothing. I knew that voice. That voice made my heart slow down. It calmed me . . . who . . . what . . . ?

"Luka, *lyubov moya.* Come back to me. I'm here. Come back. Fight the memories. Fight them, just come back."

Ki . . . Kisa . . . my Kisa . . . ? My eyes snapped shut at the soothing voice and new memories flashed through my mind . . . a boy and girl on a beach . . . kissing . . . making love . . . blue eyes . . . brown eyes . . . one soul . . . love lost . . . love found . . . a wedding . . . love . . . so much love . . .

Kisa.

Gasping, my eyes flew open, the free hand at my side shook and my skin was drenched with sweat. My other arm was elevated high, and when I followed the length of that arm, it was gripping a neck in an iron vise . . . the neck of a man, a man my head told me I knew.

Confused at what had happened, I stepped back, my hand releasing its grip on the man and he fell to the ground, wheezing, gasping, fighting for breath.

I staggered back farther until my back slammed against the opposite wall. Feet moved beside me, but I couldn't look up. I was frozen on the floor, my knees tucking into my stomach and my head falling into my hands.

"Viktor? Viktor? Are you okay?" The female voice from before made me look up, and there she was, my Kisa, my *solnyshko,* bending down, running her hands over the man's—

My stomach fell.

Viktor. Viktor, my trainer, the man who helped me to defeat Alik Durov.

Feeling as though the gulag tattoo across my chest, the bold and broad 818, was on fire, I watched Viktor's eyes close and Kisa call to the *byki* for help.

Two of the Pakhan's men ran in, and I watched them as if they were moving in slow motion. Kisa stepped back as they helped Viktor to his feet. The *byki* dragged him out in seconds and I felt a pain as sharp as a dagger's strike slice through my stomach.

My fists clenched as I realized what I'd done. *I'd almost killed Viktor.*

The door softly clicked shut and I heard the locks turning, two iron bolts being slid in place to keep me inside.

Quiet footsteps came toward me and the soothing scent of sweet flowers washed over my body and filled my nose.

Solnyshko.

Gentle fingers suddenly ran over my hand. I flinched and dragged them away as I fought back my instinct to kill, to hurt, to maim, to slaughter.

"Luka, look at me," Kisa ordered, but I kept my head low.

"Luka," Kisa repeated in a sterner voice, "look up."

Gritting my teeth, I looked up and my gaze found a set of perfect blue eyes.

Kisa. My wife.

Head tilted to the side, Kisa's eyes filled with tears and she reached out her hand to touch my face. "Luka—"

"No!" I snarled. I sank back farther against the wall, swatting away her hand. "Don't touch me! I don't want to hurt you."

Kisa reared back. I knew she was staring at me. I could feel her gaze burning through my skin. We sat in silence for what seemed like an age, my fists still taut, my blood still boiling with rage. Then, suddenly, Kisa stood, my muscles bracing for her to leave, my heart beating fast again at the thought of her leaving me alone.

But she didn't walk away. She didn't head for the door. She didn't leave. She stayed silent, only a rustling of material to be heard.

I didn't look up. Instead I focused on trying to calm the rage erupting from inside. But then a hand took mine and my palm met hot flesh.

Whipping up my head, I found Kisa kneeling beside me, the top of her sleeveless long black dress pulled down to her waist, her perfect tits on show. Her hand held mine over her bare breast and I tore my gaze away from the sight—the sight that was fucking destroying me—to meet her eyes. They were filled with a mixture of steely determination and love, fucking filled with nothing but love.

She bulldozed through all the barriers I had.

Taking control, Kisa squeezed my hand tighter around her tit, my cock hardening at the feel of my woman under my palm. Shifting her legs, Kisa released her hold on my hand, her eyes telling me not to move it from her tit, and lifted up her dress from the bottom.

My breathing quickened as her lace panties came into view, and then I fucking lost all anger when she untied the lace bows at the side, the panties falling to the floor.

I was struck mute as my wife—my fucking *beautiful* wife—straddled my thighs, her bare pussy dragging down my stomach.

My hand on her warm breast tightened as my solid dick pushed against my pants. Kisa's breathing hitched as her clit ran down my torso and her mouth lowered to my ear. "I love you, baby. I have you. You're okay. I'm here. . . ."

My eyelids shut at the relief her words brought, and just like that, I was calmed.

"Kisa . . . ," I whispered in response, my words clogging my throat.

Kisa pressed a finger over my lips. "Shh, *lyubov moya*, just . . . just . . . *love* me," she said almost silently. "Let me love you with everything I have. Let me make you feel safe, with me. Be my Luka, the boy whose soul matches mine."

And she did. I made love to her on the locker room floor, and she brought me back to myself. She chased away the demons and pain.

As we both fought for breath in the aftermath, I reached up, never moving my gaze from hers, and said, "I'm . . . I'm sorry."

Kisa's face softened. "Never be sorry. You're my husband, my heart, my soul."

The reality of what had just happened began to hit home and I shut my eyes in embarrassment. Kisa must have felt me tense as she tensed, too. Inhaling a shaky breath, she whispered, "I love you so much, Luka. Do you know that?"

The hurt and sadness in her voice was sharper than any weapon I've taken into the cage.

"Luka?" Kisa probed my silence and slowly drew back her head to look at me. Her eyes were filled with tears again. "I *love* you."

Kisa placed her finger under my chin and forced my head up. "Talk to me. Let me in." Her eyelids fluttered, chasing away tears. She sniffed back her cries and wiped at her eyes. "What happened tonight? What happened with Viktor? Why did you run from Papa and Ivan? You neglected your duty to the Bratva."

Feeling drained, I exhaled a shuddering breath.

As more seconds passed by, I heard Kisa sigh in frustration and her hands cupped my cheeks. "Look at me, Luka."

Reluctantly, I forced my gaze up and fixed my attention on her face, she was so fucking beautiful. Taking her hand, she reached down to my wedding ring, and lifted it to my face. "You see this? We're married. We vowed under God and in front of our families to be there for each other, for better or for worse." She then took my hand and, holding my index finger, ran it over my left eye. "We were made for each other. That means sharing your pain, telling me when and why you're unhappy."

The sadness on Kisa's face was too much. Squeezing our joined hands, I brought them to my lips and kissed the back of her hand. "I'm happy with you. I . . ." I took a deep breath and added, "I never knew I could be happy before you."

Kisa's tears splashed onto her bare chest. "*Solnyshko,* don't cry," I rasped out.

"But you're not happy. I hold you when you sleep. I see you when you pace, dark thoughts plaguing your mind." Kisa kissed my cheek and gazed into my eyes. "You're getting worse, *lyubov moya.* Something's on your mind." A quiet sob slipped from her throat and I instinctively pulled her into my chest.

"Don't cry," I begged in a cracked voice. "I can't see you cry."

"Then tell me what you see in your mind. Tell me what is haunting you from being happy in our new life?"

"362," I pushed out. "I promised vengeance on those who wronged him. On those who put him in the gulag." My fists clenched behind Kisa's back. My hands were beginning to shake. The frustration, the anger was coming back as I pictured 362's bloodied dead face.

Kisa stiffened in my arms. "Our papas are searching for the men responsible."

"It's been *too* long," I said, harsher than I intended to.

"I know," Kisa said quietly.

"I have to do this. I have to make it right." I tensed, knowing what I was about to say. "I have to kill them. I have to, to move on."

Kisa froze in my arms. I knew she hated the idea of me killing again, but she would never understand what 362 had done for me.

"I don't even know his name. He died as a number. A fucking slave. His grave has no name." I inhaled through my nostrils thinking of the unmarked headstone. "The man that kept me alive as a gulag child, the man that taught me how to survive and freed me as a man. He was my brother and he has no name in death." My fists shook with the fire igniting in my stomach. "He has no honor. He lost it when he died under my 'duster's spiked blades. I am the one he asked to restore that for him. *Me.* No one else."

Kisa pulled back without saying a word, but I could see the understanding in her eyes. Her gaze traced down to my chest and over to my right arm. Her fingers lifted and ran over my skin. "Your arm needs cleaning."

I glanced down and saw my skin was ripped from Viktor's finger-nails, drying blood covering most of my scarred skin. My eyebrows pulled down and I asked, "Was he hurt bad?"

Kisa's roaming finger stopped. "He'll be okay."

My head lowered and Kisa wrapped her arms tightly around my neck, her body flush against mine. Unclenching my fists and exhaling a long sigh, I wrapped my arms around her bare back, kissing along her slim neck.

"We'll find out who 362's captors are, Luka. I promise. We'll figure out a way for you to live, out here on the outside. How to make you into the best *knayz* you can be."

2

TALIA

I usually avoided this place like the plague. It smelled of death. That was the only way I could explain it. The scents of blood, sweat and dead animals permeated every inch of this underground hell making it almost impossible to breath in the thick stagnant air.

Straightening my shoulders, I walked through the training gym of the Dungeon, forcing myself to nod politely at the new fighters' trainers and sponsors filling up every inch of spare space. Well, I say "fighters." They were mostly rapists, murderers, and generally just sick mother-fuckers used by various mobs and career criminals to make a quick buck. No one would miss them if they died in the ring. In fact, it would be a blessing to society, in my opinion.

I didn't mind my job. I was good at it. I was the sponsor recruiter for the Dungeon. My duty was securing the sponsors, arranging collections on gambling debts and finding only the best fighters for our enterprise. And I never failed to deliver excellent fighters, season after season. That didn't mean the sight of these men didn't make my skin crawl. I generally worked from home, thank God. Being in this place of death day by day would drive me insane. I had no idea how Kisa did it. I sighed in relief that I was finally getting a break. I was getting to leave Brooklyn for the next couple of months. I was using my long overdue vacation days to just check out of this life for a short reprieve.

After everything that had happened over the last year I needed a breather. I needed to not be Talia Tolstaia, the great Ivan Tolstoi's daughter, just for a while. I needed to be somewhere new. I just hoped my father wasn't going to flip his shit when I told him I was going.

Heading into Kisa's office, I walked through, shutting the door behind me. Kisa was sitting behind her desk typing away on her computer. "Hey, Kisa," I called, and moved to sit in the chair in front of her.

Kisa lifted her head from her work and I frowned. "You okay? You look kind of green," I said, seeing Kisa run her hand over her clammy head.

She batted her hand in front of her face. "I'm good, Tal. Just feel like I may be coming down with something."

"You sure? Seems you've been like this a while," I questioned.

Kisa threw me her usual bright smile. "Yeah, honest."

Lifting off my chair, I took the register of new fighters and their sponsors for the Dungeon's fighting ring and laid them on her desk. "Here's all the information you'll need while I'm gone. If you need anything else, I'll only be a phone call or an e-mail away."

Kisa took the folder and placed it in a drawer before leaning back in her chair. "Thanks, Tal." Her eyes dropped to the table, then she looked at me again. "I wish you weren't going. I know you'll only be a couple of hours away, and Christ knows you deserve the rest, but I hate the thought of not seeing you every day. It'll be weird."

Moving around the room to drop my ass to the edge of her desk, I winked playfully. "It's my winning personality, Kisa. You're addicted to me."

Kisa laughed and patted my knee. "I am. There hasn't been a vacation in our lives that we haven't gone on together."

My smile faded and I squeezed her hand on my knee. "I know, *dorogaya moya*. But after this past year—Luka coming home, my parents coming to terms with the fact their son was turned into a straight-up killer, and now the recent news that the Jakhua Georgian's are back in Brooklyn to probably start a war with us, I just need a fucking time-out from it all, you know?"

Kisa exhaled a long breath and nodded her head. "I know what you mean. It's been intense." Kisa glanced away and I caught her blue eyes shimmering.

Leaning forward, I placed my hand on her shoulder. "Hey, what's wrong?"

Kisa didn't move for a few seconds, but then looked to me again. "Luka's been having nightmares again. He's not in a good place lately, Tal. I don't know what to do."

My stomach tensed. "Why? What's wrong with him?"

Kisa got to her feet and stood before me, throwing me a dismissive smile. "Nothing for you to worry about." I went to argue that fact, but Kisa pulled me to my feet and wrapped me in her arms. "Go on your break, Tal, relax, find your happiness again, and come back refreshed. You never know, by the time you return everything might be back to normal—the Jakhua's may be dead and buried, Luka may have made a full recovery, everything swimming along nicely."

I hugged Kisa back and, after a few seconds, she pulled away. Her lips pulled into a wry smile. "One can dream, hey? One thing's for sure, there's never a dull moment in the wonderful world of Volkov!"

"Yeah," I replied, forcing a laugh. Then I hesitated knowing there was something more she wasn't telling me. She was acting weird.

Kisa rolled her eyes at me as I stared. "Tal, go. I've got everything covered here."

I headed to the door, but stopped to say, "Do you think Luka will be okay?"

Kisa wrapped her arms around her waist. "I'm sure he will. I've left him in bed today. He had a rough night. I'm going to meet with our fathers this afternoon to see if they can help him."

I frowned. "What needs to be done? You're being very vague, Kisa."

Kisa gave me a tired smirk. "Just something from his gulag days, a piece of information that's been playing on Luka's mind. I'm hoping our fathers can shed some light on it. It's what Luka needs to finally embrace his training as the future pakhan. I think my father's getting antsy about how distracted Luka is. I think he's doubting whether he has what it takes to lead the brotherhood one day."

Walking back to Kisa one last time, my stomach rolling at yet another arising issue my brother now had to overcome, I gave her a tight hug and kissed her cheek. "Anytime you need me, you call. And if you need a break yourself come to see me. You shouldn't have to take all of this on either. It's starting to make you ill." Kisa tensed in my arms. "Promise me, Kisa," I pushed.

She nodded against my shoulder. "I promise, Tal. And . . . thank you," she whispered.

With both hands on her shoulders, I pushed her back to stare her straight in the eyes. "You're my sister, Kisa. That was true even before you married my brother. It's been me and you, always. Sisters 'til the end."

Kisa wiped a stray tear that had fallen and she waved her hands at me in a shooing motion. "Go. Get on the road to avoid traffic. Rest. Eat lots of chocolate and, most importantly, have some fun. We don't have enough fun round these parts."

I let out a single laugh. "I've got to tell my father I'm off first. My mama knows the score, we've planned it together, but we figured suddenly surprising my father that I'm taking a break would go over better than giving him time to talk me out of it. You know he'll try and guilt me into staying."

Kisa chuckled and said, "I've always envied you, Tal. You do what you want, when you want. I could never do that. I was too busy trying to be the perfect Russian daughter." She huffed to herself. "For all the damn good it did me."

I sobered at Kisa's compliment, and something down deep caused me to confess, "I wouldn't envy me too much, Kisa. I may live on my own terms more than most in this life, but you've got the one thing I'd give anything to have. Sacrifice *anything* to have."

"What's that?" Kisa asked, her face now confused.

I fought a lump in my throat. "Love. You've got someone who adores you probably more than you do him. I'm on my own, have always been on my own. I'd give anything to have that soul-shattering type of love. But how that'll happen in this life is beyond me. Who the hell's going to date the daughter of a Bratva boss?"

Kisa's eyes filled with sympathy. "Tal—"

I held up my hand. "Shit. I'm talking nonsense." I paused, then forced a smile. "I'd better go, Kisa. I'll see you soon, okay?"

I left the office before Kisa could say anything more, all the time rubbing the dull ache of loneliness in my chest that my little confession had brought on.

I needed this break.

I'd earned this break.

I wanted to be normal.

I wanted to be plain old normal Talia from Brooklyn, if only for a little while.

3

LUKA

My body ached from lack of sleep, but I forced myself out of bed. Kirill, the Pakhan, had told me I had to be in his office this afternoon. He was meeting with the Five Families of the Cosa Nostra, the Italian Mafia here in New York. Kirill wanted me to meet all the bosses at a neutral location; he wanted to introduce me as the Bratva's future leader. He said he wanted them to see me in person. He'd smiled when he'd informed me of that. Said he couldn't wait to see the fear on their faces when they saw the future of the Volkovs enter the room.

Walking to my side of the closet in the bedroom I shared with Kisa, I pulled out one of the damn designer suits I had to wear whenever I was on Bratva business. Minutes later, I looked in the bathroom mirror as I straightened my tie and my hands dropped to my sides. I felt like I was going fucking crazy. Every nightmare was of me killing 362, of his brown eyes glazing over with death. Most of my days were spent trying to find out who he was, where he'd come from, and so far I'd come up with nothing.

Turning from the mirror, I made my way downstairs to find Mikhail, my personal guard, and head of the *byki*, waiting in my town car.

Without speaking, he drove me straight to Kirill Volkov's house. I stepped out and strode into the huge hallway, heading toward his office. When I was just outside the door, I heard my father and Kisa's voices coming from inside. But just as I was about to enter, their hushed conversation brought me to an abrupt halt.

"Have you discovered something about 362? Have your leads brought in new information?" Kisa asked.

There was silence in response, and my heart began to pound. My hand tightened on the doorknob when my father cleared his throat.

"We've known for several months about 362's identity, Kisa."

"What?" Kisa whispered in shock. "Months? Yet you haven't told Luka?"

"It's a delicate situation, Kisa," my father spoke, "one that's recently arrived at our door. And we can't make an already bad situation worse"— I heard a chair creak—"especially not for him. Not for 362." My father spoke "him" and "362" like they were poison in his mouth.

"I don't understand. I don't . . . what?" Kisa mumbled. "Who is 362?"

My father then replied coldly, "He was a Kostava."

Kisa must have reacted to that name, as my father then added, "It's true, Kisa. Of all the people, of all the families in the world, the one man who finds my son in hell and befriends him, is a fucking Kostava."

The conversation came to a stop, but all I could focus on was that they knew. They'd known all this time who 362 was. And they'd fucking kept it from me.

Feeling a surge of anger rip through me, I slammed my shoulder into the door and burst into the room. Kirill was beside his desk, my father and Kisa sat before him.

All three turned to me as I stood in the entrance of the office, my nostrils flaring with the intensity of my erratic and rapid breathing.

"Luka—" Kisa whispered, her face white. But I ignored it, my gaze fully focused on my father.

"You've known all this time?" I thundered. I stormed forward until I towered over him. I almost cooled when I saw a flicker of fear run through his brown eyes, but then I reminded myself he'd kept information from me. Information I desperately wanted.

Kisa touched my arm, but I wrenched it free from her light grasp. "No! Don't!" I snapped at my wife, and looked back at my father and Kirill. "I want to hear this from *their* fucking mouths! I want to hear why they kept this from me. Why they didn't tell me the only fucking thing I've ever asked of them!"

My father held out his hand. "Luka—"

But I was too far gone. A pained roar ripped up my throat. Moving to the desk, I gripped the edge with both hands, and flipped it on its side.

"Luka!" Kisa screamed, but I'd already begun to pace, feelings of betrayal making me lose my fucking mind.

My feet pounded the floor as I ran my hands through my hair. "For months you told me you didn't fucking know!"

My father shot to his feet and I turned to stare into his face. "I killed him! I fucking killed him!" I held out my hands to my father. "With these two fucking hands. I murdered him. I murdered him—"

"To save me," Kisa interrupted. My eyes immediately fixed on hers. I stepped forward and Kirill got out of his seat. He edged toward Kisa, like he didn't want me to get near his daughter. That only pissed me off more. Kisa nodded at her father and he backed the fuck off.

Kisa reached out to cup my face. My rigid body relaxed as my wife's palm connected with my hot skin. "Calm, baby. Listen to your papa."

Kisa pushed her fingers through her hair. My eyes squeezed shut as I breathed slowly and steadily through my lips.

When my eyes opened again, Kisa glanced to my father's tense face, then back to me. "Luka. 362. He was a *Kostava*."

A thick fog clouded my mind as she spoke those words. A Kostava? I had no idea what that meant, who that was. The name didn't mean anything to me.

Kisa's forehead dropped to mine. "Luka—"

"I don't understand . . . ," I whispered, my head beginning to ache from trying to remember something, *anything,* about that fucking name.

"You don't understand?" Kisa questioned, her blue eyes glistening with worry.

"I don't understand why him being a Kos . . . Kos . . ."

"Kostava," she offered.

I nodded my head. "A Kostava is so bad." I glanced down, wracking my brain. "I don't remember why it's bad." My stomach tensed with anger. I knew I should've known this, but the memory just wasn't there for me to find.

"I should know this, right, *solnyshko*?" I asked Kisa.

"Your memories are still in pieces." Kisa stroked my hair. "Don't worry. We can explain. We can tell you the family history that's been lost."

I nodded, feeling like a million needles were running over my hot skin. I looked to my father and saw him curse. When I faced Kisa again, her blue eyes were boring into mine. My hand lifted to run down her face. "Tell me," I begged, "tell me about him, *please*. . . ."

Clasping my hand, she entwined her fingers through mine. With a squeeze of her hand, she led me to take a seat. When she tried to sit beside me, I pulled her down onto my lap instead. As soon as she was in my arms I relaxed.

As Kisa's eyes stayed glued to mine, she pressed a soothing kiss on my cheek. Kisa faced Ivan. "Ivan, I think it's best if you explain this."

I listened to every word out of my father's mouth. Every part of the story in fine detail. I learned about the Kostavas. Fractured pieces of my family's history were suddenly put into place. But all I could hear, all I could focus on was that 362 finally had a life to me. I knew where he came from, who he was, who his family were. But more important . . .

"He has a name," I whispered into the room as my father finished explaining why they'd kept 362's identity from me. Kisa's hand landed on my cheek and I glanced up, repeating, "362 has a name." I took a deep breath and said, "Anri. His name was Anri Kostava." My eyes closed just hearing his name said aloud. Then they snapped open when something else my father said hit home.

"He was a twin. Anri had a twin brother."

In a flash, I stood, placing Kisa back on the seat, and began pacing. My mind was instantly focused, my will, driven. "What was his brother called? What was Anri's twin brother's name?"

My father watched me carefully. He didn't say the name, until my gaze narrowed, daring him to keep that piece of information from me.

"Zaal. Zaal Kostava," my father said reluctantly. I nodded, committing that name to memory.

"And where is he now? A gulag? Is he alive and fighting to the death in a fucking prison too?" Silence roared in my ears as my father refused to divulge Zaal's situation. Bones burning, I turned to the nearest wall, and sent my fist straight into a large mirror, shattering the glass to the floor. I swerved and glared at the Pakhan and my father. Pointing a bloodied finger at their faces, I snarled, "You will tell me where he is! I need to know this."

My father stood and approached me. "Luka. Stop!" he boomed, and I froze. My jaw clenched as I fought to rein back my rage.

"Tell me!" I growled in a guttural voice.

My father stood strong, his expression ice-cold. "This family will never help a Kostava," he replied grimly. "No son of mine will ever help one of *them*."

"Then Zaal *is* alive?" Kisa said from across the room. My father's shoulders tensed.

That was a fucking hell *yes*. Hope sprung in my chest.

"Where is he?" I demanded.

"Luka—"

"Where is he!" I turned and paced once again. "I don't give a fuck who he is to us. Zaal is the brother of the man who saved my life. The man I had to kill because fucking Alik Durov threw him into the cage to kill me! When he should have been free!"

I stopped right before my father, and pushed, "Now tell me where he is. *Now.*"

My father's shoulders slumped and he glanced back to Kirill. The Pakhan raised his eyebrow and sat forward, catching my attention. "We have no solid proof, Luka. But our sources have reports of a man Jakhua has in his clan." The Pakhan laughed a humorless laugh. "I say a man. More a savage fighting dog, really, from what I gather. A man conditioned to Levan Jakhua's every command. Drugged to kill. A mountain of a man Jakhua has experimented on for so many years he's lost all humanity. He is insane, unsalvageable. A prototype, a demonstration of some obedience drug he's started to sell on the black market." Kirill's face hardened. "Started to sell to other crime organizations in *my* fucking city. Just one of many reasons his pitiful mob needs to be squashed."

My muscles seized with anger. Zaal had been experimented on until he'd gone insane. A forced killer. Just like me and Anri had been. But he was alive. He was still fucking alive.

In an instant, a decision was made.

Suddenly stepping up to my father, I said, "I'm going in to the Georgian stronghold to get him. I'm getting Anri's brother out from that piece of shit Jakhua."

My father's nostrils flared and his face dropped, filling with redness. "Never. No Tolstoi will ever help a Kostava!"

I stepped even closer to my father, my chest brushing against his, staring him down. "Anri wasn't a Kostava to me," I informed pointedly. "His family name means fuck all to me. You need to get that straight, right now." I pointed to Kisa without looking away. "He freed me from that gulag so I could reunite with my family and marry my wife." I inhaled slowly, and added, "I promised 362 retribution as he died. And I *will* honor him by saving his brother and slaughtering those who captured him."

My father's cheek twitched. "You go in, and you'll start a war with the Georgians."

I walked over to Kisa and nudged my head toward the door. Kisa followed me to the exit without question. I then turned back to my father and Kirill. "Jakhua came back to Brooklyn to take us all down, we know this to be the truth. The fucking war's already begun. Me going in for Zaal just speeds up the conflict's beginning."

As I turned the doorknob, my father said, "I'll gather our best men to help you. I won't see you killed over this. But if you get that Kostava scum out of there alive, take him the fuck away from me and Brooklyn. Or I'll kill him myself. I never want to lay my eyes on that family ever again."

I nodded my head once. "Understood."

With that, Kisa and I left the room. Kisa, clearly seeing the look of determination in my eyes, reached down and took my hand.

I wrapped my fingers through hers, then drew to a complete stop. She cupped my cheek. "What is it, *lyubov moya?*"

Leaning forward, I pressed my forehead to hers. "I'll kill him, Kisa. If I get a chance, I'll slaughter Jakhua in Anri's honor."

I could see the sadness on Kisa's face. She never wanted me to kill again. But it was who I was. I just wasn't sure if she'd ever be okay with this side of me.

"I know you will," she said quietly.

I closed my eyes and exhaled in relief. As they opened again, I whispered, "I love you, *solnyshko.*"

"I have you, Luka. Whatever you need, I have you . . . always," Kisa said in return, then kissed me on my lips.

4

221

I rocked in the corner, clawing at my skin. The pain hadn't gone. The poison never cooled. Every minute, I spent fighting the pain, the rage.

I couldn't sleep. The venom inside my veins kept me awake. I couldn't remember anything of my life. Nothing but the face and voice of my master.

Lifting my head, I heard Master laughing across the room. He was sitting next to a strange man. He looked familiar.

Had I seen him before?

I couldn't remember. The poison took all my memories away.

Lifting my hands, my muscles ached as they moved under the heavy chains wrapped around my wrist and ankles. My eyes stung, my head ticked as the pain swamped my mind.

Pressing the heels of my hands into my eyes, I tried to breathe, just as a voice made my head snap up.

My eyes met with Master's and I began to pant. He'd want me to kill. I'd get to kill . . . stop the fire in my veins.

"221, *davdget*." He ordered me to stand and my feet pressed flat to the ground. I forced my body to straighten and bowed my head.

Laughter rang out around the room.

"221, stand before me," Master demanded.

Turning obediently in the direction of where he sat, I walked forward, ignoring the inner spikes of the cuffs around my ankles and wrists ripping into my skin.

Master was sitting in the room surrounded by many men. There was a ring in the middle. I was standing in the center of the ring, when Master walked beside me.

I gritted my teeth as he put an arm around my shoulder. "You've all been gathered here tonight to witness the effect of the drug you're interested in purchasing." A hand clapped over my chest and I growled as the hit sliced pain down to my stomach. My hands clenched together as I fought back the scream ripping up my throat. My skin was too itchy to touch. Too on fire to touch!

"This is 221, my prototype for the Type A drug. He answers to my every command. The drug offers one hundred percent obedience from subjects to their masters. It also provides muscle-building components, in addition to a chemical that erases the memories of who they once were. High levels of testosterone and other hormones create a conditioned response to kill, a need so strong in the subjects, it can drive them insane if their urges are not met." Master laughed. "Perfect weapons against any rivals."

Master stepped away, and I felt a guard move toward me. Reaching out, he unlocked the shackles round my wrists and ankles. As the chains fell to the floor, the need to kill began to take hold. When Master removed my chains, it was always time to kill.

Black metal hit my open palms and I immediately gripped whatever was in my hands. I looked down. The guard gave me two black sais. I rolled the metal in my grip. It felt familiar. My head tilted to the side as I studied the sharp blades. I knew how to use these weapons. The guard stepped back out of the ring.

I breathed, the room silent as I waited for Master to speak. I could smell sweat and hear the murmur of low voices. My muscles tensed as a surge of heat spread through my body.

"A demonstration!" Master shouted, and the voices around the room grew louder.

"221, *mzad*." Master commanded me to ready myself, and my legs parted, my feet heavy on the concrete ground. My head snapped up.

A door opened behind me. In my peripheral vision, I saw the men in the room all sit forward, visibly excited.

My eyes stared straight forward, when Master commanded, "221, *t'avis mkhriv*."

I turned, obeying the command, and a man stood before me holding a long chain with razors on its links. Rage built in my chest. *Klavs, klavs, klavs*—kill, kill, kill—I thought to myself. I gripped my sais tighter as the man smiled at me.

Klavs! KLAVS! I screamed inside my head.

The man began spinning his chain to the side, the heavy links smacking off the hard ground. The man before me was big. But not bigger than me. He couldn't beat me. I would win. I always won.

"221, *sikvidili.*" Master ordered me to prepare to bring death. So I readied to bring nothing but death and pain.

"Now, gentlemen. As most are here from, or associated with, the Arziani gulags, and I set up this ring as an example of how the drugs work, 221 will not stop until I command him to, plowing through anyone put in his way."

My skin shivered in anticipation as Master's voice raised in volume. The chain belonging to the soon-to-be dead man before me kept spinning and spinning, gaining more and more speed.

"Let's start this show, shall we?" Master announced. The room fell to silence. "221," Master called, and every part of me braced for the attack. Seconds passed, then Master ignited my blood when he ordered me to kill. "*Klavs!*"

Letting my rage take hold, I rushed forward, sais braced as I stalked the dead meat. Lifting his hand, my prey swung the chain, heavy metal aiming for my head. Shifting to the side, I dodged the chain and plowed the long blade of my right sai into his side. Turning, the man had fallen to his knees, his chain falling to the ground. I approached his back and stared at his neck and hairless head. Bracing behind him, I raised both sais, and with a loud roar, sent them through either side of his skull.

Warm blood sprayed against my chest, the fire in my body pumping faster and faster. The man's body dropped to the floor with a thud, blood pouring from his wounds.

Reaching for my sais, I ripped them from his head. Needing to see more blood run at my feet, I spun the sais in my hand then plunged them into the back of his neck and the front of his throat.

Stepping back, the flames inside pushing at my mind, I began to circle the ring.

I needed more. Needed more blood.

The men in the room were talking in loud voices, the sound stabbing at my mind. I circled and circled waiting for more.

I needed more, when—

"221, *shech'erda!*" Master's loud voice cut through to my ears, ordering me to halt. My feet ground to a stop and my head bowed.

Excited murmurs rippled through the crowd.

"You see, gentlemen. One hundred percent obedience *and* effectiveness." I breathed hard through my nostrils. My feet wanted to move, but Master's command held me in check.

"Those who came from the gulags, I'm sure you'll be happy with what you've seen. And those who have come from our other enterprises, please, allow me to demonstrate the Type B drug."

Sounds of the doors opening again caught my attention. Quiet footsteps entered the ring. Then men started murmuring again, shifting in their seats.

"547 is the prototype for our Type B drug. It too offers obedience. A full willingness by the slave to do anything, and I mean *anything*. It's infused with hormones that increase the woman's libido and makes her pussy wet for hours, promising your clients endless fun. It also boasts a powerful contraceptive, so no unwanted pregnancies will occur.

"221," Master called. My head snapped up. "Center of the ring."

Turning, I walked to the center of the ring. My hands gripped on to the sais, and my teeth gritted with the need for more blood. But as I stood in the ring, I felt someone was here with me. Someone I didn't want to kill.

"221, drop your sais and take off your clothes."

Opening my hands, the weapons dropped to the ground and I pulled down my pants.

"547," Master called, "suck his cock."

Keeping my head down, a female with dark hair dropped to her knees and took my cock in her small hands. Gritting my teeth at the feel of her warm hand stroking my dick, I fought back a roar. Without looking up, her hand started jerking my cock, faster and faster. My cock hardened and a growl ripped from my chest when she opened her mouth and swallowed me whole.

Grunts and snarls tore up my throat as her hot mouth sucked harder and harder. The venom in my blood flared. It burned hotter and hotter as her mouth sucked harder.

"547, *shech'erda*." Master ordered her to stop, the female releasing my cock and dropping her hands.

It hurt. . . . I needed to come. I needed to come down her throat.

"221," Master called next, "fuck 547 from behind . . . *hard*." He laughed, then ordered, "And make her fucking bleed."

Growling at Master's command, I dropped to the floor on my knees. The female turned, pushing her wet cunt in my face. Reaching out, I gripped her hips, my fingers clawing into her flesh. Taking my cock, I aimed it at her hole, and in one hard thrust, rammed it inside.

My head snapped back as her cunt wrapped around me. The feel of it took over, the venom in my blood pushing me to take her harder and harder, faster and faster. I plowed into her over and over again, feeling pressure build in my thighs and travel up to fill my balls. Teeth gritted and jaw aching, I couldn't hold back the roar that thundered out my throat as heat filled my body and I came, shooting into her cunt.

I breathed hard, and started moving again, my cock hardening as her cunt gripped it tight. Blood covered my cock. I'd made her bleed. I'd done as Master commanded.

"As you will see, gentlemen, both subjects won't stop until ordered."

I pushed harder into the female's hole, the fire igniting again in my thighs.

Suddenly, the sound of a door bursting open filled the room. The crowd jumped to their feet as men holding guns entered the room and began to open fire.

I thrust faster into the female, when Master shouted, "547, *ak' movida*—come here; 221, Get your sais and . . . *sasaklao!*"

Slaughter. Master ordered me to slaughter them all.

I pulled out of 547. The female ran to Master and I picked up my sais. The crowd was rushing for the door; the guards opened fire on the invading men.

"*Klavs!*" Master ordered again. Gripping the sais in my hand, I ran at the men firing guns. All I saw was a red mist as I knocked the first two to the ground, straddled their thighs, sinking my sais into their chests. They gurgled as blood drowned their throats, choking them out.

Rising to my feet, I fixed my gaze on my next target. But gunfire around me began quieting. Looking around, Master's guards were lying dead on the ground.

Roaring in rage, I focused on the men with guns. They were running back down a narrow hallway, running from my sais. I had to follow them outside. I couldn't let them live.

Raising my sais, I picked up my feet to run after the men. Cold air began flowing down the hall. But I picked up speed, following the men toward, then out of, an open door.

Fury coursed through me, the harsh beat of my heart thumping in my ears.

Klavs, klavs, klavs, my mind told me, my boiling blood thickening in my veins.

I would kill them all. Kill them all for Master.

Rushing through the open door, I barely felt the cold wrap around my naked skin. The invaders turned toward me and dropped their guns to the ground. I froze. I stared at their empty hands. Opening my clenched fists, I dropped my sais to the ground.

They ran at me in twos, but I knocked them down one by one. My fists crunched noses, broke arms, and snapped ribs. My knuckles bled, but they kept coming and I kept plowing them down.

A man came running at me. I stood my ground until he was only feet away . . . then as he reached to strike me, I dodged his fist and clutched his throat. Using the poison fueling my flesh, I roared and lifted him off the ground. Squeezing hard, I watched his eyes widen. I squeezed my hand tighter, hearing his breathing cut off. Blood drained from his face, and just before he took his last breath, I twisted my hand and snapped the invader's neck.

Dropping his body to the ground, I whipped my head up at the sound of a van door opening. I braced when a man stepped forward. He was dressed like how Master dressed. The invaders swarmed around him, but his eyes focused on me.

"*Knayz,* he can't be brought down. We need to kill him. He's too far gone."

The man stopped and growled, "No. We take him."

"He can't be stopped and we're running out of time."

"No!" the man snarled, but his eyes never left mine. He reached for his shirt and began unbuttoning the front. "I'll take him."

A man beside him stopped dead. "But you're the *knayz*. The Pakhan ordered you not to fight."

But the man kept coming, shedding his shirt to the ground, now only wearing a white vest showing his cut muscles. He approached me, fists clenched, his jaw tensed like mine.

I rushed forward and raised my fist to strike, but the man ducked and rammed his fist in my stomach. Pain sliced through me.

He was strong.

Gasping, I turned and swung, landing a hit on his lip. Blood immediately ran down his chin. But he came at me again. Grabbing my hair, I fought to get free. The man's strength matched mine. He lifted his leg and sent his knee straight into my jaw.

Rage surged through me. I needed to kill . . . *Klavs!*

Storming toward him, I wrapped my arm around his waist and took him to the ground. His fists hammered into my ribs, but I pressed my forearm against his throat and pushed down. Face filled with anger, he reached up, hands gripping each side of my head. I pushed down harder, cutting off his breathing. His fingers clawed into my scalp, and with a strength I'd never encountered before, he began lowering my head. I fought back, pressed down harder against his throat. His face reddened from lack of air.

He would die. He would die.

His hands gripped tighter, and just when the fucker was running out of breath, he lifted his head and slammed it against mine. My arm slipped off his throat and he spun me on my back, wrapping my hands behind my back.

I fought to get free. My skin scorching from the poison in my veins. I couldn't stand the feel of its heat.

"Now!" the man called. "In his neck, now!"

I thrashed against his hold, but I couldn't break his grasp.

Klavs . . . Klavs . . . my mind ordered, Master's words flooding my head. They wouldn't stop, the words kept stabbing at my brain. The poison, the pain, the hold. I couldn't fucking break free!

I heard footsteps beside me, then a pain suddenly stabbed in my neck. I roared and rammed my elbow into my captor's ribs. I thrashed to get free. Rolling to the side, I jumped to my feet, but I couldn't see straight. My skin was too hot and dripped with sweat. I tried to walk but my feet wouldn't move.

The man who'd fought me got to his feet. I blinked away the blur in my eyes. My gaze went to the man. His face was pale as he stared at me. He was mouthing words, firing orders to his men, but only the sound of my own breathing filled my ears.

I tried to reach for the man, my mind telling me to fight, to kill, to create carnage. But as I stepped forward, my knees buckled and I hit the ground hard. Arms grabbed me and began dragging my limp body across the hard ground.

I tried to pull away but my muscles wouldn't move.

I lifted my eyes, the man was still staring. My skin crawled, my muscles tensed and I wanted to kill. Slit his throat, slice him with my sais.

I heard van doors open, and I was dragged off the ground. My eyes began to close, then suddenly everything faded to black. . . . The last image I saw was the man looking to the sky and taking a deep breath. I remembered his face, remembered it so if I awoke, his would be the first heart I'd make sure I stopped.

5

TALIA

Tolstoi Country Estate
West Hampton, New York

Sitting at the window of the living room, I stared out at a dark overcast sky. The light from the lighthouse circled lazily in the near distance, beckoning sailors home. Round, round, round, its hypnotic rhythm relaxed me as I sipped my coffee.

Ilya and Savin, my personal *byki,* walked in the grounds, my gaze catching the flicker of their movement in the moonlight. Both were dressed in black and as quiet as the night.

I felt safe.

I'd only been here a couple of days, and already I felt at peace. The beach, the salty sea air, this colonial-style house and most important, away from my Bratva cage in Brooklyn.

Taking another sip of my coffee, my free hand subconsciously lifted to run over the necklace I always wore around my neck. My *babushka's*—my grandmother's—necklace, the necklace she'd given me just before she died a few years ago. This delicate chain of gold had been my *dedushka's*—my grandfather's. It was the Tolstoi crest given to him as a boy. All *Vor V Zakone* received them from their fathers, all Thieves in Law, she had told me. It was a statement of honor. One he passed to her to keep close to her heart when he was gone on business.

I ran the pad of my thumb over the pendent and remembered the woman I'd regarded as my best friend, who just "got me." *Babushka* was the world's biggest romantic. And she'd loved my *dedushka* with all her heart, only to lose him at a young age. She never got over him and lit a candle every day at church in his honor.

All she had left of him was this necklace. A necklace she'd given to me as a symbol that one day I would find my true love, too.

She had wanted that for me so badly—to love another as fully as she had loved him.

I desperately wanted that, too.

I heard the back door open, and Ilya and Savin entered the room, each standing at opposite windows.

I rolled my eyes. "Surely no one threatening is going to be here in the Hamptons . . . in winter. It's the reason we came out here. Practically no one else around." My father hadn't been happy about my wanting to leave Brooklyn for a while. With the new Georgian threat, he wanted me close for protection. But with my mother's help, eventually he caved. Our compromise for my vacation—our summer home in the Hamptons. I was good with the deal. It was far enough away from home, and quiet enough for me to finally relax.

Neither of my *byki* listened to my complaint about their patrol. My father had made sure I had my guards with me. I didn't ever know much about Bratva business, but I knew Savin and Ilya were checking we hadn't been followed. I got that we were on high alert. I got that I was a huge target for the Georgians. From what I could surmise from Savin and Ilya's quiet whispers was that the boss of the Jakhua clan was insane. And he was to be feared. He was a genuine threat to our position in Brooklyn. That meant I had to endure their constant surveillance.

Leaving the guys to their searching of the house, I looked out onto the rough sea crashing against our private beach, at the tide always chasing the shore, unable to stay away too long.

It made me feel poetic. What was it about the sound of waves rolling and the sea foam kissing the sleeping sand that was so soothing?

Noticing headlights traveling up our private country road, I frowned. "Ilya, Savin, someone's coming," I called out.

My heart beat a little faster, nerves swelling in my veins a little more than usual. I placed my coffee on the table beside me. No one knew we were here. Papa hadn't told anyone for the sake of my safety.

Unless . . .

"Who could it be?" I asked Ilya, and moved to the center of the room.

Ilya waved me over to stand by him and pushed me behind his back. He looked to Savin. "Did you get a phone call from Mikhail or the *knayz*? Are we expecting anyone?"

Savin shook his head, watching the TV monitor as the car came to a slow stop at the security gate. The buzzer pressed and Savin answered the call.

"Yes?" he said curtly.

"Savin, or is that Ilya? It's Kisa, can you let me in?"

I frowned as I saw Kisa lean to the camera, her face coming into view. I nodded my head to Savin, and he opened the electric gate.

Why was Kisa driving herself? And more than that, why had she left Luka in Brooklyn?

I made my way to the front door. Wrapping my long gray cardigan around my pink tank and black leggings, I opened the door just as Kisa stepped onto the porch.

She looked pale and worried, so I stepped back from the door. "Come in, sweetie."

Kisa entered the hallway and I quickly hugged her in greeting. Ilya and Savin placed themselves in sight. Moving away from me, Kisa slipped off her jacket and I watched her curiously. "Kisa? Are you okay?" I asked. I hadn't seen her in a few days. She looked bad then, but she looked worse now.

She turned to me but her eyes were vacant.

"Kisa?" I prompted, and reached out to touch her arm. She was wearing a creased thin white sweater, a skintight pair of jeans, and Chucks. Kisa never ever looked anything less than perfect and polished. She was dressed too casual, looked too rumpled and tired. Something was seriously wrong.

"I—" Kisa had barely opened her mouth to answer me, when another set of lights flared at the gate of the private road. Savin immediately sprang into action and moved to the surveillance camera.

"It's a van," he reported to Ilya. "One of ours."

I turned to question what was happening, then Kisa sighed, seemingly in relief. She pressed her hand to her forehead, breathing out through her mouth.

"Kisa? What's happening? Who else is coming? Why are you here?" I rapidly asked in an increasingly shorter tone.

Her blue eyes snapped to mine. "It's Luka," she said, just as I heard Savin utter a "Yes, sir!" The electronic gates opened once again.

"Luka? Why?" I had to know, but Savin and Ilya were already opening the front door and rushing to the graveled driveway.

Kisa headed toward me and, taking my hand, pulled me away from the door. I let her lead me to one side. I could see by Kisa's expression that she was preoccupied; no, *worried*. My stomach sank. Something bad had happened tonight. Something big.

Savin came running through the door. His eyes quickly sought mine. "Ms. Tolstaia, where's the basement key?"

"Why?" I asked, but Savin's cold, piercing expression told me there was no time for explanation.

My eyes narrowed at *everyone's* lack of explanation. Quickly, Kisa moved into the kitchen. "In here," she said, urgently summoning Savin.

The sound of vehicle doors opening outside drifted to the hallway. Voices were raised and orders were quickly issued. Savin came rushing back through to the hallway, unlocking the always-locked door that led to the basement.

I'd never been down there; in all these years coming here in summer I'd never even opened the door. It was Papa's private place and so it was forbidden. I had never thought to question him.

As the sound of people approaching came through the doorway, I moved beside an anxious-looking Kisa. Placing my hand on her back, I asked, "Why's Luka here? Please tell me what's happening. I'm starting to freak the hell out!"

With glistening eyes, she looked to me, whispering, "Luka went into the Jakhua Georgian headquarters tonight. I don't know how much you know about them being back in Brooklyn, but it's a delicate situation, and—"

My stomach flipped and my heart pounded in my chest. "What? Why would Luka do something crazy like that?" I interrupted.

"Because of 362." This was all she said in response, then her eyes misted over.

I shook my head in confusion, holding up my hand. "I don't understand, I don't—" My sentence was cut off when several of my father's *byki* rushed through the door, dragging an enormous, unconscious naked man in their arms. My eyes widened when I scanned the massive lapse body.

Stepping back from the fray, I held my breath as the *byki* took the man downstairs. My eyes were glued to the entrance of the basement, my mouth parted in shock.

Above the commotion, I suddenly heard Kisa gasp. I followed her gaze to the doorway. Luka had stepped through. He was shirtless but for a bloodied vest, his dress pants dirtied and torn. His large body was covered in purple and black bruises, his face swollen and bloodied. He looked like hell. He looked the same as he did when he'd killed Alik Durov in the Dungeon's cage six months ago.

"Luka!" Kisa cried, and rushed forward until she stood before him. She lifted her hands but stopped herself from cupping his face. "What have you done? You weren't meant to fight! You're hurt," she whispered, and his gaze softened as it fell on her.

"*Solnyshko,*" he said, and wrapped her in his arms.

"You got him," Kisa said, quickly forgetting her frustration at Luka being hurt. Her light voice was laced with relief.

"Yes," Luka replied, and his arms tightened around her waist.

Kisa gripped his arms. "I was so worried. I thought . . . I was terrified you'd be hurt. That you wouldn't come back to me." She stepped back, allowing her gaze to slowly drink in his body. "Luka, what happened? You know the *knayz* doesn't fight shoulder to shoulder with his men. He commands. He stays back. He needs to be protected."

I frowned as Luka's jaw clenched at Kisa's words. He ran a nervous hand through his messy fair hair. "No one could subdue him. He came at us like a rabid dog. I knew . . ." Luka's fists clenched then unclenched. "I knew I was the only person who could stop him, without having to shoot him." His face dropped as if lost in his thoughts. "I . . . I know how he feels. Only I know how to fight his level of strength and skill."

He fixed his gaze on his wife. "Something inside of me instinctively reacted to his rage. Whatever demon is within him, lives in me, too."

Devastation swept through me. Luka was struggling more than I had realized.

"It'll be better now, *lyubov moya*," Kisa soothed. "You got him. You got Anri's brother back from Jakhua."

The sad expression on Luka's weary face cut me to the quick. His hold on Kisa further stabbed at my heart. She was his gravity, the one thing that kept him grounded, sane. "He . . . he . . ." Luka rasped through a tight throat. "He looks just like him. It was like seeing a ghost when he ran out onto the docks." Luka's eyes lost focus. "His size, his hair, the weapons he fought with, his features, are all identical, except . . ."

"Except what?" Kisa asked as she pulled back to search her husband's wrought face.

Luka lifted his fingers to his eye. "He has green eyes. 362, *Anri,* had brown eyes."

Luka's face seemed to contort at something, a memory perhaps? "I've . . . I've never seen a man so gone. He was filled with more rage than any fighter I've faced. He never stopped coming at us, killing anyone in his path." My brother's eyes filled with tears. Luka swallowed and pressed his forehead to Kisa's. "I don't know if he can be saved. I don't know *how* to save him. The drug he's on . . ."

Kisa wrapped her arms around Luka again, but my attention drifted back to the basement.

I don't know if he can be saved. . . .

Luka's words ran through my mind. He knew this man's brother? I wanted to ask one of the many questions that were popping in my brain, but now was not the time. Luka looked destroyed.

Noises, sounding like heavy chains rattling, drifted upstairs. Silently moving closer to the open basement door, my curiosity won out and I found myself at the top of the steep unfamiliar wooden staircase leading down.

I quietly tiptoed down the stairs, my heart racing at what I might see. As the wall gave way to a view of the open basement, I stilled, drinking in my father's idea of a basement, a "private space"—rubber flooring covered every inch of the space, the walls, the floor, everywhere. And chain links were bolted to the walls, a single plastic chair the central feature of the sterile room. And the stench of bleach was so overwhelming I flinched as I inhaled each breath of stagnant air. There were no windows, so no natural light, just a solitary lightbulb hanging from the ceiling. The room was a black box.

Nausea built in my stomach when I realized what the room was used for—the Bratva's enemies. For interrogation, torture. It made sense. No one lived close. Screams could go unheard. Cell service was nonexistent, the grounds completely secure. No one would ever suspect that in this perfect white wooden colonial mansion was a hidden torture room.

My breath caught in my throat as I took in the sight. Then the *byki* stepped away from whatever they were doing by the far wall. They were all covered in blood, sweat, and dirt. They looked as though they'd taken one hell of a beating.

As they cleared away from the object of their attention, my eyes fixed onto the huge dark man they'd just dragged in. That they'd carried unconscious through the front door. My heart raced as I stared at his naked body. He was one of the tallest and bulkiest men I'd ever seen. His muscles were many, ripped and taut. And a large chest tattoo stood out through the heavy coating of blood. I scrunched my eyes to see what it said. My eyes widened as I read the numbers "221" in bold black ink. The numbers took up all of his chest. It was an identity tattoo, exactly like the one Luka had . . . just different numbers.

God! I thought as I continued to stare at the man's battered and bruised sleeping form. Even out cold he radiated power . . . danger. I'd never seen anyone like him. It both scared and intrigued me.

Who are you? Why are you beaten? I asked in my mind as my eyes traveled farther down his body. He was naked, scars littering every inch of his skin. Burn marks, and other strange markings covered his torso and chest. Then my eyes drifted lower. His long flaccid cock was bared and hanging low on his thigh. I swallowed at the sight and I could feel my face flush as I struggled to turn my gaze away.

He looked like a scarred blood-covered slave of some kind. Like something you'd see in a fucked-up Roman-era movie.

My thighs clenched together and I felt heat spread throughout my body and down between my legs. The reaction I was having was new and terrifying but I couldn't look away. I was transfixed, my mind racing with thoughts of why he was so important that he was brought here to be interrogated.

Then I frowned as my gaze focused on something else. He was caged and chained to the wall. His wrists and ankles were in short chains, ensuring he couldn't escape. Even though he looked to be the most dangerous man I'd ever laid my eyes on, my heart cracked at the realization that he wouldn't be able to move, that he would be in pain.

Noticing the *byki* beginning to move back toward the stairs, I crept back to the hallway, following the sound of Kisa and Luka talking in the kitchen.

Pulling myself together, I tried to shake the image of the man slumped brokenly on the floor, and joined the others.

Kisa saw me enter as she cleaned Luka's wounds, his hands gripping tightly to his waist. As I saw them in the kitchen, and heard the *byki* moving to clear the van from the driveway, anger bubbled up threatening to erupt.

"Why did you bring that man here?" I blurted, my voice betraying every emotion I was feeling.

Kisa's blue gaze found mine and I saw sympathy flood her expression.

"We needed to get him out of Brooklyn. This was the only place I knew where we could bring him to be safe," Luka replied. I crossed my arms over my chest.

"And who is he, Luka? Who is this man you brought to our family's house, disturbing what was meant to be my one real chance to get away from it all?"

"All of what?" Luka asked, his face marring with confusion.

"This!" I bit back, louder than I meant, and gestured to the basement. "A man you seem to have stolen from our enemy. All the Bratva shit I wanted to escape from for a couple of months. The violence, the fighting, everything! I've only been here a few days and you bring this to my door!"

Silence reigned after my outburst. Kisa dropped the rubbing alcohol she was holding. "Luka had to do it, Tal. He *had* to. He needed to honor his friend that died in the Dungeon's cage."

My eyes widened.

362 . . . 362 was the friend Luka had to kill in the cage?

I could see Kisa had realized that I'd made the connection. I briefly closed my eyes. That man chained in the basement was . . . "He's 362's *brother*?"

Luka's sad eyes looked to me. "He had a twin. An identical twin."

Luka looked down at the floor as though he could see through the partition to the man chained up in the basement.

"What?" I whispered, in shock.

Kisa, seeing Luka's head hanging low as if in exhaustion, said, "He and his brother were taken as children, their family massacred and they were . . . they were . . ." Kisa pressed her hand to her stomach and took a deep breath. "They were experimented on for many years. Used as subjects for developing drugs. Anri, 362, was not completely susceptible, but Zaal was."

Zaal, I thought, sounding the name in my head of the newly incarcerated man. His name is *Zaal.*

"He's under the influence of some new drug, Tal. We're not sure what it is or what it does, but Levan Jakhua has used him as his pet killer we believe since he was eight."

This time bile rose to my throat as I imagined Zaal going through all that hell. "*Bozhe moy,*" I whispered. Kisa nodded her head. "Does our father know?" I asked. Luka's head snapped up.

"Yes," he replied with a curl of his upper lip. "He's been no help." I stepped back, instinctively moving away from my brother. Darkness filled his expression.

Kisa pressed her hands on either side of Luka's face. "It's okay. You got him out."

"Why hasn't our father been any help?" I asked. I watched Kisa's face pale. I stilled, suspicion on my mind. "What?"

Luka looked my way and declared, "He's a Kostava."

It took me a moment to digest what he'd said. My heart started to race. A Kostava, I must have misheard. . . . "What did you say?" I asked again, my voice barely audible. My hand instinctively lifted to hold my necklace in my hands.

Luka wore a stormy expression, looking every inch the Bratva *knayz*, and repeated, "He's a Kostava. He and Anri were the Kostava heirs."

I stepped back, my eyebrows dragging down, as I absorbed my brother's words. "What have you done?" I whispered in shock. I gazed upon my brother, who'd now risen to his feet. He looked like a stranger to me at this moment in time.

"I can't believe you would do this!"

I watched as Luka seemed to radiate rage and I squared my shoulders. Stepping forward, feeling my hands shake with the depth of my anger, I said, "You're shaming this family saving a Kostava and bringing him here, to our home!"

Luka's fisted hand slammed down on the granite countertop and he roared, "I am honoring Anri's death! I'm seeking the revenge he didn't get the chance to fulfill!"

Luka marched round the counter to meet me toe to toe, and snarled, "Anri was my best friend. He taught me to survive." His chest rose and fell from his panting, and he said, "He may not have been my blood, but he was still my brother!"

Feeling like I'd been stabbed in my heart, I fought back a sob. Luka's dilated brown eyes never moved from mine. I nodded. "I get that I don't understand, *cannot* understand, what you went through. I never will. I get that the animal in the basement's brother saved you and helped you survive, but he isn't your blood. You do all of this, even defy our father for him, the brother, the sibling, you never had. But he isn't your sibling." Luka's expression remained unchanged until I whispered, "But I am. *I'm* your blood. *I'm* your sister. And when you were taken, it was me who cried for you, prayed for your lost soul. It was *this* sister who mourned my big brother, the boy who would always protect me and read to me as a kid, and tell me that family was the most important thing in our world."

Luka's head tilted to the side and he blinked furiously, but no words came from his mouth.

I shook my head and began to walk away. "I get that you feel you need to do this for your dead friend, but I'll never support you bringing that monster here. For the first time, you have disappointed me."

"Talia!" Kisa called loudly as I walked to the staircase.

Stopping, I turned back and asked, "How long is that man to stay chained up in the basement?"

Luka was still standing in the same spot. He coldly replied, "As long as it takes."

I laughed without humor at his evasive answer, then said, "Careful, Luka. You worry you can't be in this life, that you're not fit to be a Bratva boss. But you're sounding more like a Russian *knayz* than you're giving yourself credit for."

Marching up the stairs, I beelined to my bedroom. Passing Luka's patrolling personal *byki,* I slammed my door shut and pressed my back against the hardwood. My eyes stung as I pictured Luka's furious face.

He was, is, my brother. . . .

Feeling drained by the twists and turns of the day, I took a quick, hot shower, dried my hair, and lay down on my bed. I stared at the ceiling waiting for sleep that never came.

But as hours passed, my anger gave way to calm, and I found myself torn.

Luka had survived. He'd returned when all hope was gone and a fucking Kostava had been his salvation in that gulag hell.

Running my hands down my face, the memory of the Kostava monster downstairs filled my mind. My heart actually hurt when I pictured him tied up in chains, his large body bloodied, limp, riddled with scars and incision marks. How unkempt and unclean he looked, like he hadn't taken a shower in months. Like he'd known nothing but abuse and cruelty.

And the tattoo across his chest, the slave identity number that signified he'd been taken as a child, taken and made to endure unspeakably evil things at the hands of the Jakhua Georgians.

Derr 'mo!

No matter how hard I tried to hang on to the hatred drilled into me against the Kostavas since birth, I wasn't a monster. I wasn't unfeeling. And that man, that dark, huge animal of a man had clearly been through hell.

B'lyad! I screamed internally.

I counted the cracks in the ceiling tiles and tried to think of something other than the naked Kostava but nothing worked. What the hell was wrong with me?

Sitting up in bed, I spotted my laptop lying on the desk. Walking to the desk I brought it back to my bed, deciding to check my e-mails, to press on with contacting fighter providers for the Dungeon's cage. Anything to distract my busy mind.

After my laptop powered on, I was just about to hit the e-mail icon, when my eyes fell on the surveillance program for the house. The entire house was wired with links on all of our devices, just in case.

I knew Ilya and Savin would have switched on the surveillance cameras as soon as we arrived at the house; I was sure the basement camera would have been turned on as well. After all dangerous enemy number one was now kept there.

I couldn't stop myself, one light tap on an icon and my screen was filled with 250 pounds of ripped and brutal Georgian.

My heart raced as I watched him, my eyes were glued to his unconscious body, his position unchanged from hours before.

I struggled to catch my breath as I watched his wide chest rise and fall. From the camera's perspective, the features of his face were perfectly showcased. And under all the blood and dirt he looked sort of . . . beautiful.

Swallowing, I really studied him. His black hair fell below his shoulders, a gentle wave to the thick, matted strands. Black eyebrows framed his eastern European face. His nose, at this moment, was swollen and bloodied, as were his lips. But I could see defined high cheekbones and dark stubble covering his face. Even under the swelling and blood I could see that his lips were full. His skin was a dark olive, the evidence of his Georgian heritage, and he was nothing but hard muscle. Every inch of his tall frame, perhaps six foot six, corded with protruding veins and roping brawn.

Moving back to lie against the pillows, I brought my laptop to my lap, not able to draw away my eyes. Kisa's words from earlier filled my mind.

They were twins . . . children . . . family massacred . . . experimented on . . . subjects for developing drugs . . . under the influence . . . new drug . . . Jakhua . . . his pet killer for . . . since he was eight . . .

Remembering his name, I whispered, "Zaal" to the empty room, wrapping my tongue around the pronunciation and running my finger down the picture of his unconscious form, splayed out on the black rubber floor.

Then his cheek twitched. The first bit of movement I'd seen from him since the *byki* dragged him in the house.

Pulling back my hand, I watched in fascination as his finger started to move, his legs began to stretch, and a low moan slipped from his bruised lips.

I gripped my laptop tighter and tighter the more Zaal moved.

Then suddenly, in the perfect view of the camera, his eyes shot open. Bright green eyes, captivating and beautiful green eyes. I gasped as those eyes searched the dark basement, the solitary lightbulb casting a dim glow over his body. His eyes flickered around the space, and for one split second, he looked lost. He almost looked . . . afraid.

My chest constricted as Zaal's gaze seemed to look directly into the camera, his captivating jade green eyes colliding with mine.

Feeling like he could see me, I lost control of my breath. My heart beat so loud, I could hear its pounding bass rhythm in my ears.

Zaal suddenly broke connection, his face contorting into a feral expression as a loud roar bellowed from his mouth. His large body quickly moved, lurching forward, only for his arms and legs to be wrenched backward as the tight chains restrained his movement.

Zaal lowered his head only to find the shackles fastened around his wrists and arms. Turning his attention behind him, he began pulling on the chains, testing the strength of the links.

With every heave, his strong muscles cording with strain, he would scream a deafening roar. When he couldn't get free, he began to pace. His expression was bone-chillingly severe and he watched the wall before him, as though waiting for someone to enter.

His head ticked, his fists clenched, he wrenched at the chains. I couldn't bear it. I couldn't watch him fall apart. As another frustrated bellow thundered out of his throat, I slammed my laptop shut. I had enough.

I tried to calm my breathing, but I was convinced my lungs had a mind of their own. I tried to calm my heart but it was racing too fast. And I tried to cool down, but my body burned with sympathetic pain. Pain of what demons must possess Zaal Kostava.

I suddenly remembered Luka, specifically, the night of the Dungeon's finals, now many months ago. He was raw and rough, but there was still something in his eyes. A flicker of humanity trying its best to push through. And he had Kisa. He had our parents, Viktor, and Kirill. He had me.

But Zaal. Zaal was nothing but unleashed aggression. His wrists were sliced and bleeding raw as he'd wrenched on the chains, and he never stopped trying to break free. It was like something tortured him, driving him to never stop.

Placing the laptop at my side, I ran to the bathroom. With trembling hands, I turned on the cold faucet and splashed the icy water on my face.

Who could do that to another person? I thought in sadness. *Who could morally condition someone to be that brutal, that wild? That pained and insane?*

But as I lifted my head and my brown eyes stared back at me in the vanity's mirror, I remembered the broken and scared look in Zaal's jade green eyes as his gaze lasered straight down the lens of the camera.

Yes, he was vicious. Yes, he was wild, but in that split second there was something more. Something of the real Zaal Kostava still lived inside him. I was sure.

Walking back to my bed, exhausted and wrought, I slipped under the covers. I closed my eyes, but my mind still wouldn't switch off.

Before I knew it, I'd reached for my laptop, and with a deep breath, I opened the surveillance icon. Zaal's frantic pacing immediately filled the screen.

Placing the laptop on my side dresser, I lay back on the pillow watching Zaal, the only living heir of the Kostavas, gradually lose his mind in my papa's basement.

As the next two weeks passed, I became completely obsessed.

My days centered around Zaal, watching him slowly breakdown. Watching him shake, sweat, and strike out at anyone who went near. I watched Luka try to talk to him, to calm him down. But Zaal would only snarl and lash out. I watched as he endlessly vomited, like he was going cold turkey off heroin. And I watched nightly as the *byki* subdued him with Tasers, in order to drug him to sleep, just to attach IV packs of food and fluids to keep him alive.

And I watched as Luka gradually lost hope that Zaal could be saved, until my father and the Pakhan called him back to help in the igniting war with the Georgians only a couple of days after he and Kisa arrived.

Fourteen days had passed and Zaal had made no progress whatsoever.

Racking pain filled my chest when his strength waned, when he couldn't move off the floor. He would sleep for hours, lying prone on the cold ground.

I lost all hope, my obsession with this man dominating my entire life. Then one day Zaal had stopped moving altogether. His lifeless body, one day, had chosen not to wake up.

And that was the day everything changed.

6

ZAAL

"Come here, Son." Turning from playing in the garden, I saw my father calling me to the table to eat. I ran toward my father, and he led me to the porch where my mother, sisters, and brothers already sat. My grandmama sat at the head of the table and winked at me.

I laughed.

Father said a prayer, and then told us to eat. As I picked up a piece of bread from the basket, a loud crash sounded in the house. Father looked toward the house. He snapped his finger and thumb, ordering the guards to go and find out who it was, but they didn't move. They stared at my father and their eyes narrowed. My brother looked at me and frowned.

"Move!" my father commanded. Instead, the guards lifted their guns . . . lifted them at the table. My sisters screamed, my baby brother cried . . . but my twin reached out and took my hand. I looked at him and he looked at me. I squeezed his hand. Be strong, *he mouthed,* keep strong.

"What are you doing?" Father asked the guards and rose from his seat, just as tens of men came flooding from the house, all dressed in black. They all held guns . . . guns aimed at us . . .

Bullets . . . blood . . . death . . . blood . . . screams . . . guns firing . . . piercing . . . slicing . . . death . . . death . . . death . . .

My eyes snapped open and I tried to breathe. But all I could see was *blood . . . so much blood . . . blood choking my throat . . .* I gasped as the image of running blood filled my mind. . . .

Darkness came, and when my eyes opened again, I was hot, too hot.

Sweat poured from my forehead into my eyes. But I couldn't move my arms to wipe the sweat. Couldn't move them even though they ached. Poison was burning my flesh from the inside; venom and something else crawled slowly under my skin, clawing to get out.

I couldn't stand it. My stomach convulsed but no vomit came up my throat. There was nothing there, just pain. My muscles were squeezing in my thighs and back, pulling so tight they were snapping, trying to break from my skin. My saliva boiled in my throat. I couldn't scream, couldn't make a sound.

I lay on the floor, eyes watching the black walls as pictures and strange faces passed through my mind.

I couldn't remember if even I knew them. *Did I know them?*

Then a face stabbed at my brain. My body jerked. *Master. Where is Master?*

Darkness came and went. I tried to scream as knives stabbed right through my stomach and came out the other side. My body shook as each blade sliced through, but I couldn't move. I was too hot, too hot, but then I was too cold, too cold inside. My blood turned to ice, trying to push through my veins. My muscles froze, I was trapped on the floor.

My eyes suddenly closed, darkness pulling me down.

"Tie him to the table," the man's voice said, and someone threw me on a metal bed and strapped me down.

What are they doing? *I was scared, so scared. I managed to turn my head, looking for help.*

Then I saw him on a bed beside me. The boy's brown eyes looked at me, and he mouthed, "Dzlieri. Be strong. Keep strong." His fingers reached out trying to touch mine, and I did the same, but they didn't meet. "Dzlieri, be strong, keep strong," he mouthed again. I nodded my head as a man approached my table.

He ran his hands over my body, then the boy's. "Identical in every way but their eyes." He smiled. "They'll be perfect."

Two men held me down, then flipped me on my back. My head was forced down to the bed. I couldn't move.

Fear ran through me and I could feel my hands shaking. But as I lifted my eyes, the boy was in the same position as me, two men in white coats holding him down. His head was facing mine. His eyes met mine and he silently told me to be strong, keep strong. And I did. I didn't even scream when a long thick needle was pushed into my spine, when we were cut open, when we were beaten. Neither did the boy. We held each other's gazes and never broke away.

A voice snapped me round. Voices—no, a single voice, the same voice that I heard every day. He was speaking in a strange language. *Did I know what he was saying?*

"Turn round and fight it," he said. My eyes squeezed shut when I understood him. I couldn't turn, couldn't turn round. I wanted to growl, turn and cause him pain, but my muscles were weak, aching. I couldn't keep my eyes open.

I was floating, my breathing slow, air was dragging into my lungs. Everything was still. I waited for Master. But no Master came.

My cheek was flat to the ground, my eyes were shut. But I was numb. My heart beat at a steady pace. It didn't race or stutter. There was no pain, no fire inside.

But I was too tired. I couldn't move, my blood was no longer hot. The knives were no longer in my stomach. There was nothing.

I lay for a long time until the sound of a door creaking open caused me to still.

Quiet footsteps approached. The scent of something sweet filled my nostrils, and for the first time in a long time, my body wanted to move.

My eyes stayed closed, my back to the approaching person. My hands clenched into fists and I waited, teeth gritted for them to get close enough. They had me chained. But were they Master or the guards? The sound of their footsteps, I couldn't recognize.

I waited and waited until the person kneeled behind me, their breath shaking with fear. I hated fear. Someone told me once that fear made you weak.

Readying to strike, a hand suddenly pressed against my back and I fought back a hiss at the contact. Not reacting, the hand ran down over my arm and along my waist. It was soft, and I frowned. I didn't understand. *Had Master sent a female to me? Was this a test?*

Anger about my confusion pierced my brain.

It was a test, had to be a test.

I had to kill. . . . Master always wanted me to kill. . . .

As the hand ran across my back, warm breath drifting over my skin, I snapped.

Jerking from my position lying down, I roared, rolled around, and reaching out, grabbed the attacker's arms and crashed them to the ground, my body braced above them to strike.

My blood pumped with the need to kill and just as I raised my hand to smash into the face of my attacker, not even feeling the heavy chains around my hands, I glanced down.

And froze.

Huge brown eyes stared up at me, too wide and afraid. The strange female's mouth was open, big pink lips trembling as her eyes moved to my fist in the air. My nostrils flared at her smell . . . my heartbeat thundered and my muscles twitched.

Long blond hair.

I stared at her and felt her shaking beneath me.

Her lips moved and I focused there.

"D-don't h-hurt me," she whispered.

My head moved to the side as I heard her voice. Her voice was strange, *sounded* strange, like the man that used to come in here telling me to fight. To fight the poison.

She tried to move so I pinned her down further. She gasped and the blood left her face. "Please," she begged, and the rage inside me built.

Who was she?

Why was she here?

Master didn't give me a command. I didn't know what to do.

"I-I'm not here to hurt you," she said. I moved my face closer. Her skin was lighter than mine, and she smelled so good.

I moved my eyes along her body. She was small. Too small. I'd kill her easily. Snap her neck in a second.

"Please," she begged again, and her eyes went to my fist. Eyes narrowed, I lowered my fist and she inhaled a long breath.

I stared at her. Suddenly, heavy footsteps ran down the stairs. I snarled at the men approaching as anger invigorated my numb muscles.

Klavs, klavs, klavs, I thought when two men, dressed in black, entered with guns held high.

Guards. Enemy guards.

Klavs, klavs, klavs.

"Talia!" one of them boomed. *They were talking to the female.*

Gripping the woman by her arms, I pulled her to my chest, and moved back against the wall. Pushing her down on the ground, I stood in front of her, trying to rip free from the chains.

The guards were circling, guns aimed at my head. I growled, trying to swipe out with my hands. The chains held me back. Anger surged through my veins. I threw my head back and roared.

"Talia, get the fuck out from there!" one of the guards said, shouting to the female. I tried to understand what he said, when suddenly I knew.

He wanted to take the female from me. He wanted to hurt her. Wanted her for himself.

Running forward, I held my hands out trying to grip the man by his throat. He jumped back and the female screamed.

Pain shot through my head. Screams, females screaming . . . blood . . . guns . . . bullets. Thundering out a bellow, I dropped to my knees and gripped my head.

"Get out!" I heard the female say.

"Miss. *Move!*" the guard commanded. I tried to stand. I pressed my fist to the ground to try to lift myself, but I fell back down. The pain in my head was too much.

"I said leave! That's an order!" the female repeated.

The men were silent, when the female again said, "Leave! *Pereyti teper!* Or so help me God I'll have you punished for insubordination!"

"*B'lyad!*" one of the guards shouted in response. "We'll be watching. If he does anything to you, we're coming back in to kill the fucker! I don't care what the *knayz's* instructions are. Keeping *you* alive is our priority. Those are your father's orders." I heard the footsteps leave and the door slam shut.

The pain left my head, but my heart still beat too fast. Muscles weak, I fell back to the floor. I could feel the female nearby, but my body was numb. I could barely move.

Forcing myself to turn, the woman was sitting in the corner where I'd put her. Her brown eyes were looking at me in fear. Her hands were still shaking.

I crawled closer, but the chains were too heavy. Collapsing to the ground, I stared at the female's eyes, but darkness was taking me again.

Darkness was pulling me down. . . .

7

TALIA

Zaal's body slumped to the floor beside me, and I pressed a hand over my frantic heart, trying to calm down. I closed my eyes and inhaled through my nose. I'd been wrong. So damn wrong. Kostava wasn't dead, he was *very* much alive.

I thought back to early this morning. Thought back to the moment I'd looked at Zaal's lifeless body on my laptop screen. Thought back to the moment my heart chose to control my head. . . .

As I heard the front door close from downstairs, Ilya and Savin off to patrol the grounds, my palms twitched with the knowledge that it was just me in the house. Just me and Zaal.

My stomach filled with butterflies at seeing his beautiful face again. Checking in on him each morning had become my daily ritual.

Jumping from my bed, I made sure the bedroom door was locked and I ran to my laptop. Zaal had fallen asleep early last night before I'd gone to bed, after minimal movement all day. But I knew he'd be awake right now, right this minute. He was no longer pacing the floor and snarling at anyone who came near as of this week. Rather, he'd sit against the wall, his head often hanging low, his large body twitching and sweating. But he didn't move. His jade green eyes were dull when he stared off into space, his attention fixed on nothing.

I didn't know why, but I watched him, watched him lying there like a broken and abused animal. My chest would ache and no amount of rubbing over the skin could soothe it.

I'd always felt kind of trapped, mentally and emotionally lost in this Bratva life, and staring at Zaal Kostava, the man I was conditioned to hate, just broke my heart. Because he mirrored how I felt. Especially of late, I felt broken and scarred on the inside. He looked broken and scarred on the outside. I felt a connection to the Kostava. I supposed he and I were kindred spirits.

Opening my laptop, I expected to see Zaal in that same slumped sitting position, tied up in chains, hair matted and dressed only in the black pair of sweatpants Luka had insisted he wear when he was drugged that first night.

I clicked on the desktop icon, chose the camera for the basement, and waited with bated breath as it connected. As Zaal came into view, my heart immediately fell. He wasn't sitting up as expected. He was still sprawled on the ground, body eerily still.

I leaned in closer willing him to move. But two hours passed and he hadn't even flinched. A deep pit had formed in the center of my stomach. He looked . . . what if . . . ?

I swallowed a thick lump in my throat and felt an unfamiliar hollow feeling in my heart. I knew he'd been getting worse, his demeanor had changed dramatically over the past few days. But he was strong. I thought he'd survive. I thought it was another phase of his recovery. He'd had several over the past couple of weeks.

Leaving my laptop on the dresser, I jumped off my bed. Hands on hips, I stared at the locked bedroom door and forced myself to do something I vowed I would never do.

I needed to see him up close.

I reached up and palmed the necklace lying on my chest. I thought of why my father had disapproved of Zaal's rescue. Of why Luka had had to bring him all the way out here to the Hamptons rather than to a holding cell in Brooklyn. But no matter how much I tried to persuade myself not to do what my heart was urging me to do, a pair of jade green eyes would dominate my mind, taking it captive, and with it all rationality. Derr 'mo! Those eyes! The sadness they held. The torture, the hurt and confusion shining in their depths, calling to me.

I had to go. He needed me.

Eto piz 'dets! This is fucking crazy! I thought silently in Russian.

Rushing to my door, I took a deep breath at the top of the stairs and frantically ran down. Savin and Ilya, clearly back from patrolling, came busting out of the kitchen.

"Ms. Tolstaia?" Ilya enquired, "What's wrong?"

Pushing my hand through my hair, I said, "I was at my window and I think I saw someone outside. Maybe more than one. I can't be sure?"

Savin straightened and immediately pulled out his Glock. Ilya moved toward me. He looked me straight in the eye and ordered, "Stay here!"

In seconds, they'd run out of the house. Knowing I had only a short amount of time, I hurried to the hidden safe, entered the passcode, and retrieved the basement key.

With shaking hands, adrenaline fueling my reckless plan, I arrived at the basement door. Without overthinking any rebuke from Savin, Ilya, or Luka, I entered the dark room and quietly closed the door behind me.

Pausing on the tiny landing, I inhaled a shuddering breath. Move, Talia, *I told myself, just move. He needs you.*

Leaving the key on a ledge, I placed my trembling hand on the handrail and began my cautious descent. With every step on the wooden stairs, my heart beat louder and louder.

When the expanse of the dark room came into sight, and my gaze fell on an unmoving Zaal Kostava, it took all my self-control not to rush over and beg him to awaken.

I couldn't hear his breathing. His back was facing me, his oversize body curled into a fetal position, like the pain had been too much to bear. His bloodied and bruised arms and legs were completely stiff.

Reality hit home—he'd died.

Derr 'mo! What had Jakhua pumped him full of? Had whatever was leeching from his system for the past two weeks been too much for a person to bear? Even for a man as formidable as Zaal?

Folding my arms over my waist, I walked silently toward his comatose form, flinching as I saw the chains that held him so tightly in place. His tanned skin was pale and, finally seeing for myself that he was gone, I fell to my knees beside him and my shoulders sagged.

I'd watched this man for weeks; long hours spent in fascination, and as much as I tried, I couldn't hate him. I wanted to, felt obliged to . . . but, hell, it had been impossible.

How could anyone hate a man breaking so badly? A man who had never known love? A man filled with such pain? A man kept chained in the darkness?

An urge hit me. I needed to touch him. I had to, something within me told me to reach out. No person should die in such a way. Alone, with no caring person there to offer comfort in their final hours.

My mind raced with the scant information I had about his life. He was now twenty-nine. That meant he'd endured over twenty years of being experimented on like some clinical rat. Twenty-one years of being subservient to the man who had caused the demise of his family. Twenty-one years of killing, on instruction, anyone in his path.

Lifting my hand, I hesitantly placed it on his bicep. I gasped at the coldness of his skin. It felt like ice. My eyes closed as I offered a prayer to God to save his dark soul. Opening them again, I studied the mass of tattoos, cuts, and scars, and every finely toned inch of his muscles.

I'd never seen anyone like him. He was . . . he was perfect. Yet, savagely imperfect at the same time.

My hand drifted farther down his body, and across the brightly colored skull tattooed on his back. I knew he probably had these forced upon his flesh. Luka had told me how the gulag owners wanted him to look more aggressive by sporting sinister tattoos. It seemed that Levan Jakhua shared exactly the same whim. And they worked. The artwork of images of death made him like something from your nightmares.

Then my gaze met the slave number on the top of his neck where his long hair had parted, a smaller version of the "221" branded on his chest.

My hand traveled to touch the black ink and a flood of tears blurred my vision. "I'm sorry," I mouthed, "I'm sorry you had this life."

I went to withdraw my hand. Was moving away to tell the byki that the captive had died. But just as my palm went to move, it fell from Zaal's ice-cold skin. Before I knew it, strong hands were gripping my biceps, and a familiar pair of jade green eyes were suddenly boring into mine. Two hundred and fifty pounds of prime muscle were pinning me down. . . .

I shook my head and glanced at Zaal, now sleeping. I couldn't help but remember the feeling of his huge body towering above me, his sharply featured face so primal and raw. At first I'd been terrified, but when Savin and Ilya had found me, their mutual looks of rage as they met my eyes, all fear vanished as he pushed me back to protect me.

This monster, this animal, this apparently unsalvageable man had protected *me*. And now, alone, here I sat with him. My obsession in the flesh. My forbidden addiction.

It should have been my chance to get away. I knew he'd be sleeping for the next few hours. Hell, I knew his daily routine down pat. But as my *mind* tried to convince me to go, my *heart* kept me rooted to the spot.

Glancing to Zaal, I edged closer. Taking the chance while I could, I brushed back his dirty matted black hair from his face. My lips parted and I drew in a sharp breath as his features were revealed.

With my forefinger, I slowly traced his broad forehead, then his nose and, finally, his jaw. He was beautiful, exotic, and every inch a man. But he was severely unkempt, his hair dirty, and his body still peppered with weeks'-old bloodstains.

Looking about the sparse room, there was nothing in here to clean him with. I couldn't leave him like this, soiled and riddled with filth.

Determined, I got to my feet and headed up the staircase. As I opened the door to the basement, Savin and Ilya were suddenly in my face.

They were livid.

"What were you thinking by going down there?" Savin asked coldly. "He could have killed you."

Ignoring Savin, I walked around him and headed into the down-stairs bathroom. Searching the cabinets, I quickly found a bath sponge, body wash, shampoo, conditioner, some towels, and a hairbrush. Gathering them in my hands, I headed to the kitchen, and located a large bowl.

Ilya walked to the counter. His eyes fell on the items lying on the top. "You can't be serious?" he asked incredulously. I didn't say a word as I ran the hot water and filled the bowl to three-quarters full.

"Miss Tolstaia, you're not going back down there. We can't allow it."

My back stiffened and I turned to face Ilya, who'd been joined by an angry-looking Savin. "I'm going to say this as politely as I can, guys. I've known you both my entire life, your fathers served mine honorably. I both love and respect you as friends, and as my guards, but I *will not* be ordered around by you. I'm not twelve, and I don't need your fucking permission to do anything."

I lifted the bowl and set it next to the other items. Seeing a shopping tote bag on a hook, I filled it with the products I'd need and pulled it over my shoulder. Looking at my *byki,* I added, "Yes, I'm a woman in the Bratva. I'm controlled by my father, my Pakhan, and now, my *'knayz'* brother. But I'm telling you now, I refuse to be spoken to like a fucking errant child by you two." My eyes narrowed. "I'm going back down to the basement to clean the man who has been left down there to rot for two friggin' weeks. The man I believed had died alone on that God-awful hard rubber floor, and there's sweet fuck all you two can do about it."

I lifted the bowl and walked around them. Ilya cussed and Savin stepped in my path. "He's a Kostava," he said in a deadly hush. "You're a Tolstoi. Yet you help him? The *knayz* helps him? I don't get what the fuck is going on. He should have been slaughtered when he was found. Hung up and paraded through the streets."

For a moment I felt a flash of shame. Real shame that I was about to help the enemy. But something stronger overcame this shame—a need to help Zaal. A need to get close to him. I couldn't explain it. Of course, it was irrational, it was wrong, but I *had* to. He had no one else.

I was it.

Ignoring the men, I headed for the basement, and Ilya called out, "We'll be watching that monitor, miss. If he so much as touches you the wrong way, we'll come down and I won't hesitate to kill him."

It wasn't a threat. His words were a promise.

Mu'duk, I muttered under my breath, and resisted telling him to fuck off. When I reached the small landing of the basement, I saw the switch that controlled the security camera directly before me. Turning to bolt the two inner locks of the basement door, I then smiled directly into the stair's camera hanging from the ceiling, and cut the live feed. Last thing I needed was Ilya and Savin watching me wash Zaal down.

When I walked down the stairs and returned to Zaal's side, I set the bowl down and carefully began to wash his body. Blood and dirt eventually gave way to tanned skin. I gently washed every inch of him, and when I reached his face, it was to find a pair of unfocused green eyes, staring up at me.

My hand froze but I stared right back.

My heart raced and my cheeks flushed with heat.

Zaal studied me, his eyes widening, then he began to move.

Quickly shuffling backward through fear of what he might do, I stopped when he dragged his lethargic body into a slumped sitting position. His gaze dropped to the bowl and then to his half-washed torso.

He looked back up at me and I could see confusion clouding his features. He watched me and I watched him. The room seemed to increase in temperature and a powerful magnetic tension formed between us.

Zaal's attention fell to the sponge in my hand. His black eyebrows pulled down and, lifting his hand, he ran it over the clean side of his body.

Swallowing, watching his array of facial expressions communicate without words, I slowly shifted onto my knees. Zaal's eyes snapped to mine and he tensed. Perhaps he perceived me as a threat?

I held up my sponge, and his wary eyes narrowed. Edging closer, I nervously whispered, "I was cleaning you."

The clean hand moved to the soiled and sweat-ridden side of his body. He fixed his gaze on me once more and dropped his hand. He focused on me blankly. I moved ever closer. His nostrils flared, his hands clenched, the chains attaching him to the wall rattled at even this slight movement.

But I kept moving forward until I was within touching distance. Stopping, I held up the sponge and gestured to the bowl of hot water. Clearing my throat, trying to chase away the nerves starting to overwhelm my body, I said quietly, "Can I keep going? Can I continue to clean you?"

He didn't react, but his cheek twitched, then twitched again. I didn't know if that meant he wanted me to or not. Deciding to continue regardless, I carefully dipped the sponge into the soapy water. Zaal's torso was on full display and he tensed, as though I was about to strike him.

My heart fell again.

Had he not had any human contact at all? Had no one ever cared for him? Touched him? Spoke to him other than to issue a command to kill, or to pump him full with drugs?

He didn't move as I approached very slowly, but his eyes watched me like a hawk. Holding out the sponge, I said just as quietly, "I'm going to run it along your arm, is this okay?"

There was no answer, just another twitch of his jaw and a narrowing of his green eyes.

Averting my attention from his face to his large arm, I pressed the sponge against his skin and met hard muscle. My lips parted and my heart raced. I could feel him watching me; I blushed under his scrutiny.

The deathly silence in the room only intensified the mood of the situation and his wet skin bumped in my wake. He was solid muscle. His skin was nearly golden in tone, but my chest tightened at seeing the mass of jagged scars marring his skin up close. They were everywhere, more than I'd realized. Round marks that looked like they'd once been open holes, red raised scars that looked like burn marks. I'd seen them through the surveillance feed, but up close? They were horrific. I didn't even want to imagine how they could have been caused.

Swallowing back my shock, I glanced at Zaal, who was still watching me. His head was angled slightly to the side. I tried to cast him a smile. And when I did, his lips parted, the top boasting a perfectly shaped cupid's bow.

Snapping myself from my stupor, I sank the sponge into the bowl and made quick work of his arm and tattooed back. Reaching for the towel, I dried him off, then said, "Can I clean your front?"

Zaal didn't move from where he sat, prompting me to shift to place myself in front of him. His chains were in the way, but at least he could move his arms, baring his packed torso. Eyes widening, I drank in every sculpted inch as he allowed me to clean his broad chest.

The bold 221 tattoo glared at me; his black hair was clumped and fell in knotted disarray. Offering the sponge for him to see, I shuffled on my knees until I was positioned between his legs, cradled in close proximity to his imposing frame.

For a moment I entertained the certainty that this close, if he wanted to, Zaal could easily kill me. If he was truly the untamed savage, the crazed monster he'd been acting for the two weeks here at the house, he should kill me now.

But when I found myself mere inches from his face, my eyes met those stunning jade irises, and any fear I had fell away like butter sliding off a hot knife.

Electricity seemed to crackle between us as we breathed the same air. Zaal stared and stared, until, raising the sponge, I pressed its wet warmth to his chest. This close, with my ear hovering just below his mouth I caught his sharp inhale of breath.

My thighs clenched at the desperate sound and warmth spread between my legs. I could feel myself blushing, and my hands trembled.

Overcome with a heady attraction, I focused on the task of cleaning the traces of blood and dirt from his skin. My hands ran over his muscled chest, over his bulging traps that sat perfectly on top of large round shoulders.

My breath came in short quick pants as my hand slowly traced down his washboard abs, showcasing more muscles than I knew it was possible to produce. Eventually, I found my sponge at the waistband of his sweatpants.

I paused. He needed cleaning desperately, but I wavered. I knew he was naked beneath his pants. I must have hesitated too long; Zaal suddenly moved, his chains clattering off the hard floor. I jumped back at the sudden movement and my frightened eyes darted to meet his. Once again, Zaal was watching me carefully. His long rough fingers slipped under the elastic of the waistband, then slowly pushed the pants off his waist and over his thick thighs. The pants stopped as the chains from his ankle shackles prevented him from freeing himself completely.

Our fixed attentions hadn't dropped as he removed his pants. I was transfixed by his expression, the parting of his lips and the slight color that had graced his defined tanned cheeks.

My heart drummed. He was naked. I hadn't expected him to remove his pants. I wasn't exactly sure how to proceed.

Finally, inhaling a shuddering breath, I reached out and dipped the sponge in the bowl. Lifting my hand, I drained out the water with a squeeze of my fist, and feeling breathless at what I might find, I risked a look down.

My hand froze, suspended in the air as I met the sight of his tapered waist, his muscles forming a sharp and overly defined V that led to a dark cropping of hair and . . .

I sucked in a breath as my gaze landed on his cock, his long, wide, and very hard cock. And the more I stared, the more it hardened, standing flush to his lower torso.

Hands shaking, I looked up to see his eyes blazing. His face wore a furious expression. It should have frightened me, but as his hips lifted, it was obvious why he looked so severe—he wanted my hands to intimately touch him.

Inching forward, I ran the sponge over his calves and his strong thighs. I cleaned both front and back, feeling relieved when they were relatively clean and needed no more attention. My hand ran farther north, only to be met with what unnerved me.

I closed my eyes and took a deep breath.

What are you doing? I was all over him, having blatantly used the excuse of washing him down to touch him.

Suddenly I felt sick, and wrong. *Really* fucking wrong.

Deciding to leave, no, *needing* to leave, I went to withdraw my hand, when firm fingers gripped my wrist. My eyes snapped open.

No words came from Zaal's mouth. His grip was anything but hurtful. But I could see he had no intention of letting me go. And as fucked up as it made me, I didn't want him to let go of me.

My eyes lowered to his hand on mine and then rose to his face. His jaw was clenched. He wore a pained look. I opened my mouth to speak. A whoosh of air slipped through my lips, my words resisted their formation, when suddenly Zaal pulled me in closer. Gasping at the sudden movement, my knees shuffled on the rubber flooring. Never breaking Zaal's stare, he slowly lowered my hand and the wet sponge to the base of his long cock.

Zaal's hand paused as the sponge connected with his hard length and I grew wet between my thighs. Every part of my skin seemed on fire as I felt him beneath the sponge. Felt his cock, hot, long, hard, and desperate.

Then Zaal, controlling my hand, slowly dragged the sponge upward, a deep grunt slipping from his mouth as I reached his tip. Body rigid and eyelids hooding, he pushed my hand back down to his base. His chest muscles jerked as his hand and my hand together moved the sponge back up, then down, faster this time. Losing all rational thought, I curled my hand further around the sponge, the action gave me tighter purchase of him. Zaal dragged in a breath and a growl tore from his throat.

My pussy pulsed inside my jeans when Zaal's back hit the rubber wall, his huge thighs tensing with every stroke of the sponge.

Zaal's eyes fluttered to a close; his ridiculously long black lashes landed on his high cheekbones. As his guttural growls and grunts grew louder, his hold on my wrist slackened, but it didn't matter. I was lost to him, addicted to watching his full lips part, his long breaths stuttering in the silence of the room and his hips rolling, meeting my strokes thrust for thrust.

My breast ached to be touched as I worked my wrist faster and faster, stroking him until every sculpted inch of his body became taut.

As I pumped him harder, my thighs clenched together searching for some kind of release. Then Zaal's breathing changed and his hand fell away. But I didn't stop. As I glanced up from his swelling cock under my attention, his eyes snapped open. I almost faltered at the searing, hungry way he was viewing me. I froze, caught in the intensity of his primal glare. My hand worked still faster. I saw his green eyes darken and flare; Zaal stiffened, and releasing a harsh roar, came all over his stomach, the white streams of his release splashed over his tanned skin.

Breathless, I released a moan as I watched him fall apart. Zaal's body jerked as I worked him down, until I slowly released my hold.

Zaal sat against the wall, his body exhausted with its release. Placing the sponge in the bowl, I brought it back to his stomach and gently wiped away the obvious evidence of his release.

Next, taking the towel, I wiped it over his legs and stomach until he was dry. My heart still hadn't calmed, and I couldn't look him in the face. But feeling him watching, I couldn't resist glancing up. Zaal was studying me, watching me dry his freshly washed skin. My pulse raced, and a warmth spread in my chest. He was . . . *beautiful*. Zaal was the most amazing man I'd ever seen.

I fought to rein in my reaction. Unexpectedly, Zaal reached forward and took my hand. I froze as he examined my palm, my wrist, then every single one of my fingers. I frowned wondering what he found so fascinating. Then he coaxed me closer with a pull on my arm. I followed. What choice did I have? I was captivated, completely drawn into whatever Zaal wanted from me.

My knees were almost flush to his parted thighs. This close, I could feel intense heat radiate from his chest. I could see the glistening sheen of sweat on his chest caused by his release.

Zaal squeezed my hand, then brought it to his face. I sucked in a shallow breath as my palm connected with his rough stubbled cheek. Zaal's eyes darted to mine, as if, somehow, they were trying to speak to me.

I tilted my head to the side, my long blond ponytail falling over my shoulder to land on his chest. Zaal's eyes flickered down, his lips parted, then once more he watched me.

He held my hand, unmoving, against his cheek. When he did draw it back, he took four of my fingers and began running them down his cheek. He repeated the motion over and over, my fingertips grazing against his unshaven skin. His eyes seemed to plead with mine, but for what?

The desperate look on his face was so earnest and forlorn that I had to fight for breath. It was at that moment I saw the *man* before me. Not the Jakhua killer, not the forbidden Kostava heir, but the residual spirit of the man he was without the poison of the drugs. Somehow it shone through, even though he appeared nothing more than a freak, a monster created at the sadistic hands of a bitter, twisted tyrant.

Zaal jerked on my arm again, recalling my attention to him. His head bowed like he was urging me to understand him. I wanted so badly to know what he meant.

I wanted him to talk. *Christ,* did I want him to speak.

Then I wondered for a moment if he *could* talk. Lord knows what Levan Jakhua had done to Zaal's body over the years. My stomach sank. Maybe he had ruined Zaal's ability to speak. Maybe he had taken his voice away.

Zaal began moving my fingers down his cheek again, across his forehead and along the other side of his face and I refocused on this strange action.

His eyes then darted to the bowl. And it dawned on me. I understood what Zaal wanted. He wanted me to clean his face.

"Your face?" I asked. He stilled on hearing me speak. "You want me to bathe your face?"

His beautiful, hopeless eyes closed for a fraction of a moment. He was saying "yes."

Wiping a stray tear that had escaped the corner of my eye, I withdrew my hand and moved to the bowl. I reached in the bag I'd brought down and retrieved a small facecloth. Seeing a bottle of water behind Zaal, I used the remnants of the water to dampen the cloth, adding soap. Zaal watched me the entire time. His previously stern eyes had softened. And the almost-kind look in his eyes, set against the raw, intimidating features of his face staggered me.

I inched closer to the position I was in before. And I noticed something for the first time. Zaal's chest rapidly rose and fell the closer I got to him. I was bringing something out in him. He was *affected by me,* and I couldn't believe just how much I was affected by *him.*

Taking the cloth, I pressed it against his cheek. Leaning in, I felt his warm breath ghost over my face. I saw the veins in his neck stand out with every soft stroke I made. And this close, with the removal of the weeks' worth of dirt and grime on his face, certain features came to light. His skin was smooth, his lashes so dark; it was almost as if kohl liner had been applied to his upper eyelid. The effect of it framed his jade eyes perfectly. Jade eyes that never once moved from mine. Jade eyes that on closer inspection, completely stole my soul. The color was breathtaking, his irises pure bright green, no flecks of brown, just the cleanest and most beautiful of colors, heightened by his dark Georgian features.

But what held me captive, what stirred something inside me was something quite inconsequential. Three small beauty marks, three delicate moles lying just to the side of his left eye. They made him appear human, not the animal, the fierce wild monster he'd been conditioned to be. These three moles promised me that here sat a person. Underneath the scars, the muscles, and the tattoos was a hurt and lost man.

I washed Zaal's face. Even when it was clean, I didn't want to stop touching his face. I didn't want to stop running my hands over his high cheekbones, along his broad forehead, and across his strong jaw. It was apparent he craved my touch as much as I loved to touch him. When I moved to withdraw my hand, Zaal lifted his hand and placed it over mine.

My palm was flat to his cheek.

We breathed in unison.

There were no words, no sounds, just my skin connecting with his.

Before long, Zaal's eyes closed. By the shallow breaths he was taking, I knew it wouldn't be long before he fell to sleep. His body was exhausted, the result of dispelling whatever hard drug was flowing through his veins.

Yet his hand didn't move off mine. Zaal's head was angled just so, as though he was leaning into my touch.

My heart skipped several beats. I couldn't take the feelings coursing through my body. I couldn't take what being in Zaal's presence was making me feel. Like something I had to keep at bay was clawing its way to the surface.

Once I was assured he slept, I gently removed my hand from his face. A sudden wash of emptiness flowed through me. Lifting the washcloth, I slipped it back into the bag. I then pulled his sweatpants up as far as I could manage.

Zaal didn't stir.

As I moved away, I stared down at the remaining heir to the Kostava clan. Any hate I'd harbored had disappeared.

Confused, and more than disturbed at the events of today, I picked up the bowl and my bag, and walked to the stairs. I tried not to look back, but my heart physically ached at the thought of leaving him down here in this hell of a basement alone, no light to comfort him, no *me* to press my palm to his cheek and help him relax.

Unable to stop the pang of guilt ripping through my chest, I forced myself to reach the top of the stairs and open the door. I raced to the bathroom, deposited the dirty water, and moved to the kitchen to lock away the key. But as I walked into the room, Savin and Ilya were both staring at me, both wearing the same look of disappointment on their faces. I glanced down to the cut surveillance monitor beside them, the screen now filled with nothing but white noise. I shook my head at their anger.

Ilya moved forward as if to speak, but I held up my hand. "Don't," I ordered with a hard voice. "I'm going to my room."

Turning on my heel, I ran up the stairs and into my bedroom. In seconds I was in the shower, my mind drowning me in the memories of what had just happened.

I pictured Zaal's eyes softening as I cleansed him. His hand moving my fingers against my face, silently begging me to wash his face. And then him falling to sleep as he pressed my palm to his cheek; drifting off to sleep fully trusting me, a stranger.

I ran my hands down my cheeks. I felt torn. Because I *felt*. I felt something for *him*, my enemy. Heat coursed through my body as I remembered stroking him, remembered his hand guiding me to make him come, his stuttered breathing, and the look of pure pleasure that spread across his face as he released on his stomach.

Unable to fight back a moan at the memory, my hand slipped down my soapy body to where I needed it the most. My fingers ran across my clit and I cried out at how badly I needed release, too. The memory alone of his grunts and rumbled growls brought me to the edge. My back braced against the wall as I circled my fingers faster and faster, long moans slipping from my mouth. Then when I imagined him staring in my eyes as his jaw clenched, he roared and came, white streams of his cum in contrast with the olive tone of his stomach. I cried out as pure pleasure ripped through me. My body curled inward at the force of how strong I came, gasping for breath in the aftermath.

Standing under the heavy spray of the water, I washed away the wetness that was coating my inner thighs. I jumped out, toweling myself off.

As I lay on my bed, a wave of shame took hold. I squeezed my eyes shut, feeling like I was betraying my own blood. What would my father say if he knew what I'd just done with the enemy?

But no matter how hard I despaired, I couldn't seem to regret Zaal. I wanted him.

But I knew I couldn't go down there again. I owed it to my family.

In ten minutes I'd dried my hair and crawled into my bed. I just wanted to curl up and forget it all for a while.

As soon as I pressed my cheek against my palm searching for sleep, the memory of Zaal doing the same stirred a need in my body, a need for *him*.

Lifting my hand to my laptop on the dresser, I pulled it open to find my guards had reattached the surveillance feed. I fell into a fitful sleep watching a now-clean Zaal sleeping deeply.

His usually pain-riddled face now expressed nothing but peace.

8

TALIA

I didn't leave my bedroom all day. In fact, I never even left my bed. I'd forced myself to stay away from the basement. I'd forced myself to stay locked the fuck away, period. I'd forced myself to fight my instinct to run to Zaal.

I'd tossed and turned all last night, memories of my *babushka* plaguing my dreams, filling me with guilt. Memories of her stroking my hair as I fell asleep as a child, telling me about how she met her true love . . .

"I was only a child really, Talia. But one look at your grandfather and I knew. I knew he was my soul's other half."

"You did?" I whispered in awe.

Babushka smiled. "I did. It was his eyes. He had the kindest of brown eyes." *Babushka huffed a laugh. "Of course, I knew who he was. He was a Tolstoi, every Russian knew the Volkov Bratva, but I remember seeing those eyes and knowing that as violent as his life was, he was not."* I watched as Babushka's eyes filled with water and my stomach sank. She missed my grandfather so much. I could see the racking pain in her eyes.

"Babushka?" I whispered and she pulled me closer into her side.

"Your dedushka was my life, Talia," she said in a sad voice, *"And one day, a man will enter your life and you will know, without a doubt, that he is yours. I can't explain it, but something will snap within you and from that day forth, you'll be his and he'll be yours."*

I smiled against my babushka's chest, and echoed, "I'll be his and he'll be mine."

"*A good Russian boy. A man from our way of life. A man your papa will approve of, will welcome into the Bratva to stand by his side. A man your family will be proud to have as their son.*"

"*I can't wait,*" I said excitedly, and closed my eyes, trying to imagine what my true love would be like. I smiled further just picturing my father shaking my love's hand, with a proud and happy smile on his face, my heart full with the knowledge that I'd chosen my true love well . . .

I blinked fast, trying to chase the tears from my eyes. Trying to swallow back the nausea creeping up my throat. But *Babushka's* words stabbed at my brain. *I can't explain it, but something will snap within you and you'll be his and he'll be yours.* My heart beat at a furious rate as Zaal's face flashed in my mind and, at that one simple thought, my heart swelled and filled with warmth.

Something within me had snapped.

The minute my hand had touched Zaal's skin, and those jade eyes had seared mine, I knew something within me had fundamentally changed.

Sighing in shame, I gripped the comforter in my hands and fought back my tears.

Why him? Anybody but fucking him!

You can't do this, Talia. You can't have him. You can't want him like this! I scolded myself as I jumped from my bed, unable to sit in this goddamn room any longer, hiding, shying away from the overwhelming pull to the man in the basement. I showered and dressed, all the time replaying last night's dream in my head. I thought of Babushka and guilt took its firm hold. She would be so ashamed of me. *Me!* Her favorite. I knew I was letting her down. And I couldn't fucking bear letting her down.

Running down the stairs, I reached the kitchen, brushing my hair back from my face in nervous frustration. My hands were trembling and my legs had the consistency of Jell-O as I drank in the darkening sky outside the large-framed windows.

Just breathe, I told myself. *Take a deep breath, close your eyes, and breathe.*

I sucked in a breath. I closed my eyes. But all I saw when my eyelids drifted shut was him. His large olive-skinned body, his long black hair, and those green eyes. Those soulful green eyes that would fix on me as though he could read my mind, speak directly to my soul.

Shivers broke out along my skin at the mere memory of his taut body, at the sight of those three beauty spots beside his left eye that had me transfixed.

Snapping my eyes back open, my hand drifted to my precious, treasured necklace and I felt my eyes sting with betrayal once more.

I had to forget about him.

He wasn't mine to have. He *couldn't* be.

It was a stupid naive obsession.

The whip of the winter wind thrashed against the house windows' glass as I stood motionless in the center of the vast kitchen. It howled and whistled and my hands curled into fists, only to slam down on the granite top island with my anger bubbling up inside.

I breathed hard, ignoring the throbbing of my now-injured hand, trying to rid my attraction to the damn man out of my mind. But the more I tried to expel the vision of him in my head, the more prominent his features became, every inch of him in perfect, infallible detail in my mind.

Whipping around, I searched the room for a distraction, my muscles jerking like a drug addict trying to avoid their next fix. My head told me to not go down and see him again, to not give in. My head told me to not go to the security room and check in on him on the basement's surveillance feed.

But my heart propelled me forward, and with a careless abandon I found myself in the *byki*'s small security office staring eagerly at the main screen.

I stayed that way for a while; staring, trying to avoid the inevitable craving I knew I was going to cave into viewing.

Because I was obsessed.

I was obsessed with 221, and could no longer lie to myself that it was just intrigue, that it was simply a harmless bit of self-indulgent interest. It was more. I knew it was more.

I fucking *hated* myself for the fact that it was more.

Slowly reaching out, my index finger found the On button for the feed and the large screen came to life. And there he was, lying on the black rubber floor, wrapped in chains and static in motion.

As soon as my eyes found his slumped, broken frame, my heart raced in my chest and my lungs seemed to squeeze at the sight. My skin grew hot, and an ache formed between my legs. I wanted to touch him again. I wanted to hold him in my arms.

I stood there like a statue glued to the ground for what could have been hours, and as the minutes ticked by, the gold necklace around my throat suddenly felt like an open flame brandishing my skin. It was burning me, burning me with guilt.

And just like that, I knew I had to get away from this place. I needed distance. I needed to clear my mind. I needed to pull myself together, get *away* from the temptation.

Shit. I needed a Goddamn drink. Or two.

Seeing my *byki,* Ilya and Savin patrolling on the far west of the property's extensive grounds, I knew it was my chance to get away alone.

Without hesitation, I ran to the kitchen closet that held the car keys and took the nearest set I could find: the Mercedes. Running toward the front door, I slammed my hand on the button that opened the electric security gate and, grabbing my purse, burst out of the front door and beelined for the Merc.

In seconds I was at the blacked-out C-Class 250 and, with a lead foot on the gas pedal, roared out of my family's isolated Hamptons mansion, quickly hitting the open road. Destination: Brooklyn.

As the miles passed by, the trees a blurring stream of brown, a dull ache set in my chest.

I needed this, needed to breathe the Brooklyn air. And I needed my best friend. Keeping my eyes on the dark country road, I reached into my purse and pulled out my cell. In seconds I'd found her name and the call connected.

"Hey, girl!" Kisa's soothing voice greeted. "I was just thinking about you."

"Kisa," I said anxiously, "can you meet me for a drink in a couple of hours?"

Kisa paused then asked, "Tal, what's wrong? Where are you?"

"I'm driving back to Brooklyn. I . . . I just need to get back for a while, is all."

More silence. Then, "Talia, you're worrying me. Why are you coming back so soon? Has something happened?"

I sucked in a breath, and explained, "Kisa. I need to talk to someone. I'm going insane. And I'd really like a long fucking drink of vodka to accompany that chat. So? Can you meet me?"

"I'm at the Dungeon, Tal. I'll be here awhile more."

My heart fell, but I exhaled a relieved sigh when my best friend offered, "How about we meet at Brighton Beach for a walk? It's close to the Dungeon, I can get away easier."

I rolled my eyes at Kisa's alternative plan, but couldn't stop the laughter bubbling up my throat. "You never were one for the bars, were you, *dorogaya moya*? Always been the good girl," I teased.

Kisa laughed in return, clearly easing her worry for me. "And you've always had to be the rebel, haven't you, Tal?"

My laugh turned into a guilty cough. Kisa was right. I'd never walked the "good old Bratva" woman's line. My father had given up trying to keep me in check. I was his little girl and could wrap him around my little finger. But this, what I was doing with 221? I knew he'd never forgive that.

"Tal? Do you want to meet at the beach?" Kisa asked, breaking my inner self-chastisement.

"Yeah, we can meet at the friggin' beach," I agreed, "but, Kisa?"

"What?"

"Make sure you pick up a bottle of Grey Goose and bring it with you, okay?"

"Tal—"

"Don't worry, Sandra Dee," I interrupted. "I'm not going to make you drink. That liter of Russian perfection is all mine."

Kisa's light laugh filtered through the car, instantly making me feel better. "Tal?" Kisa said as her humor faded to silence. "Drive safe. I'm worried about you, girl. You don't sound right."

With a steady voice, I assured, "Don't worry about me, Kisa. I'm good, as always. Nothing ever fazes me for long. Whatever this is, I'll get over it."

My unyielding grip on the steering wheel told an entirely different story.

By the time I hit Brighton Beach night had fallen, bringing a blanket of darkness. As I drove slowly through my hometown, past the gloomy abandoned streets, past the boarded up stores and bankrupt restaurants, the rundown shell of houses and the homeless people huddled on the floor, I shook my head.

It was like another world out here. If you were a part of the Bratva, if you were Russian, Brighton Beach was a haven. No cops interfering with business, hoards of loyal people from the motherland, sharing culture and wealth. But if you were any other nationality, you were forgotten, a piece of nothing to the Mafia that controlled the dingy streets.

Because in the world we—that I—lived in, the Mafia, the soviet brotherhood, was paramount. No one fucked with us. No one threatened our slice of East Coast Americana. Brighton Beach may look like some rundown hell to most, but to the Volkov Bratva, this was the land we ruled. My father and Kirill Volkov were the kings of this fucked-up kingdom.

Seeing the beach on my left, I pulled my car to a stop at the abandoned dark section Kisa and I had come to as kids, and cracked open the door. The icy wind whipped around my hair awarding me the jolt of reality I'd been searching for.

Locking the car door, and leaving my now powered-off cell in the passenger seat, I walked onto the freezing sand in my Gucci boots and, almost meeting the tide, slumped down to the ground.

I stared out at the vast sea of darkness, breathing in the salty air and tried not to think of what Savin and Ilya would be doing right now, finding me gone. And I was *really* trying not to think of the broken man I'd left on the cold basement floor.

Hearing a cough behind me, I turned my head to see Kisa heading my way, wrapped up in a thick parka and clutching a large bottle in her hands.

I smiled as she approached, her arms hugging her waist, her long brown hair whipping around her face. When her eyes met mine, she shook her head. "Talia Tolstaia, I love your crazy ass to pieces, but it's freakin' freezing out here!"

Pushing myself off the ground, I walked to my best friend and wrapped my arms around her. "You're the one that wouldn't meet me at a bar, so technically, it's your fault we're freezing our asses off right now."

Smiling wide, Kisa linked her arm through mine and she guided me to a cluster of rocks, hunkering us down behind their shelter to escape the severe bite of the wind.

Without breaking her hold on my arm, she passed me the sealed bottle of Grey Goose and watched with amusement as I cracked it open and took a long heavy swig. My chest burned as the alcohol ran down my throat, and all the air fled my lungs at the vodka's strong taste.

After a few more long sips, I immediately felt more relaxed. Screwing the cap back on, I tipped my head back to the full starry sky and sighed. "That feels better," I said quietly. And it did. Away from the presence of 221 I could breathe, I could think more rationally.

Kisa's arm tightened in mine. Her beautiful face turned my way, and she asked, "What's going on, Tal?"

My eyes were fixed on the crashing of the waves, when 221's beautifully stern face entered my head. I dropped my gaze, frustrated with myself when my stomach flipped and filled with butterflies.

"Tal? You're scaring me now. What's wrong?"

"I just needed to get away."

Kisa was too quiet in reply. I met her gaze to find her frowning. "But you went to the Hamptons to get away from everything here. To disconnect from Brooklyn for a while. Now you need to get away from the Hamptons, too? I don't understand."

"I know," I replied quietly, "I'm ridiculous."

Kisa's gloved hand found mine and squeezed my fingers. "You're not ridiculous. But what's happened to make you need to leave?"

My free hand sunk into the cold sand beside me and I filtered the grains though my fingers like a sieve. I wanted to tell someone.

"Talia, please. You've never hidden anything from me before. I know you. I can tell something is on your mind." Kisa's blue eyes searched mine, then she added, "Just because I'm married to Luka doesn't take away my loyalty to you."

I threw Kisa a watery, grateful smile. Kisa nudged her head in my direction urging me to divulge. Unscrewing the Grey Goose, I drank another few sips, and whispered, "It's 221. I needed to get away from 221."

Kisa tensed and sorry spread over her face. "Shit, Talia. I didn't even think."

I nodded my head then took another drink. I gripped the neck of the bottle and the laugh that tore through me was humorless. "He's haunting me, Kisa. I can't believe Luka brought him to the country house where I was staying. I just never expected to feel this strongly toward him. He's all I can think about. He's all I can concentrate on." My hand subconsciously lifted to run over the "Tolstoi" engraving on my favorite gold necklace.

My heart raced as Kisa said nothing. Finally, I turned to my best friend to see her watching me sympathetically. "I never even thought how hard it would be for you having him there." My eyebrows pulled down and Kisa squeezed my hand. "Of course you don't want him there. After all the family history, of course you don't."

I opened my mouth to tell her she'd misunderstood me, but Kisa looked out over the sea, lost in her own thoughts. "It's Luka, Tal. He's got a one-track mind over saving that guy. It wouldn't have even occurred to him that you'd detest the very sight of him. That it was disturbing your life to this extent."

Even surrounded by the freezing cold wind, my cheeks filled with heat. Kisa had it wrong. *So* wrong.

I opened my mouth to explain that when Kisa laid her head on my shoulder. "I'm sorry you're getting dragged into all this revenge business of your brother's, Tal. But . . . but Luka needs it. He needs to help 221 more than you can understand, despite how offensive that is to your family. It's healing him."

Kisa's sad voice drifted on the wind to my ears and I stopped what I was about to say.

This fascination, I would have to keep to myself. With a final sigh, I laid my head on top of Kisa's. I was lost. Alone and lost.

"Tal?" Kisa asked moments later.

"Yeah?"

"Where's your *byki*?"

I grimaced when I thought of the trouble I'd be in with Savin and Ilya when I was found. "Erm. I kind of left them at the Hampton house and came back to Brooklyn without informing them."

Kisa's head whipped up, and an admonishing, but humored smile spread on her lips. "Talia! Seriously, girl. You *are* a rebel! Your father will flip if he finds out you sneaked off."

I rolled my eyes. "I know. Twenty-four and still have to answer to daddy dearest. How pathetic."

Kisa playfully slapped my arm. "With the rival threats of late it's necessary. It's for your protection, not punishment."

"I know," I said indulgently, and patted Kisa's hand. "Come on, *dorogaya moya,* time to get off this beach. It's fucking freezing!"

Kisa laughed as we walked back toward our cars. I suppressed my groan seeing Kisa's *byki* standing dutifully by her Lincoln. She was going to be the perfect Bratva wife when Luka eventually took the pakhan mantle.

"How you doing, Kisa?" I asked as we casually headed over the sand. "Have I missed anything since I've been away?"

I felt Kisa's arm tense for the briefest of moments within mine, but she shook her head in dismissal. "Nope, nothing new. Just the same old same Volkov life. Fighting, death, and extortion. You know, our honest family's business."

Unable to hold back my laughter, I nudged my shoulder into Kisa's and we both chuckled all the way back to the road.

When we hit pavement, I saw Kisa's *byki* eyeing me strangely. They knew I was alone without my guards. That clearly wasn't going over well.

Throwing the guards a wave and a huge smile, I greeted, "Evening, boys!"

Kisa, laughing again, pulled me in for a hug. I went to move back, but she held on tighter. Frowning, I held her back until she pulled away. I went to ask her if she was truly okay, when she pressed a kiss to my cheek and whispered, "I miss not having you around, Tal. Brooklyn's not the same without you."

My chest filled with warmth. "I'll be back soon, Kisa. Can't leave you in everyone's favorite death-match ring alone. You need me to brighten your day."

"You joke, but it's true," she said meaningfully. Kisa stepped back toward her car, but asked, "You're going back to the Hamptons, aren't you?"

I let my eyes drift into the distance and the empty, almost post-apocalyptic feeling of the Brighton Beach streets. "Yeah, I still need a bit of time alone." I met Kisa's eyes and said, "You give that big brother of mine a kiss for me, okay?"

Kisa's face lit with pure love at the mention of Luka. "I will. He misses you, too, you know. Even if he doesn't show it so much." Kisa hesitated before she got in her car. "Are you okay to drive? You haven't drunk too much, have you?"

I waved my hand, dismissing her concern. "Nope. I'm good. I'll take it easy, I swear."

Kisa nodded, but I could see she was still worried for me. "Okay. Call me when you get back."

"Will do!" I said cheerily.

In minutes Kisa was gone. And I was still thinking of a six-foot-six, 250-pound Georgian.

Shit.

Screw this, I thought as I jumped behind the wheel. I needed a club. I needed a bit of normality. I needed to be the Talia of old for a while. I needed to see if another guy could make me forget 221's face.

9

TALIA

Club Synz was teaming with hundreds of hot bodies, all dancing, kissing, brushing against one another—a promise of what would come as the night wound down and the comforts of home came calling.

I sat at the bar nursing a mojito.

Acid music pumped through the speakers so loudly I could feel the heavy bass vibrating through my chest. Staring into the clear liquid of my drink, I twirled the straw and watched the sprig of two mint leaves dance in the funnel I'd created. Then there was the lone lime segment chasing the paired and connected mint leaves down to the bottom of the glass. It never quite caught up, bobbing just above as if it were watching them have all the fun.

I couldn't help but think it was a metaphor for my life. Always watching other people fall in love. Always finding love out of my grasp.

221's face then appeared in my mind *yet again*. His long hair. His green eyes. That long black hair, his hand holding mine, the feel of his length under my palm . . .

Shit!

Suddenly, the chair moved beside me, making me jump. My hand flew to my chest and my heart skipped a beat. I glanced to the side to see a young dark-haired guy sporting black geek glasses and an expensive three-piece suit slip into the neighboring leather seat.

Holding up his hand to signal the bartender, he flicked his blue-eyed gaze my way, a slow grin instantly pulling on his defined lips. Forcing myself to smile back, I watched in rapt attention as his eyes dropped to my bared shoulders, over my white strapless top and down to my skin-tight Armani jeans. His nostrils flared as he drank in my over-the-knee boots and my long blond hair that fell to the middle of my back.

A few seconds later, his eyes once again met mine, and knowing he'd been caught, he quickly cleared his throat in embarrassment. The grin he was wearing immediately spread into a wide smile, which show-cased his perfectly white teeth. He was pretty damn good to look at—tall, broad . . . attractive. He looked like a lawyer or someone who just got off work. Or a professor . . . yeah, a hot-ass professor.

He was cute. My type before . . .

Talia, you need to get 221 out of your mind! I admonished, making my-self look over at Mr. Professor once again.

"Hey," he shouted over the music.

"Hey," I replied just as the bartender flicked his chin at Mr. Professor, clearly impatient to take his order.

Turning, Mr. Professor placed his order of a double Grey Goose vodka on the rocks. Pausing, he flicked his gaze to my drink and, smil-ing, added, "And another mojito for this beautiful lady."

The bartender moved away to make the drinks and Mr. Professor turned to me. "I didn't catch your name," he shouted as the music switched to a heavy dance beat.

Pushing myself to respond, I replied, "That's because I never gave you it."

He nodded and pursed his lips. "Okay, point made." He leaned in closer, his strong musky cologne filling my nose. "But don't I deserve it after buying you a drink?"

On cue, the bartender placed our drinks down on the counter and Mr. Professor passed him his credit card without taking his eyes off me. Reaching out to grasp his glass of Grey Goose, he raised it high, nudg-ing his chin in the direction of my mojito.

Sighing, I lifted my glass.

Throwing me another heart-dropping grin, he leaned forward and said, "Cheers . . . ?" His request for my name hung in the air.

Shifting forward on my seat, I leaned slightly forward, and informed, "Talia."

Mr. Professor nodded. "Beautiful name for a beautiful lady."

Tilting my head to the side, I asked disinterestedly, "And yours?"

"Brandon."

Brandon, I thought. Such a normal, bland American name.

Bright lights from the dance floor reflected off the lenses of Brandon's Tom Ford glasses. Clinking my cold glass against his, I toasted, "Cheers to you, too, Brandon."

I took a small sip and the ice-cold drink ran down my throat, the strong white rum adding to my already growing buzz. I coughed. This drink was *strong.*

As I placed my glass down, I faced Brandon again, only to find him already watching me. "What?" I asked.

His hand moved to stroke his stubbled cheek. "I haven't seen you here before. Have you just moved to the city? Pretty girl like you could do well here."

Brushing back my hair from my shoulder, I shook my head. "Brooklyn born and bred."

"Really?" he asked, and took another drink. Swallowing, he asked, "And what is it you do here in Brooklyn, Talia?"

My face adopted the same neutral expression I was used to displaying.

Shrugging, I replied, "I help run the family business." Brandon nodded, and I returned the question. "And you?"

"Import and export, mostly."

"Sounds *interesting,*" I said sarcastically, and Brandon dismissively waved his hand.

"Hmm . . . It pays well," he said with finality, then his fingers found their way into the bottom of my hair.

I remained still as he stared at the gold strands and I took a deep breath willing myself to find him attractive. His top lip hooked into a crooked, disbelieving smirk. Dropping my hair, his index finger then lifted to trace the edge of my jaw. I felt the need to push his hand away. Even as hot as he was, I found his touch repulsive.

"You're one of the most beautiful women I've ever seen, Talia. Do you know that? Do you have any idea how gorgeous you are? All that long blond hair, your tanned skin, your dark brown eyes . . ." I stilled as his gaze turned hungry and stared predatorily at my lips.

Pulling back, Brandon reached out for my drink, and brought it to my mouth, the sugar-coated rim kissing my bottom lip. "Drink, Talia. Drink this, then I'm going to taste it on your tongue."

His free hand dropped to my leg and drew lazy circles, traveling farther and farther north. I tried to be into it. I really did. But I felt like I was betraying 221.

I felt like I was betraying myself.

Brandon's head dipped and his bright blue eyes met me over the rim of his glasses. *"Drink."*

Tipping my head forward, I opened my mouth to accept the drink. I took a small sip. I didn't think I could stomach any more, and Brandon pulled the glass away and threw me a devastatingly handsome smile.

His hand lifted to stroke my hair. "Do you feel more relaxed?"

"Mmm . . . ," I mumbled, slightly jarred at how forward Brandon had suddenly become. His mouth approached my mouth and, to my shock, dusted a soft kiss on the corner. Pulling back, seemingly happy at my shocked-still state, he took my hands, and asked, "Dance with me?"

Brandon pulled me from my seat. I grabbed my purse, throwing the strap over my shoulder. Brandon guided me through the heaving mass of hot bodies, the two of us immediately merging with the frenzied mob the club had morphed into.

Brandon kept pulling me along, his pace picking up the deeper into the throng we penetrated.

I frowned, wondering why we were headed to the other side of the dance floor. "Brandon?" I called, but he obviously hadn't heard me over the too-loud music.

I tried to pull on Brandon's hand but his grip tightened and he *still* didn't look back. Fear immediately drenched my body as we fled the dance floor and headed for a darkened exit door.

"Brandon! Stop!" I shouted, but my plea was drowned out by the sound of the heavy bass.

Brandon pushed through the exit door, dragging me with him until I staggered into a dark and secluded alley. Hearing the exit door slam behind me, I swung around just in time to see Brandon loosen his tie and crack his neck.

My heartbeats sounded like cracks of roaring thunder in my ears. I backed up, trying to get away, only to hit a wall. I froze, my eyes darting to Brandon . . . Brandon who was stalking . . . his expression no longer seductive and friendly, but cold and damn-right fucking insane.

Quickly glancing to my left, I couldn't see the entrance to the alley; a tall wall blocked me to my right. But as I turned and moved to run, a strong hand gripped my throat and rammed me back against the cold brick, the impact of the contact knocking the breath from my lungs.

Brandon smiled, cold and sadistic. He shook his head at me, *tutting.* "You made that far too easy, Talia. Don't you know you should be careful when talking to strangers?"

All the blood drained from my face as he spoke, his hand tightening its grip. Brandon's all-American accent had vanished, only to be replaced with a thick Eastern European accent. It wasn't Russian, but close . . . Georgian?

My stomach fell. *Georgian.*

"You're . . . Georgian?" I rasped out of my restricted throat and watched as Brandon's head tilted to the side and his blue eyes narrowed behind his black glasses.

He moved in closer to me and I lifted my hands to claw at his hands. "And how did you know that, Talia? How did you pick out that I'm Georgian?"

Christ, was the city now teeming with Georgians!

I gasped for breath and Brandon's smile widened. "Now you listen to me. We're going to take a trip." Brandon reached into his pocket and pulled out a small syringe filled with a clear liquid. "But I'm going to give you something so you won't try to get away."

My hands began to shake and I started thrashing in his arms, trying to escape his grip. Brandon's hold on me tightened to the point that I could no longer breathe. "Calm down, bitch. Or I'll really give you something to be sorry for."

I watched as he brought the syringe to his lips almost in slow motion, biting off the lid to reveal a fine needle. Gaining purchase on the syringe, he lifted it toward my upper arm and I closed my eyes, not wanting to witness what he was doing.

Suddenly a loud crash sounded and a strong hand slammed down on my shoulder, pulling me to the side until I was ripped from Brandon's hold. I was crushed against a hard chest. My eyes flew open as I coughed and sputtered, air finally finding its way back into my oxygen-starved lungs.

Strong hands kept me upright. Jumping back in fear, I tried to push away from their hold, when I met a familiar pair of blue eyes. "Ilya," I croaked, wincing at the pain of my sore throat. But Ilya, my personal *byki,* my Bratva guard, didn't even look at me.

Hearing another crash behind me, I twisted my head to the right to see Savin, my second guard, smash the heel of his palm against Brandon's nose, blood immediately spraying on his shirt. The sound of crunching bone assaulted my ears.

Brandon stumbled and instinctively reached for his nose, the syringe he'd tried to inject in my arm falling to the ground.

Savin reached into his back pocket and pulled out his Russian army knife. He smiled as he held up the blade, moonlight reflecting off polished steel. Without hesitation, Savin lunged forward with the knife and drove it into Brandon's side . . . right through his kidney.

Brandon called out. Not giving him any chance to retaliate, Savin thrust Brandon back against the opposite wall, forearm to throat to keep my attacker in place.

"Who the fuck are you?" Savin hissed, danger radiating from every pore.

Brandon coughed, bringing up blood that spilled from his mouth, and spat out, "No one you need to worry about."

Savin, on hearing Brandon speak, looked back at Ilya and hissed, *"Georgian."*

Savin got closer to Brandon's paling face. "You're the deliverer we've heard about? The Jakhua deliverer?"

Brandon, this time, lost his smug grin. His reaction said it all. He was exactly who Savin had accused him of being.

"What's in the syringe?" Savin asked, but Brandon remained quiet. Savin, clearly losing his patience, sank his knife into Brandon's lower stomach, slowly, inch by slow inch. Brandon gasped and cried out, then gritted his teeth.

He still said nothing.

"Last chance," Savin threatened.

Brandon jerked his chin arrogantly and said, "I will not say shit to a Russian cunt like you." He looked over at me and smiled. "A daughter of the Bratva, *Talia*? I wish I'd known that before, it would have made the game that much sweeter—taking down the Bratva whores, one wet cunt at a time. It would have raised the price on your body. There's a high stake on capturing a Volkov *printsyassa* . . . a lot of buyers would pay the earth to take their revenge out on your sweet pussy."

Out of nowhere, Savin lifted the knife and hammered it into the side of Brandon's neck. I tried to scream out in horror. I wanted to look away. I really tried to, but Brandon's glazing eyes remained fixed on me as the blade cut deep.

Yanking out his knife, blood pouring from the wound, Savin thrust the blade in Brandon's neck three more times—blows to the front, back, and far side. Savin stepped away and Brandon's gurgling body fell to the floor. A pool of blood rapidly began to form. Freeing myself from Ilya's grip, I slapped my hand to the wall behind me and vomited all over the alley floor.

I closed my eyes and took a calming breath. But my breathing came hard, its warmth turning into a white mist as it fought with the icy air of a winter night.

Ilya crossed his hands at his front, scanning the alley for any other threats. I knew that face. He was angry with me. Ilya's jaw clenched as he stared at me without speaking. His fair hair was ruffled and his blue eyes blazed with rage. Straightening where I stood, a heavy silence reigned.

The sound of a vehicle door slamming shut in the distance echoed farther down the closed-in alley, followed by the sound of approaching heavy feet. Savin suddenly emerged from the darkness, the same scowl of fury Ilya was wearing on his sharply featured face. His hands were now clean of blood.

The sound of gurgling stopped, and I couldn't bring myself to look at Brandon, dead on the ground. Brandon who wasn't really a Brandon at all. He was a Georgian. A fucking member of the Georgian mob, and I . . .

Christ!

I stared at them both and shook my head. They stood, stoic, silent, and unmoving. It broke me.

Minutes passed by. Neither of them uttered a word, which told me just how livid they really were. I'd snuck out of my house without them, come back here. I'd broken the rules. Judging by their furious faces, they were beyond pissed at me.

"Speak," I demanded out of frustration, and placed my arms across my stomach. My hands had started to shake as the cold wind slapped at my bare skin. "Look, I'm—"

"Do you want to get us killed?" Ilya interrupted in a low, dangerous voice. He'd lost his *byki* shield. The one Bratva decorum demanded.

The question made me step back. "What? No! Don't be stupid, Ilya, I just . . . I needed to get away for the night. It's all been too much at the house. With Zaal. I needed to clear my mind—"

"Well, you got that, miss. This cunt almost made your mind real fucking clear." He edged closer. "If your father had found out you had sneaked past us tonight, what the hell do you think would happen to us?"

Savin was watching me coldly as Ilya spoke, eyes narrowed, but I could see his agreement with his fellow guard in his harsh glare.

I was shaking "It was one night, Ilya. *One* night where I wanted to do what *I* wanted without the surveillance."

Savin laughed, but there was only viciousness in that laugh.

"Don't you dare laugh at me, Sav. I just wanted a night at a bar where I could be chatted up by *normal* guys. Where I could have a damn drink without being watched."

What I said clearly irritated him, because he stepped forward and got right in my face, his dark features sharp. "That guy, that cunt lying behind you in a pool of his own blood, the 'normal guy' that was chatting you up, is a fucking trafficker. A fucking deliverer for the Jakhua *Georgians*."

I opened my mouth to talk, to say anything in response, when Sav grabbed my shoulders, spun me round to face Brandon's corpse. "That fucking dead guy there on the ground was going to drug you, and once you were drugged up to the fucking eyeballs, he was going to drag you out of Brooklyn in the back of his van and you'd be on a boat from the docks within the hour, off to fuck knows where—to whatever piece of sick shit had put in an order for a twentysomething blonde to be his bitch slave!

This is the underground world of Brooklyn, Miss. There's danger every-where!"

As Savin spat out his answer, it dawned on me what he had said. Brandon . . . Brandon was a . . . a Jakhua *trafficker*? My hands reached up to my burning cheeks and Ilya took an arm in his grip to steady me.

I met his eyes. "I'm not feeling so good. I'm burning up."

He frowned. "Did he get you with the needle?"

I shook my head, knowing I'd have felt it, when . . . the mojito he'd bought me . . .

"He bought me a drink. I think he drugged it."

Panic began to paralyze me, when Ilya pushed, "How much, Ms. Tolstaia? How much did you drink?"

"Just a couple of sips. I barely took any of it," I replied, and watched as my guards' tense shoulders relaxed. I inhaled again hoping that the cold air would cool me down.

"Can we just go home? To the Hamptons," I pleaded.

Savin, the harsher, more dangerous of my two guards, stood in front of me, blocking my path. "Promise me you won't do that again. You won't go anywhere without us." His voice brooked no shit. He wasn't really asking me not to do it again, he was straight up *telling* me.

"I don't get a choice, do I? Once you tell Papa, I'll be ordered back here to Brooklyn. When you tell him I went to the Georgian enemy in the basement, too."

Ilya stepped forward, his face now less stern. "Talia. Let's go back to the Hamptons. Your father has too much to concern him without us mentioning this. *Any* of it."

I closed my eyes and breathed a sigh of relief.

I heard Savin say something to Ilya about the syringe Brandon had tried to inject me with. I heard them talking in low whispers, then I heard them scoop it off the ground.

As I pictured the mass of people tonight in the club—men with women, women with women, men with men—my heart felt like it physically cracked down the center. I could see their happy faces as they danced carefree. I wanted someone to dance with. Someone to look at me the way Luka looked at Kisa, the way she always looked at him. Like they were the reason their worlds turned.

I pictured me alone and washing Zaal. I could see my hand running down his rugged face, I could feel him lean in, his breath drifting past my face. My heart kicked into a sprint.

"Ms. Tolstaia?" Ilya called. I quickly blinked away the vision.

"I'm ready to go," I said abruptly, giving up any fight lingering within me. I set off down the dank alley, walking ahead of Ilya and Savin, feeling the heat of their bodies behind me.

Stopping dead, my arms crossed over my chest, trying to block out both the cold snap in the air and the humiliation I felt.

I turned to my guards. "I'm sorry," I said quietly. "I won't pull anything like this on you again. I shouldn't have put your lives in danger like that. I . . . I couldn't live with myself if something ever happened to you both because of me."

Nothing was said in return to my apology, but I could feel the tension leave the three of us as we approached the bulletproof black Lincoln my *byki* used. A thought suddenly occurred to me, and I turned to ask, "How did you find me? How did you know where to come looking?"

Ilya and Savin kept their neutral expressions, and I knew why they weren't explaining it to me.

Without anger, I said, "You've got a tracker on me, haven't you?" They stood, not meeting my eyes, instead focusing on nothing over my head and I glanced down. My purse. There must be a GPS in my purse.

I couldn't muster the will to even be annoyed.

I moved toward the Lincoln, and Savin brushed past me. He opened the back door of the car and I silently slid inside.

Both of my guards slipped in next to me, shielding me in the center of the backseat. Both of them were in full protection mode, fixing their attention out of the windows, checking for any more potential threats.

I laid my head back against the heated leather seat and closed my eyes. Then my chest constricted as my thoughts drifted back to Zaal. But this time I didn't fight my want of him. I embraced it. I'd tried to get away from him tonight. From my obsession, from my inexplicable draw to the forbidden slave. It hadn't worked. In fact, it only served to remind me of the life I was in regardless. One of danger, violence and death. There was no point in fighting who I was, the life I belonged to.

I would never be normal.

Therefore I would no longer crave normal.

And because of that, I knew when I arrived back in my Hamptons home tonight I'd be going to see Zaal.

I had to touch him again.

There was no choice.

I had to be close.

Because something inside me had snapped, and just as my babushka had proclaimed, I knew I would never be the same again.

10

ZAAL

"You think it will work this time?" Master asked the man who wore a white coat.

I started shaking at Master's voice. He was cruel. He would punish me if I ever remembered them, he'd punish me if I didn't do as he said.

"I fixed the chemical balance, so it should work. We'll see."

"It took the dog weeks to recover from the last shot." I stiffened. Master was angry and my hands shook harder.

I stared at the ceiling. I was strapped down, I couldn't move. The man in the white coat came closer. My body froze. My chest tightened and I couldn't breathe.

He hurt me.

He always hurt me.

My eyes widened when I saw what he held in his hands. A needle. A long needle. I tried to lift my hands to stop it going into my arm. The straps held me down. I kicked my feet and thrashed my body trying to escape. The man in the white coat stepped back.

"221, stop!" Master's voice echoed in my ears. I stopped moving.

Don't hurt me, don't hurt me anymore, I pleaded in my mind.

Someone laughed as I tried to breathe. *"You've got him well trained."*

Master laughed. I recognized his laugh. He laughed at me when he hurt me. He laughed at me when he made me bleed, when he hit me, when I cried.

"He's a weak dog that I broke. Stripped him of his name and that fucking family he belonged to. Now he's mine. Now he heels only to his master's voice."

The laughter got louder, but Master's command kept my body unmoving on the bed.

The man with the white coat again came closer but he stopped. He was look-ing at Master. "If I remove the straps will he stay down when I inject him?"

"He'll do anything I command." Master paused. "Watch."

The man in the white coat unfastened my straps. I wanted to move, until Master ordered, "221, stay still. Do not move or you will be punished."

At his command, my shoulders pressed into the bed. Not even my fingers could move.

"Impressive, Levan," the man in the white coat congratulated.

"What will be even more impressive is if this shot works. It'll clear any memory of who he was, and fuel his rage, yes?"

"Yes . . . flawlessly," the man confidently replied. I could see the white coat out of the corner of my eye. I didn't want to see him inject me, so I closed my eyes. A sharp pain spread through the arm. The man in the white coat pushed the needle harder and deeper. I wanted to scream, I wanted to run away, but Master had ordered me not to move.

A hot feeling suddenly filled my arm; the hot feeling quickly shot through my body. I gritted my teeth as the liquid turned to fire in my veins. It hurt, it hurt so much.

My body shook. Something was stabbing my stomach. I couldn't stand it. It was making me angry; so angry I needed to scream out the pain, I needed to get it out.

But I couldn't move. . . . I couldn't move. . . .

Snapping my eyes open, I blinked and my body jerked. I blew out a breath. I could move?

I *could* move.

I squeezed my eyes shut to chase away the nightmare. Master had been there. Master and a man in a white coat, both hurting a boy. Hurt-ing a child who was . . . who was—

Hearing breathing beside me, I sat up, braced to kill, when I saw her. The golden hair, the brown eyes . . . *her.*

I shook my head and squeezed my eyes shut trying to remember. Water. Water. She'd washed me. She—

Opening my eyes again, I reached out and, taking her arm, pulled her closer. She let out a shocked cry and her eyes grew big. She looked scared. I didn't want her scared. I thought she must have been like me. She must be Master's, too. He never let females that weren't his near me. Ever.

I had to protect her.

Remembering her from before, I picked up her hand and stared at it. It was so small. Her fingers were so little, and they had a strange color on the end.

Her hand was hot. It was so soft. I ran my fingers over her palm and heard her breathing change. I saw her light skin go red. I wanted to touch it.

Lifting my hand, she went still. I moved my fingers closer and pressed them against her skin. It was soft like her hand. No, softer. And it was warm.

Her hand moved in my hand. Before she could pull it away, I picked it up and pressed it against my cheek.

I closed my eyes. It felt just like last night. I felt just as good.

Her breathing got faster and faster, and I opened my eyes when her other hand pressed on my other cheek.

Something inside of me cooled. The rage that always ran through my veins calmed. It was still there, I could feel it bubbling under the surface, but her warm hand had calmed it. I took a deep breath. There was no pain, no poison, just the feeling of *her.*

"I . . ." My eyes snapped open when she spoke. Master did not let us speak. But her voice . . . it sounded strange. It made me want to listen, even if it was forbidden.

I watched her swallow. I watched her eyelashes flutter and my chest tightened. She was . . . she made me feel . . . I was unsure . . .

"I came to wash your hair," she said. I closed my eyes. Her voice. Her voice was different, sounded different to Master's, but I . . . I liked hearing it.

Suddenly, I felt her hand touch my hair. When I opened my eyes, she was kneeling up in front of me. Her gentle hands were touching my hair.

"It's so long," she said. I frowned. Her hair was long, too. Was my hair being long bad?

I did not allow my eyes to leave her face. I couldn't look away. Her face was . . . it did something to how I felt inside. My chest tightened. My stomach clenched, and I felt my cock get hard. I wanted her to touch me again. I wanted her to stroke my cock again like she did before.

But I forgot wanting that from her when her lips moved and she smiled. My lips parted and I dropped her hand. But her smile dropped, too.

No. I didn't want that.

"Are you okay?" she asked again, her kind voice washing over me. It made me feel warm. I couldn't remember the last time I felt warm. It was always cold in my cells. In *this* cell. I didn't want to be cold anymore. I liked feeling *this* way. With *her.*

A pain stabbed at my head, causing my body to bend forward. I saw someone smiling in my mind, it felt like I knew them. I heard people laughing . . . and it was warm. . . .

Gasping one final time, the pain left me. The female was next to me, touching my arm. Master's female's face wasn't smiling anymore. But I needed her to smile.

I turned her quickly, and holding her by both arms, I pulled her to my chest. A shocked sound came out of her mouth as I held her against my skin.

My cock hardened again. I liked her against me. I glanced down to see her tits pushing against my chest. I heard her breathing change and a redness crept up her neck and onto her face.

Smile, I wanted to tell her. I wanted to see her smile again.

Releasing one of my hands from her arm, I touched my fingers to her lips. They were pink and full. I wanted to touch them further, but I wanted her to smile more. Master and his guards didn't smile.

I nodded my head toward her mouth, tapping my fingers against her lips. She frowned and reached up to take my hand. "What do you want?" she gently asked.

I pulled my hands free and tapped on her lips again with my fingertips. She sighed and leaned her head farther forward. "Tell me. Tell me what you want."

I wanted to speak, but I couldn't. Master never allowed me to speak. I shook my head at the female and sat back on my heels.

Master's female moved away and came back with her water. She held up some bottles. "Will you let me wash your hair?"

I touched my hair with my fingers. I couldn't understand why she wanted to wash it. Her hand touched my shoulder. "Will you let me? I'd like to," she whispered.

Then she smiled.

Lurching to my knees, I brought her close and touched her lips and nodded my head.

Her eyes searched mine to understand, then she sucked in a breath and her lips spread into another smile. "You want me to smile? You like it when I smile?"

Nodding, I moved closer and ran my fingers along her lips. She let me touch her. She let me look at her smile, then she pressed her fingers to my mouth. She swallowed, then asked, "Can *you* smile?"

I pulled back and bowed my head. Master wouldn't allow it. She followed me, and putting her finger under my chin, lifted my head. Confusion filled her eyes and her smile had disappeared.

I didn't understand why her eyes were confused.

Her hand ran through my hair. "Let's wash this, shall we?" she said in a broken voice.

I nodded and sat back. I didn't understand why she looked sad.

I watched her get the water bowl and searched with my eyes for her chains. She didn't have any. I next searched for her identity number. I couldn't see one.

My eyebrows pulled down. I didn't understand why she was here. All Master's females wore chains, collars, or cuffs. She had none. Then my heart started to beat faster.

Had Master given her to me? Was she mine to keep?

Master's female moved behind me and I heard water sloshing in the bowl. But I didn't want her behind me. I wanted to watch her, look at her face. I wanted to feel warm. She made me feel warm.

Reaching behind me, I took hold of the female's wrist. She froze and stopped breathing. I tugged on her arm and patted the floor in front of me.

She breathed out and relaxed. "You want me to stay in front of you?"

I nodded. She carried the water in front of me and smiled. I relaxed and she pulled out the round soft object that she'd cleansed me with yesterday.

Dipping it in the water, she pulled it out and the most amazing sound in the world slipped from her lips: a laugh. "This may get you wet. I hadn't thought through how to actually do this down here."

I was staring up at her, but I was frozen, my muscles seized on hearing her laugh. It didn't sound like Master's laugh. It didn't make me angry, it made me feel. It made me feel full.

Water suddenly wet my head, the drops falling down my chest and onto my stomach. Master's female leaned down to meet my eyes. "Is that okay?" She was smiling. She wanted me to answer, so I nodded my head.

Straightening, she continued to wet my hair. I heard the sound of something opening, and Master's female put something that smelled *nice* into her hands, then onto my head. Her fingers lifted my long hair. She started running them over my head. She shuffled forward until she pressed against me.

I wanted to touch her. Lifting my hands, the chains rattled as I placed my hands on her waist. The female stilled, her fingers in my hair stilled, too. She took a deep breath, then continued. I closed my eyes at the feel of her touching my hair. The movements were making me relax.

My hands gripped her waist. She was so small, so soft.

I heard her breathing hitch and her fingers tightened in my hair. Eventually she stopped, and pulled back. I looked up at her face; it was flushed.

"I need to rinse it off now." She held up the soft object, dripping with water and squeezed it over my head. I closed my eyes as the water ran down my face. My hair stuck to my face.

The female then took a towel and began drying my hair. She sat back and frowned. Something flashed across her face and she said, "I'll be right back."

She went to move and panic shot through my body. I reached out and took her hand. She jumped and whipped her head back. I looked up at her, silently begging her not to leave me. I didn't want to be alone in here again. I couldn't protect her if she left.

She bent down and cautiously put her hand on my face. "I'll be right back." She looked down at my chains and her face looked sad again. "I promise, I'll be right back."

The reassuring look on her face convinced me she would return. I released her arm, but my skin shivered as she walked away, then disappeared up some stairs. I breathed in and out, in and out, never moving my eyes from the stairs.

Come back, come back, come back, I said in my head. I didn't want Master to take her from me. I wanted him to have given her to me.

I heard a door close, and then her feet came down the stairs. As soon as her brown eyes met mine, I exhaled and my shoulders lost tension. But she was watching me strangely. Something was in her hands. I tried to see what it was, but I couldn't see in this darkness.

Master's female bent down before me, her long blond hair falling over her shoulder. She swallowed, and said, "I want to release you."

I frowned. She pointed to my chains. "I want to release you from these chains."

My stomach tightened and I shook my head. Master did not let me go free. And I didn't want her to get into trouble. The only time Master released me was to kill.

I froze. Did Master want me to kill?

Did I have to kill now?

The female moved closer. "No one will hurt you, I promise. I just want to get you away from the water so I can comb your hair." Her hand reached out and, taking my wrist, she slid back the shackle. She flinched, and her voice caught. "I don't want you to hurt anymore." Her finger lightly ran over the scars and fresh sores from my chain. "I want to heal your wounds. I want to look after you."

I looked into her eyes trying to detect deception. I couldn't see any. Was it true? Was I being released so she could care for me?

No one ever cared for me.

No one ever spoke to me unless it was to give me orders or call me a dog.

No one ever touched me unless it was to bring me pain.

"I promise you won't be hurt. There's no more pain here." I stared into her brown eyes. Trusting those brown eyes, I nodded. She lifted the key to the chains, but then stopped. I looked at her face and she said, "You won't hurt me, will you? When you're free, you won't hurt me?"

I frowned and my stomach felt empty. She feared me. I didn't want her to fear me.

Edging farther forward, I lifted my hand to her cheek and pressed my palm flat to her warm skin. Her eyes fluttered closed, then opened and met mine. "I can trust you, you won't attack me, right?"

I nodded my head, then slowly held out my wrists. She took a deep breath. I could see the pulse thumping in her throat. She was still scared. But I wouldn't hurt her. I . . . I liked Master's female.

The female unlocked the chains, and as they released, they clattered to the floor. The female paused as I stared down at my freed hands. I could move them without the pressure. I could move my fingers without feeling pain.

"I'm going to release your ankles now, okay?" the female whispered. I nodded, but still stared at my wrists. I heard the chains from my ankles hit the floor. The female stood up and stepped back.

I looked up, feeling something in my stomach.

The female was watching me. I watched her back, hoping she wasn't still scared, then she took a deep breath and held out her hand.

I stared at her hand, her tiny fingers, and my heart began beating too fast. I stared at that hand and met her eyes again. "Take my hand," she said.

Leaning forward, unused to the freedom in my arms and legs, I reached out and put my hand in hers.

Feeling the wetness of the water beneath my feet, I stood and stretched my body. I swayed, feeling strange, weak. The pain, the poison in my blood had calmed. It felt too strange.

The female's hand squeezed mine and I glanced down to see her watching me. She seemed so small, her head having to tip back to meet my eyes.

She swallowed, her face pale. "Are you okay?" I studied her small hand wrapped around mine, then nodded. She pulled on my hand. "Come over here, out of the water."

I walked forward, the lightness of my legs without the chains at first difficult to get used to. The female slowly led me to the chair that sat in the middle of the room. She pointed to it. "Sit down and I'll comb through your hair."

I stared at the chair, but backed away. Master didn't allow me to sit anywhere but the floor. Said that I, 221, had to always sit below him.

I sat on the floor and bowed my head. I didn't want Master to hurt her for my breaking the rules. I wanted to keep her. He would take her away from me if I disobeyed his commands.

The female remained standing, but I could feel her as she stood in front of me, then she bent down. "Can I comb your hair while you're on the floor?"

I nodded.

She moved across the room and returned holding something in her hand. She kneeled in front of me and said, "This may be a bit painful. Your hair is very matted."

Something ran through my hair, sometimes getting stuck. It felt spiky. It pulled at my head, but she was gentle. Her touch was like a whisper.

Staring at her stomach, I lifted my hand and ran my fingers down the black clothing covering her top half. Her hand stopped in my hair and she sucked in a breath as my fingers explored.

I wanted to touch her again.

I wanted to feel her warmth.

As if hearing my thoughts, she whispered, "You can touch me again. If you want?"

Lifting my hands, I lay them around her waist and I heard her breathing change. My thumbs traced her hips over her clothing, but I wanted to feel her skin. Wanted to feel her skin against mine.

The female began combing through my hair when I moved my hands down to the bottom of her clothing, and dipping my hands underneath, my palms touched the bare skin of her stomach.

The female jumped and gasped, but she didn't move away. I stared at her bare stomach. Her skin was so pale, so light, and it was soft, all of her was soft. I'd never felt anyone so soft.

Hearing her breathing turn heavy, I looked up and caught her watching me. Her lips were parted. I gripped her waist tighter and ran my thumbs over her flat stomach.

I stared up at her and dipped my head forward. I wanted her fingers in my hair again. I liked her touching my head. I liked touching her, too. Master never let me see anyone. I was always alone. I liked being with this female more. I didn't want to be alone anymore.

Hearing her shaky breath, she reached for the spiked object and began running it through my hair. I closed my eyes, tipping my forehead against her stomach. I inhaled the scent of her skin and my cock hardened. She smelled good. Her bare skin smelled too good. As her hands ran through my hair, my nose pressed against her torso and I inhaled again. A low growl left my throat.

Wanting to taste her skin, wanting to taste her, I lifted her clothing further and licked along her stomach.

The female released a breathy moan, and whispered, "Oh, God . . ." Her hands tightened on my head. She stilled for a moment; so did I. I didn't want her to push me off. I wanted to stay close. I wanted her to tend to my hair.

She pulled in a deep breath and started combing through my hair again. I groaned as it stopped hurting my head and started feeling good.

I ran my mouth across her skin. But I wanted to see more. Lifting her clothing, I ran my fingers upward.

I wanted to see underneath her shirt.

I frowned when I found her breasts covered with a black material. The female moaned as I ran my hands over the front of the material and pulled it apart. Freeing her tits I dropped the material to the floor. The female released a shocked cry as her tits were freed. I groaned as my hands cupped them, her red nipple hardening as my thumb ran over the flesh. The female, now breathless, folded her arms over my head, pushing my mouth around her mounds.

As soon as her taste touched my tongue, need surged through my body.

More. I needed more.

Reaching out my hands, I gripped the back of her thighs and pulled her spread legs over my lap. She shouted out as her cunt landed over my cock. Lifting one hand, I grabbed the clothing covering her tits and pulled it over her head. My nostrils flared as I glanced down to her bare top half. My heart beat louder, my blood rushed faster, and I ran my finger down her body from the bottom of her throat to the waistband of her pants.

She was perfect.

She had no scars. Master hadn't hurt her.

Relief ran through me knowing that she hadn't endured pain like me. The man in the white coat hadn't strapped her down, hadn't cut her, hadn't injected her with the needle that brought venom to the vein.

Moving my hands from her front to her ass, I dragged her forward, the warmth from her cunt immediately rolling over me. I groaned as my mouth sucked on her tit, the feeling of her sitting on top of me taking its hold.

The female's hands raked through my wet hair. They slid right through, her sharp nails on my scalp making me grunt and thrust my hips.

No one had ever put their fingers through my hair. No females Master ordered me to fuck had ever touched me that way. They didn't care; they didn't want me. I didn't want them. But I wanted her.

Releasing one tit, I moved to the other and flicked my tongue over the nipple. Her hips began to roll over my cock faster and a growl rumbled in my throat.

It felt good.

Gripping her ass harder, her cunt getting hotter, I snapped my head back. The feel of her against me was too much.

The female gripped my hair, and when I brought my head back down, she was watching me, big brown eyes watching me.

She was so beautiful and she looked at me like she cared. No other female had looked in my eyes before, no one looked me in the eyes. Master said I wasn't worthy.

I studied her pale skin. Her blond hair fell forward on my chest as her forehead leaned forward to meet mine.

Her breathing was short, and she rocked faster. Her full tits bounced, but I couldn't take my hands off her ass, my eyes off her eyes.

"Oh, God . . . ," the female whispered, her eyes fluttering and her body starting to jerk. "Oh, God, God . . . I'm . . ."

The female's hands fisted my hair and she threw her head back. I couldn't stop watching as her pink lips parted, her hot breath drifted over my skin and a long cry raced from her throat.

Her hips ground harder against my cock. As her cunt jerked back and forth, I gripped her ass. My thighs tensed and I snarled as pleasure built at the base of my spine. Then I came. Thundering out a shout, I tucked my head into the female's neck. Her skin was damp and warm. I pressed my cheek against her shoulder and breathed in her scent as her hands stroked over my head and through my hair.

I closed my eyes, calmed by her touch. Slowly, I wrapped my arms around her back, keeping her close.

My stomach fell when I thought of Master coming to take her away from me. I didn't want to lose her.

I thought of the other females he owned and what he made them do. They would fuck other males, several males at a time. He would make *me* fuck them. Hard. Rough. Unleashed. He would try to make them cry. He would laugh. He wanted me to make them bleed.

The females wore no clothes and had their number tattooed on the back of their necks. I stiffened. Did this female have her number there, too? Was she forced to fuck men, too?

Loosening my grip, I pulled back. I looked at the female's face. Her eyes were confused. She bit her bottom lip. My gaze dropped to her smooth body, her pale skin. There were no marks, no numbers.

"Are . . . are you okay?" she asked softly. I frowned.

Why did she talk? Did she not fear Master's punishments? I was forbidden to talk, never to raise my head, only to follow his commands and to kill.

I waited for the poison to return to my blood. I waited to feel pains in my stomach. I waited for the need to kill to overwhelm my body. But nothing happened.

No poison.

No pain.

No rage.

I didn't understand what was happening to me. Nothing made sense.

"Please," the female whispered, and shuffled back off my lap to bend down and look in my eyes, "are you okay?"

Gripping her arm, I spun her around and lifted her hair off her back. She let out a fearful cry when I did so, but I needed to see her number. Her neck came into view. There was no number. I searched her back, her arms, and her wrists. No number.

Confused, I sat back. Why didn't she have a number?

The female turned to face me, her brown eyes wide. I stared at her. I squeezed my eyes shut, trying to remember what the other females looked like. But I couldn't remember their faces. Something stopped me from remembering. I remembered fucking them. I remembered their numbers. But I couldn't remember *them* . . . yet I remembered every-thing since I'd met her. Every part of her face, every strand of her long blond hair, every inch of her soft pale skin.

The female suddenly moved, catching my attention, and retrieved her clothing. Without breaking her gaze, she pulled it over her head.

Her cheeks were red, and she was shaking.

She stood, and my heart seemed to stop. She was leaving. I didn't want her to leave. Her brown eyes filled with tears, and she turned in the direc-tion of the stairs. I'd hurt her. I hadn't meant to. I didn't want her to go.

Something inside of me made me lurch forward and I wrapped my hand in hers. She looked back, her lips trembling.

My chest tightened.

Something inside of me made me pull her forward. She gasped, but that didn't stop me. I wanted to hold her, touch her. When her stomach hit my chest, I wrapped my arms around her waist.

I heard her sniff and closed my eyes, hoping she wouldn't leave me. I always felt fire, my mind stabbing with hurt and pain. But since she had been brought to me, I hadn't felt any of it.

She took the fire and pain away.

She made me feel . . . safe.

The female didn't try to pull away. Instead, she ran her hand down my cheek. I pulled back and looked at her. Her eyes softened and she said, "What is it? Tell me please? What were you looking for on me?"

I took a couple of steps back and lifted my hand. Taking my finger, seeing she was watching me, I traced my finger over my identity num-ber on my chest, 221. I was 221.

The female's eyes were still watching me as I lifted my head. I nudged my head toward her body and pointed to her chest.

Her eyes widened and the redness drained from her face. "You want . . . you want to know my number?" she asked.

I nodded my head. I tapped the back of my neck and pointed at her neck, too. A fast breath left her lips.

The female carefully moved forward and gently got down to her knees. She reached down for my hand and threaded her fingers through mine. I stared at our joined hands and felt warmth wrap around my body.

"Look at me," the female said. I lifted my head.

She brought our joined hands to lie over her chest. With my palm against her skin, I could feel her heart racing.

I gazed into her dark brown eyes and she explained, "I don't have a number." My eyebrows pulled down. She didn't have a number? I didn't understand. Her hand squeezed mine. "My *name* is Talia. I have a name, not a number."

My eyes dropped as I tried to understand how she had a name. Her hand tugged on mine. "Do you understand? Do you understand that I don't have a number?"

I nodded my head slowly. I saw her take a deep breath. Her eyes fell to my chest, to my number. "Do you . . . do you know *your name?*"

Confusion fogged my mind. My name? I had no name. I was 221. I was Master's 221.

The female's hand pressed against my cheek. As soon as it touched me I felt calmer, warmer. "Listen to me," she whispered. "You're safe. You've been freed from that man."

My body tensed. I didn't understand. Why was she saying these things?

"Do you understand? You've been freed," the female repeated. I looked into her eyes, but I could sense in her no lie.

Dropping my head, my heart beat faster as I thought of the word "free." I was free? From Master. From . . .

But when I looked around the dark room, it looked like everywhere else I'd ever lived. Chains. Chains trapping me to the floor. Darkness, no light, and only me for company. I was always alone.

"Look at me." I did as the female asked.

"Do you know your name?" she repeated. I moved my hand to trace my number, when she stopped me, gripping my hand. She stared at me for a long time and asked, "Can you speak?"

A pain flashed through my head and images came to my mind. . . . *Master hanging me to a wall with my hands behind my back. I had spoken my name. I had tried to speak. . . .*

"You'll never speak again!" he shouted. "You'll never say that fucking dog name again!"

I opened my mouth, but Master pulled the chains tighter. I cried out in pain as my arms pulled further back, my shoulders on fire with pain.

"You're not that name anymore. You won't speak ever again. You'll be silent. You're 221, and you're under my command!" The chains pulled harder and harder until my arm snapped from the socket and I screamed out in pain. My body hung from the wall, my head bowing forward to Master.

Don't talk. Don't talk ever again, *I told myself. Master will bring pain if you do. . . .*

I gasped as sweat poured from my head. The female moved in closer and wiped at my face with her hand. "Breathe," she soothed, "breathe."

I looked into her eyes and saw them shining.

I could talk. I *used* to talk. But I wasn't allowed to talk now.

She sat back and watched me. "Your name?" she whispered, wiping the wetness from her face.

I glanced down and my stomach clenched as I tried to push words from my mouth. I opened my mouth. The female held her breath. My eyes searched the room for Master. I'd be punished if I talked.

"It's okay," the female again soothed. "Speak. No one will hurt you. You're safe. You're finally safe." I wanted to speak. I wanted to please her. I didn't want her to leave.

I cleared my throat and it felt raw. But I could feel my voice. I startled—I had a voice. Master wasn't here to take my voice.

The female's hand squeezed mine, still lying over her heart. She repeated, "My name is Talia, who are you?"

Squeezing her hand back, I forced my voice to work. It croaked, "2 . . . 2 . . . 1 . . ."

The female sat back and sucked in a breath. A few tears streamed down her cheeks, but as I was about to back away, thinking I'd hurt her, her lips moved and she smiled even though her lips trembled.

"You speak," she said in relief. "You can speak. And your accent . . ." She blushed, but shook her head, lip curling. She seemed . . . happy?

"Can you say my name?" she asked. I concentrated on her mouth as she said, "Talia."

I listened to the sounds. I rolled them around my mind, and said, "Tal . . . Tal . . . i . . . a . . ." A relieved sigh burst from her mouth. She moved until she was right in front of me.

I stared at her face, her pretty face, her soft eyes, entranced by the way she looked at me. I put my finger to her heart, then put my finger over mine, and I asked, "You are . . . for me?"

A whoosh of air passed through her parted lips. Her words caught in her throat. Her dark eyes shone brightly as water filled them, soaking her long black lashes.

Slowly, her hands moved to each side of my face and threaded in my long wet hair. I held my breath, heart beating loudly. Then, she did something I'd never felt before, she pressed her lips to my forehead.

I swallowed at the feeling this press of her lips brought to my heart. The sun. Something inside of me told me it was like the feel of the sun shining on my face.

I frowned as that thought crossed my mind. I did not remember standing out in the sun, head tipped back as it warmed my face, but something inside told me that I had done it once, or a lot, I did not know.

The female broke away. Her finger drifted down and traced over my number tattoo. Her long lashes fluttered, and she said, "This is a slave number given to you as a child. What was done to you was sick, twisted, and very, very wrong. They, that *man,* called you by this number your whole life. But you *had* a name. You still *have* a name."

I stilled, something long forgotten trying to push through to my mind.

A name. A name? *I have a name?*

I'd always been 221.

I am 221.

I am Master's 221.

I am—

"Zaal," the female said suddenly. My body tensed, a wash of pain stabbing at my flesh. "Your name is Zaal. Do you remember?"

I clenched my jaw as it hurt to think of that name. *Zaal.*

I slumped, out of breath. Tal . . . *Talia's* arms wrapped around me. I thought of what she'd said. I was free. Master wasn't here. I had a name. *Zaal.* So much raced through my head. I pulled away. I turned my attention to my chains against the wall and felt ice cold.

I wasn't free. She was lying.

Talia sat back in surprise and abruptly, I moved. I could see the hurt etched in her face, but she was *lying. . . .*

"Zaal—" she spoke, and reached for my arm. I pulled it back with a snarl, giving her my back.

Anger ran through my veins, fire building in my stomach. Master was punishing me, I knew this. Giving me this female, getting her to make me believe I was free. I was being punished. He was punishing me for something. I just didn't know what I'd done wrong.

Getting to my feet, I walked back to my chains. The water with which Talia had cleansed me was still pooled on the dark hard surface.

I sat beside my chains, on the cold wet floor, my back against the wall. I kept my head down. Master would soon be here to punish me.

"Zaal?" Talia's voice questioned. She had quieted, her voice barely above a whisper.

My chest tightened as she called me that name. *Zaal.* A white-hot pain burst into my head on hearing the name Zaal. It took my breath away, causing me to rock back and forth. I pushed my hands against my eyes to stop the pain.

A hand pressed to my cheek and stayed there until the pain passed. I opened my eyes. Talia sat before me. She was looking at me with sadness in her eyes. A lump crawled up my throat and I rasped, "Why . . . why are . . . you . . . doing this . . . to me . . . ?"

Her face scrunched in anguish and she sat back, her lips trembling. "Doing what?" she whispered. Her voice was shaky.

"This . . ." I told her, my hand over my aching chest. "You hurt . . . this. . . ." I tapped my finger over my heart. It felt bruised, cracked at her deception.

I'd trusted her.

She paused, her pretty face frozen until she glanced away, her lips pursing. "How?" she asked quietly. "How do I hurt your heart?"

"You . . . lie," I replied. I watched her snap back to face me, seemingly in confusion. I picked up a chain, lifted it beside my arm and showed her the marks on my wrist. "I am not free."

I didn't know how long I'd been in here, in this new cell, but I'd been chained. My wrists and ankles bled. Food had been thrown in a bag at my feet twice a day. I pissed in a bucket in the corner. Just like I did with Master.

"No," Talia said. Her voice crackled. "You are free. Your captor isn't here."

More pain pierced my chest as she continued to lie. "Chains," I said. "I am not free. I am kept in chains, in darkness. I am not free . . ."

The dark cell went silent. Talia didn't say anything for a long time. Then she stood. I didn't look up. I knew she was leaving. But her feet didn't move.

"Zaal?" she called. "Take my hand."

I shook my head. Still she didn't walk away. I felt her watching me. When I lifted my gaze, she was staring at me. Her hand had remained outstretched.

"Why?" I asked. "Why take your hand?"

A single tear ran down her cheek. "Freedom," she replied. "I want to show you freedom."

11

TALIA

You are . . . for me?

Even now as I held out my hand for him to take to get him out of this fucked-up torture cell of a basement, I couldn't shake those words from my mind. I couldn't remove the image of his face, looking up at me with such hope, such relief that I was his.

You are . . . for me?

In that moment I was every hope he'd had. I could see it; see it in those sea green eyes. He moved me. Completely moved something inside of me with those simple, earnest words.

He hadn't moved; he stared at my hand like it was a forbidden fruit he so badly wanted to savor. He was shattering my heart as, internally, he warred with himself. His conflicted eyes flitted from side to side; he wanted to believe me. He wanted to believe in me so badly, it shone like a desperate beacon in his green eyes.

I edged forward and pushed my hand closer to his. "Take my hand, Zaal. Let me show you the truth. Trust me, always trust me. I won't ever lie to you. I *promise.*"

He glanced down at the heavy chains spooled at his side, then back up to my face. He was frowning. An accepting expression passed across his face, which made me believe he *was* going to *trust me.* His hand lifted, but stopped in midair. His jaw and fist clenched simultaneously. Then he made my heart swell; he took a leap of faith and wrapped his big hand in mine.

We stayed there, suspended in our relative sitting and standing positions hands joined. After rolling to his feet, Zaal's huge frame towered over me. His hand still held mine, and by the tight grip, I knew he wouldn't let go. He was so fierce and untamed in his looks and demeanor. But his tight grip on my hand told me how fearful he was about the concept of his freedom . . . about putting his trust in me . . . when, in his tortured mind, I might lead him to nothing but more punishment and more pain.

He took a deep breath, and rasped, "I am weak. I feel weak."

Sighing, I tipped my head to the side. "I know. But you're getting stronger. Each day, you're getting stronger again."

Stroking my thumb over the back of his scarred hand, I watched his muscles tense. Our gazes met; something indescribable, palpable passed between us. I said, "Come with me."

Zaal nodded, and I began leading him toward the staircase. When we reached the bottom step, he paused, then ground to a halt. I glanced back to his wary face; automatically I squeezed his hand.

He took a deep breath and once more he began to follow me, this time up the stairs. When we reached the top, I opened the door. Bright light immediately flooded the space. Zaal, as if blinded, stumbled backward, his back hitting the wall.

I whipped my head around to see him squinting, his free arm shielding the light from his face. He was panting like he'd just run a marathon, but his hand hadn't released mine. No, quite the opposite. It had become iron tight, verging on the point of being painful.

"Zaal?" I asked, and rushed to where he was hiding in the shadows. "What's wrong?" I continued.

I gently lowered the arm shielding his face. His eyes were blinking rapidly. He pointed to the ray of light illuminating the floor. "Light," he rasped.

I frowned in confusion. "Light?" I questioned.

He nodded his head and swallowed hard. As I stared at his face a stark and devastating realization hit me. "You're never out when it's daylight?"

Zaal stared at the ray of light, dust particles dancing in its beam, and said, "I am always in darkness. Chained in the darkness. I kill only in darkness."

I knew he'd been kept like an animal. But no name, head always bowed, punished until he lost his voice, and brought up in darkness since a child? Daylight-deprived? It cut me more deeply than any knife could possibly do. To have been kept out of the sun . . .

My thumb ran over his hand again. His jade green eyes met mine. "There's no need to fear the light. Let me show you."

I could have sworn Zaal's heart beat so loud that I could hear it in our cocoon of silence. For a moment I didn't think he was going to leave the comfortable familiarity of the basement. Thank goodness, he found the courage to step forward, his feet moving as though testing new waters.

I walked through the door into the hallway. Zaal's impressive frame filled up every inch of the doorway. He looked down at the threshold between the basement and the hallway. I noticed a sheen of sweat glistening over his body.

He caught me watching and announced, "I have never walked out of my cell alone, free from my chains."

Chasing away my building tears, I tightened my hold on his hand and assured, "You're not alone." His eyes widened. I stepped closer, somehow instinctively knowing he needed me beside him.

Zaal took long deep breaths and brought our joined hands over his heart. "Talia," he said on a relieved sigh in his strong Georgian accent, the sound bringing a wash of peace over me.

I waited until he took that first step. And with his hand iron tight in mine, he stepped over the threshold. Eyes searching, Zaal drank in the expanse of the hallway. His head flinched at the bright light and his eyes stayed narrowed. His bare chest rose and fell with what I presumed was adrenaline surging through his body.

I pulled Zaal further into the body of the house. Just as he seemed to let himself relax, the sound of the front door opening echoed off the wooden walls. Savin and Ilya walked through.

Zaal tensed.

My head whipped to my *byki*.

Savin and Ilya drew their Glocks.

"Guards," Zaal snarled, pushing me back against the wall. His huge body blocked mine from Savin and Ilya. His body crouched in preparation for a strike.

"What the fuck?" Ilya cursed.

When Zaal heard Ilya speak, he tensed. All I could see was his back. Every muscle was braced for the fight. This was the Zaal that Luka had brought to the house weeks ago. This was the violent monster Jakhua had created. The stone-cold killer. The product of over-experimentation.

"Guards," he snarled again.

"Zaal!" I called out. My voice seemed to have no impact on his rapidly rising anger.

"Talia. Are you hurt?" Savin asked.

"No! Don't hurt him!" I called from behind Zaal. "He thinks you're Jakhua's guards!"

I carefully moved to the side of Zaal and placed my hand on his back. He tensed and his crazed, still-blinking eyes darted to me. His face was flushed, and it was clear to me that the brightness of daylight was adding to his agitation.

He gripped my wrist and pulled me to his chest. His strong arm wrapped around my waist and he shouted, "Mine!" to Savin and Ilya. I saw Savin's face tighten in alarm. But hearing the protective, possessive word slip from Zaal's lips had my thighs clenching and my heart soaring.

I wasn't afraid.

"Miss," Ilya warned, motioning for me to step away.

I held out my hand to my *byki,* and ordered, "Leave." They stared at me like I'd gone insane. "Leave!" I shouted. Zaal's grasp on me became too tight. He was losing it. I could feel it in his shaking limbs and erratic breathing.

"What?" Ilya exclaimed. "We can't do that, miss. He could kill you!"

"You can. He's safe, but he thinks you're guards. The guards Jakhua employs. I've let him out because he's safe." Ilya glanced back at Savin. "Please, leave . . ." I begged.

"Fuck!" Ilya snapped. Lowering his gun, he turned to face Savin. "Outside," Ilya ordered, before looking back at me. "You have five minutes to explain who we are before we come back in. And if he comes at us again, I'll blow his fucking head clean off."

When the door slammed shut, Zaal let out a frustrated growl and dragged me across the floor. He slammed me against the wall. His face was contorted in rage, his jade eyes lit with fire. "Guards," he hissed. "Master's guards. You lied. . . ."

"No," I whispered. His eyebrows twitched. "My guards," I explained, then pushed, "They're *my* guards."

Zaal stilled. A frown pulled on his red face. "Your guards?"

I nodded. Timidly lifting my hand, I pressed it against his cheek. As soon as my palm met his face, tension left his shoulders. I'd observed that when I did this, it soothed him. "You were freed from your Master weeks ago. You were brought here to safety."

He blinked and searched my gaze. "To you." My stomach flipped at the want in his eyes. He thought I was his safety. That he was brought here to me.

"No, Zaal. *For you*. You're free. Nobody owns you now."

Lips parted, Zaal inhaled a shaky breath. "No Master?" he asked in bewilderment. I shook my head for emphasis.

His head lifted to look around the hallway. I could see the confusion racking his brain. "I'm free?" he asked again.

"Yes," I whispered, my fingers stroking over his cheek. He let out a deep exhale and straightened. I watched with bated breath as he placed his hand on his arm, on the tens of scars, and then slid his fingers to the shackle wounds on his wrists and ankles.

I watched as those fingers traced the permanent red circular marks, and I watched as he lifted his head. Zaal met my eyes with unshed tears in his. "I am free."

The sight of those tears dropping over his dark stubbled cheeks was my undoing. "Zaal," I croaked through a thick throat.

I wanted to tell him who he was. Where he'd come from. I wanted him to tell me what had been done to him for years, for decades. I wanted to tell him what Jakhua did to his family. But he was, in many ways, just a child.

He couldn't understand. He was like a caveman, seeing the world for the first time.

I took his hand and, meeting his eyes, said, "Come with me."

Zaal tightened his hand on mine. I led him from the hallway into the large living room. He stopped at the doorway. Zaal drank in the large area filled with plush furnishings, the large feature windows overlooking our beach.

He swallowed hard.

I began pulling him toward the kitchen. Zaal stopped dead as he looked at the appliances, the countertops. I watched him and tried to imagine what this was like—seeing everything for the first time.

I couldn't. I couldn't even begin to comprehend.

"This is where the food is prepared," I said. I moved to the fridge. "Are you hungry?"

Zaal pressed his hand against his stomach. "I am always hungry," he replied. "Master feeds me very little. I have to earn my food."

I stared at him in silence. "How?" I whispered, unsure whether I really wanted to know the answer.

"Killing," he said, as if it was an ordinary everyday activity.

I swallowed and stepped forward. "Do you kill a lot?"

Emphatically, he nodded his head. "It is all that I do."

Blowing out through my mouth, I pointed to the fridge. But Zaal's attention kept drifting to the windows overlooking the beach. I leaned back against the fridge and watched his eyes try to interpret the scene.

Quietly, I moved beside him, and placed my hand on his arm. He tensed and whipped his angered face toward me. I stilled, and he seemed to remind himself I was no threat, his expression softening. "Would you like to go outside?" I asked nonchalantly.

He blinked, then blinked again. But he shook his head. His gaze drifted to the window. Taking his hand, I led him to the window. Releasing my hand, he edged forward and pressed his hands to the glass.

A warm feeling stirred in my stomach as he stared out of the large pane of glass. His eyes were flitting over everything in sight. Perhaps he was committing it to memory?

Did he think he would be captured again soon? That he would never see this sight again?

Zaal looked out for minutes, in a happy silence. I wanted to give him more. "Zaal. Come with me," I prompted, and led him up to a bedroom. Luka and Kisa had been staying in this room. Luka still had some hooded sweatshirts hanging in the closet. Zaal stood in the center of the room. His eyes taking in the furniture; the bed, dresser, everything.

Choosing the biggest hooded sweatshirt I could find, I walked to Zaal and unzipped the front zipper. "Put this on," I instructed.

Zaal looked at the sweatshirt and then at me.

I couldn't help but smile at the lost look on his face, over something as simple as a sweatshirt. A wisp of a laugh slipped from my mouth. Suddenly, I found rough fingers stroking my lips.

Zaal was staring at my lips in fascination. "What is this called in your language?" he asked.

I wrapped my hand over his fingers, and replied, "A smile."

"A . . . smi . . . le . . ." He sounded out the word as he moved closer to my lips. The task of breathing became difficult as he stood a mere hairsbreadth away. His head leaned in closer, and for a moment, I thought he would kiss me. Instead he drew back and pressed his fingers to his own lips.

Finding my stolen voice, I asked, "Do you smile, Zaal?"

He paused, then shook his head. His expression changed from confused to enquiring. He asked, "Why do you smile?"

My heart beat at double speed. "When something makes you happy. When you *feel happy*."

"Happy . . . ," he whispered. Then he took the hooded sweatshirt from my hands. "You were happy giving me this?" He looked down at the sweatshirt, clearly with interest.

Not wanting Zaal to think that I was laughing at his naivety, I took the sweatshirt, held it out for him to slip on, threaded it over his arms and, moving to his front, zipped it up. He still awaited my answer, so I replied, "I am happy that you're finally free."

Zaal paused, then lifted his hand. He ran it through my hair. "Your hair is soft," he observed.

Perplexed by the sudden change in conversation, I responded by running my hair over the ends of his long jet black hair, and said, "Now so is yours."

He followed my fingers through his almost-dry hair. His eyes met mine, and he asked, "You took care of me?"

I swallowed as my throat felt too full with such attraction for this man. "Yes," I whispered, "I took care of you."

His head dipped again and his finger ran down my cheek. His finger continued south, over my breasts, my nipples aching under his touch. Then his finger tapped over my heart, before moving to tap over his. "Because . . . you are . . . for me."

Time stopped as he said those words again. Though on this occasion, they weren't a question. To him, I could tell it was fact. In his eyes, I was his, I was for him.

"Let's go to the beach," I announced, unable to earth the electricity crackling between us. His eyes widened, but before I gave him a chance to resist, I guided him out of the room and down the stairs.

As we turned the corner into the living room, Savin and Ilya were standing in the center. Zaal tensed. I turned around and, standing on my tiptoes, pressed my hand to his cheek. "They are here to protect you, not cage you."

Zaal's eyes narrowed as they focused on my *byki,* but he wanted to trust me. I could see that Zaal was placing his trust in me.

Zaal, this time, took my hand. My heart bloomed as I cast him a smile. I heard his breathing hitch, so I smiled even wider.

I tried to lead us past Savin and Ilya, but Savin stepped forward. "Miss, a word, please?"

I stared at Savin, his dark gaze was stern. "What, Savin?"

His eyes flicked to Zaal then to me. "In private, please."

"It can wait, Sav," I replied, then he said, "does the *knayz* know you're doing this?"

I stiffened. Anger and a hint of guilt built in my stomach. "He's in Brooklyn, summoned by the Pakhan. He doesn't need the hassle. He has enough to deal with."

Savin nodded, his mouth tight. He knew that I knew what I was doing was wrong. But I continued without hesitation. "He wants this *situation* made right." I glanced back to Zaal, who had moved closer to my back, a protective gesture. "I'm helping to make it right," I concluded.

Zaal followed me to the back door, and his breath blew faster. I didn't look back. I just opened the door, the winter wind off the ocean lashing at my face.

Zaal's hand tightened in mine, but I stepped through taking him with me. The wind whistled loudly, but at least the sun shone bright. I stopped and Zaal stepped beside me. His eyes squinted at the sun. The look on his face as he scanned our private beach was like seeing someone coming home after the longest time. To me, it was the look of freedom.

"Do you want to walk farther?" I asked. Zaal looked at me, nerves played across his dark features, but he nodded.

I glanced down at his bare feet. I worried that he'd be cold, but he didn't seem to feel the winter chill. I didn't think anything, not even a damn hurricane, would register with him at this moment.

"I'll show you the ocean," I offered. We walked past the swimming pool and onto our private wooden walkway. The air was filled with the sound of waves crashing onto the sand. Zaal kept pace behind me. His breathing was erratic, and his muscles were tense. He flinched at the bright light, but I had a feeling nothing was going to stop him from reaching the beach.

When we reached the end of the dock, I turned to Zaal and dropped my hand. A panicked look swept over his face. I ignored it and kept going.

I shouted, "Have you ever seen sand before?"

I pointed at the smooth beige sand. As I expected, Zaal shook his head. I smiled. It got his attention. "One of the best feelings in the world is to walk on sand."

Zaal stared down at the sand, studying it closely. I rubbed my hand down his arm. "Go," I said, "feel the sand. Meet the ocean."

Zaal was understandably apprehensive. His face paled slightly, but as I nudged my chin encouragingly in the direction of the beach, he stepped out.

As soon as his large feet sank into the sand, a gasp escaped his mouth. His toes wiggled, and he bent down to scoop the sand up in his hands. He remained crouched, hands buried under the soft sand for a good while.

A tidal wave of emotion washed over me, stealing my every breath. My hand clutched my chest and my eyes stung.

I, Talia Tolstaia, the twenty-four-year-old daughter of a Bratva boss of New York, was getting emotional for a Kostava. A Kostava who had no idea who the hell he was.

Legs feeling weak, I dropped down to sit on the edge of the wooden dock, wrapping my arms around my waist.

Zaal had his head bowed, a statue on the sand. I tasted salt on my lips, from the spray of the sea.

Zaal lifted his head. His eyes were closed. The sun kissed his face. I too felt the sun on my skin as though I was attracting its rays. I felt as though I was feeling it for the first time with him—the warmth. I was feeling the wind wrap around my hair. I was right here in the moment.

I sighed and Zaal opened his eyes. Those pearls of green fell upon me. Zaal stood slowly, and bowed his head at me. I smiled through trembling lips and though no smile pulled on his lips, it was shining from his eyes.

Zaal turned. His huge body, sculpted from vast muscles, his long black hair wild and free, slowly made his way to the endless rush of the waves.

I wrapped my arms around bent legs and rested my cheek on my knee. Zaal was walking to the tide. When he met the sea foam, I watched it pass over his feet. From here, I couldn't hear him or see his face, but I could see his shoulders relax. Then he knelt down and pushed his hand into the salty ocean. It would be freezing at this time of year, but he didn't even flinch.

Like he did with the sand, he stayed awhile touching the water, as if in prayer. Over fifteen minutes passed by. The entire time I simply watched him in silence.

Suddenly, Zaal stood and deeply exhaled. When he turned to face me, his green eyes were bright; my heart ceased to function.

He was smiling. It was small, it was faint, but it was there.

And in that moment I knew—I was losing my heart to the object of my family's deepest hatred.

Zaal walked toward me. My thighs tensed. Everything about him was raw; his wild long hair, his dark stubble, his deep olive skin. He was everything I could have wished for.

"Did you like the beach, Zaal?" I asked, and raised my head.

Zaal closed his eyes. His lip hooked up in a small smile. I gasped at the sight. When he opened his eyes, he dusted his fingertips over his mouth. "I feel . . . *happy*."

I placed my hand over my chest and closed my eyes, too overcome by what he'd been through, when fingers ran through my hair.

I opened my eyes. Zaal was looking at me in concern. "Why do you look sad?" he asked in his clipped English. A part of me then questioned how he knew English. That thought vanished as soon as he moved closer still to me.

I shook my head. "I feel sadness at how you've been treated."

His black eyebrows pulled down. I knew he still couldn't understand the gravity and the magnitude of what he'd been through. I knew he didn't remember what was done to his family. He was the embodiment of living in the moment, living for now. Of course, I adored that Zaal was embracing and savoring life for the very first time.

"Ignore me," I said as I waved my hand.

"You are tired?" he asked.

I nodded my head. "Yeah, I've barely slept these past couple of weeks."

Stepping back onto the dock, Zaal reached down and lifted me up in his strong arms. I couldn't help but laugh as he did so. He placed me down in front of him and put his hand in mine. "We rest," he said with finality.

I let him lead me back to the house, then I led him up the stairs. I walked him to a spare room. As we entered, I hung back at the door. "You can sleep here." I pointed to the bed. "You have a bed, Zaal. No more sleeping on the floor."

I turned to leave the door, when Zaal suddenly reached for my hand. I turned my head to face him. Raw fear was on his face. He pulled me to his chest. "Where do you go?" he asked, his accent thicker as panic laced his voice.

"My room," I whispered. My pulse picked up speed at the desperate look of need in his eyes.

His hand dropped and his fingers laced through mine. "I come with you."

I knew this had to be it. This was the moment I stopped myself from falling off the cliff. This was the moment I called Luka and told him that Zaal had got rid of whatever fucked up serum was in his body. That it was time to come and get him.

Or, I'd jump off the cliff, arms wide and free-falling. I'd follow what was leading my heart. Zaal, the Kostava who had seized control of my soul.

Stepping closer to Zaal, I ran my hand down his chest, my eyes following my fingers, and I chose to fall. "You go where I go."

Without looking at his face, I turned and walked to my room. As I entered through the door, I released his hand and walked to the window. I drew the blinds. The sun was fading now, the bright winter's day drawing to its end. I paused as my hand hung on the blind's chain. I was exhausted. I felt exhausted, conflicted, confused, yet at the same time, every cell in my body was zinging to life. Lustful adrenaline surged in my blood, igniting every sense. The cause: *Zaal*.

Taking a deep breath, I slowly turned. Zaal was watching me. I knew that look. He wore that look when I'd bathed him, when I'd stroked his cock. Wore it as I'd washed his hair, then straddled his lap.

Reaching my bed, I pulled a nightgown from my dresser. My eyes flitted back and forth to Zaal, who remained standing, waiting patiently at the door. My body was so aware of his overwhelming presence, that my large bedroom suddenly felt full, stifling. But *right*.

Throwing my nightgown on the bed, I walked to Zaal and took his hand. I led him further into the room. He followed and I pointed to my right. "The bathroom's in there. You'll probably want to have a shower." My face flushed red as I remembered riding him in the basement. My breasts ached and my nipples hardened at the memory. I wasn't sane around this man.

Zaal's eyes bored into mine. His lips rubbed together as he watched me. Suddenly his finger was brushing across the apples of my cheeks. "You are red." His eyes narrowed, studiously taking in every detail. "Why?"

I shook my head, trying to dismiss his question, but he edged in closer. I almost moaned aloud when his hard torso caressed mine. My gaze fell to his olive skin, then the dark edges of his identity tattoo. I felt my panties grow damp. "Tell me," he said roughly. His thigh brushed against mine and I could feel his hardness. I closed my eyes and fought with all I had to rein in my desire. "Talia . . . ?" he pushed.

Shyly, and looking for something to do with my fidgeting fingers, I ran my fingertip over the zipper of his sweatshirt. "You may need to clean up before you sleep."

I saw his head nod in my peripheral vision. Reluctantly dropping my hand from his chest, I walked to the bathroom. I'd assumed Zaal had followed, but when I turned to show him the shower, I was alone.

I moved back to the bedroom to see where he was, and I ground to a halt. My lips parted and a shaking breath slipped from their depths.

Zaal.

Zaal stood beside my bed, free from clothes, his black hair hanging low and free over his chest. Every inch of his body was ripped and raw with tight muscle . . . and his hard cock . . . his large wide cock was erect, flat against his lower torso. His clothes were lying in a heap beside the bed. Zaal's head was downcast, waiting, just waiting for me.

I swallowed at the sight of him. I fought for breath at his savageness; his brutal, primitive presence, and I lost my sensibilities.

Driven by instinct, I stepped forward, Zaal's eyes immediately snapping up to meet with mine. His nostrils flared, his taut traps flexed, and his hands clenched at his sides. It was predatorily, and I felt like I was his prey. Though I wasn't afraid. No, the opposite; turned on, compelled, drawn in, but never afraid.

Zaal's cheek twitched as I approached, and I stopped just inches away. I fluttered my eyes from the view of his chest to his eyes; his eyes were already fixed on mine.

"Zaal . . . ," I whispered, hearing the longing clear in my tone. "Do you not want to cleanse?"

His pectoral muscles, marred with deep scars and ink, pounded heavily as his breathing grew labored. "You," he rasped. My stomach and thighs clenched. Reaching down, he picked up my hand and laid it flat on his torso. I gasped when he began to steer my palm over his abdominal muscles, his jade eyes blazing with need. "You cleanse me," he said, his clipped English and heavy Georgian accent growing thicker. "You touch me."

He pushed my hand ever lower. My breath hitched as my palm ran over the head of his cock. "Zaal," I moaned as my free hand lifted to rest on his bulging bicep. I was overcome by him, by this inexplicable pull between us.

Zaal's hand over mine, we placed our joined fingers over his hard length. His jaw clenched and a growl rumbled in his throat. His eyelids grew leaden. I watched in fascination as his long black lashes swept against his high cheeks, his tongue licking along his full bottom lip.

My index finger, free from his hold, ran along the tip, pre-come kissing my skin. Zaal stilled, a deep groan surged from his lips, and before I'd known it, his strong hands had fisted the material of my thin sweater and ripped it in two.

Instantly, my breasts were bared.

Zaal panted as if he couldn't draw his next breath without touching me. And my tether was strained. I thought of the necklace around my neck, its significance, the memory, the giver of the gift. But I became lost in that trusting sea of jade. The pull of Zaal's draw, and the truth that I'd never felt this viscerally connected to another person in all my life, well, I tried to push it away . . . but could not.

Zaal was without restraint, tormented by the primal need to take. To take me. To own me. I could see it in every tense muscle, every protruding vein. He wanted to fuck me.

And, Lord forgive me, I wanted that, too. Damn the consequences, I wanted the man I'd sworn to always hate. I was fired with need.

Leaning to his side, I lifted Zaal's red scarred wrists, once manacled by shackles and chains. I brought them to my breasts, my hands covering his as I silently urged him to touch.

Long calloused fingers grasped at my flesh. Hot shivers traveled like flares to the apex of my thighs. His touch alone sent me close to the edge. If this flicker of pleasure was a taste of what was to come, I wasn't sure there would ever be any going back.

For a moment I had to question whether this betrayal with Zaal—against my family—was worth it. I cast my gaze across his identity tattoo, the scars from Lord knows what, and then his face, open, trusting, and handsome. Those beautiful innocent eyes. I sighed deeply, a sense of accepting peace flowing through me. It was worth it. Pure instinct told me *he* was worth it.

I chose to follow my heart.

Zaal's face flushed as his hands explored. Meeting his gaze, I couldn't look away from his hungry face as I snapped the button of my jeans. But Zaal looked down to watch, his hands palming my flesh more and more, his fingers grazing over my erect nipples.

I rolled my jeans down my legs and kicked them to the side of the room. Nerves overwhelmed me, engulfing my skin with hot shivers.

Tension built to a heady storm as our body heat clashed. Zaal's rough hand still stroked my skin, his fingers tracing south.

I stood only in my black lace thong, a flimsy barrier from being completely bare, completely vulnerable.

My heart drummed.

My thighs clenched.

My pussy pulsed.

And then he moved. He moved until he was flush to my front. Flesh to flesh, sharing space. "Talia . . . ," he whispered, his warm breath skirting down the side of my neck.

"Zaal . . . ," I whispered in reply, my eyes closing at his nearness.

Taking a deep breath, I lifted my head. Zaal hissed through his teeth as he glanced down. He towered over me, dwarfed me with his sheer size.

Zaal's hands smoothed up over my waist, teasing me inch by inch. A low rumble sounded in Zaal's throat, making my pussy flood with wetness. Then his hands skirted over my breasts, up the sides of my neck, and landed on my cheeks.

We stood there, suspended in the moment; his hands cupping my cheeks, breathing in each other's air. The pulse in my neck raced, then my eyelashes fluttered in anticipation of what was to come.

Our desperate gazes met.

He took a deep breath.

Then he whispered, "You are . . . for me?"

And I knew I was done.

Trampled, heart-flattened, done.

You are . . . for me? Four simple words that smashed through any barrier between us.

"Zaal," I moaned and, with my hands threading over his broad round shoulders, I lifted to my tiptoes. Zaal's eyes widened in surprise as I drew in my mouth toward his. His hands, on each side of my face, tightened. His breath slipped through his lips with a nervous exhale.

Eyes remaining open, I brushed my lips over his. Zaal stilled. He panted into my mouth, which hovered in anticipation next to his. Zaal's warm sweet breath caused my pussy to ache with need.

I expected Zaal to crush his lips to mine. That a man of his size, with such a primal persona, to overpower me, to control me, to dominate me. But he stayed still, body tensed. I pulled back slightly, only to see his eyebrows drawn. His pupils were dilated, the whites of his eyes shining brightly. His nostrils flared. The three moles to the left of his cheek had me entranced as they twitched with nerves.

Then it hit me—Zaal didn't know why my lips were touching his.

I sighed. The heat of realization melted in my chest. He'd never been kissed.

Zaal's hands were cupping my cheeks like his grip was the only thing keeping him grounded. Keeping him from falling.

Smoothing my hands up the sides of his thick neck, I threaded them through his now-soft ebony hair and lay them on his cheeks. Zaal's eyelids lowered, his anxious eyes fluttering to relax at my touch.

"Zaal?" I whispered. His eyes bolted open, that jade green stare catching mine. "Have you ever been kissed?"

Frown lines laced his forehead. His cheek twitched. "I . . . I don't understand. You speak . . . differently from what I know."

English, I thought. He struggled with understanding English.

Zaal's face searched mine. He was Georgian. I didn't speak Georgian, but most Georgian Mafia knew Russian. I prayed he did, too.

"*Potzeluy,*" I offered. Zaal froze, his gaze drifting above my head. His expression was one of deep concentration, as though he was trying to remember how he knew the word. "Do you know the word?" I pushed.

His head dropped and he nodded. "I think . . . I think . . ." His head lifted and he pulled me to his lips with his hands still on my face. My heart fired off beats like a cannon in battle. His lips moved until they hovered next to mine. "They, our *lips* meet. They meld." A crease between his eyebrows formed. He asked, "How? How do I know this?"

I swallowed as his panicked eyes searched mine for an answer. Before I could reply, his face paled. His hands shook against my cheeks. Zaal's eyes squeezed shut. His lips parted. "I think . . . I think someone used to kiss me . . . before I belonged to Master?" Sweat beaded on Zaal's forehead. My stomach fractured at the lost look on his face. "Tal . . . Talia . . . who would have done that?"

I didn't know what to do. Did I tell him the truth or did I soothe him? I chose the latter. He was shaking, flustered. I wanted to make him feel safe.

"Shh . . ." I hushed, then moved my mouth to caress his lips and pleaded, *"Potzeluy menya."*

Kiss me.

Zaal tensed. He whispered, "I will try."

In seconds my lips melded to Zaal's. A long moan resonated in my mouth. I used the grip on his cheeks to pull him closer.

A deep hum sounded in Zaal's chest. Wasting no time, I pushed my tongue into his mouth, his taste bursting onto my tongue. For a moment, Zaal's palms slipped from my cheeks, the deepness of the kiss catching him off guard.

I kept going. I took from this primitive man what I wanted, what I needed. At first, the kiss was clumsy, as his innocent tongue tentatively met mine. I became breathless the more our tongues dueled. Zaal became more confident. His grip tightened and he pulled me to his hard chest, the impact knocking precious air from my lungs.

I pulled back, gasping for oxygen. But Zaal stayed close, his pupils wide, dark, and love drunk. I panted, still at the edge of his swelling mouth. His lips were red and flushed. I flicked my tongue out and ran it along the seam of his bottom lip. Was it possible? Zaal's hard cock seemed to swell even more; its length pressing hard against my stomach. I cried a breathy moan and captured his bottom lip between my teeth, before releasing it and staring into his eyes.

Zaal froze. Completely froze; causing my body to follow suit.

His green eyes blazed and his hands dropped. With a sudden, almost deafening snarl, his large hands yanked at my panties, ripping the black lace thong in two.

The chill in the air beaded my nipples and washed over my clit. Zaal stepped back. His stormy gaze dropped to between my legs. His hand gripped his cock.

Beads of sweat dropped down onto his damp chest. And those eyes, they roved, they devoured my naked body. They shone bright, flaring with need. As I watched his scarred tattooed hand stroke his long cock, my thighs grew slick with wetness.

Zaal growled low as my hand lifted, then skirted down my stomach. My heart raced as fast as a hummingbird's wings. Then I reached the top of my pussy. Zaal's hard breathing seized as my fingers crept lower, down to run along my folds.

And he broke.

Whatever control Zaal had, snapped. He plowed forward.

With a shocked gasp, Zaal took me in his powerful arms and crushed his mouth to mine. The grunts and groans pouring from his mouth caused me to claw and rip at his back. I wrapped my legs around his waist. Zaal's cock met my pussy, its length dragging along my folds, scraping against my already-swollen clit.

Tipping my head back, I cried out. Hands losing purchase on his burning skin, I raked his hair. My fingers wrapped around the long strands and I ground against his length.

Zaal's mouth broke away from mine, a loud roar sounding in my ears. Suddenly, Zaal's knees dropped to the floor, his firm grip not releasing me as he took me down also.

The head of his cock probed at my entrance and I cried out against his neck. Zaal groaned. Hands holding my waist, he flipped me onto all fours, his huge body closing in behind me.

I called out in shock, but lost all rational thought when his head lowered and his wet tongue swiped my pussy, licking over my folds, to finally land on my clit. He was relentless in stroking, probing, and sucking.

I could barely see, my skin shivering as he assaulted my clit, sucking and swirling his tongue. My juices flooded into his mouth. When his tongue stiffened and plunged into my hole, a white light blistered behind my eyes as I broke apart. I came so hard my arms gave way and my forehead touched the carpet.

I came, wave after wave cresting and stealing my breath. But Zaal never stopped, savoring every ounce of pleasure I could give. He lapped at my wetness, his strong hands spreading my pussy to reach every last drop.

I fought for breath, trembling on the ground, when I suddenly felt Zaal behind me. I felt his wide hard cock brace at my entrance, his rough fingers grasping my hips.

Desperately needing to see him, I turned my head. My heart missed a beat at the sight. Zaal, every muscle in his huge body protruding and strained, stared at my pussy. His face was primitive, tense with need, flushed with need. His teeth were gritted and a look of intense desire took hold in his eyes.

Then, as if sensing my stare, he glanced up, and that look he was wearing so strongly ebbed away, only to leave adoration in his beautiful expression.

"Zaal . . . ," I whispered as his hands flexed on my skin. His jaw clenched, and releasing one hand, he guided his cock to my entrance. I thanked the lord I was on the birth control shot. I wanted Zaal raw. I wanted him flesh to my flesh.

I never moved my gaze from his. He never moved his from mine. But as the head of his length pushed into my hole, my wet warmth engulfing him, his traps and neck corded as he slammed himself inside me.

I screamed out as he roared, the joined sounds of our sex echoing off the bedroom's walls. And then he began thrusting. Hard, rough, and fierce. Zaal's untamed hair hung over his face, masking the wild expression on his features. He looked every inch the unpolished savage I'd believed him to be.

Zaal's cock pounded into me. The sound of his slapping hips against my ass made my clit throb more and more. His cock stroked against the spot that was always out of my reach, pleasured shivers shooting up my spine.

I was so close to exploding, but as I looked into Zaal's face, his eyes now closed, lost in our moment of pleasure, I knew I didn't want to be on my knees. I didn't want him braced behind. I wanted to see those jade eyes. The very eyes that had triggered my obsession with a Kostava. I wanted to feel his powerful body thrust on top of me. I wanted him nursed between my open thighs.

Fighting the building pleasure taking hold, I murmured, "Zaal . . ."

But he was lost in a haze of pleasure. Lost as he fucked me, owned me, possessed me.

Zaal ripped a roar from his mouth as my core squeezed hard, choking his length. Lifting on my weakened hands, I forced myself forward, Zaal falling out from within me.

His eyes snapped open as I rolled onto my back. His face screamed predatory danger; pupils dilated and teeth gritted in frustration. He reached down to my waist to flip me back on all fours. I held up my hand.

Panting, searching for air, I shook my head vigorously, stopping him dead in his tracks. "Stop . . . Zaal . . . please . . . ," I breathlessly begged. He stilled.

"I need . . . I need . . . you . . . ," he fought to say, his English pronunciation nearly unintelligible as he fought to remain calm.

I stared at his rolling muscles, sweat dripping on his olive skin and that huge cock, rigid against his stomach.

"Take me like this," I said through broken breaths. Zaal's cheek twitched. His forehead creased in confusion.

I slowly lay down on my back, spread my legs, and held out my arms. Zaal's gaze ran over my begging body, lingering on my wet, open center. My breasts ached at the thought of him back inside me. I needed to feel him fill me. I needed him to own me.

Then a wash of insecurity filled Zaal's face. A thought suddenly struck me: he'd never taken anyone like this before. The Jakhuas truly did treat him like an animal, only letting him fuck from behind.

"I don't understand?" Zaal's guttural and desperate voice confided.

My heart dropped at the apprehension spreading across his face, as he clenched his fists by his side.

"Come here," I prompted, coaxing him to come closer with my fingers. Zaal, breathing too fast, bent on all fours and, with the power only a predator could possess, crawled slowly over my awaiting body.

He stared down at me, the ends of his long hair tickling my breasts. He stared into my eyes, waiting for further instruction.

I pressed my hand against his face. His cheek nuzzled against my touch. "Take me like this," I whispered. His eyes widened. I smiled, and heard a hiss pass through his clenched teeth. "Take me as you look into my eyes, with your skin brushing against mine." Zaal hung on my every word as I guided his oversize chest down over my breasts. I whispered into his ear, "Come in me, like this."

A growl built in his throat as he lowered himself down. His thighs lay in between mine. Skirting my hand down between our bodies, I palmed his cock, slick with my wetness. Zaal groaned, his mouth dropping open at the feel. Placing his rigid cock at my entrance, I pushed the head inside and said, "Take me."

Zaal's eyes met mine as he thrust forward and filled me to the hilt. Zaal's strong arms braced on either side of my head, but as he rocked back and forth, I noticed he wasn't as rough, he was filling me, taking me, but he was *feeling* me, slowly and deliberately owning me.

Zaal's eyes watched my mouth as I licked along my lips. His breathing hitched at the sight. Guiding my hands up his taut arms, Zaal lowered to thread his arms under my shoulders. I gasped as his hard chest pressed against mine.

This close, I could make out every line of his handsome face, the three moles to the left of his eye humanizing this man. Zaal stared at my lips and his thrusts paused.

We lay here breathing each other in, joined in the most primitive way. I smoothed back his long black hair from his face, and felt a fissure in my heart. This, right now, in this very moment, something soul-shattering passed between us. He'd come into my life like a storm. A storm I didn't want, one I'd prepared all my life to hate, to fight. But it brought with it refreshing rain. It cleared the skies and brought out only warmth.

Zaal was saving me, liberating me from loneliness.

My throat was chock-full with emotion as I lay here, staring into his eyes. Then Zaal took a long breath, traced his nose along my cheek and whispered, "*Potzeluy.*"

Kiss.

Feeling my body fill with warmth, I cast Zaal a watery smile and guided his mouth to mine. His long hair cocooned us, protecting us in our own space. His full lips were like butterfly wings, whispering against my lips. This was in stark contrast to the animalistic rage and primal presence he exuded.

But when his tongue pushed through to my mouth, my tongue

tentatively meeting his, Zaal's hips moved, his length pushing harder into me.

We kissed. He thrust. My hands explored. My palms met hot skin: his shoulders, his waist, and his back. With every sensation of my touch, Zaal's pace increased. His lower abdomen dragged over my clit. Crying out, such sensitivity almost too much to stand, my hands gripped on to his ass. Zaal roared into my mouth.

He devoured me with his mouth.

He dominated me with his strength.

But my heart, my heart was giving itself to him. With every thrust he made inside me, another piece of my heart broke and melded into his.

Zaal's hips moved faster and faster, his movements jerky and erratic. Pressure built in my spine. I almost came undone as Zaal's moist lips dragged across my cheek, peppering me with kisses and swipes of his tongue. He traveled to my neck and I cried out as his damp chest grazed against my hard nipples.

"Zaal," I moaned, my voice hitching.

"Talia," he grunted back. My fingers kneaded his ass, driving him even further into me.

I couldn't take it. I couldn't take the desire surging through my veins, the want and need for this man lit me up from the inside. Zaal's skin brushed against my clit; pounding, circling, teasing. I dug my nails in, bit down on Zaal's shoulder, and burst apart, as the most intense orgasm of my life tore through my core.

I came, coating Zaal's cock. The walls of my pussy clenching, I gripped Zaal's dick until he began to snarl. The sounds pouring from his mouth were vicious and raw, but everything told me how he felt— that he was feeling the same magnetic draw as me.

Zaal's unrelenting hips suddenly stilled. His head whipped back, neck corded. He thundered as he came, his cum bathing my pussy with warmth. It was enough to take me over again, but my attention was fixed on Zaal's face . . . on the pure pleasure our joining had brought to him.

As the last of Zaal's thrusts jerked into me, he dropped his forehead to my shoulder. I ran gentle fingers down his spine. My eyes were closed as he shrouded me with his warmth. Then it was just us.

Joined.

Replete.

Melded.

As we lay in each other's arms, a tear slipped from the corner of my eye. The betrayal to my family was complete; realized and profound. But so were my feelings for Zaal.

Weeks of watching him pace back and forth in the basement, held captive in chains, gave birth to my *obsession*. Watching him leech whatever drug they'd pumped in his veins, as he lay—broken—on the floor, had given birth to my *compassion*. Watching him slumped against the wall, shackled, with lost and lonely eyes, gave birth to my *affection*. But lying here, taken and warm in his arms; well, that had opened my heart.

Zaal was in my whole heart.

The hammering of his strong pulse began to slow. His soft breaths on my neck evened out. My hands continued to trace the ridges of his spine. Then Zaal lifted his head.

My eyes met his, and my heart cracked.

Tears filled his eyes, a disbelieving expression possessed his face. "Zaal?" I asked, my voice barely above a whisper. "What's wrong?"

Two tears fell over his cheeks and trickled down his olive skin, then down onto my chest, rolling over his identity ink. My heart constricted at this devastating sight, then completely shattered when he sucked in a stuttered breath and asked, "I . . . I am truly *free*?"

Wrapping my arms around his neck, I held him tight due to the look of utter disbelief on his face.

"Yes," I assured, and nuzzled into his neck. "You're *free*, Zaal. That man can't hurt you anymore. You're safe. You're free. There's no more pain."

His arms around my back tightened as I spoke those words. His breathing was heavy and I could feel the water from his eyes dropping into my hair. "Shh . . ." I soothed, stroking my hands through his hair.

Zaal stayed like that for minutes, still buried inside me. Eventually he lifted his head. I swallowed at the way he stared at me like . . . like I was his everything. "Because . . . of you?" he asked.

I held my breath.

"What?" I whispered.

"Free . . . because of *you*?"

I pressed my hand to his face. "No. My brother freed you. I was already at the house when you were brought here." I glanced down. Redness filled my cheeks. "I watched you in the basement. After weeks spent watching from afar, I . . . I finally had to see you in person."

Zaal's frown was prominent as he mulled over what I'd divulged. I stroked my finger along his cheek. "Do you remember anything about the night you were freed?"

Zaal's face contorted as if he was in pain. His hold on me tightened. "I . . . I remember pain, rage. I remember the chains and wanting to kill. Then venom and pain leaving my body. Then weakness, confusion." His top lip hooked into a flicker of a smile, and he added, "Then you." He exhaled through his nose. "Your small hand on my skin."

Zaal's panicked eyes fixed on me. "Why did your brother free *me*?"

My body froze at his question. Zaal's tense jade irises implored me to answer. But I didn't know what to say. He was still weak, still recovering. I wasn't sure he should hear about his twin brother, his family, the experiments he'd been forced to endure, from my mouth.

Distracting Zaal from his question, I bent his head and pressed a kiss to his forehead. "Shh. Let's get some rest. All will be explained in good time."

Zaal's tense body relaxed with a relieving exhale. I palmed his cheeks. "Shall we go to bed?"

Zaal's face expressed confusion again. He looked around us. "We are already on the floor." I frowned at his strange reply, then my stomach sank. *We are already on the floor. . . .*

God, I thought. My stomach turned over. He'd never slept in a bed. It was why he took me on the floor. He didn't know any better.

"Zaal." I spoke with authority to command his full attention. "You're free now. And you'll sleep in my bed, with me."

His face showed no understanding, so I pushed slightly on his arms. "Stand, and I'll show you," I directed, but Zaal didn't move. "Zaal?" I pushed harder, but he still didn't move.

"You will stay with me?" he asked. I caught a tinge of panic in his voice.

My heart bloomed, and I rolled my head to kiss his arm. "I won't leave your side," I assured.

Zaal's green eyes shone, but he pulled back, his length slipping from within me. I moaned at the sudden feeling of loss.

But suddenly I gasped. My head lifted to stare at Zaal. His fingers were running over my clit and further down. I jerked, still too sensitive, when two of Zaal's fingers pushed within me. I was rooted to the floor. When, unexpectedly, he pulled out his fingers and promptly sat back on his heels.

I was so turned on I could barely think straight.

Gathering my wits, I shakily got to my feet. Zaal was still on the ground, his eyes watching me like a hawk. I moved toward him and held out my hand. He took it without hesitation. Rising slowly to his feet, Zaal's six foot six height eclipsed the fading sunlight streaming through the blinds at my window.

Walking behind him, I ran my hand over my bed. "We sleep in here." Zaal's assessing stare narrowed when it met the comforter.

Releasing his hand, I walked around him. Then he lightly grabbed my wrist. "Where do you go?" His voice betrayed an edge of panic, so I stroked my finger along his forearm. I blushed as I stated, "I'm going to cleanse myself."

He looked down my body, clearly wondering why. Then he fixed his gaze on my pussy and his cum coating my thighs. His face turned stormy. He pulled me back, wrapping me tightly in his embrace. "No," he ordered aggressively. "You stay with me, like this."

My pulse raced, blood coursing through my body. The way he dominated, he owned, he possessed inflamed my already tingling skin. A finger lifted my chin. I found myself falling into his deep green gaze. "Do not cleanse," he said in his strong Georgian accent.

"I won't cleanse," I assured in reply. His hold on me relaxed.

Leaning over Zaal, I pulled back the comforter and climbed into bed. Zaal was standing beside the bed, looking down. I tapped the mattress and said, "Climb in, Zaal. Rest with me."

It took a few seconds, but Zaal did climb into the bed next to me. Immediately he held me in his arms. I inhaled the musk of his warm skin and turned to look him in the eyes.

As we stared at each other, somehow I felt different. This man, and what we'd just experienced, had changed me. *He* was changing me. A small smile spread on my lips as I caught sight of those beautiful three moles on the side of his face.

Zaal drew in a breath. Inching closer, he whispered, "*Potzeluy.*" I closed my eyes.

Without hesitation, I pressed my mouth against his. It was soft, it was tender. I felt like my prayer had been answered.

As I pulled away, Zaal's fingers stroked over my hair. Adopting a serious expression, he repeated quietly, "You are . . . for me?"

Ignoring everything but Zaal and I, our magnetic attraction, and what we'd just shared, I tipped my forehead to meet his, whispering, "Yes, Zaal . . . I think I am . . . *for you.*"

12

LUKA

"One, two, three, four."

I slammed my fists forward, ripping into the flesh of the newly slaughtered pig hanging from the rafter of the gym. Viktor, my death-match trainer from my Dungeon days, counted my reps beside me.

My bladed knuckle-dusters sliced into the pink flesh of the swine, the dripping blood and the cut of the skin almost humanlike as I let the power of my punches loose.

"Drop and give me fifty," Viktor ordered. I did as commanded, falling into my push-ups position. I pushed off the floor, eyes focused forward as Viktor counted me down.

The familiar smells of the gym filled my nose, the sounds of clang-ing metal, grunts, and punching bags being struck brought me back to life. But a rip of guilt also sliced through my chest. Kisa had no idea I'd been training again. She had no idea that I'd called on Viktor to get me match fit again. To be Raze ready.

In the weeks that I'd been back in Brooklyn, the street war between the Bratva and the Jakhua Georgians had begun. Our men were being targeted, shot, killed, beat. And it incensed me. Fueled the constant rage I'd fought to rein in.

As the *knayz* I was forbidden to fight. The Pakhan wanted to secure the safety of his future successor. But me? I wanted to be on the streets. I wanted to fight among the men. I wanted to take the lives of our enemy. I wanted to be a part of the war, not watching from the sidelines.

Fuck. I needed the violence. Something dark within me still craved it.

And more than that, I wanted Jakhua. Anri's revenge would not be complete until that fucker had died under my blades. I wouldn't move on until that mission had been accomplished. Right now that fucker was in hiding. But at some point he'd show his face, and when he did, I'd be prepped and ready to take him out.

"Fifty," Viktor called, ending my push-ups. I jumped up, only to start my next set of reps on what was left of the decimated pig carcass. I was ten reps in to my routine when I felt someone watching me.

Lifting my head, I searched the gym, and my eyes fell on Kisa standing near the entrance to her office. My stomach rolled. She was meant to be out for the day. She was never meant to know I was training again. She wouldn't understand why I needed this.

Halting in my training session, sweat pouring down my face, I breathed hard as I stared at my wife. Her expression was unreadable as she stood motionless just watching me in my gym shorts, my blood-covered 'dusters firmly on my fists.

"Shit, been caught," Viktor muttered under his breath from beside me. He threw Kisa a guilty wave. She waved back, then turned to go into her office. When the door shut, I dropped my head and felt Viktor's hand land on my shoulder.

"You better go sort that out, kid," he said. "I'll clean up here."

Nodding, I slid the 'dusters off my fingers and headed for the office. As I walked through the mob of this season's recruits perfecting their skills, I couldn't help but size each one of them up. And I automatically knew I could take them all. For most, there wouldn't even be a contest. I would slaughter them in seconds. I tried my hardest to push those thoughts from my mind.

It was no longer my life.

I reached Kisa's office, and with my hand hovering over the knob, I took a deep breath and walked in. As the door shut, I stepped forward, unsure of how Kisa was going to react to finding me training.

I walked before her desk and slumped down in the seat opposite. I stared at the table, hands gripping the edge, not saying a damn word. Kisa didn't move for several seconds, until she leaned forward and ran her finger over my wedding ring.

I watched as her finger traced the edges of the gold ring and I held my breath. "How long have you been training?" she asked. Every one of my muscles tensed.

Briefly closing my eyes, I opened them to look up at my wife and confessed, "Awhile." *Four months to be exact,* I added in my head.

"Here?" she asked. I nodded my head. "Under my nose, hiding in plain sight, or is it only in the shadows or when I'm gone?"

I sat back in my seat at the anger in Kisa's voice. She was rarely pissed at me. Clearly my training had pissed her the fuck off. "You wouldn't understand," I replied.

Kisa's angered face immediately filled with hurt. And I immediately felt like shit. "I would, Luka. I would understand," she whispered. "If you'd talked to me, I would've understood."

Her cut voice made me look up at her beautiful face. I could see pain written all over it. And it cut me to shreds. Sighing, I stood and moved around her desk. When I reached Kisa's side, I pushed her chair back and sat before her on the edge of her desk.

My taped-up hand ran down her soft cheek and she leaned into my palm. "I need it, *solnyshko.* I need to train, to fight. This was my life for so long that it's all I really know. It's part of me now. Here, in this gym, I feel more at peace than I do when we are with our fathers. I tried to not come here, but I couldn't. I had to come back."

"*Lyubov moya,*" she whispered sympathetically, and shuffled forward on her seat. Kisa's hands ran up my thighs. I stared down at her and sighed.

This woman was my world. The woman God created perfectly just for me.

Kisa rubbed her lips together and cautiously informed, "I saw our fathers outside." She didn't add anything else, just let that information hang in the air.

I stiffened and clenched my jaw. "They saw me," I confessed dejectedly, "they saw me sparring in the cage, saw me break a man's nose and knock him out cold." I glanced up at Kisa as I remembered finding my father and the Pakhan watching me ringside in shock as I towered over the man I'd forced to the ground.

"I could see their disappointment," I said. "My father hadn't said a word. He just watched me wipe the spattered blood off my chest before walking out of the gym. The Pakhan followed. I disappointed them, I could see it in their faces. I'm not the man they want. I *shame* them, Kisa." Kisa's hands tightened on my thighs and her head tipped to the side.

Spurred on by her touch, I said, "They don't want this man I am now, *solnyshko*. They want the Luka from the past. The promise of that kid they knew years ago. They don't want this." I pointed to my cut knuckles and my identity tattoo. "They don't want the fucked-up monster who can't shake the conditioning from the gulag."

"Luka," Kisa whispered, and got to her feet. Her hands pushed through my hair as she stood flush to my chest. She guided me straight to her lips. Kisa's sweet taste immediately exploded in my mouth and made me feel better. I moaned against Kisa's mouth, and as she wrapped her arms around my waist, I pulled her further against my chest.

Kisa finally broke away then threaded her arms around my neck. Her eyes met mine. As I got lost in her blue understanding stare, I said, "I can be the *knayz*, Kisa, I know I can. But I have to be the heir *on my terms*."

Kisa's arms tightened and she said, "Papa and Ivan don't want their Bratva's inner circle to be violent."

My jaw clenched when I thought of the Bratva set up before I returned. "Alik Durov fought in the Dungeon, in the cage. He fought our rivals and enemies on the streets. No fucker threatened the Bratva with him as *knayz*. And they should fear me just the same, if not more. Instead, I'm on a fucking leash. People will think me weak, Kisa. Jakhua attacks our men daily. But I'm expected to sit in an office with Kirill and my father, pushing pens and watching it all happen from behind a mahogany desk." My muscles burned that sad truth.

Bringing my hand to my chest, I said, "I could lead our men on the streets, attack our enemies until they crawl back into the holes they slid from." I leaned forward, my blood pumping faster just imagining it. "I could make the Volkov Bratva unrivaled, Kisa. I could make us stronger than ever. I just need that chance. I need our fathers to trust in me, in the man I am now. Violence included."

Blood drained from Kisa's face. She lost all color. Moving backward, she slumped back on her seat. I watched her in confusion.

"Kisa?"

"You want back in the Dungeon?" she whispered brokenly. "You want to fight like Alik did in the cage, on the streets? Even now you want that? Even now you have your life back? Now you have me. Do you still want to kill like him, too?"

I bent down, my knees hitting the floor. By the look on Kisa's face, I knew I shouldn't have said anything. "No, baby," I assured. I pushed her brown hair back from her face. "I fucking hated Durov. There's not a single day that goes by that I don't remember killing him and feeling fucking fine with it. But"—I took a deep breath and confessed—"at least he got to be who he really was."

Kisa was motionless waiting for me to continue.

I tried to think of a way to explain myself better. Taking her hand, I said, "I don't want to fight in the cage anymore. But I don't know who I am without the fight, if that makes sense. I am the fight. I am death. It's who I am. It's who I was molded to be."

My eyes dropped to stare at the floor when Kisa didn't say anything in response. Why the fuck she was with me was a mystery to me. I was fucked in the head. I was irredeemable. She deserved better than me. She'd been forced to be with Alik Durov for years in my absence. And she'd hated it. He'd hurt her, made her life hell with his need for blood and violence.

I sucked in a painful breath. I wasn't much of an improvement on that cunt. I needed those things, too. Probably just as much.

Suddenly Kisa crouched to the floor. Her arms wrapped around my shoulders and I immediately sagged into her chest.

"I love you, *lyubov moya*. Since birth and until the end," she whispered, pushing any self-hatred I had to the side.

I sighed as she said exactly what I needed to hear and held her tight. "I love you, too, *solnyshko*. Always."

Kisa leaned back, searching my face, and I couldn't stop myself from kissing her again. I broke from her mouth and pressed my forehead against hers.

We stayed there awhile in silence until Kisa pulled back. I reached out and took hold of her wrist, suddenly remembering she'd been to the doctor this morning. I'd noticed she'd been sick and off color lately. It was worrying the hell out of me.

"How was your doctor's appointment?" I asked.

Kisa stared at me, her blue eyes seeming to lose focus. With an abrupt squeeze of my hand in hers, she quickly smiled and said, "Just a stomach flu, baby. Nothing to worry about."

I sighed in relief, and got to my feet. I offered her my hand, too. Sliding her palm over mine, Kisa got to her feet. I wrapped her in my arms. "I'm glad it's nothing serious. I love you," I whispered. "More than I know how to express."

Kisa tensed for a brief moment, her breath hitching. Then she held me right back.

13

ZAAL

They started off as images. Pictures of people and places I didn't recognize. They began invading my dreams at night. I watched them as if I was standing on the side. People; men, women, children, both boys and girls. They were happy. They made me feel warm. There were two boys. They looked the same; same hair, same build, same face, but one had brown eyes and the other green.

I couldn't erase their faces from my mind. But every time I thought about them really hard, red-hot pain would slice through my brain . . . then came other images . . . images of blood, of guns, of screams that tore my stomach apart. I couldn't stand them. The screams ignited the fire in my veins, causing me to lose control. But a little girl's screams were the worst. . . . She would scream and I would see two little arms reaching for me to help but something was holding me back . . . then the screams would stop and a pit would form in my stomach.

I wouldn't be able to breathe, and my heart would break, impossible anger tearing me to shreds.

I lay in bed with Talia, my eyes wide open and my arms wrapped around her small waist. I didn't want to close my eyes. I didn't want to rest and have the dreams come back. I didn't want them in my head. I had no idea what they meant but knew they made Talia cry.

She would always cry. When I didn't understand what she wanted me to do, her eyes would fill with tears. She would look at me with her big brown eyes and go quiet.

I didn't like her crying. My stomach would tighten and my chest would burn. I liked her smiling and when her lips would show her teeth. I liked the mole on her lower left cheek and when her long blond hair would lay over one shoulder. When she would stare at me, her cheeks flushing red. When she would put her hand on my face and cool my scalding blood. I liked it when she stroked my long hair, and when she kissed my lips, her tongue pushing inside my mouth.

I liked being with her, and not being with Master. I liked being free with Talia, in this protected house.

But my favorite was how she made me feel. How fast my heart would beat when she lay with me. How I could breathe when she held my hand, her thumb stroking the back of my hand.

And fucking her, though it was different from all the times before. It wasn't the same with her as it was with Master's females. I looked into her eyes. Her hand would stroke my back, then rake through my hair. It was slow. It meant something to me. When we were together I felt full. I only ever remember feeling numb and empty; killing and fucking for Master. Talia made me feel alive. There was no man in a white coat injecting me and making me feel nothing but rage. There was just Talia, and she was all I wanted.

Talia moved in my arms, her face coming into view. I drank in her face and my chest seemed to grow bigger. Her face looked peaceful as she slept. Her big eyes were closed, but still beautiful. Her little nose twitched as she dreamed. Her pink lips parted as she slowly breathed in and out, in and out.

I was tired. I fought the pull of sleep, but with Talia's soothing breathing and warm touch against my body, my eyelids won the battle to close. As I drifted off, I held her to my chest, refusing to let her go. . . .

I lay in the sun by the stream. I loved being outside. I loved the feel of the sun on my face, of the birds singing in the trees.

I heard footsteps crunching the long grass behind me, and suddenly the sun was blocked from my face. I knew who it was, and I didn't even open my eyes as I felt him before me. "Move," I said. A foot kicked my leg. A laugh tore from my brother's throat and I felt him drop down to lie beside me.

"You're always out here," he said. I rolled my head to the side and opened my eyes. His face, identical to mine, was looking right at me.

I shrugged. "I like the sun. I like the warmth. I hate the darkness. If I could live in forever sunshine, I would."

My brother nodded with a smirk on his face, then looked up at the clouds in the sky. We were always together, him and I. Wherever he went, I went. Mama used to say we were a team, better together than we'd ever be apart.

"Papa's called a meeting today," he said. I closed my eyes. "He wants us to be with him. He's meeting with the men from Kutaisi. They're all coming here."

A shiver ran down my spine. "I don't want to go." I thought of the head of that clan. "The man, the leader always stares at us. He makes me feel strange. I hate him."

My brother was silent for a moment, then said, "I feel like that around him, too."

I snapped my eyes open and turned to my side. My brother did the same, the two of us lying on our sides so we could talk. "You do?" I whispered.

"Yes. He . . . he makes shivers go down my spine."

I took a deep breath and looked into my brother's brown eyes. "I think Papa likes him."

My brother's eyes narrowed. "I think he does, too."

"I don't trust him," I admitted. My brother reached out and laid his hand over mine.

"Nor do I." I took a deep breath and I could feel my cheek twitch in nerves. "But we have to go. We have to become strong men to lead our clan."

My brother released his hand and I stared at his face. "You'll lead. You're the oldest. You're the heir."

He laughed, and it made me smile. "By four minutes."

I shrugged, but his hand squeezed mine. "No, brother. You're my twin. Grandmama says we share strength. We'll lead together. We will always be together. We're stronger together. You know this."

Losing my smile, I nodded my head. "I know. But you'll always be my older brother to me." My brother smiled. We both lay down on our backs.

"Papa wants us to cut our hair," my brother said. I turned my head to face his. "I told him we liked it long. Grandmama agreed. I think we'll be able to keep it long." He looked over at me and smiled. "It's long and black, like Georgian warriors of old used to wear."

"Yeah," I agreed, "we'll never cut it and we will always be warriors."

"You and me," my brother said.

"You and me," I agreed.

"And me!" a little voice called from behind us. I smiled and rolled onto my knees. A little girl was hiding in the grass. Her long black hair stood out against the tall green grass.

My brother rolled his eyes, then closed his eyes, his face soaking in the hot sun. But I stretched up, smiled at my little sister hiding in the field.

"Mmm . . . did you hear something, brother?" I said, and heard my sister's giggle from a few feet away.

My brother grunted, too busy falling asleep.

I crept forward and said aloud, "It sounded like Zoya. Didn't you think it sounded like Zoya?" I played along.

More laughter came from just in front of me. Two brown eyes appeared in the grass, so dark they looked like darkness itself.

"Mmm . . . I wonder where she could be?" I said, and pretended to search the grass. When her giggles became too loud to ignore, I couldn't help but smile. In seconds, my five-year-old sister jumped from the grass and ran straight at me. Her laughing face was the last thing I saw before she launched into my arms, knocking me back, near my brother.

My brother cracked one eye and, smirking, shook his head at my sister. Then he went back to sleep.

Zoya pulled back and her little hands pressed against my cheeks as she sat on my lap. "Sykhaara," she said to me, using Grandmama's pet name for me, "my sweetness," "I came to get you. Papa wants you both home 'now'!" I laughed as she imitated our papa's deep voice. She laughed when I laughed. "He said some men are coming and you have to dress up and meet them. 'You have to learn the family business'!" she imitated again, her little hands on her hips.

My brother laughed at our little sister as he stayed in his position beside us and Zoya nodded her head meaningfully. Her eyebrows pulled together and she asked, "Who are the men?"

I tapped the end of her nose. "Papa's friends."

"Ohhh," she replied, "so they're my friends, too?"

My brother this time sat up. His face was serious. "Yes, they're your friends, but just be careful, okay, Zoya. They're dangerous men."

Her face was serious and she nodded her head, repeating, "Friends, but be careful. They're dangerous."

"Yes," I said, but that hollow feeling was back in my stomach. The three of us walked back toward the house, Zoya in my arms.

Her finger pointed to my face. "One, two, three," she counted tapping the side of my left cheek.

"What are you doing?" I asked. She prodded my upper cheek.

"One, two, three," she repeated, "the moles beside your eye."

She reached out and put her hand on our brother's face. "You don't have them."

"No," he said, reaching out and tickling her ribs. Our sister screamed and laughed until our brother stopped and ruffled her black hair.

"It's okay," she said, and tapped his shoulder. "He has one for each of us." She pointed to me, "one," then pointed to herself, "two," then pointed to our brother, "three." She nodded her head proudly. "One mole for each of us."

I turned her face to look at me. "And what about the babies? What about your other brother and sister? I don't have five moles. I don't have enough for all of us."

She scowled. "Uh-uh. They're babies. They cry and cry." She put one of her hands on my face and one on my brother's. "You're mine. My big twin brothers. The babies have each other. Papa said when you're big and strong you'll protect me and no one will hurt me because you'll scare them all away."

My brother moved over and whipped her from my arms. He threw her in the air and she squealed. He pulled her to his chest, kissed her on her cheek, and said, "And that's true. We'll always protect you."

"I know," she said smugly, and pointed that little finger between the three of us again. "One, two, three . . . Zoya, Zaal, and An—"

I gasped and my eyes snapped open. I lurched forward. Sweat poured from my body. My hands were shaking. I looked down at my hands, they wouldn't stop shaking. I blinked and blinked and searched for air, the little girl's words circling my mind. . . .

One, two, three. Zoya, Zaal, and An—

Pain stabbed behind my eyes as I tried to remember more. I shouted out in frustration. The pain blocked something in my mind, something I wanted to remember.

You'll forget them all, Master's voice ordered. A chain whipped along my back, hands tied behind my back as I hung off the wall. You're mine. You have no past, no family, no other thought than to kill. You're a killer. You'll kill for me. Only me.

"Zaal?" Talia's soft voice suddenly cut into my racing mind. Her hand landed on my shoulder. I closed my eyes, trying to use it to calm.

I could feel her moving beside me. Suddenly, she spread her legs over my lap and placed her palm on my cheek. "Shh . . ." she soothed. "It was only a dream. You're safe, you're here with me."

Papa said when you're big and strong you'll protect me and no one will hurt me because you'll scare them all away.

"Zaal!" Talia pushed, and raked my damp long hair back from my face. "Look at me. Please."

I did as she ordered and locked on to her brown eyes. I swallowed and asked, "Who am I?"

Talia froze, her face paling. I slipped my hands on her bare waist and asked again, "Talia. *Who* am I?"

"Zaal," she whispered. I shook my head.

"No!" I released my hands and gripped the side of my head. "In my head. Pictures, people. Who are they?" I pulled my hand into a fist and hit it against my chest. "Who am I? Zaal? Who is *Zaal*?"

Talia's hand on my face began to shake, but she was frozen on my lap. My heart began to pound. It was too fast, beating too fast. Talia knew something.

"Zaal," she whispered. Fear in her voice.

My stomach churned. I'd made her upset again. I didn't want Talia to be upset.

Pressing my forehead against hers, I asked, "Why do you get upset? Why do you always get sad over me?"

Talia's mouth opened. But no words came out. I gripped her face, and smashed her lips to mine. I pushed my tongue into her mouth. Talia groaned, her fingers fisting my hair.

My cock hardened under Talia. She moved forward until her cunt was over my dick. I growled when I felt the wetness, the warmth spreading over me. Running my hands down her back, I lifted her ass, and in seconds pushed her down on my cock. Talia screamed out and her head fell into the crook of my neck. I closed my eyes as her cunt sucked me in, the feel too much.

Fire ran through me as I pushed Talia up and down, her nails scraping against my scalp. I closed my eyes, trying to forget my dream. I pounded her pussy harder and harder, but the more I tried to lose myself in Talia, the more my brain tried to remember.

Pain so strong tried to shoot down my spine. I bowed my back, but my cock thrust harder in Talia. It felt too good to let the pain in. I panted. My chest heaved and I gritted my teeth as my head ached. My body fought against both pleasure and pain. I couldn't take it, couldn't take the confusion.

Snapping my head back, I released a rage-fueled roar and, gripping the back of Talia's thighs, pushed her on her back, my cock still fixed tight inside her cunt. Talia shouted in surprise as I smashed my chest against her breasts. Eyes forward, my arms tensed and braced at each side of her head. I slammed forward, Talia's legs wrapping tightly around my waist.

My nostrils flared with the severity of my thrust and I shook my head trying to fight the pain.

Below me, Talia moaned. I built up speed, the bed smashing off the wall. Talia's hands grasped my hair. She forced me to look down.

Sweat was dripping down her chest, strands of her blond hair slapping against her flushed face. Her eyelids were cast, and her mouth was slightly open. I slammed into her even more.

I squeezed my eyes shut when her gaze met mine. Shame ran through me. I was being too hard. I tried to slow, but Talia's hands gripped my arms.

"Fuck it out of you, *zolotse*. Take from me what you need." I fought to control the urge to fuck her hard . . . then I stilled as I heard what she said, *zolotse,* my gold.

"*Zolotse* . . . ," I murmured, getting harder still off the endearment. Talia's face flushed red, but her brown eyes never moved from mine. *Zolotse.*

My head fell to her chest. Talia's hands pushed through my hair. I panted and tried to rid myself of my rage, my confusion, my frustration, but I couldn't. It wouldn't go.

Then Talia's mouth moved to my ear and she whispered, "Use me. Use me to rid yourself of the rage, take it out on my pussy."

I stilled, and at her words, my cock swelled until it hurt. "Talia," I growled.

"Do it, Zaal. Take me, *zolotse.*"

At the use of that word, something snapped inside me. Seeing the open look on Talia's face, I broke. Tensing my neck, I thundered out a groan and plowed forward, Talia raking my back with her sharp nails.

I tucked my head into her neck, her scent enveloping me. And I took. I rammed into her over and over again. Possessing her. Owning her. Talia whimpered and moaned, but her pussy tightened like a fist and our skin burned with heat.

"Zaal . . . ," Talia moaned. "Yes, baby, fuck me."

My cock swelled at her words. Talia's breath shortened. Her moans grew louder and louder. Her head threw back, her back arched, and her pussy clenched my dick.

My cock twitched. I couldn't take anymore. Gritting my teeth, I threw my head back, and stilling, my muscles strained, I came so hard I gasped for breath. My body shook as I flooded Talia's cunt. Then I slumped to her chest, our bodies drenched with sweat.

Since she'd freed me from my chains, we spent day and night together like this. We fucked, but gentle and slow. This time I lost control. I felt weak. I was weak. The images in my head were making me *weak*.

Lifting my head, I looked into Talia's eyes. My heart sank. Her brown eyes were wide and weary. Her cheeks were red with how hard I'd taken her.

Racked with shame, I pulled out of her. I lurched backward until my back hit the wall. I stared down at her lying there on the bed, my seed dripping from her thighs. I dropped my head in my hands.

I'd hurt her.

I never wanted to hurt her. But my head. I couldn't control my head. I couldn't stop the pain.

Feeling the bed dip, I froze when Talia's soft hand smoothed across my chest. I kept my head down as her finger traced over my identity tattoo. 221 . . . 221 . . . 221 . . . I was 221.

I sucked in a breath. I knew who 221 was.

He was a killer.

He was Master's killer.

He was the man that lived in chains and darkness.

But Talia called me Zaal. I did not know who Zaal was. A man freed from Master, a man with unexplained dreams and nightmares. The man who craved to be near Talia.

But there was more.

I could feel there was more, more to know, to understand.

Hearing Talia inhale a long breath, I felt her fingertip run along my knee. I raised my head. Talia was staring at my tattoo, then her glassy eyes drifted to meet mine.

I lifted my finger, and ran it over the smooth skin of her arm. "Who am I, Talia?" I asked, my voice broken. "Who is 'Zaal'? I don't know who he is." I breathed in through my nose and pressed my hands against my head. "It causes me pain. I am in pain."

Talia's face contorted as though she was in pain too. But she finally nodded as if she had decided something, and moved to the table beside her bed. She picked up the object she called a phone.

Her back curled inward and I saw it shaking. Then suddenly she spoke. "Luka," she said quietly, "I need you to come here now, and bring Kisa with you. It's Zaal. He's ready."

Talia sat on the seat beside me. Her hands were fidgeting in her lap. She was nervous. I took a deep breath as we stared out of the windows, the sea waves crashing against the shore. I closed my eyes listening to those waves, imagining my feet in the cold sand, the breeze wrapping around my body and the sun shining on my face.

My eyes snapped open as I instantly thought of my dream. The boy laying in grass, his brother beside him. I shook my head from the memory. If I thought too hard the pain would return.

Talia shuffled beside me and I turned to her. "Why are you nervous?" I asked. Talia stilled and her brown eyes looked to me.

"I'm waiting for my brother and his wife to get here. They should arrive any minute." Talia then looked up and met the gazes of her guards. The men were looking at her back, concerned.

The guards did not like me. They would stare at me with narrowed eyes and curled lips. I didn't give a fuck. I didn't like them either. They were guards. All guards I had ever met were weak and unfeeling. They punished for their own enjoyment.

Though they seemed to like Talia. They tried to protect her. From what, I did not know. She never talked about her life with me. She never told me anything. I realized that since she had freed me from the basement we hadn't talked of much at all. We had fucked. I'd held her in my arms, but not much else.

I didn't understand why.

I opened my mouth to ask Talia again why her brother freed me. Just as I did, a bell sounded. I lurched forward at the sound and the guards left the room.

When Talia and I were left alone, I reached for her arm and turned her to face me. I narrowed my eyes. "You are afraid. Why?"

Talia's eyes darted to the side. Unable to stand it, I picked her up and placed her on my lap. I placed my palms on her cheeks and made her look up. Her bottom lip trembled. Unwilling to see her upset, I leaned forward and pressed my lips against hers. She whimpered into my mouth, her hands wrapping into my hair. Pulling away, I held her against me, the heat in her cheeks warming my palm.

"Talia—"

"Talia?"

I jerked at a male voice calling her name and jumped to my feet. I eyed up the male standing before me. He looked familiar. His hair, his eyes, his build.

The male glared at Talia. My hands fisted at my sides. My chest rose and fell. Suddenly, a female entered the room. Her eyes looked to me, then the man, and finally to Talia.

The female's eyes widened when Talia's hand fell on my arm. The male's eyes narrowed and his head tilted to the side.

Why did I know him?

"Zaal," Talia's soft voice called. I pulled my gaze from the male's stare to look into her face. She lifted onto her toes and pressed her hand against my face. She looked pale and my heart dropped. I didn't understand why she was so worried. I didn't understand what I'd done wrong.

"This is my brother, Luka." Talia pointed at the male who had been glaring. "He's the person who freed you," she explained.

My eyes widened. My attention was naturally drawn back to the male. Talia's fingers stroked down my cheek. I moved my gaze back to her. "Zaal, my brother, Luka, he is like you."

I frowned and Talia edged closer. She placed her other hand on my cheek, cupping my face. I leaned in to press a kiss to her lips. I could feel her lips trembling. Her hands were shaking on my cheeks, but I felt every part of that kiss. Felt her intense sadness.

She was sad for me.

My stomach sank. It was as if her kiss was telling me that something bad was about to happen. As Talia broke away, she ran her hand down my neck, over my chest and down to grip my hand. Feeling eyes watching, Talia turned us to face her brother.

Talia brought us forward. Every cell in my body was alert as the man stared at me. He was dressed in a shirt and pants like Master. He looked like Master. The female behind him, the female with the bright blue eyes moved closer to the male who looked like Master.

Talia brought us to a long seat and urged me to sit. I followed her lead, but my eyes never left the male. He was tall, broad, and strong. He had scars on his face and arms. I looked down at my arms. They were like mine.

Talia's brother and the female slowly sat on the seat opposite us. The room was filled with tension and silence. It made me want to get up and leave.

The male watched me, then turned to Talia. "How long?"

I tensed when the question came from his lips. Talia flushed red and bowed her head. "Awhile."

The male's face hardened and his jaw clenched. "And you didn't think to tell me?"

Talia was silent. The finger wrapped around mine tightened. The female next to her reached over and got the male's attention. She shook her head at him. The male's eyes focused back on me. His hard eyes flickered to Talia, but not for long.

I pulled on Talia's hand and her head lifted. Brown eyes met mine and I stroked my free hand down her face to make sure she was okay. Talia cast me a small smile and turned back to her brother.

"Luka," she said quietly, her voice timid as though she was afraid of what he might say, "Zaal has been free of the drug for weeks. He has been gaining strength each day." Her eyes fell, then fluttered nervously back up. "That's why he is out of the basement. He changed when the drug left him. I have . . . I've been caring for him." She sucked in a deep breath. "I've been with him."

Talia glanced up at me and brought our joined hands to her mouth, her lips pressing a kiss to the back of my hand.

"Talia," the female opposite whispered as though she was shocked, attracting my attention. She smiled sadly at her friend and then smiled across at me. But I watched the male. I watched his unmoving expression.

"Luka," Talia said, her voice suddenly seeming more powerful than before, "I asked you to come here today because Zaal has started having dreams, flashes of people and pictures he can't explain. He wants to know why you freed him from Jakhua. He wants to know where he's from. He wants to know who he is." Talia's voice never wavered, and she added, "I know some, but not much. I thought this would be best coming from you. That's why I called you here today. It wasn't for any other reason."

Her steely gaze lay upon her brother, and I felt my chest swell with pride that she was by my side. "I didn't want to get anything wrong. It's important he hears it correctly. The whole truth, from someone who was there for part of it."

My hot blood pumped in my veins as I listened to Talia speak, then it froze to ice, my lungs squeezing all air from my chest.

. . . he wants to know why you freed him from Jakhua. He wants to know where he's from. He wants to know who he is. . . .

Talia's brother rose from his seat. He walked toward us. Talia squeezed my hand so tightly that, for a moment, I thought she might fear her brother. Rage spiked in my blood at the thought of him taking her from me. I jumped to my feet.

I was taller than her brother.

Bigger.

I had size, but there was no fear in his eyes as he fixed his attention on me. My muscles tensed as he approached. One thought controlled me: protect Talia.

"Get back," I snarled as he approached.

But he didn't. He just kept coming. I braced on my feet and ignored Talia's nervous breathing behind me. My head lowered in anticipation of the strike. Suddenly, staring me right in the eyes, the man ripped off his shirt, threw it to the ground, and halted only feet away.

My body couldn't move, too overcome by the picture before me.

818. His chest read *818.* His tattoo, his identity ink, just like mine.

The man lifted his hand and traced his number with his finger. "I am like you," he said roughly. He took a step closer. "I was taken from my family as a child and forced into a gulag. I was made to fight against my will. Pumped full of drugs until I felt nothing but rage. Injected with more drugs to forget my home, my family. I lived only to kill. I was trained to maim, to slaughter, to annihilate. I was Raze, a champion death-match fighter. I was 818. I was death."

I swayed on my feet. Never had I met anyone like me. Never had I met another with this tattoo who wasn't a slave girl.

A shot of pain pierced my head and my hands gripped the side of my skull. A number pushed through to my mind, but I could not make out what it was 2 . . . 3 . . . 6 . . . no, it was scrambled, it was—

"Shh . . . ," Talia soothed, her hand running up my chest. I cracked open one eye and flinched at the bright light of the sun.

I wrapped Talia in my arms, gaining strength from her touch. I looked over her head at the man, at 818, and asked, "A gulag? I do not know what that is."

Darkness swept over his face. "It is an underground prison. We were kept in cells, like you. Chained up, like you. We were forced to learn how to fight to the death, like you. The only way to survive was to win our matches. I won all mine. And I survived. I got free."

The male swallowed as he said this. Something made him step back. I pressed my hand on my chest. "I am free now?"

He nodded. "I came and freed you from your Master, Jakhua. You were on a drug they are selling. It makes you want to kill. It makes you angry, so angry that the only way to ease it is violence. You have been tested on by Jakhua since you were eight years old. Jakhua uses you as an example of how his drug works. He takes away your free will. On the serum, you do anything he asks of you. You kill anyone he commands, and forget anyone from your past."

My heart stuttered as I tried to understand what I was being told. "Eight years old," I rasped. "A child?" The man nodded and Talia sniffed back tears. She cried, her head tucked against my stomach. My hand on her back tightened and I asked, "How old am I now?"

"Twenty-nine," Talia whispered from my hold. Her head lifted. "You are twenty-nine, Zaal. That man, that sick man you call 'master' has held you captive for over twenty years."

I staggered back. My legs hit the long seat behind me and I dropped down in disbelief. Over twenty years.

My eyes closed as I pictured Master's face. I thought of his short dark hair, his harsh brown eyes. I thought of his mouth, his hands, his fists. Too many fractured images raced through my head—screaming. I was screaming, my arms held out for someone. Blood. Blood, so much blood.

And I felt rage. I felt a rage burn in me that I couldn't explain.

"What happened?" I asked coldly, and looked up to 818. "Why did you free me?"

818 walked back to his seat and sat down. His shoulders sagged, but his dark eyes met mine and he asked, "Do you remember anything before you belonged to your master?"

I shook my head, but remembered my dreams. Remembered the two boys that looked alike. The little girl. My eyes widened. The little girl tapping my face counting *"one, two, three . . ."*

I lifted my hand to my face, to my left cheek and felt for the moles. Talia was suddenly before me, on her knees. She watched my hands. "Do you remember something, Zaal?"

"One, two, three . . . ," I said, my eyes still picturing the little girl's dark eyes and hair. Talia's eyes narrowed in confusion, but as she moved my fingers from my face, her thumb stroked over that same spot.

"Your three moles?" she asked.

"One, two, three," I murmured. I looked into her eyes. "Three of us walking. Two boys and a little girl." I forced my mind to remember. I touched my long hair. "The boys had long black hair." My breathing increased as I remembered. "They looked the same."

"Yes," 818 confirmed. My eyes snapped up.

"Who?" I grunted, my hands beginning to shake.

818 swallowed and said, "Your brother, your twin brother, Anri."

I stared and stared as 818's words carried into my mind. . . . *your twin brother, Anri, your twin brother, Anri . . .*

I tried to remember but nothing else came. Frustration built in my chest. I barked, "Continue. I want more. I need to hear more." Talia gripped my hand, but I couldn't look at her. I needed to know more without distraction.

"I knew him," 818 suddenly said. "I knew your brother."

I stilled. "How?" I asked.

"He was in the gulag, the Georgian underground prison, with me. He was the best fighter we had." 818's eyes misted with water and he rasped, "He was my best friend."

818's face dropped as he spoke those last two words. Frustration built in my veins. "I do not remember him," I snapped. "I do not remember knowing him." I breathed through my nose. "What else?" I asked. "Tell me more."

818 lifted his head, took a deep breath, and said, "You are from Georgia, eastern Europe."

"Where are we now?"

"We're in the United States, *zolotse*. In New York." I looked to Talia and my heart sank. Her beautiful eyes were staring up at me, her sadness shining through.

"I do not know any of this, Talia. I cannot remember anything and it hurts." I pressed my hand on my heart. "Inside of me feels empty."

"I know," she soothed. Talia got to her feet and sat in my lap. Her palm pressed against my cheek and she pressed her lips to mine. As she pulled away, I took a long breath. "Let Luka tell you about your past. Your memories will return. Don't force them, just let them return of their own accord."

Luka cleared his throat. "You were the prototype for the drug you have been on. Your memories are still within you, but it will take you time to get them all back."

"You know this?" I asked, my eyes noticing the many scars on his flesh.

"I'm living it," he replied, "and I was not on the same drug as you. Your drug was far worse, much more powerful."

My fingers clenched. My teeth started to grind at that information, but I nodded my head for Luka to continue.

"You had a large family, Zaal. Two sisters and two brothers. You were the eldest, with your twin. You had a sister who was five, and a younger set of siblings, a baby girl and a baby boy."

I worked on breathing, though it was a challenge. "Go on," I pushed.

Luka continued. "Jakhua was a family friend, the boss of an allied

Mafia family. Then one day, he came into your house . . ." Luka took a deep breath. My stomach tightened. I felt I should know this. I knew this piece of information was important.

"Go on!" I bit out. Luka's brown eyes met mine.

"And he killed them all. Massacred your family, right in front of your eyes."

Talia went absolutely still and turned her face into my neck. I breathed in and out, in and out. No memory returned, but anger did. Anger for what Jakhua had done. For taking away my family.

"He spared your lives, Zaal. Took you and your twin, Anri, with him to experiment on. He put you through test after test to see if the drug worked. Eventually after a few years, with you, it worked one hundred percent." He left that hanging in the air.

"And him, my brother?" I inquired.

"Only partially. He would forget things for a time, but the drug never lasted long enough to take all his free will. Jakhua needed subjects with full obedience. He knew your brother wouldn't give him that. So he sent him to the gulag, where I met him a few years later."

My muscles ached and I felt exhausted. I clutched on to Talia, praying for a memory, any flicker of my past. But I was numb. Nothing was there in my fucked-up mind.

Talia, feeling me tense, stroked my skin, pressing kisses to my neck.

"And my . . . my brother?" I asked. The room went completely silent. Luka dropped his head, ran his hand through his hair. He looked up and rasped, "He died recently. Died in a death-match cage. In a fight."

My chest squeezed. My cheek twitched. I waited for the pain of losing a sibling, but nothing came. It was like my brain had switched off.

The female beside Luka laid her head on his shoulder, whispering in his ear. Luka turned into her touch and she kissed him on his cheek. Luka's tired eyes met mine and I said, "You were there."

Luka nodded his head. "I made him a promise that I would seek revenge on his captors. We found out it was Jakhua, then we found out about you. I freed you because that is what Anri would have done if roles were reversed." Luka's eyes blazed with a sudden flare of fury. "And next I'll kill Jakhua. I'll get your brother his ultimate revenge."

I sat, staring at Luka. His female's eyes were glistening as she watched me. I glanced down. Talia was curled against my chest, but her beautiful big eyes were studying me carefully. It was like she was waiting for me to break.

I lowered my head at the female who was keeping me whole. I pressed a kiss to her head. "Are you okay, *zolotse*?" she whispered brokenly.

I nodded without words. All three of them were staring at me like I should react. Truth was, I didn't feel anything. I had a list of events that had happened in my life, but it didn't feel like my life. I felt like Zaal and Anri were strangers to me.

I was still 221.

I wasn't Zaal.

Talia sat up further, but I couldn't meet her eyes. "Zaal?" she asked again, but my eyes drifted to the staircase leading to the bedroom I'd been sharing with Talia. There I was happy. I had her and she had me.

Here, I was lost, numb. I didn't know who I was meant to be. I didn't know the family I used to have.

Talia made me someone. I was her Zaal.

But alone, I was nothing more than a number. Than Master's *dzaghii*, his dog.

Lifting Talia in my arms, I placed her on the seat and got to my feet. "I am tired," I said. I walked toward the door.

"Zaal?" Talia called, and ran up behind me. I turned and she pressed her small body against my chest, questions swimming in her eyes.

I lowered my head and pressed my forehead to hers. I breathed in her scent and felt warmth flood through my body. Since I had awoken drug free, I had needed her as much as I'd needed the old drug. But right now, I needed to be alone.

"I need to rest. I need. I need . . ."

"To be alone," she said, finishing my words.

I pressed my lips to her forehead and said, "It is not because I do not want you. It is because I need to think I—"

"It's okay," she whispered. "You go and sleep. You're still recovering and today has been a lot for you to take in."

I headed to the stairs, but turned back to Luka and asked, "Zaal is my first name. What was my family's name?"

Luka's eyes shot to mine. Tensing his jaw, he stated, "Kostava. You are Zaal Kostava from Tbilisi, Georgia. You and Anri were the heirs of the Kostava clan, a Mafia family."

I soaked in those words and I wrapped my mind around that name, Kostava. Zaal Kostava.

Leaving Talia in that room took more strength than I ever could imagine. She was a part of me now. As I walked up the stairs to the bedroom, my hand felt empty without hers clutching mine.

I walked into the room and stared into the emptiness. My pulse raced and my palms began to sweat. Being alone again brought memories of being back in a cell. I fought the urge to go back downstairs.

I wanted to remember and rest.

I needed to find out who I really was.

Remember exactly how Master had taken my life from me. Exactly what he'd done to my twin brother and me.

I strode to the mirror hanging on the wall and stared at my reflection. My black hair ran down over my shoulders, my skin was marked with scars and marks. Then I looked to my face and I remembered what Luka had said. I had a twin. Anri. We looked exactly alike.

Then I looked to my left cheek and the three moles beside my eye. *One, two, three. One, two, three,* the little girl's voice sounded in my head. I could almost feel her little finger tapping at my skin.

A sister. My sister. Dark eyes and dark hair, clutched in my arms.

My heart sped up as I tried to remember more. But nothing else came. That was all I had to give, for the moment.

Going to the bed, I removed my hooded sweatshirt and climbed under the comforter. I closed my eyes, Luka's words echoing in my head: *he killed them all. Massacred your family . . . right in front of your eyes . . .*

And my name . . . *Kostava. You are Zaal Kostava from Tbilisi, Georgia. You and Anri were the heirs of the Kostava clan, a Mafia family . . .*

14

TALIA

My strength drained as Zaal walked out of the living room and up the stairs to our bedroom. I closed my eyes and took a deep breath. *Our bedroom,* I emphasized in my head. Because that's how it was for me now. It may have only been weeks, but it was weeks of days full of just him and I. I'd taught him about life. I'd showed him the sun, but he'd shown me true freedom. He'd shown me what it was to feel wanted, needed, vital to someone else's happiness.

A deep sigh sounded behind me. I knew I had to face Luka and Kisa. Luka's face was stone when he'd seen me be affectionate with Zaal. I hadn't told Luka he'd changed. I had lied to my brother repeatedly when he'd called in to check on Zaal's progress.

And I'd done it on purpose. I'd wanted Zaal to myself. Just for once, I'd wanted to have something that wasn't Bratva owned.

Zaal was mine.

In this house he wasn't a Kostava. I wasn't a Tolstaia. We just *were.*

Inhaling a long breath, I slowly turned to see Kisa and Luka staring at me. Luka's expression was stern, but Kisa's was sympathetic.

Silently, I moved toward them, then sat back in the large sofa cushions. Luka's gaze was cold. Shaking my head, I said, "Just get it over with, Luka. You're disappointed in me. You think I've lost my fucking mind."

I caught Luka shift on his seat in my peripheral vision. "I am pissed,

Talia," he said. I raised my eyebrow at how much he sounded like my father. Betrayal of my family now ran through my blood—I got it. I went against the golden rule—*never* betray the family.

Then Luka added, "But not because you're with him. But because you led me to believe he was unchanged. I've been going crazy, believing that he was gone in the head with whatever fucked-up drug they've pumped in his veins for twenty years. For weeks I've been preparing to come back here and kill him, because I thought it was better than leaving him living as Jakhua's monster. I owed Anri that much. His brother would be better off dead than alive, as nothing but a mindless killer."

I swallowed at Luka's answer. Kisa cast me a smile as Luka threaded his hand through hers. I instantly felt guilty, my readiness to argue with my brother vanishing to dust.

I ran my hands down my face and groaned. "I just wanted him to myself, Luka. He was weak and so lost. In fact, I thought he'd died. I'd been watching him on the surveillance footage and could see his gradual change. He was first feral, then weak, then nothing. I thought the cold-turkey drug detox had been too much too soon. But then I went down to see him. I don't know, so he wouldn't be alone, I guess. The change in him, God, it was night and day. On the drugs he was an animal, attacking the guards left, right, and center, pacing the same patch of floor like a pit bull. But when the drugs were gone, he stayed slumped against the wall, his sad green eyes staring at nothing. He was so broken, so lonely and lost . . ." I cleared my throat, remembering him bound, dirty, and matted, in chains.

"I couldn't leave him." I flickered my gaze to my brother and Kisa, then added, "And then he responded to me. He trusted me, and we've grown close." A smile curled on my lips. "He's beautiful. Inside and out."

"Oh, Talia," Kisa said softly. I met the eyes of my best friend. "You love him," she said. My lips parted to argue the case. But as a pair of jade green eyes drifted through my mind I couldn't . . . I couldn't deny Zaal, couldn't deny the impact he'd had on me.

Kisa rose from her seat and came to take me in her arms. I hugged her back, but as she pulled away I could see concern all over her beautiful face. "You don't approve?" I asked. Kisa held my hand.

She shook her head. "Talia, I'm not one to judge. I loved your brother my whole life. You know this. But through grief and duty to the Bratva, to my papa, I was claimed by Alik Durov." Her eyes fell and she shook her head. "But Talia, you know that my father and your father won't accept your being with a Kostava. Under any circumstance."

I glanced to Luka, who was watching us. "Luka?" I asked. He ran his hand down his face.

"Kisa's right. They won't accept it. He's not Russian. He's Georgian. Worse still, his family murdered one of our own."

Devastation cut through me. I lowered my eyes. "So you're saying all I have with Zaal are the next few weeks until I have to return home?" Neither of them said anything in response. But it told me everything I'd asked. To them my situation was hopeless.

But quite frankly, I didn't give a shit what anyone had to say.

Standing, too consumed with concern for Zaal, I decided to go to bed. I refused to accept that I had limited days with Zaal, but if somehow I lost the fight to keep him in my life, I wasn't going to waste a single second.

I released Kisa's hand. She got to her feet. "Talia," she called after me, sympathy for my situation lacing her voice.

"It's okay, Kisa," I said in comfort, throwing her a smile. "I'll be fine. Because what other choice is there? We're Bratva women, stern Russians who brush anything off. I'll work it out. I always do."

Kisa's eyes closed and opened only to showcase the pain she felt for me. I glanced to Luka, who had his hands in his hair. "You're just lucky you found your soul mate at birth." Kisa's eyes sought out her husband and that love, that breathtaking connection they shared pulsed between them. "And that when he was lost, he returned to you." My stomach gripped in envy and I added, "Where for me? Because I've fallen for the enemy, I get to cherish him, hold him, then am expected to let him go all because the great Volkov powers that be don't approve. Question is, how the fuck do you live knowing the person meant solely for you is still out there living and breathing without you by their side?"

Luka got to his feet and I stilled. Since he'd returned, Luka had made no attempt to hold me. He'd never showed any emotion toward me. I watched him approach. Kisa stepped back, a floored expression on her face.

Warily, Luka stood before me, rocking uneasily on his feet. Shock filled my veins as his big arms lifted. Unable to hold back my gasp, Luka wrapped them around me and brought me to his chest.

I held him. I held my big brother and took solace in his embrace. I'd missed this. As kids we were so close. He'd hold me all the time. For the first time since he'd returned, it felt like maybe, just maybe, my brother, my childhood hero, was rising from his darkness once again.

I soaked in his warmth and whispered sternly, "Luka, I believe it was meant to happen. Even if it won't be welcomed."

Luka pressed a kiss to the top of my head and rasped, "What was meant to happen?"

"Everything," I said back. "Your journey brought me Zaal. He's shown me what real love is."

Luka's hold tightened. I felt Kisa's hand on my back. After a few more seconds, I withdrew from his arms. Luka was watching me with concern.

Subconsciously I reached for my necklace. I ran my hand over the Tolstoi name and laughed a humorless laugh. "You know, *babushka* gave me this as a talisman to find my true love. It was *dedushka*'s. He gave it to *babushka* before he left for that trip to Moscow, as a way to keep him close to her heart until he returned." I caught the gold of the necklace glinting off the beaming sun shining through the window. "I wonder what she would have said knowing that the love I found was the son of the man she hated most."

Unable to take the pain this knowledge brought, I whispered a brief "Good night," and dashed up the stairs.

Quietly, I cracked open the door, to see Zaal lying fast asleep on the bed. His huge body seemed to dwarf the king-size bed. My chest clenched in pain. He was mine. Every fiber of my being had claimed him as mine. My heart, my soul, my spirit. At this point, I didn't give a fuck what anyone else thought.

I stripped off my clothes, careful not to make a noise. Zaal was lying on his back, his long black hair hanging over his pillow. His muscles relaxed as he slept. He looked so peaceful. I hoped he would get the rest he craved.

Attracted to him like a magnet, I snuggled into his side, the heat of his body instantly warming me. My head lay on his chest and I listened to his steady breathing. It soothed me. Suddenly, as if needing to touch me, even in his sleep, Zaal slid his arm over my shoulder and pulled me close.

As I closed my eyes, I remembered everything Luka had told Zaal tonight. And I felt sick. His history was so sad, so violent. A wave of protectiveness embraced me, and lifting my chin, I stared up at Zaal's handsome face.

His eyelids fluttered in sleep, and running my finger down his stubbled cheek, I whispered, "Zaal Kostava, you've stolen my forbidden heart."

15

ZAAL

"Boys, come here!" Papa's voice called Anri and me in from the garden. We looked at each other and smiled. I set off running, sprinting through the long grass.

I was fast, but so was Anri. I could hear him running behind me, picking up speed. I laughed as we rounded the corner and our house came into view.

Grandmama was sitting on the porch. She started laughing as she saw us approach. I pushed myself harder, then Anri was suddenly at my side. We looked at each other and started laughing. We both reached the porch at the very same moment.

I stopped in front of Grandmama. She put down her tea and started clapping. "My boys!" she exclaimed, and opened her arms for us. Both Anri and I ran into her embrace. She kissed us both on the head.

Footsteps sounded behind us and Grandmama pushed us back. Papa was waiting at the door and called us over.

We ran to Papa and he smiled wide. "Come with me, boys." Papa led us into the house and through to his office.

A tapping on the wooden floor seemed to follow us. When I looked around I saw that Zoya was running our way, dressed in a pink dress and clutching her white stuffed toy rabbit.

"Sykhaara!" she shouted with a giggle, and jumped into my arms. Anri reached over and ruffled her hair. "Where are you going?" she asked. Papa leaned forward to kiss her on the cheek.

"I have something for your brothers," Papa said proudly.

Zoya's face lit up. "For me, too?" she shouted in excitement.

Papa shook his head. "Leave me with your brothers. And if you're good, I'll take you to town tomorrow and buy you anything you want."

She nodded her head. I placed her on the floor. She ran back to Mama who was watching us with proud eyes as she fed our baby brother and sister.

"Anri, Zaal, in my office."

We sat in Papa's large office, on the sofa opposite his chair. Papa sat down in his black chair, smoothing out his expensive suit as he did so.

"Anri, Zaal. When I was your age, my papa controlled our clan. The Kostavas have always been strong. We've always been feared and we always will be.

"But years ago I made a decision for our clan that took us from Moscow and brought us back to Georgia. I issued a command that many took offense to and it cost us our standing in Russia, and with the rest of the Vor V Zakone.

"I still stand by my decision, but it's no secret it has damaged this family's reputation. This is our home. Georgian blood runs through our veins. But in order to rule strong, we need to be back in Moscow. And we need to claim our slice of New York, too."

We both nodded, listening to every word our papa said. He spoke of our clan all the time. He spoke about regaining our place in Moscow after the murder of our rival's boss. Mr. Jakhua, another Georgian boss, and my papa were always in meetings. They always planned to overthrow the Volkov Russians. My papa hated the Volkov Russians. He said they were greedy and needed taking out.

Anri and I hated the Russians. Papa taught us how to hate them.

Papa leaned forward. "When I was eight, I began listening in on business meetings of the family. You are both eight, and there's no better time to start than now. You'll learn the family business, then when you're older and I'm gone, you'll both rule our clan." Papa smiled and sat back proudly. "Two male heirs. I have two strong young men to carry the Kostavas back to greatness."

Anri elbowed me in the side. I smiled as he nodded in pride.

Papa stood and opened up his safe. He pulled out two black boxes and gave one to each of us. Papa sat back down and pointed at the boxes. "All the men in our family get one at your age. It's tradition." He waved his hand. "Open."

I carefully opened the box at the same time as Anri. A gold necklace sat on a bed of velvet. I ran my hand over the emblem and Papa leaned forward. I looked up and he pulled his necklace out of his shirt collar.

"It's the same as mine. My father had one, too." A smile spread on his lips. "Be proud to wear them. You're the future of this family. You'll fix my mistakes."

Anri stood and clutched his necklace to his chest. "We will get revenge for you, Papa. When we're older we'll take back Moscow for you. We'll take New York."

I stood beside Anri and did the same. "We swear it, Papa. We'll make them all pay."

Papa stood, and with a hand on each shoulder, asked, "Who will you destroy?"

We took a deep breath, and recited three names we knew by heart, "The Volkovs, Tolstois, and Durovs."

Papa smiled and threw his arms around our shoulders. He led us out of the door. Mama and Grandmama rushed over to help us put our necklaces on. They beamed with pride. My mama stepped back and put her hands to her mouth. "My sons," she beamed, and ran her hand over the necklaces on our necks.

"Dinner. We celebrate!" she said, and scooted us all out into the yard.

Anri pulled on my arm and we snuck into a doorway. He laid his hand on my shoulder and said, "We are strong. We must remain strong to be the heirs Papa wants us to be."

"I will," I replied, "we will," and Anri put his hands on my cheeks.

"We're brothers, Zaal. Until the end. We'll always be together. We're stronger together."

He gripped my hand and we walked toward the table. The whole family was there. Two seats were free at the top of the table beside Papa.

Zoya saw us coming and ran toward us. She jumped into my arms. "Zaal! Can you sit beside me?"

I nodded my head. As the eldest brother, Anri sat beside Papa with me next to him.

"Come," I said to Zoya, and sat her down on her seat. I slid in next to Anri. Papa made a toast. The servants brought the food.

Suddenly a loud crash sounded in the house. Papa clicked his fingers to the guards. "Go see what it is."

But the guards didn't move.

My papa dropped his fork and rose from his seat. He glared at the guards. "Go and see what that was. Now!"

All of us were still around the table. The guards rolled their necks. They smirked at my papa, then they raised their rifles.

A crash sounded again. Suddenly, Mr. Jakhua, my papa's friend, entered the yard, with lots of guards following him.

A hand suddenly grabbed mine. When I looked down, I saw it was Anri's. I was shaking. Shaking so bad. Anri squeezed my hand and mouthed, "Dzlier. Be strong. Keep strong."

I nodded as my heart began to race.

Then Zoya crawled into my arms, tucking her face against my neck. She whimpered. My papa stepped toward Jakhua. A guard suddenly jumped in front and pointed a rifle to his chest.

My mama cried out, my baby brother and sister beside her started scream-ing, too.

"Levan! What the fuck is going on!" my papa shouted. But Levan flicked his finger to his guards.

The guards rushed toward our table, and I froze. Zoya started crying against my neck. I held her close with one arm as Anri kept tight hold of my other hand.

The guards rushed to my mama and my grandmama and hauled them to their feet. Two guards took my baby brother and sister. They were screaming for Mama as they were dragged behind.

Anri jumped to his feet, as did I. I held Zoya in my arms. We tried to back away. Guards came for us. I gripped Zoya tighter, her arms locked around my neck. I fought for air as fear stole my breath. Then, out of nowhere, a guard rushed forward and wrapped his arms around Zoya.

Zoya screamed against my neck. Everyone was screaming, the sound deafen-ing my ears. Dropping Anri's hand, I reached for my little sister. But the guard was stronger.

Her terrified dark eyes met mine and tears fell down her face. "Zaal!" she screamed. Her hand reached out for me to save her.

"Zoya!" I screamed back, but a guard grabbed me from behind.

The place was in chaos, my family screaming, guards shouting, and my papa fighting to get free. My head whipped around searching for my brother as my feet left the floor, the guard holding me in the air.

He was beside me, fighting to get free. "Anri!" I called. His brown eyes found mine.

"Zaal!" he called back, gripping on to his necklace. "Dzlier. Be strong. Keep strong." Tears fell down my cheeks, but I forced myself to keep strong.

"Zaal!" Zoya called, her little arms trying to reach me from across the yard.

Jakhua stepped forward, stared at me and Anri, then clicked his hand to the wall against our house.

The guards holding my grandmama, Papa, Mama, Zoya, Dmitry, and Lena, dragged them to the long wall that stretched around the back of the house.

Anri and I were kept back. Jakhua walked toward us. I watched my papa's face pale. "No!" he shouted. "Get off my boys!"

Jakhua stood beside us and gripped our faces in his hands. He forced us to look forward and he hissed, "Watch, boys. Don't you dare move your eyes."

Mama and Grandmama held our brothers and sisters against their legs, trying to protect them. But Zoya, kept her head facing us, all the time watching me.

Her pretty face was scrunched up and she called out, "Zaal!"

I roared and fought to get free. I wanted to be with my family. I could hear Anri doing the same. Trying to get to our family.

"You fucked us all when you murdered the Tolstoi, Iakob. And I don't plan on being stuck here in Georgia forever. The Volkovs have banned us from every good trade route, and it's all your fault. I should never have backed you in killing Matvei. I've made new connections with the Arzianis. They have enterprises in the U.S. and in Moscow. You, the Kostavas . . . you're done."

My papa shook his head. My eyes focused on my family's terrified faces, my gaze lingering on Zoya's crying eyes. Then Jakhua lifted his arm, and a second later, dropped it. The guns began to fire.

The sound of my family screaming hit my ears first. Anri and my screams added to the chaos. Then the blood started to pour. Red liquid pooled on the pavement and ran down the back wall of the house.

My heart pumped too fast. My whole body shook as my family, one by one, slumped to the ground. Dead. All dead.

When the gunfire stopped, silence reigned. I could hear Anri breathing heavily. I was panting, too. I stared straight ahead. When the guards moved aside, my knees grew weak and I fell to the ground.

Blood. My family dead, drowned in their own blood.

My hands shook. A rage built up my throat. Then, with tears in my eyes, I screamed. My heart broke as I looked at my family on the ground . . . my little brother and sisters . . . Zoya's body trapped underneath my grandmama's, her hand reaching for me, now still and lifeless.

Anri screamed beside me as I vomited on the floor.

Blood. All I could see was blood.

Jakhua then moved before me and Anri. He spoke to the guards. "Knock them out. Get them in the van. We're done here. Leave the bodies. They can rot in the sun."

I held my stare at my dead family. Then I felt a hand grip on to mine. I looked to the side, my eyes blurred with tears. Anri's devastated face stared back at me.

I wanted to speak, I tried, but no words came. I was racked with pain, so much I didn't think I would breathe ever again.

I was staring into Anri's eyes when everything went black.

I woke strapped to a bed, my brother beside me, and the pain started again . . .

My eyes snapped open; darkness prevailed. I was panting. My heart beat too fast. With crystal clarity, the images from my dream played over and over in my mind. . . . Blood, guns, Jakhua, my brother, Anri, my sister, Zoya, crying, her hand reaching for me to save her . . . but I couldn't save her. I couldn't save any of them.

My stomach lurched and I fought back vomit. I wanted to move. I wanted to dive off the bed and scream. I wanted to rip someone apart. Rip Jakhua apart like he ripped apart my family. I squeezed my eyes shut as my numb body refused to move. My mind held me prisoner as it replayed their deaths in my head. I could see it so clearly. I could smell the tinny smell of fresh blood, the smoke from the rapid gunfire. And I could see the lifeless open eyes of my parents, and Grandmama. I could see the tiny lapsed bodies of my baby brother and sister strewn on the bloodied floor. And I could see Zoya's tiny hand peeking out from below my grandmama. But I couldn't see her face.

And Anri. I could see every part of his face, identical to mine.

My stomach knotted so hard I thought I'd never breathe again, the crack in my soul so great I thought it would never heal. Before I had no feeling, no memories of my past. But now? Now I was feeling everything, every loss, every horror in my mind. Every memory was a dagger in my body, one I couldn't remove.

Tears were pouring from my eyes. An ache, so painful it stole my breath, ripped through my body. More memories poured into my mind—the necklace, my brother, Anri. *Fuck!* Anri, him holding my hand.

I looked down at my hand. It still felt so real. I could still feel Anri's fingers squeezing, telling me, *"Dzlieri.* Be strong. Keep strong."

More tears fell. When I saw the horror I felt reflected in his eyes, his dark eyes, dark eyes like Zoya's, Zoya who had died, my little Zoya, crying my name and reaching for my hand until the very end.

I couldn't handle it. Couldn't take this wave after wave of agony that crushed my soul. I wanted the images to stop. I wanted my family's pain to stop.

I wanted it all to fucking stop!

My body tensing and pain convulsing my chest, I turned toward Talia. I knew she was beside me, her hand lay on my stomach.

I focused on that hand. I focused on the warmth seeping into my skin.

I wasn't alone. No longer alone. I had Talia. I had Talia in my heart.

Hearing her soft breathing, I rolled onto my side, my eyes blurring through a mist of tears. I lay on my arm, just watching her sleep. I could see her sleeping form lit by the dull light from her bedside table lamp. She knew I hated the dark. She knew it without me having to tell her it. I blinked away my tears and focused on her long golden hair, on her pink mouth parted by sleep. I squeezed my eyes shut as another stab of pain sliced my heart.

I reached out and laid my hand on hers. I wanted her to wake. I needed her hand on my face. I needed her mouth on mine, I needed her to wrap her arms around my waist.

I gripped her hand, but still she slept on. My eyes wandered over her body. My chest clenched with how much I wanted her. She was beautiful. So fucking beautiful.

My gaze drifted down her neck to her chest and her tits. Then I stilled, my eyes wide as my gaze met the gold necklace around her neck. I gasped for air as I recalled my papa handing similar ones to Anri and I. He wanted us to restore the clan's reputation, to make the Kostavas great once more. . . .

Papa stood, and with a hand on each shoulder, asked, "Who will you destroy?"

We took a deep breath, and recited the three names we knew by heart; "The Volkovs, Tolstois, and Durovs." My blood rushed like fire through my veins. The necklaces we were given were gold, the pendent showing our family crest.

I stared at Talia's necklace, it looked exactly the same. Breath held,

I leaned forward and studied the pendent. There was a crest. My pulse pounded as I made out the emblem—a wolf, a shield, and then I stopped dead when my eyes read the family name engraved along the top.

Breathe, breathe, I told myself, but I couldn't breathe. Releasing Talia's hand, my fists clenched at my sides.

It couldn't be. She can't be. No!

I remembered waking in the basement. I was trapped in darkness, I was held in chains. Captured. Left to die.

I shook my head as pain and rage filled my muscles. The name on Talia's pendent pierced my mind. With each and every stab, the fire burned and burned. They'd exiled my family. They were the reason Jakhua turned on my father, the reason my family had died.

Papa's voice sounded in my head, *"Who will you destroy?"*

"The Volkovs, Tolstois, and Durovs."

Tolstoi.

No longer able to rein in my fury, a roar ripped from my throat. I lurched my body over Talia. She'd lied. She'd deceived me. I wasn't free. . . . I was a fucking captive of the Tolstois!

Talia's brown eyes snapped open in shock. I gripped both of her wrists, lifting them above her head. She gasped as she tried to move, the blood rushing from her face. But she wasn't going anywhere. She couldn't move.

Her frightened brown eyes met mine. "Zaal, what? What's wrong?"

She pulled on her arms, trying to break free, but I snarled and hissed, "*Tolstoi* . . ." Venom and hatred fueled my anger.

Talia's face turned even whiter and her eyes grew impossibly wide. Her bottom lip began to tremble and her hands began to shake. "Zaal . . . please," she begged. Her plea, for a moment, made me flinch. I hated when she was sad.

Tolstoi! My mind pushed. Anger regained its hold.

"Tolstoi," I growled threateningly.

She shook her head. "Zaal."

"Fucking Tolstois!" I roared. "The enemy!" Talia flinched and cowered underneath my body. "You're the fucking enemy!" I thundered, but Talia only cried more.

"No!" she whispered brokenly. "Don't."

Klavs, klavs, klavs, sasaklao, I heard in my mind.

I should have killed her. I was a Kostava. Tolstois should die under my hand. But I couldn't. It was Talia.

Wrenching back, I pushed off the bed. My hands gripped the side of my skull. The pain was too much, grief consuming my heart.

"Zaal!" Talia cried and scurried to the end of the bed. I whipped my head to face her. Her face was red and blotted from crying. She stared at me, and my heart ached. It was Talia. My Talia.

But she was a fucking Tolstoi!

With shaking arms, she held out her hand. "Please," she begged, "take it . . . trust me . . . let me explain."

I stared at her hand. But all I could see was Papa giving me and Anri our necklaces, telling us to avenge the family. The guards pointing rifles, gunshots, blood . . . Zoya . . . Zoya's dark eyes begging me to help. But I couldn't . . . I couldn't save her. . . .

New images invaded my brain. A narrow cold bed, Jakhua's cold smirk, his laughter, needles, pain from being sliced open. Anri screaming beside me. Chains, beatings. More needles, more pain. Then darkness, anger, nothing but red-hot anger, and the constant craving to kill.

Body shaking, my neck corded and bulged with tension. My teeth gritted. I clenched my fists so hard my nails drew blood on my palm. I screamed to the sky and ran out of Talia Tolstaia's room.

I thundered toward the stairs. Tolstoi guards were running to meet me, guns held high. Roaring at the memory of guards firing on my family, I charged. They were nothing to me. I plowed my fist into a guard's face. Lifting him in my hands, I raised my knee, thrust him down, and snapped his back.

Another guard fired at me; the bullet hit the wall. But the sound of that bullet incensed me, ripping me straight back into the past. Reaching out over the narrow staircase, I gripped the guard's neck, and slammed my head against his. The guard faltered, collapsing on impact. I placed my hands around his neck and twisted. It snapped, and I threw his lifeless body on the floor.

I raced down the stairs. I had to escape this hell. When I rounded the corner at the bottom of the staircase, I saw the outside door. Pushing forward, I made for the exit.

As I passed through the living room, movement to my left caught my eye. Him. Luka. 818. A motherfucking *Tolstoi*! He stared at me, chest bared, only sweatpants covering his legs, just like me. I lowered my head. Anger wrapped around me, surrounding me with fury.

"Zaal," Luka said coldly, "calm the fuck down."

I rolled my neck from side to side as I watched Luka brace to fight. I curled my lip in disgust. I began pacing, back and forth, back and forth.

"Zaal—"

"Tolstoi!" I thundered, watching Luka's face. "You are a fucking Tolstoi!"

Luka's jaw clenched and his eyes darkened. "I am like you," he said in a deathly tone. "I was taken from my family, too. I fought to survive. Killed night after night until I could break free." He stepped forward, the movement irritating me. "I fought with your brother, alongside him. I fought with Anri, he was my best friend, my brother."

He was my best friend, my brother. . . .

I convulsed with even greater fury as those words ignited in me. "No," I growled, "you are a fucking Tolstoi. You are the enemy. An enemy I swore to my father to destroy!"

"Anri was my friend, not an enemy! Family means nothing in the cage!" Luka bellowed back.

I snapped. I charged forward, gripping Luka by the throat. But he fought back, his strength nothing like I'd ever encountered before. His arm slammed down on mine, the force knocking my arm away. He pushed on my chest; I stumbled back. I paced again, my body remembering the kill . . . remembering bringing death.

I wanted it.

I craved it.

"How did he die?" I hissed.

Luka stilled, and my eyes bored into his. "How did he fucking die?" I boomed. Luka lifted his hands, as if in surrender.

"Me," he said quietly. My world stopped. "I killed him," he said. "He died at my hands."

Heat, so intense, flared at my feet and traveled through my body like hellfire. He killed Anri? A Tolstoi killed *my* brother.

Heaving forward, I rushed Luka. I tackled him to the ground. My fists struck his face over and over, but Luka hit back. I ignored the pain and agony of his blows as we fought for dominance on the ground. In blind fury I just kept hitting.

"I had no choice!" Luka snarled as he rolled me on my back, his hand tight around my throat. Sheer strength kept me pinned to the floor. His dark eyes pierced mine. As he spoke he seemed to make me a promise. "I had no choice but to kill him. We were forced to fight. I had to get my revenge on the man who had me captured and taken to the gulag."

I flailed, but Luka's incredible strength held me down. "Anri understood that only one of us would be walking away from that cage. It was him or me. I won, but, as he drew his final breath, I promised him his revenge." He leaned down farther and tightened his grip on my throat, making it even harder to breathe. "I got you out. I set you free. We put you in the basement to get you off the Georgian drug. You fucking survived. And next, I kill Jakhua. I promised Anri, and now I promise you, Zaal. I don't fucking fail."

Luka released my neck and sat up. "Our families may be enemies, but Anri was my brother. I was 818 and he was 362. No family names divided us. No family history tore us apart. Pain and revenge brought us together."

I panted for breath through gritted teeth. My chest was covered in blood. My ribs ached. "He would never have befriended a fucking Tolstoi," I spat out in a guttural voice.

Luka tensed. Then raising his fist, he slammed it against my jaw, and pushed down on my head. I wrapped my arms around his neck. Either of us could twist and it would be the end. A neck would break. One of the clans would lose the heir.

"Anri was my brother too. He taught me how to survive. He told me to be strong, keep strong. And I did. And I am. I'm strong. I'm fucking Raze. And I'll slaughter you here and now, if you threaten my family."

As those words poured from his mouth, my arms fell away from his neck. Luka rose, feeling me pull away.

Be strong. Keep strong. Be strong. Keep strong . . .

Blistering agony possessed my mind as Anri's familiar words struck home, struck at my heart. My body ached. Confusion set in. He was a

Tolstoi. But he *knew* my brother. I could see that absolute truth in his eyes.

Jerking my legs, I knocked Luka off me. I staggered to my feet. Luka stood and turned to face me, his brown eyes darker still. His body ready to strike.

I caught movement from behind me. I saw Luka's female huddled in the corner. She had been watching us fight. Tears were flooding her eyes. Luka's gaze flickered to her, then immediately back to me. "I killed Anri to save Kisa. She's my wife and the woman I've loved all my life. I had more to live for at that moment in time, but he died a warrior. He died giving all his heart."

Footsteps pounded into the room. Talia's two guards came running in. They looked just like they'd woken up. Each of them held a gun, pointing in my direction.

"Don't shoot!" Luka ordered, but the guards did not lower their weapons.

"He didn't remember you either," Luka said suddenly. I held my breath as an agonized ache sliced down my spine. "But if he'd known you were alive, he would have never stopped until he freed you. He was the most honorable man I've ever met. He saved me, and I want to save you, enemies or not. I want to save those he loved. I think maybe he befriended me because, deep down, he remembered having a brother. He wanted a brother again."

Gasping for breath, I stumbled back. My mind was crammed full of thoughts. Too many thoughts to handle.

Footsteps ran down the stairs. But I needed to get out. I watched Luka, the guards, and his wife. They were all looking at me.

Reaching the door that led to the beach, I pushed on the wood until the door broke off its frame. Cold air slapped against my bare chest, but I ignored it all to run out into the night.

I ran and ran until grass gave way to the wood of the dock. I ran until the wood ran out and gave way to the freezing cold sand. I tried to run on, but my legs gave out. As my knees hit the soft sand, I threw my head back and screamed. I screamed for my family. I screamed for my brother dying in a cage, and I screamed with the venom flooding my veins for Jakhua.

He would die.

I would slaughter him.

I would honor my family by slitting his motherfucking throat.

When there was nothing left inside of me, my hands fell forward, plunging into the soft sand. Tears poured from my eyes. The icy wind whipped my hair around my face and clung to my bare skin. But I was beyond caring.

I was empty.

Light footsteps sounded on the dock. They were running. Then they stopped. I felt her behind me. I knew who would be there.

A Tolstoi, Tolstoi, the enemy that stole my heart, made me human again.

Feeling drained, I staggered to my feet. I looked out onto the thrashing sea, its waves rolling and crashing on the shore. I breathed in the salty air, then noticed crying from behind me.

On a deep breath, I turned. I immediately froze. Talia stood on the edge of the dock, watching me. Her long blond hair blew to the side in the wind, her body covered in black clothes.

Her dark eyes watched mine, an agonized expression on her face.

Talia Tolstaia. *My* Talia Tolstaia.

I tried to find hate. I tried to despise.

I found only warmth.

It was her warmth. She was mine.

She had cleansed me. Cared for me. Cried for me. She was . . . *for me.*

Salty tears dropped down my cheeks. My heart squeezed tight. She was in my heart. The feel of her hand as it lay in mine. Her warmth, her smile, her touch.

My heart was in the enemy's hands. Betrayal of my family brought me to my knees. I had nothing left to give.

"Zaal!" Talia cried suddenly, her cracked and broken voice carrying off in the wind. I looked up as Talia ran onto the sand, her legs bringing her toward me.

Her chest heaved. Her hands shook. She staggered to a halt and stared intently into my eyes.

She was in pain. As much pain as I felt.

She was like me. No, she was a *part* of me.

Talia stood, watching me. She was as still as a statue. My mind told me it was wrong. My memories told me it was wrong. But in my heart, it felt *right*.

I needed her.

I needed *my* Talia.

Pushing myself to stand, I watched Talia brace for my wrath, her arms rising in defense. I took a step forward. Even above the strong wind, I heard her breathing hitch. I saw her body flinch. I lifted my head. Our gazes met. Talia's lips parted. I took another step forward. Talia tensed, then I dropped to my knees and threw my arms around her waist.

I held her tight. As tight as I could without hurting her. My cheek pressed against her stomach. I could hear her heart pounding. A feeling so consuming built in my stomach, and then unable to hold it back, it ripped from my throat.

I was crying.

Releasing all the pain I'd just been hit with. All the pain from the memories muddying my mind, I fell apart on this sand. I clutched on to Talia, like I couldn't get close enough. My chest ached with everything pouring from my soul, then instantly spreading me with warmth, Talia's arms wrapped around my head, drawing me closer to her soft body.

I could feel her crying, too; shaking, sharing my pain. Then Talia dropped to her knees. My chest hit the cold sand, as my head rested in her lap. I shuddered with the severity of my sobs. I released twenty years of grief that had been trapped inside my mind.

And Talia cradled my head, she rocked me back and forth, she stroked her hand through my hair.

She did not speak, just sat there with me. A Tolstoi comforting a Kostava.

After I didn't know how long, my tears ran dry and a raw, blistering ache throbbed in my chest. Talia's hands slowed on my head. The strong wind died down. I could hear Talia breathing and I took a deep breath.

Unclasping my hands from her back, I placed them on the sand and forced myself to my knees. My hair covered my face as my swollen eyes stared at the sand.

Talia was silent.

Taking a deep breath, I lifted my head. Talia's face was so sad, so hurt. It shattered any contempt I had left within me.

Talia lowered her head and said, "I should have told you."

When I didn't say anything in response, she raised her head. Immediately I noticed the necklace was gone. A tear dropped in the place it used to be. I looked into her eyes. "I tried to hate you." She sniffed, and I stilled at her words. Her shoulders sagged and defeat seized her body. "But I couldn't," she confided in a whisper. "I couldn't hate you. In fact I was obsessed and then it turned to something deeper. I committed the ultimate of all sins."

I held my breath, waiting to hear her finish that sentence. But Talia edged forward, her knees brushing against mine. A small smile spread on her lips, and her fingers traveled to my neck, then up to rest against my cheek.

We breathed in the same air, her palm warming my cold face. Her head tipped to the side and the look of affection in her eyes was my undoing.

She leaned forward, and pressing her lips to the side of my mouth, whispered, "I fell for our greatest enemy. I fell in deep, and I gifted him all of my heart, all of this enemy Tolstaia heart."

I closed my eyes and fully absorbed what she had said. She'd gifted me her heart. Talia's hands underneath mine were shaking. Opening my eyes, I said, "Your hands are cold."

She froze, then a nervous laugh burst from her lips, and she threw herself into my lap. Her hands wrapped around my neck. Tucking my nose into the crook of her neck, I breathed in her scent.

"Zaal," she whispered, and clutched me tighter.

Her whole body was trembling as she held me close. I gently pulled away. "You are cold," I declared. Her lips chattered and her skin was icy to the touch.

"You needed me," she replied softly, her fingers combing through my hair. Taking a deep breath, Talia lost her laughter, and said, "I was extremely close to my grandmother, Zaal. As a child, and right up until her death a few years ago." I froze as Talia began to mention her family. Talia shuffled on my lap, moving in closer.

"She and I were kindred spirits. She was feisty, and never walked the line"—Talia laughed—"just like me. I've never been good at obeying my father's strict rules." Talia's fingers stopped stroking my hair. She was lost in her memories. "I grew up knowing only the story my family told me of our family's conflict. The one where the Georgians used to be part of the *Vor V Zakone,* the soviet Thieves in Law, until they turned coat. I knew how the Kostavas, the Jakhuas, and the Volkovs all worked together as one unit. And I was told the story of how the Volkovs took the turf in New York, but banned the Georgians from joining them, taking the territory as their own, leaving the Jakhuas and Kostavas to run Moscow." Talia sighed, shook her head, and continued, "And I know that your father, out of anger for this slight against his faction, organized to murder the Volkov bosses when they were next to visit home. But my grandfather ended up going alone to Moscow on the fated trip when Jakhua and your father planned the murder to send a message. It was my grandfather your father shot and hung from a street post for everyone in Russia to see. And it was my grandmother that lost the love of her life that day, all so the Georgians could show their strength against the Russians."

I tensed listening to the story from the Russian point of view, but as Talia's hand began moving through my hair again, I tried to relax.

Talia shifted again, laying her head against my chest, and said, "I imagine your family hated being left out of the New York business. And I imagine after they were hunted down after my grandfather's murder and forced back to Georgia, all trade routes cut by the Volkov Bratva, that your family and the Jakhuas became more resentful toward us than ever." Talia's hand slid down my face from my hair and she lifted my chin with her fingers, lifting her head to meet my eyes. "I imagine growing up as the Kostava heir, you were filled with an intense hatred for my family."

I nodded silently. Talia's lips tightened.

"I know this because I've had a great hatred for your family my whole life, Zaal." Talia laughed a humorless laugh. "And I can honestly say it has brought me nothing but pain." Talia's finger stroked over the moles below my left eye, and asked, "If it's okay with you, I'd like to let go of that hatred now. Those people back then were not us. It was a lifetime ago, a history that we can't change." Her chin dropped. "I know your version of that story will no doubt differ from mine, but I pray it ends the same. With you wanting me, with you being with me despite our surnames causing a drift."

I stayed unmoving for the longest time, listening to the sea, feeling the cold wind hit my skin. Talia didn't say anything more, but I knew one thing: I felt exactly the same.

Taking Talia's freezing hand, I got to my feet, pulling her with me.

As we stood wrapped in the wind, Talia looked up at my face and asked, "You feel the same? Even after you remember your family?"

I nodded my head, unable to speak. I felt drained, numb. But I knew I wanted this female above anything else.

"You need to rest," Talia said on a relieved sigh, and took my hand. She turned to walk us back to the house, but I needed to express something from the heart. I pulled on Talia's hand. She turned to face me, her beautiful face confused.

I lifted my hand over my chest and rasped, "To me, you are *not* a Tolstaia."

Her eyes softened, and stepping closer, she replied, "To me, you are not a Kostava." She lifted higher on her toes, and said, "You are my Zaal, the man whose soul has stolen mine."

Then she kissed me. Her cold lips met mine; soft, tender, caring. She pulled away and stroked my arm. "Let's go inside. I need to care for you and hold you while you sleep."

Warmth spread in my chest. I let this female, *my* female, guide me into the house. As we entered the door, Luka rose from the long seat. He watched me with wary eyes. Squeezing Talia's hand, I let go, and walked toward her brother. The guards all stood around him, more guards than there were before. All holding their guns.

But Luka's eyes did not leave mine.

Standing before him, I said, "You have my gratitude for freeing me from Master."

Luka's face hardened. "He isn't your master anymore. He's nothing but a fucking dead man walking."

I nodded at Luka. I went to walk back to Talia, when he announced, "Anri would be proud of the man you've become. You're like him in every way. Your looks, your strength, your loyalty."

I closed my eyes for the briefest of moments, before taking a deep breath and making my way back to Talia.

We entered the bedroom and Talia took me into the shower. She cleaned me slowly with a washcloth, then patched up my cuts and bruises, before brushing out my hair. All the time she touched me, I touched her back. As she cleansed and cared for me, she peppered my face with kisses, told me, without words, that she was mine, and I was hers.

As we climbed into bed, I faced Talia on my pillow. Memories now were a trickle, a gentle stream in my mind.

Talia watched me. I shuffled closer, wrapping her in my arms. I closed my eyes, relaxed my heart with the female I should never have wanted, and confessed, *"Ya khochu byt's toboy vsegda."*

Talia stilled in my arms, then with a press of her lips on my chest, whispered, "I, too, want to be with you forever."

16

LUKA

Brooklyn, New York
One week later
"You're really doing this?"

I turned to face my father as I stood in the center of my living room.

"I'm going," I replied coldly. My father slowly sat down on the sofa.

I hadn't seen him since that day in the gym when he'd seen me training. When I'd arrived back here from the Hamptons last week, he was away on business. This evening I found him waiting at my door. He was here to discuss tonight's plan to take out Levan Jakhua. We'd finally got a tip-off for where the Georgian bastard was hiding from our insider. I'd been given permission for this sting from the Pakhan in my father's absence.

It seemed he was now here to hear about it in person.

Refocusing on the here and now, I watched my father cross his legs, reflecting the calm demeanor he always wore, as his eyes fell upon me. "And you're going to kill him? *You?*"

My jaw clenched as I anticipated the argument that was going to come. I walked to my papa and sat down on the seat before him. "My *byki* will go in to where he's hiding. I promised you I wouldn't fight, and I won't. They'll bring Jakhua out to me." I looked up at my father. "Then I'll slit his fucking throat."

My father's hand rubbed over his short graying beard, and he nodded. "And Kisa knows you're doing this?"

"She understands what I have to do to avenge Anri," I replied vaguely. He nodded again.

We sat in silence until I asked, "Papa? Why don't you want me to fight?"

My father's hand stopped on his face, his brown eyes looked into mine. "Luka, you will never understand this until you have children, but the day you were taken from me"—he patted his chest—"something within me died."

A hollow pit formed in my stomach. My father rarely showed emotion. Since I'd gotten back to Brooklyn after being freed from the gulag, he hadn't really known how to treat me. I supposed that was because he no longer knew me. I'd left him a boy, and I'd returned a damaged man. Fourteen years of raising me had been lost. I'd never really thought about it that way before. Maybe he was just as lost as I was.

He sat forward. "When Kisa told me you were back, when she stood in our private box in the Dungeon and told me my son, my lost son, was the man killing Alik Durov in the cage, I couldn't believe it." His eyes lost focus. "You were savage, wild, but highly effective. You slaughtered Alik Durov. You slaughtered anyone that came into your path. You were unstoppable, the most effective killer I'd seen, well, *since* Alik."

I stiffened at the mention of Alik Durov, but my father's expression softened. I was looking at my real father. Not the Bratva boss, but Ivan Tolstoi, my father.

"I watched that boy slowly go insane, Luka. I watched it happen before my very eyes. With each kill, he thirsted for blood, the bloodlust slowly took control. And as for all the fucked-up things he did in private? I had no idea. But that boy lived for the kill. Sought out our enemies and tortured them. Killed them in the most sadistic ways imaginable." He sighed. I thought he looked tired. "We may kill in this life, Luka, but we're not beasts. We adhere to a code, even when it comes to the death of our rivals."

"Papa—" I went to speak, but my father held up his hand.

"When I saw you kill Durov, you no longer resembled my serious and respectful son I'd known as a child." His eyes met mine. "You looked like Durov. That same need for the kill was in your eyes." He sat back and dragged his hand down his tired aging face. "It still is, Luka. That look. That look is still there. Every single day." Silence hung in the air, and he added, "You're going to be the pakhan, Luka. Of that, we are certain. But I refuse to watch my son become like Durov. I've just got you back. I won't lose you again. Especially to the demons you hold inside. I won't lose you to yourself."

My chest tightened at the flash of vulnerability in my father's eyes. I stood and walked toward him. I kneeled at his feet. "Papa, I'm back. And I'm not Alik Durov. I'm your heir, and I won't let you down. You have my word on that."

Water built in my father's eyes. He lifted his hand and tapped it on my cheek. "You're my life, Luka. My legacy," he said through a tight throat. "I lived with a void in my heart when you were gone. I thought that thinking you were dead all those years was the hardest part of losing you." He shrugged. "Turns out it wasn't. Because living with the knowledge that I could lose you all over again? All because you crave to be in the fight? I fear, this time, would kill me."

"Papa, I'm not going anywhere," I assured. "And I won't ever let you down. I swear it to you. I swear it on our family name. I'll"—I fought back a lump in my throat—"I'll make you proud, Papa. Just give me a chance."

My father reached forward and took me in his arms. Pressing a kiss to my head, he rasped, "You already do make me proud, Luka. You already do."

He held me for several seconds before he pulled back. Getting to his feet, he fixed his tie and walked to the door. Before he stopped, he asked, "How is Talia? She's seemed distracted the few times we've talked."

My head lifted, and I caught the concern on his face. "She's good," I replied, leaving any mention of Zaal from the conversation.

He nodded. "Good. She needed this rest."

With that he walked out the door, and out of my house. I sat on the floor, replaying the conversation, until a throat cleared behind me. I looked back and Mikhail, my personal *byki*, was behind me.

"You ready?" I asked. "Do we have a location for the cunt?"

Mikhail nodded. "He's hiding out near the docks."

I got off the floor, and walked past Mikhail. We got in the town car, the van filled with *byki* up ahead.

Twenty minutes later, we rolled up to the docks and the warehouse Jakhua was meant to be hiding in. I glanced around the dark and run-down area; the place was desolate.

Mikhail looked at me in the rearview mirror. I lifted my hand and Mikhail gave the order to send in the *byki*. They filed out of the van and into the warehouse.

I waited for the gunfire.

I waited for the screams, but there was only silence.

Something came through on Mikhail's earpiece. His pale blue eyes met mine in the mirror. My blood ran cold.

"What?" I asked.

"There's something inside."

In seconds I was out of the car and striding across to the warehouse. I burst through the door, only to be met with a huge empty space.

My eyes drifted up to the rafters. Two bodies hung by their necks, their stomachs gutted and their throats slit. I walked closer, my feet walking straight through the pooling blood.

I looked at the men, trying to place them.

"Fuck!" Mikhail hissed from behind me.

I whipped my head around. "What?" I asked, my pulse beginning to slam in my neck.

Mikhail paled.

"What?" I thundered. Mikhail held his head high.

"These were two of my men."

I frowned and walked toward him. "Why would Jakhua kill them? Why would he set us up just to see two fucking corpses?"

Mikhail shifted on his feet. "These two men were brought back to Brooklyn today. They switched protection detail. They had families, and they'd been away for weeks. I decided to bring them home and have them patrol on home turf."

I shook my head and opened my mouth. Mikhail spoke before I could. "They were at the house in the Hamptons. They've been patrolling up there. They were assigned to the Kostava, to your sister."

I tensed, every muscle in my body filling with scalding blood. I looked up at the corpses and my stomach instantly sank.

Talia.

Zaal.

"Who informed you of tonight? Who gave you the tip-off?" I asked Mikhail. He paled and looked up to one of the fucks swinging from the roof.

"Andrei," he replied, and pointed to a corpse.

My hands shook with rage. It was a setup, a motherfucking setup! Ripping a knife from my jacket, I launched it into the heart of the betrayer hanging from the ceiling. The *byki* stepped back as I fumed with rage.

"Give me your phone!" I ordered Mikhail. He passed it over and I called the house in the Hamptons. All I got was a dead tone.

"The line's dead," I said. The *byki* shifted uncomfortably. Shaking with red-hot anger, I roared and threw the phone against the wall, smashing the fucking thing to pieces. I ran toward the door, the *byki* following behind.

"Get to the Hamptons! That motherfucker's set us up. Fucking betrayed by one of our own. Jakhua's gone back for Zaal! That bastard's gone back for his man."

As I ran out the door, fear, real fear, surged through my blood. Talia . . . that fucker was going to kill my sister.

My mind locked down. My blood ran cold. Only one thing ran through my mind.

Jakhua's imminent death.

17

TALIA

Waves crashed on the shore, the sound lulling me into half sleep. Zaal laid his head on my lap, and I stroked through his long hair with my fingers.

Zaal's hand traced down my stomach, his beautiful jade eyes looking at me with complete adoration.

He was getting better. He looked better. Several days of rest, since finding out about his family, had brought the color back to his cheeks. And he was talking more, remembering more.

"Tell me about them, *zolotse,*" I said quietly, not wanting to disturb the heady peace we had found in this room.

Zaal glanced up at me, and swallowed. I leaned down and pressed a kiss to his head. "Tell me about your family."

"I only remember some things," he replied, his accent becoming thicker as emotion took hold. "I remember only certain things about each one of them, about me as a child."

"Tell me," I pushed again, and linked my hand through his for comfort.

Zaal closed his eyes. I could see them moving behind his eyelids. His hand tightened in mine and I knew he was pulling images, fractured memories, from his mind. He'd told me he saw only pictures. Only felt certain feelings when remembering them.

But it was something. I feared with the drugs he'd been subjected to for years that he'd have no memories at all. We still weren't sure about the damage to his body, his mind, but just having something to hold on to, it was a blessing straight from God.

Zaal's eyes opened. He fixed his gaze on mine. "I remember I liked to lie in the sun," he rasped, a small curl of his lip gracing his mouth. "I remember my brother coming to sit beside me." His hand suddenly squeezed mine and his brow furrowed. "I remember us always being together. He was always at my side, I think. Papa's two boys."

I fought back the lump chasing up my throat. This man. This six foot six, 250-pound man spoke with such reverie about his lost brother. With such softness and affection in his husky deep voice.

"What else, baby?" I asked, still stroking through his hair.

His eyes crinkled at the corners as he pushed himself to remember. "I had a sister Zoya." He sucked in a deep breath and his body tensed. "She . . . she followed me everywhere, called me her *sykhaara*."

"What does that mean?" I asked soothingly.

Zaal's lip lifted in a fond smile. "My sweetness."

Adoration filled his eyes when he said, "She was five. She had long black hair, and such dark eyes they almost matched. A brown so dark it looked like coal. She would always be with me. Told me I would protect her when she was older, when me and my brother led the family."

My soul splintered when the tiniest tear slipped from the corner of his left eye. His haunted stare searched for mine, and when it connected, he said, "They ripped her from my arms, Talia. The guards, our own traitor guard, ripped her from my neck." He took a shuddering breath. "She cried my name, her hand reached out for me to save her." More tears fell, and his hand trembled. "And when they fired their guns, and Jakhua forced me to watch, Zoya's dark eyes were still watching me, like . . . like she expected me to save her."

His voice broke. I shuffled down the sofa to take his face in my hands. "You were eight, Zaal. A child."

He tried to breathe, his chest rapidly rising and falling. Then he added, "When their bodies were piled up, they were like slaughtered cattle. When they had all been killed and left outside to rot in the hot sun, I saw her arm on the ground. Zoya was trapped under my grandmama, her little dead body was hiding from view. But her hand was still reaching out for me. She'd wanted me to save her, expected me to, right until the end."

Tears tumbled down his cheeks, but his face was unchanged. He looked up at me and the devastated expression in his eyes destroyed me. "I let her down," he whispered. "I couldn't save her. And I have to live with that forever."

I wrapped my arms around his chest, squeezing him tightly. Zaal held on tight. He always held on tight. Like he was the Earth, and I was his sun.

"He killed them all, Talia. Killed them like they were pigs. My family."

"I know, Zaal," I soothed, and just held him in my arms.

A few minutes later, with Zaal's fingers wrapped in my hair, I felt his chest move. I looked up to see a whisper of a smile on his lips.

I melted.

I stared at him waiting for him to speak, when he murmured, *"Sykhaara."*

"My sweetness," I said, remembering the translation.

"She did not even understand what it meant."

"Then why did she call you it?" I questioned.

"My grandmama called me and Anri it. We were her favorites. Her Georgian princes, she would say."

It made me smile. Zaal noticed. He tipped his head to the side in question. "Like I was close to my *babushka,* you were close to yours."

"How did she die?" he asked.

I inhaled and explained, "Heart attack. We found her one day in her chair, it was the anniversary of my *dedushka*'s death." I shook my head, the pain of that day still strong. "My mama always said she died of a broken heart."

Zaal was quiet as he contemplated my words, no doubt thinking about who was responsible for my *dedushka*'s death. With a sigh, Zaal said quietly, "I do not remember my papa well, Talia. I wear the name Kostava, though I find, apart from a few strong memories that seem set on repeat, I do not know the man at all." Zaal patted his chest. "But know that I am not my papa. I am not vengeful toward your family."

I held Zaal tighter. My affection for this man swelled to fill my every cell. He was perfect for me. In every single way.

"She would make me dance," Zaal suddenly rasped, breaking the heavy silence, and turning the direction of the tense topic.

I lifted my head and asked, "Who?"

His eyes narrowed as he thought something over in his head and he answered, "My grandmama." His eyes then widened. "She is how I know English. She had lived in America before she married my grandpapa."

A smile broke on my face. "I always wondered how you knew English."

"It was her. She said to lead the family we should know English. And Russian."

My chin rested on Zaal's packed stomach, and I asked, "She taught you to dance?"

I could see Zaal searching his mind for more memories, when he said, "Yes. She said we needed to be real gentlemen." He exhaled like the memory took effort to remember. "We would dance to her favorite song, a song she heard in America."

"What was it? The song?" I pushed eagerly.

He racked his brain and said, "I'll Walk . . . I'll Walk . . ." His lips pursed and his forehead creased as he pushed the memory. Then his beautiful green eyes lit up. "Alone," he said. "'I'll Walk . . . Alone.'"

My breathing paused in disbelief.

"What?" Zaal asked, my face obviously showing my surprise.

"It was one of my *babushka*'s favorites. It's by Dinah Shore."

I lifted myself from Zaal's arms and reached for my phone on the coffee table. I scrolled to my music and found the track. Zaal sat up in interest, and as I turned my head, I just had to pause.

He was so damn beautiful.

My heart raced as he sat there in black sweats and a white T-shirt. His olive-skinned muscles stood out against the paleness of the white and his long hair hung in front of his face. I loved his hair, I really did, but I loved his face more.

Zaal was staring at me. "What?" he asked.

"You're so handsome," I said quietly, and felt the blush build on my cheeks. *"Takoy krasivyy."*

Zaal regarded me strangely, as if he had no idea why another person would ever regard someone as handsome. I sat with that thought for a second, and realized, he probably didn't.

Getting to my feet, I walked toward him. Zaal sat up looking at me. His sitting down was almost the same height as me standing.

Reaching up to my hair, I pulled on the band keeping it in a ponytail. My long hair fell down over my shoulders and I held it in my hand.

Zaal frowned. "What are you doing?" he asked.

"Can I do something?" I asked. Zaal regarded me warily. I leaned down and ran the back of my hand across his face. "I love your long hair, Zaal, but I want to see your face."

The frown never moved, but when I raked my hands through his hair, his hands laid on my thighs, his eyes closed, and a low hum sounded in his chest.

I smiled at him and gathered his hair to a knot at the top of his skull. Finished, and wanting to survey my work, I stepped back, and all the air escaped my lungs.

Zaal was looking up at me, and I felt like I was seeing him for the first time. With his long black hair brushed off his face, his regally beautiful face—high cheekbones, dark eyebrows, full lips—staring up at me like I was the most beautiful girl in the world, a stark reality hit home.

I'd more than fallen for Zaal. He now completely owned me. In every possible way. He was in my every cell, my every breath, my every heartbeat.

Zaal rose to his feet, and with his newly visible face, I stared up at him, struck mute and lost for words.

Zaal leaned down, and giving me exactly what I needed, met my lips with his. It was soft, gentle, and more meaningful than any rushed, passionate embrace could be; it told me everything I needed to know. I owned him, too.

Zaal pulled back, and sliding my hand down to his, I asked, "Would you dance with me?"

Zaal stilled. His perfectly framed eyebrows pulled down. "There is no music," he rasped out.

Moving to the sofa, without breaking his hold, I pressed play on my phone, the device connecting to the house's speakers.

In seconds the crackling sounds from the 1940s old recording drifted through the speakers. Zaal sucked in a quick gulp of breath, his eyes fluttering closed. I laid my hands on his broad chest, the beat of his heart hammering underneath. At my touch, Zaal opened his eyes, his gaze glossy.

Dinah Shore began to sing about her love, who was at war, and her promise that she would wait for him, that she would never love anyone else, never give up her heart. As those words filled up the room, Zaal reached for my hands, laying one on his shoulder, and clasped the other one in his hand.

Zaal began to lead, his feet moving slowly and unsurely at first, but as the song played on, he became more steady and self-assured.

Zaal's eyes never left mine, something indescribable passing through them as he moved me around the room.

I lay my cheek to his chest, lost in this moment of simplicity and joy, a rare occurrence in our complicated life.

"I remember this," he said quietly, and my eyes drifted to a close. "I remember being good at this," he continued, and huffed a single laugh. "And I remember Anri was not. He would always step on Grandmama's toes."

I listened to every word he spoke, relishing the happiness in his voice in this moment of pain-free joy. Zaal's arm around my waist squeezed me tighter and I could hear his heart hammering.

Zaal's breathing increased, and his stilled feet brought us to a stop. Opening my eyes, the final notes of the song coming to an end, I lifted my eyes. Zaal was staring down at me, and the look on his face made my stomach flip.

I watched him silently as he brought my hand to his chest. His long lashes blinked. Then blinked again. And with the slight parting of his lips, he said, "My heart, it is full, Talia. It is full, for you." My throat closed as those heavenly words slipped from his soul. "It used to be empty and weak, now, now it beats strong again."

Zaal leaned down. With the gentlest, most feather-light of touches, his soft lips brushed against mine. And I savored his taste. I savored his hands on my back. I savored it all. I wanted time to stop. I wanted time to freeze, to hold us captive in this moment, in this very moment.

I never wanted it to end.

The ambient sound of the speaker hissed in the background. Drawing back from Zaal, I pressed my hand to his cheek, and said, "I want to make love to you."

Zaal's forehead creased with confusion, but standing on my toes, I kissed those creases away, and whispered, "Come with me."

Linking his hand in mine, I led him out of the living room and up the stairs. No words were exchanged as we approached my bedroom. Not one sentence uttered as we entered the door. I locked us inside.

Walking to the bed, Zaal followed behind. I turned, and I trembled. Everything about tonight felt bigger somehow. More important. The air around us had thickened, making it impossible to breathe. I knew, I just knew that it was because I was in love.

I was in love with Zaal Kostava.

We'd bared our pasts, we'd fought our fates. And at the end, left over was only the purest form of love. Of need. Of *us*.

Like Zaal had said, *our empty hearts were now full.*

Zaal's hands were fisted at his sides. His eyes were luminescent with need. As he watched me, I lifted my shirt over my head. Reaching behind me, I unclasped my bra. The material fell away. Zaal's eyes focused on my heavy, bare breasts.

The tension thickened, pulsed, clogged our very air.

Inhaling a long breath, I snapped the buttons on my jeans and rolled them down my legs. A hiss tore from Zaal when my panties came down, too.

A growl sounded in Zaal's chest. I stepped toward him, until I was flush against his chest. Zaal watched me, never taking his eyes from mine.

Laying my hands on his waist, I lifted his shirt over his head. Once removed, Zaal's thick muscled body met my eyes. I felt my pussy clench and wetness spread between my thighs.

Yet Zaal stood still. Stood still and let me take the lead, let me undress him, let me love him like he deserved to be loved.

My hands drifted to the waist of his pants, and I pulled them down, Zaal's hard long cock springing into view. He kicked his pants off his feet.

Now both naked, I lifted my hand and ran it down his chest. As my fingers lingered on his toned and defined V, I continued until his hand wrapped around mine.

Walking backward, my legs hit the bed. I climbed on, Zaal's huge frame following me. Lying down on my back, Zaal's nostrils flared as he crawled over me. His body heat melted against mine and I held out my hands, welcoming him into my arms.

Spreading my legs, Zaal lay in between. His body kissed mine and I felt his length lay flush against my pussy. I moaned at the contact. Zaal, with his long hair brushed back off his face. There were no words.

I could read every part of Zaal's face.

Could see every hungry expression igniting his dark and raw features.

Gripping Zaal's wide shoulders, I pulled him down to crush his mouth to mine. The kiss started off slow, teasing, skin brushing against skin. Then as the tension built, so did the kiss.

On a low groan, Zaal pushed his tongue into my mouth. His hips moved, rocked against my pussy, his hard length dragging over my clit.

"Zaal!" I cried out, my lips breaking from his mouth on a gasp.

But Zaal's hand pressed on my cheek, his touch forcing me to stare into his green eyes. His hips rolled some more, and I was ready. He was flush against me, and I could feel he was, too.

His eyes were fixed on mine.

Mine were fixed on his.

I had to have him.

He had to have me.

Lifting my hand to smooth over Zaal's cheek, I whispered, "Make love to me."

Zaal studied my face, and skirting his hand down to my thigh, he spread me further, and slowly slid inside.

Zaal's teeth gritted as he pushed forward, inch by long thick inch. I wrapped my hands around his neck, and a pained moan fell from my lips as he filled me to the hilt.

I gasped at the full feeling, my skin damp as Zaal's hard body rubbed against mine. He was all consuming. Taking me. Owning me. Completely possessing me in every possible way.

"Talia," he groaned as his hips built up speed. But he never looked away. Our eyes stayed fixed as I met him thrust for thrust, my hips rolling to feel him more and more.

Zaal leaned down, his arms encasing my head. I bathed in his warm breath as my hands lay flat against his back. Zaal increased his speed, my pussy gripping tightly to his cock. I breathed in his scent—musk and sweat and Zaal. All Zaal.

My skin felt on fire, every part of me glowing with life.

Grunts and groans spilled from Zaal's mouth. And I drank them all in. His face tensed and his mouth parted, breathing in and out in short sharp pants.

Then Zaal's hips hit harder. I wouldn't last. It was too much. This intensity. The look in his beautiful green eyes. The look of pure need, of pure love in his face.

I didn't think it could be like this.

I never knew. I never knew it was possible to feel this strongly.

Shivers ghosted down my back as tingles shot up my spine. My clit pulsed and Zaal's cock within me brushed over my G-spot deep inside. My pussy clenched and my nipples hardened, my back arching off the bed.

Zaal's nostrils flared and his lips tightened. His thrusts pumped faster still, and I knew this was it, knew he was about to fall . . . fall over the edge with me.

On a cry, and a final hard thrust by Zaal, my pussy clamped down on his dick and I burst apart at the seams. Stars glittered behind my eyes as I came, the force of my orgasm causing Zaal to bellow out a roar.

Zaal's chest was damp with sweat, and he dropped his head to the crook of my neck. My eyes fluttered closed, Zaal's length still jerking, grunts escaping his mouth. His breathing evened out and I placed my hand on the back of his head; I had to hold him close. I needed to anchor myself. My heart felt full to the brim with love, so full I felt I needed his touch to keep in control.

And I wanted him to know.

I wanted him to know how he'd changed me.

"Baby," I whispered. Zaal's head turned slightly to the side, his heavy breathing still labored. I guided his head higher, until his bright jade eyes were looking right into mine. My heart stuttered at the wild and primal sight of loose strands of long hair falling over his face. They had freed themselves from his knot and I had to slowly inhale at the sight.

Taking a deep breath, knowing I had Zaal's full attention, I placed my palm on his cheek, and confessed, "I love you, Zaal. I completely and wholeheartedly adore you."

Zaal's full lips parted.

His eyebrows pulled together. "Love?" he asked. His green eyes searched mine as if he could find the answer in their depths.

His short breaths warmed my face, and I explained, "It's a feeling. It's that fullness you feel in your heart, your soul. The tightness and breathlessness you feel in your chest. It's passion." I moved a hand to lay over his chest, directly over his racing heart. "It's the need, the absolute need to be with another, like this, joined, unwilling to be separated for anything." I blinked away the mist from my eyes, and added, "It's you and I, Zaal.

"*Love*," he whispered, rolling his tongue around the word.

"Most males and females with full hearts, hearts full for each other, say, 'I love you,' and 'I love you, too.'"

"Mmm . . . ," he replied, his head slightly shaking as if he disapproved. And my heart sank. A raw surge of pain making me breathless. He didn't love me back.

Zaal's skin had flushed as he watched me, a kaleidoscope of emotions flitting across his face. Lifting his hand, he pressed it over his heart, and then over mine. "You are . . . for me," he stated, those familiar words, so simple yet so powerful, sounding like heaven to my soul.

Tears fell, and I realized this was him telling me he loved me, too. "You like to say that better?" I asked, my voice breaking in happiness.

He nodded firmly, his harsh face straightening in conviction. "You are . . . for me. No other male. Just me. And *me* . . . for *you*. This is my, '*I love you.*' These are *my* words from *my* scarred soul. They are not borrowed words, but words from my full heart, and my heart only."

Those four simple words, "*You are . . . for me*," were the most meaningful words that could ever be spoken.

Zaal leaned down and peppered soft kisses over my face, murmuring, "You are for me, you are for me," repeatedly, until I thought my body would burst with light.

With my hands on his face, I lifted his face to meet mine. Gazing into those green eyes that had taken me captive all those weeks ago, I replied, "I am for you, Zaal, eternally. I am forever for you."

The expression that set on Zaal's face, one of disbelief and pure adoration, stole my breath. He swallowed the heavy emotion built between us, and took my mouth in the most gentle and sweetest of kisses. I wrapped my hands around his wide body, his warmth keeping me safe, making me feel so incredibly safe.

This was perfection.

This was my paradise—

Suddenly a loud crash sounded downstairs. Zaal's mouth ripped from mine. Gunshots sounded. Loud pain-filled shouts echoed into our room.

I recognized those voices—Savin, Ilya.

"No," I whispered, terror washing through my body.

Zaal froze when a rush of feet pounded up the stairs. His hand found mine, and just as he was about to pull me from the bed, the door burst open, the wood cracking off the wall. I screamed as men flooded into the room; men with rifles all aimed at our heads.

Zaal shook with rage. Releasing my hands, he ran at the guards. But just as he was about to fight, a man pushed through the door. A dark man with inky black hair and soulless eyes. He was dressed impeccably, and as soon as he laid eyes on Zaal, Zaal ground to a halt.

The blood drained from my face—Jakhua, his master.

Zaal's face tore apart with agony as he stood before Jakhua. I could see how conditioned he was to obey this man.

Jakhua, with a heady confidence, glanced over to me and his lip curled in disgust.

"221," he said in cold greeting. Zaal's body stiffened. I could see his eyes squeezing shut repeatedly at Jakhua's voice. My heart lurched. He was trying to fight the hold, fight the twenty-year-long leash Jakhua had on him.

Jakhua walked forward and, clicking his fingers at his guards, ordered, "Take the Russian whore."

White-hot fear spiked through my body as two of his guards walked forward. I shuffled back along to the headboard of the bed, trying to get away.

Zaal had begun to pace, holding on to the sides of his head. But Jakhua's eyes never left mine. I could feel the repulsion. My stomach rolled in response.

A guard reached out for me, but I kicked out, landing a strike to his stomach. He grunted at the hit, but a second guard was suddenly behind me, and he rammed his fist straight against my cheek. Dazed from the blow, I was unable to fight the guard from wrapping his hand in my hair, using the painful purchase to drag me from the bed.

And then I heard a blood-curdling roar tear from Zaal. Managing to glance up, my vision blurred by the pain, I saw Zaal run at the surrounding guards. He was lethal in his execution.

My desperate gaze sought out Jakhua, and I smiled at the pure look of fear on his face. His personal guards pushed him back, as Zaal knocked Jakhua's enforcers to the ground.

Jakhua looked my way, and with a smug grin, signaled something to the guards. The guard holding my hair dragged me to my feet. In a rush, my naked body was pushed through the melee and down the stairs. I could hear Zaal snarling, and crashes against the wall, but I couldn't get free.

The guards pulled me down until I hit the hallway, where they then wrenched open the basement door and pushed me inside.

My blood coursed through my body when I was pulled down the stairs. Footsteps followed behind.

I fought my screams. I needed to be strong. I thought of my father and mother, of Luka and Kisa, and what they'd endured. I wouldn't give these bastards the satisfaction of hearing or seeing my fear.

I was pushed against the wall, the wall only weeks before I'd watched Zaal slump against. The guards held out my hands and made quick work of shackling me. The chains were heavy on my limbs and they tightened them until my arms hung above my head.

I almost passed out from the pain, but I gritted my teeth forcing myself to fight.

Suddenly I saw feet and when I looked up Jakhua was standing in front of me, his face betraying his rage. Unprovoked, he struck me across the face with the back of his hand. I closed my eyes at the blast of pain slicing through my head. I felt a wetness drip down my chin.

I tasted the iron taste of blood as it hit my tongue. My lip throbbed. My shoulders ached as the chains kept me suspended, the pain too much to bear.

Jakhua moved back, and he gripped my cheeks. His furious dark eyes met mine. "You're the Tolstoi bitch who's sunk her claws into my dog, huh?"

I felt anger, white-hot anger. The feeling was new but not unwelcomed. Gathering the blood in my mouth, I spat the contents in his face. Jakhua froze for a beat then struck me again, my cheek pulsing with the impact of the blow.

Suddenly the door to the basement smashed open. I saw Zaal run down the stairs, his huge body tense, his muscles rippling. His hair fell from the topknot and his green eyes burned with rage.

As he hit the bottom stair, he turned to face us. His flushed face instantly paled when he saw me chained to the wall. "Talia . . . ," he murmured, and raced my way.

The guards raised their rifles, but Zaal kept coming. Looking like a savage animal unleashed, Zaal stormed toward Jakhua. But in a split second, Jakhua had pulled out a long sharp knife from his jacket. Ripping my head back by the hair, he held the knife right against my exposed throat.

Zaal skidded to a halt. Suddenly losing all his anger, his fear was evident in his expression.

"Come any closer, I'll slit the fucking Russian whore's throat," Jakhua taunted through gritted teeth. I met Zaal's eyes. He had no idea what to do.

"Don't fucking hurt her!" he hissed. The knife pressed further against my skin. I could feel the sharp cold metal draw blood. A muffled cry slipped from my throat.

The sound prompted Zaal to step back. He repeated, "Don't hurt her."

Jakhua laughed a humorless laugh. "The animal fucking talks!" I shivered at the disdain in his voice. Zaal's jaw clenched.

"The Volkovs have cost me a fucking lot of money. That cunt, the new *knyaz,* taking you from me has lost me tens of millions in Type A sales."

I closed my eyes, trying to breathe calmly. But when the knife pressed against my throat even closer, I gasped for breath. When I opened my eyes, Zaal was pacing, hands fisting at his sides.

Jakhua pulled on my hair, my head snapping back until the pain shot down my spine. "And this bitch, this fucking whore is going to die. I'm going to kill them all."

"No!" Zaal thundered. When his green eyes met mine, my body went limp. His expression had changed, but his eyes, they told me something new. They were telling me "good-bye."

"No!" I said desperately.

Jakhua ripped at my hair. "Shut up, bitch."

Zaal tensed, then dropping to his knees, quietly said, "Take me."

My heart stopped. I felt like it frosted over inside my chest. "Zaal! No!"

But Zaal wasn't looking at me, he was looking straight at Jakhua. "Let her live, and I'll come with you, willingly."

I could hear Jakhua's heavy breathing in my ear, a heavy breathing that turned to relief as Zaal spoke those words.

"I have to make my money back," Jakhua said. "I need one hundred percent obedience. You are to go back on the drug. I need you back for demonstrations of its effectiveness."

I held my breath as he spoke those words. *No!* I tried to tell Zaal with my eyes, but his eyes were firmly focused on Jakhua.

Several seconds passed in silence. Zaal then got to his feet. He took a step closer. Then his eyes met mine. I couldn't stop the tears from pouring down my cheeks as I read the resignation in his face.

Without taking his eyes from me, Zaal agreed, "I'll come with you. I'll go back on your drug. And I won't resist, just let Talia live."

My face contorted with the same amount of pain I felt crash through my body. Jakhua abruptly stepped back, the knife removed from my throat. "Your papa would be ashamed of you, 221. Fucking a Tolstoi. Like some fucked-up *Romeo and Juliet* shit."

Zaal stepped forward, ignoring Jakhua, and I shook my head. "No!" I cried, my throat rasping with the rawness of my cries. "Please! You can't go back. You can't let him do that to you again!"

Zaal's nostrils flared. His face paled with sadness. He stepped closer.

I pushed his warm palm against my cheek. "I will gladly go, to save you. To let you live."

I shook my head again, but I could see the deep resolve in his eyes. "No, Zaal. They'll take away your thoughts. They'll steal your memories again. They'll make you kill again. You'll be back living in darkness! I can't, you can't, please . . ."

"But *you* will live," he whispered. My heart tore as I heard the break in his deep rasp. He didn't want this. He wanted to be free, he deserved to be free.

"Zaal—"

"I will happily give up my life for yours." His eyebrows pulled down in devastation. "I cannot imagine a world without you in it, you brought me the sun. I can live in darkness again knowing that you are shining here on the outside."

Racking sobs tumbled from my mouth, their severity bruising my empty lungs. Zaal closed in, and with the gentlest of touches, he pressed his lips against mine. The pain from my split lip hit my face, but I didn't care. I never ever wanted to break from this kiss.

Zaal pulled back, pressing his forehead to mine, as if he was committing this touch to memory, a memory he would lose as soon as he was injected with that fucking serum again. I couldn't stand the thought.

"You deserve to live," I whispered.

Zaal's lips spread into a sad smile. "I have lived, Talia. In the short time I have known you, I have lived more than I could ever have dreamed." His eyes stared at mine. "I have lived only because of you. I have . . . I have gained a full heart, a full heart for you."

I closed my eyes at the pain of this moment, of his acceptance of this fate. Suddenly he was ripped away. Snapping my eyes back open, I watched in horror as the guards dragged him away toward the stairs.

I thrashed in my chains, trying to get free. Zaal shook his head, telling me to stop. Stilling, and unable to breathe, I stopped. I watched as they approached the stairs.

Mustering the last of my raspy voice, I shouted, "Zaal!"

He turned his face as he reached the bottom step and, with his hand on his heart and tears in his eyes, he said, "You are . . . for me."

With those words the final dagger pierced my heart. I knew I'd be ruined for life. As Zaal began his ascent, I met his eyes, and declared in a hoarse voice, "I am . . . for you."

Zaal swallowed, closed his eyes, and as the guards forced him up the stairs he disappeared from view.

All energy drained, a crippling grief sweeping through my body, I sagged in the tight chains, sagged and cried, cried until darkness claimed me, and I could cry no more.

18

TALIA

"Down here!"

I stirred from sleep on hearing a male voice shout upstairs. I heard the rush of feet. Footsteps stormed down the steps to the basement.

I was aching, in pain, and my head throbbed.

"Shit! Talia!" I heard. Cracking my bruised eyes open, Luka ran my way. Luka and Mikhail, and *byki,* lots of *byki*.

"Luka." My mouth formed the word, but my throat felt like it was filled with razors.

"Get her down!" Luka ordered. I smiled in my head, my lips too weak to make the gesture. He sounded like a leader, finally like the man he was born to be.

A sudden pain shot through my body as I was freed from my chains. Every muscle in my body screamed as the blood began to fill them, forcing them back to life.

Strong arms held me and lifted me off the floor. Something was put to my lips. Cool water immediately filled my mouth. I struggled to swallow through a raw throat, but I forced myself. I had to tell Luka about Jakhua, about Zaal. I had to save him. Luka had to save him.

"Get her robe!" Luka called. I heard footsteps on the stairs as someone obeyed his order.

Luka poured the water over my face. A towel followed as he cleaned my face, the soft material feeling like stabbing needles.

Luka's hand pushed my bloodied hair back from my face, and he asked, "Talia? Are you okay?"

My eyes widened and filled with water. My body jerked. I tried to move. I needed to move. We needed to save Zaal.

"No," Luka said as my body arched with pain. "You need to wait. Your body needs time to adjust."

Looking into Luka's brown eyes, I cried, and rasped, "He took him. He came and took him from me."

Luka's face darkened. He pulled me to his chest. "I'll get him, Talia. This I promise you."

"But he is going to drug him again. Zaal agreed to be the prototype again, to save my life." Luka lowered me until I could see his face, his face torn with pain. "He saved me, Luka. Traded my life for his."

Just then, a *byki* came with my robe. Luka ordered them all out of the basement. My eyes widened, and I asked, "Savin and Ilya?"

Luka's eyes narrowed. "Shot."

My stomach fell. "Are they . . . dead?"

Luka shook his head. "No. They're not in good shape, but they're on their way to the hospital. They should be okay."

Luka helped me to stand, my legs aching as I tried to balance on my own. But Luka never let me fall. Instead he helped me dress, then lifted me in his arms.

As we made for the stairs, I asked, "You're going to save him, right? I don't, I don't think I could live without him."

Luka stopped. Looking me straight in the eyes, he said, "I already have men, trustworthy men, finding out where Jakhua's taking Zaal. We have men on the inside, rats in his crew. It shouldn't be long. He left himself too open risking this visit to retrieve Zaal. His tracks are already being traced. And as soon as we know where the fucker's crawled off to, I'm gonna fucking storm the place and kill every last *piz'da* there."

I swallowed at seeing my brother so violent. But right now, for the first time, I welcomed it. I wanted it.

Only Luka, Luka who used be known as Raze, could free Zaal.

As we approached my parents' house a few hours later, I opened the door and ran into the hallway. Everyone was in the living room; Mama, Kisa,

Papa, and the Pakhan. As I hurried into the living room on still-shaky feet, my mama jumped up and her face turned white.

"Talia . . . my girl," she cried, and ran toward me taking me in her arms. She gripped me so tightly I flinched. Hearing my quick inhale of breath, Mama pulled back. Her hand lifted and skirted over my face. "Talia, what did that man do to you?"

"I'm fine, Mama." I rubbed the top of her arms, and walked around her to face my father and Kirill. "Jakhua came to the house." I swallowed, my throat still sore. I said, "They took Zaal. He took Zaal again. He's going to use him for the drugs again."

Someone entered the room, and when Kisa jumped from the sofa, I knew it was Luka. But my eyes stayed on my father. "Papa, we have to go and get him."

My father stood, as did Kirill. My father walked forward and took me in his arms. "We'll kill, Jakhua, Talia. He'll pay. He's fucked with the Bratva for the last time. Touching my daughter was the last thing he will ever do."

I pulled back, my body sagging in relief. "And Zaal?" I asked. My father's face clouded over. My relief soon turned into dread.

"The Kostava is not our business. With Jakhua gone he'll find his own way."

Blood rushed so fast through my body, I could hear nothing but its pulse in my ears. As I looked up to my father, he had turned to Kirill. They were speaking in hushed whispers.

Anger seeped into my bones, and shaking, I shouted, "No!"

My father and Kirill turned to face me. My father looked at me in surprise. "No!" I repeated. "You have to save Zaal."

My father's face remained unmoved. I knew that silent expression. It was still a no. "Papa," I argued, "he saved me! Jakhua had a knife to my fucking throat. He was going to kill me, out of hatred for you. But Zaal gave his life for me, he didn't even hesitate. He was willing to give up his freedom for me!" My father shook his head, and before he could speak, I confessed, "I love him."

The room hushed to a tense silence. My shocking confession hung in the air. My eyes were to the ground, but I forced them up to look into my father's face, his face that was filled with disappointment and shock.

"I love him," I said again, pride filling my bones. I stepped forward. "And he loves me, too."

"You fell for the Kostava?" my father said in disbelief.

I lifted my head and said, "He's not just a *Kostava*. His name is Zaal. Zaal who, along with his brother, was taken by Levan Jakhua, and forced to watch the massacre of his family as a child. A child who was forced to be a slave for Jakhua for over twenty years. Zaal is not just a Kostava. He's the perceived enemy who just sacrificed himself to save your only daughter!"

I panted from exertion. I heard my mama sniffing behind me. I turned to face her. "I love him, Mama," I said with a trembling voice. "We have to save him. There's no other choice for me."

My mother looked over my shoulder at my father. I followed her gaze. He was livid. "No daughter of mine will be with a Kostava! I won't accept it." His voice lowered. "And I won't risk my men rescuing a man from that family!"

Pain shattered my heart. I stumbled back. "Then you'll lose a daughter," I said, and meant every word. I watched as my papa's angry expression faded into shock.

"Talia . . . ," he whispered. I shook my head, cutting off whatever he was about to say.

"No, he's my everything. I won't let him trade his life for mine, and do nothing to help. Don't you think that a man who would sacrifice his own life in place of another's deserves to be saved?"

Kirill stepped from behind my father and confirmed, "We will kill Jakhua, Talia, but we won't send our men in for this man. Ivan's right. We've already lost too many men in this fucking street war. I won't risk more." I stared at the Pakhan. And I knew that was that. His word was final.

I didn't know what else to do.

But then Luka stepped further into the room and stopped beside me.

"Then risk *me*," Luka stated. My head snapped up to see my brother's hard face meeting that of our father and Kirill's.

Kirill's eyes narrowed. Father stepped forward. "Luka, we spoke about this—"

"I'm not Alik Durov," he said coldly, cutting off our father's words.

Father tensed, and Luka added, "And I'm not the Luka you knew. I'm someone new. Someone the gulag created. I can't and won't leave Zaal to suffer at that man's hands again. His brother saved me. Nothing you say will stop me from feeling a kinship toward him." Luka's face hardened, and he emphasized, "I don't give a fuck that he's a Kostava. I don't give a fuck if you won't risk any of our men for him. Because I'm going in, and I'm stronger and more effective in the kill than twenty of our men put together.

"Zaal knew nothing of his family. He isn't his father. He didn't kill *dedushka*. But his brother saved my life, and *he* saved Talia's." He laughed sardonically. "So that family you hate so much, the Kostavas, the great 'Tolstoi enemy' have saved both of your children. And without Anri and Zaal, we would both be dead. You'd have no heirs to your fucking throne."

My father blanched, and Luka, looking every inch a Bratva pakhan, added, "I was locked in a cage, mind fucked, incessantly raped, and made to fucking kill. There is *no* way that I'm leaving Zaal to that same fate. He was taken as a child and forced in every way *like me*. And just *like me,* he won't ever be that boy who was captured. That boy was made into someone else, just *like me.* He'll forever be Zaal Kostava and 221, just like I will always be Luka Tolstoi, *and* 818. A part of me will *always* be Raze. And nothing will ever fucking change that."

Luka looked down at me. "I'll get him out, Tal. I swear it to you, as your brother, and as your *knayz*."

Luka turned to leave, when my father stepped forward. Luka stilled.

"Luka," our father said, and cleared his throat. "I am proud of you in this moment. I am so very proud."

The Pakhan nodded in agreement, and lifted his chin. "You sound like a true *knayz*, Luka. I've been waiting to see this rise in you. Who knew it would have been a Kostava that inspired this change."

Luka swallowed, and reaching for Kisa's hand, silently led her out of the door, to their house three doors down.

The room was stifled and tense, and I could feel a shift in atmosphere. Getting to my feet, I walked into my mother's waiting arms, when my father came forward. I braced for his wrath, for his judgment and disappointment. Instead, he took me in his arms and pressed a kiss to my head.

With glossy eyes, he stepped back. "I couldn't have lost you, too, Talia," he said gruffly, causing my resolve to crack. I pulled back, but my father turned away, and dismissed my mother and I with a wave of his hand.

My mother took me from the living room and into my bedroom. As the door shut, she sat beside me on my bed. Reaching out, I took her hand and asked, "What now?"

Mother sighed, and with the experienced strength of a true Bratva wife, she said, "We wait, Talia. We sit calmly, and we wait."

19

LUKA

The minute we entered our house, I walked into the living room and began to pace. I was going in. I was going in to the Jakhua hideout for Zaal.

Out of the corner of my eye, I saw Kisa sit down on the sofa, her fingernails in her mouth. Her face was directed toward the window, but I could see by her body language that she was stressed.

She was completely lost in her thoughts.

I focused on my wife, panicking at what she could be thinking, then I thought over the task I was about to undertake. I was going to murder Jakhua and anyone else from his clan that got in my way.

I was going to do this, and I knew how Kisa felt about me fighting. I knew she hated it, but Zaal needed me to save him. Talia needed this. Anri needed this. And *I* needed to get Anri's revenge once and for all.

I closed my eyes and tried to calm my breathing. I didn't know how to balance my need to kill, and what was best for my wife. It was hurting my head. It was making it difficult to breathe.

Hearing Kisa move from the sofa, I opened my eyes to see her making her way toward me. My wife stopped right before me, her face unreadable, and she took my hand in hers. I looked down at our linked hands, and then straight into her eyes.

I was so afraid of what she would say.

"Sit with me, *lyubov moya,*" Kisa said as she led me to the couch. She sat down, and I did, too. Kisa's hand was tight in mine. She pulled me in close and pressed a kiss to my lips.

Kisa moaned as I pushed my tongue into her mouth, loving her sweet taste hitting my throat. But then she pulled away, her eyes instantly downcast. My head tilted to the side as I stared at my wife. I had no idea what she was thinking.

Taking a deep breath, Kisa brought our joined hands to her lap, her free hand making small circles on the back of my hand.

The room was silent, apart from our strained breathing. I wondered if she wanted me to explain why I agreed to this tonight, if that's what she was waiting for. I shifted trying to think of something to say, how to put my feelings into words, but before I could, Kisa said, "It's funny." I stilled as she spoke, then she laughed a humorless laugh. "When I was young, I used to think that love conquered all." Kisa's hand shook in mine, and I edged closer to Kisa's side.

She lifted her head, her blue eyes meeting my brown. "But I now know this isn't true."

I took a deep breath at her confession, and fear filled my body. Was she . . . ? Was she done with me? Was she telling me she'd had enough of me?

Lifting her hand, Kisa ran a finger under my left eye. I couldn't speak as I watched her eyes glisten with tears.

Pushing my hand into her long brown hair, Kisa gave me a weak smile and squeezed my hand. "I now know that love conquers *most*. And I'm okay with that—*most*." She shrugged. "No one on this planet is perfect, Luka. So it shouldn't surprise me that no one can take away all their lover's demons. That I can't make you free of your painful past. I can't make you into the carefree boy you were as a child." I didn't dare move as Kisa kept speaking. She leaned forward and pressed a soft kiss on my cheek. "But I *can* hold you when those demon's rise. And I can chase them away with a kiss, with a touch, by making love."

"Kisa . . . ," I whispered, unsure what to say in response. Her words, what she was saying, they meant everything to me. Kisa placed my finger over my lips, and shaking her head, cut me off.

"I love you, Luka," she assured firmly, "and I accept the man you are now, *wholeheartedly*. I *accept* that you are the two loves of my life— you are both Luka *and* Raze. You're the passionate and considerate boy from my youth, the one who would kiss me on the beach and I'd read to each night. But you are also the strong and tortured man from my present. My fierce protector. The man who saved me from a life of grief, the man who holds me in his arms all night. That man needs me just as much as he needs the air to breathe." I swallowed, trying to absorb every word spilling from her mouth. I tried to wrap my head around that she was finally understanding me. Expressing the way I felt inside. And accepting the man I had become—the man that was both Luka and Raze.

My eyes blurred with tears, and holding my hand she pressed her forehead to mine. "Both Luka and Raze make you the man you are now. One doesn't exist without the other. Both of their life's blood runs through your veins, mixing together to be *this you*. This man right now, holding my hand so tightly, and I will love them both until my dying day, and beyond if God allows it to be the case."

Kisa glanced away and I watched her swallow her fear, her emotions. Kisa took a long breath, and smiling, turned back to me and said, "So be the man you are now, *lyubov moya*. Be both my Luka *and* my Raze. Don't fight it anymore. Embrace them as sweetly as you do me." Tears ran down our faces as she whispered, "Be at peace. *Finally.*"

I lurched forward and wrapped my wife in my arms. I was shaking with the relief of Kisa's acceptance. Hot tears fell from my eyes as I buried my face in her neck. She just held me close, never letting me go.

Minutes later, I pulled back. Something felt like it had changed between us. A peace *had* settled in my body. I looked at my wife, my beautiful, perfect wife, and I exhaled.

I lifted my hand and pressed it against her cheek, my stomach rolling at what I was about to confess. "*Solnyshko,*" I whispered almost apologetically, "tonight, I will kill again."

Kisa closed her eyes and breathed sharply through her nose. "I know." Kisa opened her eyes and tried to smile, saying, "because that's part of who you are, inside. A part of you needs to kill those you feel do wrong against those you love. *Raze* needs to kill to protect his family. And Zaal, he's your family."

My eyebrows pulled down as I wondered if all this was a dream.

But by the understanding look on Kisa's face, I knew it was real. She got me. She'd understood my biggest fear, and in only the way Kisa could, she made it better.

I could breathe.

I relaxed and I could breathe.

Kisa's expression changed and a blush coated her cheeks. Suddenly, she gripped my hand. "Luka," she said as I brought her hand to my mouth.

"Yes?" I replied.

She turned around and reached into her purse. She then pulled something out, and clutched it in her palm.

With the picture hidden in her grip, she looked to me nervously. Squeezing my hand, she said, "I have something to tell you."

I nodded, my stomach tensing at whatever she had to say. Taking a deep breath, she held out her hand, and a picture was placed in her palm. Pushing it into my hand, I looked down at the small paper square and turned it over.

At first I wasn't sure what I was looking at, then I focused on the grainy black-and-white picture and all the air in my body left my lungs. I froze, unable to move as my hands began to shake.

My eyes snapped up and met with my wife's. "Kisa . . . ," I whispered. A tear ran over my cheek. "Are you . . . Is this . . . ?"

My eyes fell to Kisa's stomach, and suddenly all the sickness, the paleness and tiredness she'd experienced of late, made sense. Taking my hand, Kisa laid it flat over her stomach. I watched her face as she smiled and nodded.

Tears streamed down her cheeks. "Yes, *lyubov moya,*" she whispered, "we're having a baby."

Overcome with emotion and pure fucking happiness, I dived forward, lowering myself to the floor, between Kisa's legs. My hands splayed on Kisa's thighs, then drifted up to land on her waist. I lifted her shirt and pressed my lips to her soft skin. Kisa's hands threaded through my hair, and I closed my eyes and just breathed. It was what we'd always wanted. A baby. A little person made by the both of us.

A family. The start of our own little family.

Pulling back from pressing kisses on Kisa's stomach, my eyes met my wife's. "I love you, *solnyshko*," I whispered, unable to express all I felt inside. "Thank you. Thank you for loving me so much. For understanding me like no one else."

A cry broke from Kisa's throat, and she held me so close. We seemed to stay that way for a lifetime; I never wanted to move. Then I heard movement near the front door and I knew the *byki* were here.

With a final kiss to my hair, Kisa guided me backward and cupped my face. "You need to go and get Zaal, Luka. You need to give Talia and him the chance to love as deeply as we do."

My eyes closed and I nodded. My hand lightly pressed over Kisa's stomach, and I rose to my feet. I stood looking at the back room, the room that held my weapons. I'd never gone into a fight without them before. But I also didn't want Kisa seeing that side of me. I wasn't sure she wanted to see me battle-ready. I didn't want her upset. Especially now.

Kisa stood and kissed me on my cheek. "Go, baby. Go be the man you need to be."

I had no idea how she did that, how she could so perfectly read my mind.

Kisa urged me to move with her hand, and I stepped forward.

My heart thudded as I walked to the back room. My head was spinning with the news.

I was going to be a father. Kisa was carrying our child.

A feeling of deep peace washed through me at the thought of seeing my love full with our baby. And my heart felt free. Free now that Kisa had accepted the man I was. She'd accepted all of me.

Completely.

Without judgment.

I was free.

Walking into the back room, I began undressing. Throwing my stifling shirt and dress pants to the floor, I moved to the closet and opened the wide doors. Only three things were waiting behind this wood—my black sweatpants, my dark gray hooded sweatshirt, and my bladed knuckledusters. The three things that defined the man I'd fought so hard to hide. The man I'd been since I was fourteen, and the man I could no longer deny.

Reaching for the hangers, I removed the pants and slid them on my legs. I removed the hooded sweatshirt and slipped it over my arms, zipping up the front.

My head looked up at the final items left in the empty closet. My fingers tensed and my blood pumped with excitement. Adrenaline merged with the anticipation of the fight, with anticipation of the kill, of bringing death to Jakhua.

Lifting my clenching hands, I pulled out the cold pieces of steel and ran my fingers over the sharp pointed blades. With breath held, I slowly slid the knuckledusters over my fingers and breathed. My eyes closed as my fingers curled into fists and the sense of being home coursed through my veins.

I walked back toward the living room when I caught sight of me in the mirror hanging on the wall. I stopped dead and stared at the man looking back at me.

This was the man I knew—*Raze.*

This was the man I held in my heart. This was me, the fighter, the one who maims. Slaughters. Kills.

Opening the door, I walked down the hallway and into the living room. Kisa was sitting on the couch. When I entered the room, her lips parted.

I stood still and watched her with wary eyes. Kisa got to her feet, looking beautiful in her black shirt and tight jeans. Her long brown hair fell over her shoulders, and her blue eyes captured me.

She stood before me, her sweet scent washing over me. A smile pulled on her pink lips. Her hands reached out and smoothed down over my gray sweater. Her hands moved down to my hands and over the spikes of my knuckledusters.

She huffed a laugh. Her bottom lip trembled.

"*Solnyshko?*" I whispered, not wanting to see her cry.

She flicked her eyes up to mine, and said, "I didn't realize until this very moment how much I've missed you looking like this."

My chest tightened. Kisa stepped closer again until she was flush to my chest. Her hands lifted and ran through my hair. "The man that with just one look I knew was my soul mate brought back to life . . . miraculously brought back to me."

I lifted my hands to wrap around her waist, and her head tilted to the side. Her fingers ran under my eyes. "All you're missing are the smudges of eye black."

I shook my head. "I'm not trying to hide who I am anymore. I know I'm Luka Tolstoi."

Kisa nodded, fighting her tears, but her hands lifted to my neck and she placed my dark hood over my head. "No," she whispered, and ran her finger softly down my cheek. "Like *this,* you're Raze."

"Kisa," I rasped, my throat now tight.

"Shh," she soothed. "Go. Go and stop Jakhua. Go and bring Zaal back to Talia, back to us all. He belongs here. With us." I stared at Kisa, unmoving. Then her hand took mine and she pressed it against her stomach. "And fight for us. Stop Jakhua for the safety of our child. For our little family, you have a reason to come back to us now, *lyubov moya.*"

I leaned forward and kissed Kisa's mouth, whispering against her lips, "I always had a reason, Kisa. You're the reason. You've always been the reason. You will always *be* the reason."

I tasted Kisa's salty tears as they dropped to my lips. With one final kiss, I pulled away and walked to the front door.

Just as I was about to leave, Kisa's voice called from behind, stopping me in my tracks. "Luka." I turned my head to see her standing in the middle of the room watching me leave. Then just as I was about to return and take her in my arms, she smiled affectionately and said, "*Raze hell,* baby."

Expelling a sharp exhale, my chest filled with fire at those familiar words. I pounded out of the door and straight into Mikhail's waiting blacked-out van.

The *byki* in the back were all sitting calmly, waiting for my orders. As the passenger door shut, Mikhail pushed a rifle into my hands. I looked up to him, and he said, "As much as you scare the fuck out of me with those bladed 'dusters in the cage, I hope you know how to work one of these. The warehouse cellar where the Jakhua cunt hides out is gonna be filled with guards with rifles. You ain't gonna get much of a chance to fight these fuckers up close."

I wrapped my hands around the rifle and said, "Don't worry about me. Worry about getting yourselves out alive."

Murmurs sounded from the *byki* in the back of the van. As Mikhail started the engine, he turned and said, "I've worked for your papa now for fifteen years." I looked at him and he was looking right back at me.

"Never, not once, in all the jobs we've been sent on, has the *knayz* or a pakhan fought beside us. Alik Durov fought in the Dungeon. He murdered on these streets for nothing more than he was a sick fuck. He treated our men like dogs, disposable soldiers for his amusement. But you, sir, *you* fight alongside us with pride, as a brother in arms. You give us pride for the Volkov family, and for our position in New York." He glanced back to the watching now-silent *byki,* and said, "You've led us in every way since you came back. And every one of our brothers here, and the rest of the Bratva soldiers, would follow you straight into hell." Mikhail shifted in his seat and added, "You'll be the best pakhan we've ever had someday, sir. And I'll be proudly standing by your side. *We all will.*"

Emotion clogged my throat at the brothers' faith in me, and I shared their pride. As I felt the steel of my 'dusters on my hands and the rifle sitting in my lap, I finally knew. I *knew* this was the life I was made for. The battle, the violence, the years of killing in the gulag, and brother to my thieves in law.

I *was* the motherfucking *knayz* of the Volkov Bratva.

And I wouldn't fail tonight.

I wouldn't fail until I wore the name pakhan in my heart. I wouldn't stop until I made us the strongest, most feared Mafia in all of New York.

I took a long deep breath.

I was finally fucking *home.*

20

ZAAL

Darkness.

Back in darkness.

I hated the fucking darkness.

The chains hung tight and heavy around my wrists and ankles. And the cell was freezing cold.

I didn't know how long I'd been back here in this hell, but it was long enough to miss the sun. It was enough to miss the light.

My stomach churned in pain. I had to close my eyes and breathe through my nose when I thought of what I missed most.

Talia. My Talia.

Anger filled my chest when I thought of her hanging off the chains, bloodied and beaten, with Jakhua holding a knife to her throat.

She was so strong. Begging with her eyes not to exchange my life for hers. But that was never a possibility. My heart, my heart would never survive losing her. It was full for her. I would take the drugs to keep her safe.

Talia would be safe.

The sound of a guard entering the cell pierced through the dark. Footsteps approached me. A bright light suddenly flared. I flinched away from the flash of white.

"Get up," the usual guard hissed, speaking in my native Georgian tongue. "Master wants to see you."

"He's not my fucking master," I snarled. The guard stepped back as I got to my feet and approached the door. I could see the fear on his face. He was weak.

I held out my hands, but the guard didn't move. "I will not move," I said. "Do what you came to do."

The guard hung back. I could hear the rattle of the keys in his shaking hands. Fury took hold, and slamming my hand against the metal bars, I roared, *"Do it!"*

The guard jumped into action and unlocked the door. I held out my hands. Gripping the chain he led me down the dank hallway and to a dark room at the end. My skin pricked as flashbacks rushed into my brain. *Needles, pain, screams . . . Anri . . . Anri . . .*

The guard pulled on the chain. He threw open a door to a room. Suddenly, everything was familiar—the narrow bed, the straps that tied me down, the single light hanging from the roof, and the smell. The smell of chemicals, of the drug, the drug they pumped into my veins, the drug that made me forget.

I didn't want to forget.

I didn't want to forget long golden hair, a pair of brown eyes and that smile. Talia's smile.

Someone entered the door behind me. I knew it was Jakhua. I could sense him. I could see his face in my mind as he ordered the death of my family. I could clearly hear his voice as he ordered his guards to shoot, and I could see that look of satisfaction on his face, as he told the guards to leave my family in a heap against the wall, slaughtered and piled up like culled pigs. And I remembered his face as he strapped my brother and me down, and pumped us full of liquid rage.

"Get him chained to the wall," he said from behind me. The guard pulled me by my chains, doing as instructed.

I hung from the wall. Jakhua ordered, "Tighter."

The guard pulled on the chains. I gritted my teeth as my arms stretched so wide that my arm muscles burned.

I breathed through my nose; in and out, in and out, trying to dull the pain. Suddenly, two feet stood in front of me. Fueled with venom and hatred, I raised my head, and met the eyes of Jakhua. His face contorted with fury as I met his eyes. Pulling his arm back, he slammed it straight into my stomach. But I didn't react. I didn't even flinch.

Redness spread on Jakhua's face. Gripping me by my hair, he wrenched back my head and spat, "You fucking dare to look me in the eye. *You.*"

My eyes never moved from his, and I hissed, "I remember. I remember, everything."

When the cunt didn't react, I said, "I remember you walking into our country house. I remember you killing my family. I remember being brought to you. Remember being tied down to a bed, along with my brother. I remember you experimenting on us. Injecting us, beating us, forcing us to fight as children. Forcing us to kill others, to learn to be savage. I remember you tying us to the wall, just as I am now, hitting us until we called you master. Beating us until we forgot our own names."

Jakhua stepped back and smirked. "And here you are again. Back chained to my wall. About to call me Master once more."

I pulled on the chains holding my arms as anger pumped scalding blood around my veins. "I'll kill you," I spat. Jakhua stilled.

"In a matter of minutes you'll be back on the drug. In a matter of days, after being chained to this wall, you'll be bowing at my feet, like the fucking *dzlieri* you are."

Gritting my teeth, I couldn't stop the furious roar that burst from my lips. But Jakhua just stood there, looking at me like I was nothing, like the dog he believed me to be.

"I'll kill you for murdering my family. I'll kill you for taking my brother from me, and I'll fucking kill you for taking her from me!"

Jakhua laughed. He walked to a table. He picked something off it—a chain—and walked back toward me. "So, you finally remember Anri?"

I froze. I watched him circle the bed in the center of the room. He'd mentioned my brother . . . the brother I barely knew, only fractured memories visiting my dreams at night.

I stayed silent as Jakhua planted his feet before me. "Funny. When I had him sent to the Arziani gulag, when he was screaming for you to help him, you didn't say a thing. You watched him with blank eyes. Eyes under the control of my drug." He leaned in closer. I could smell smoke on his breath, the distinctive scent from the cigars he always smoked.

"You looked right through him as he begged you to see him. Didn't react as he whispered in your ear, and you didn't even shed a tear as he was dragged from the room screaming your name, and you never saw him again."

At his words, my head ached, a sharp pain striking through. My eyes closed, and I could see it. I could see Anri fighting a guard to get to me, he was older than the other memories I had. His body was bigger, his hair was longer, and the tattoo, he had a tattoo. My eyes widened, and I gasped for breath. 362. I could see the number 362 in black bold letters across his chest. And his face, his face as he begged me to see him, to fight the drug, and I . . . I . . .

My heart squeezed in my chest as I remembered his words, his final words to me. Suddenly, pain ripped across my chest. I looked up to see Jakhua had struck me with the chain.

I would kill him.

Klavs. Klavs. Klavs. I repeated in my mind, trying to set the order in my subconscious for when the drug took hold. With every blow, I forced myself to commit important things to memory. Talia cleansing me. Talia stroking my hair. The feel of her palm on my face, and her telling me she loved me. That her heart was full for me.

"You are . . . for me. No other male. Just me. And me . . . for you. This is my, 'I love you.' These are my words from my scarred soul. They are not borrowed words, but words from my full heart, and my heart only."

Talia sobbed as I leaned down to kiss her soft, wet mouth, repeating, "You are . . . for me, you are . . . for me . . ." Then Talia holding my face and whispering back, "I am . . . for you, Zaal . . . eternally. I am forever . . . for you . . ."*

The blows kept coming as I kept circling the cherished memories through my head. Then he stopped. Opening my eyes, my chest raw with chain marks and blood, Jakhua stood before me, sweating and panting. His dark eyes were burning with rage. I knew it was because I didn't react.

I wouldn't. When he pulled me from Talia I died inside. I would never give him the satisfaction of seeing me weakened by his hand. I would resist until I couldn't resist anymore.

Jakhua slammed the chain to the ground. I watched him wipe his sweating brow, then saw the door open.

Every muscle tensed when a man in a white coat walked through. My heart began to race when I saw the needle in his hand. My body shivered. A cold sweat broke out on my body. It was as if my body remembered what was coming.

Jakhua pointed at me and gave the order, "Do it. The sooner that dog is under the better. I need him to kill. I need him doing everything I command without hearing his fucking mouth."

I thrashed on the chains as the man drew closer. I snarled and roared as he flicked the needle. The chains grew tighter. I shook with the tension on my arms.

Just as the man held the needle to my arm, gunfire exploded down the hallway. Jakhua snapped his fingers at the guard and the guard ran from the room, rifle held in readiness.

My hands fisted. I stared at the door. My heart pumped as the sounds of screaming reached my ears. Jakhua reached for his gun. He scurried to the back of the room. The man in the white coat dropped the needle on the floor, and the glass bottle holding the liquid smashed into the floor.

Crashes and the sound of bullets ricocheting off walls flooded the hallway just beyond the door. I pulled on the chains, and I thundered a roar. I bellowed and bellowed, wanting the fight to come to this room.

I searched for Jakhua. His eyes met mine. My lip curled and I saw the blood drain from his face. My stare was a promise. A promise that if I got free, his life would be mine.

I would kill him. I glanced to the man in the white coat cowering in the corner of the room. I would fucking slaughter them all.

Jakhua pointed his gun in my direction. I saw in his face his resolve to kill me. I pulled harder on the chains, using my feet for purchase. I needed to get free. I needed to kill. I couldn't miss my chance to kill the fucker.

I wanted revenge.

I wanted his blood on my hands like my family's was on his.

As he pulled back the safety on the gun, rapid fire sounded just outside the room. Jakhua dropped his gun as the door burst open. I smiled. I smiled as he pathetically fumbled for his gun.

Men spilled into the room. I tried to recognize them, but all were dressed in black, holding their rifles before their faces, aiming them right at Jakhua.

"Mine!" I thundered, causing some of them to avert their attention my way. "He's mine!" I snarled, just as another man entered the room, a man wearing a hood over his head, bladed knuckledusters dripping with blood on his hands.

Then he turned to face me, and I relaxed.

Luka.

Storming forward, Luka pulled back his hood and met my eyes. He turned to one of his guards. "Get him the fuck down!"

A guard ran toward me. Pulling something from his pocket, he worked on the lock. The chains pulled on my arms, but my gaze locked on one man. One man cornered in the room. One man who needed to die. Slowly. Painfully, by *my* hands.

The sound of a shackle opening hit my ears, and one of my arms dropped free. Blistering fire surged through my arms and the blood filled my muscles. Then the second shackle was unlocked. Both of my arms were now free.

Rolling my neck and shaking out my hands, the chains that had owned me most of my life dropped to the floor. I stared down at the pile of metal on the ground. My chest constricted. I was free.

My eyes shot to Jakhua.

I was *almost* free.

Luka's eyes followed my gaze and he lurched forward with his fist held high. Reaching out, I gripped his wrist pulling him to an abrupt stop. Luka's eyes met mine. I shook my head and growled, "He's mine."

Luka's jaw clenched as though he was fighting the need to take Jakhua himself. I released his arm and said, "He killed *my* family. Anri was *my* blood. The cunt is mine to kill."

Luka stared at me in silence, but eventually he nodded and said, "You're right. He's yours. Make the fucker reap what he sowed."

The guards moved out of my way as I strode forward. Jakhua stood against the wall and watched me. He never took his piss-small dark eyes from me. I stood before him, fire filling my veins.

I breathed. Just worked on breathing as the man that slaughtered my family stood before me. And I was free. No drugs depriving me of my memories, making me forget who I was.

Just me and him.

Me and the man who was about to die.

Walking to the table where Jakhua kept his weapons, the very weapons he'd used on me as a child to bring me under control, I looked at them all lined up in neat rows.

I knew what I was looking for. The weapons he'd made me train with as a child in a cage. Made me kill others in a cage to prove my strength.

My hands twitched as my eyes fell on a flash of black metal. My heart pumped as I reached for a set of black sais. Sharp and deadly black sais.

I moved before Jakhua. His eyes widened as I twirled the sais in my hands. The room was silent as the guards and Luka all watched me.

Walking to Jakhua, I lifted my right sai and placed the thin blade at his stomach. I pushed forward, all the time looking into his eyes . . . eyes that bulged as the hard steel slowly pierced his gut.

Lifting my other hand, I dropped the sai to the ground. I wrapped my fingers around his throat. I squeezed hard and made sure he looked right into my eyes as he struggled for breath.

His arms tried to hit at my back, but I didn't even feel them. Jakhua's face reddened as I slowly and painfully stole his life.

Then with the sai still plunged inside his stomach, I twisted and slowly dragged it up. The blade sliced through flesh. It tore through organs and scraped against bone in agonized slowness.

And all the time I stared into his eyes. The last face he would ever see would be that of a Kostava, the only surviving heir of the family he hated most.

Blood tried to surge up his throat. I squeezed my hand tighter, Jakhua choking as my hand tightened. Still my sai continued to cut. Then just as the life left his body, I ripped the sai from his torso, released my hand from around his neck, and watched as his body slumped down the wall, blood pouring from his wounds.

Stepping back, I looked at the guards all holding their rifles in readiness. With Jakhua's dying eyes looking at me, I ordered, "Fire!"

The Bratva's guards followed my command, raining bullets straight into Jakhua's flesh, the force of the bullets at such close proximity ripping his body to shreds.

I watched as his eyes glazed with imminent death. When the firing stopped, a weight fell from my chest. He was dead. Jakhua was *dead*.

Silence filled the room. Hearing a noise from behind, I whipped around just in time to see the man in the white coat drop to the ground. Luka stepped back from the man, wiping his knuckledusters on his pants. He'd slit the white coat's throat.

My eyes fell on Luka, then on the man in the white coat, then finally back to Jakhua. I glanced down at my hands; they were shaking. I stared at my bloodied hands, and images of my family raced through my mind. My chest grew tight. I felt like all of my blood had drained from my body.

My knees hit the ground. A pressure built in my stomach, traveling up my throat. Shaking with too much emotion, too many memories blocking my mind, I tipped my head back and screamed.

I screamed and screamed until the pressure left me. One single realization took its place as I sat, weakened, on the ground.

I was free.

I was finally *free* and completely free.

Feeling a hand on my shoulder, I turned. Luka Tolstoi was behind me. He met my eyes and said, "We need to leave."

"Where do I go?" I asked, my voice rough and raw.

"To Talia," Luka replied. Any tension, any anger I had remaining, left my body at the simple mention of her name.

I nodded and got to my feet. "Yes," I said, "take me to Talia."

"Let's go," Luka said as we pulled up to a house.

I stared at the large house and took a deep breath. It was the Tolstoi house. I looked to Luka. "I will not be welcome."

Luka sighed and opened the van's door. I followed him onto the dark street. I stood, looked at the house and my heart clenched. Talia was in that house. *My* Talia was in that house.

And I needed her. I wanted to see her again so much that all my muscles ached at the thought.

Luka laid a hand on my shoulder. I wore a sweatshirt and pants. But my skin was covered in Jakhua's blood. My hair was not smooth.

Talia liked my hair smooth.

"She's inside," Luka said, and walked up some stairs. He glanced back, and taking a deep breath, I walked behind him.

Luka opened the door and walked toward a room. I could hear voices and, with each step, my heart beat faster and faster.

I was a Kostava in a Tolstoi house.

I was hated.

My father had killed Talia's *dedushka*.

They had cause to hate me. I should not be here.

Luka walked into the room first. I heard relieved voices rushing to greet him. I remained behind the wall.

I had no family.

I did not know how it was to be in a family. I did not know how to act around people.

The room then went quiet. Luka came back into the hallway. "Come," he said, and walked back into the room.

Inhaling through my nose, I stepped forward and rounded the corner.

I stopped in the entranceway. Every face looked my way. My gaze fell on two men standing at the back of the room, one who bore a strong resemblance to Luka.

Ivan Tolstoi, I thought.

Luka's wife was there, wrapped in his arms. An older woman was there staring at me, a curious look on her face.

My pulse thundered as they all watched me in silence.

Then I heard a gasp from behind me. My muscles tensed as light footsteps approached. I briefly closed my eyes and took a deep breath. I exhaled, and turned. I saw the golden hair first, then a set of brown eyes.

Talia.

A cry of relief sounded from her mouth as she entered the room and moved before me. Her trembling hand covered her lips as tears ran down her cheeks.

She looked at me as if I were not real. Then, on a sigh, she ran forward and jumped into my arms. "Zaal," she cried, and wrapped her arms around my neck.

Holding her in my arms, her legs wrapped around my waist, I

crushed her to my chest. "Talia," I whispered back, and tucked my nose into her neck.

I held her tightly.

I never ever wanted to let go.

She was mine.

I was hers.

We were each other's.

Talia pulled back, and crushed her mouth against mine. As our lips connected, my soul filled with her kiss. Always full for Talia.

Her hands pushed into my hair and she broke away. "Are you okay?" she asked, her eyes dropping to my chest and arms.

"He did not drug me," I assured. More tears ran down Talia's cheeks.

"Are you okay?" I asked, remembering her chained up and hurt on the wall.

"Yes," she whispered.

Lifting my hand to her face, I pressed my forehead to hers and whispered, "You are . . . for me."

Talia smiled. "I am . . . for you," she whispered back, and wrapped me in her arms once again.

I would have held her forever, but someone coughed from behind us. Talia tensed in my arms. Slowly she pulled back and my pulse spiked when I saw the fear in her eyes.

Talia released herself from my arms and slid gently to the floor. Threading her hand through mine, she led me forward, straight to the two men in dark suits. Dark suits like Jakhua used to wear.

"Papa, Pakhan," Talia said quietly, "this is Zaal." She swallowed and added, "Zaal Kostava. My love."

Both men stared at me. The room was silent and thick with tension. Talia reached out her free hand and took the arm of the man with longer hair, the one that looked like Luka. "Papa," she said confidently, "I love him. I love him with my whole heart. I know you may not approve, and if you don't it won't change a thing. I love you, you know this. But I am head over heels in love with this man, and I want you to accept him as my other half."

Talia's father watched me as his daughter spoke. I was so proud, so floored at how Talia bravely fought for our love, but could also see the hatred for me in his dark stare. Talia curled herself back into my arms as her father's cold expression spoke volumes.

"Papa," Luka said from behind. I turned and met Luka's eyes. I shook my head, telling him without words not to defend me, and Luka quieted. Talia stepped to the side.

Turning back to the Volkov Pakhan and Ivan Tolstoi, I stepped forward and laid my hand on my chest. "I am Zaal Kostava. I am the son of Iakob Kostava, the man who murdered your father."

Ivan's face hardened.

"But I am *not* my father," I stressed. "I was not raised in that life. I was taken as a child, like Luka, and forced under Jakhua's control." I breathed in a long breath, and looked to Talia. "I am in *love* with Talia. I wish to stay, with Talia."

Talia's hand reached out for mine and I took it briefly. I then let go to fix my gaze back on Ivan. His face was unreadable. Then I remembered something from my childhood. Something I had seen men do to my papa in his office.

Dropping to my knees before the Pakhan and Ivan, I looked up. "I, Zaal Kostava, of the Kostava clan of Georgia, pledge my loyalty to you, Ivan Tolstoi. I swear to never betray you." I laid my hand over my heart, and I continued, "I give you my life for the life of your father. Blood for blood." I breathed out through my nose and said, "I have no family. I have no obligation to the Kostava clan. But I will pledge myself as a Tolstoi. As a brother of the Volkov Bratva. If you will have me."

I held out my hand, my head still bowed, waiting to see if Ivan would take it. He did not move, but then I heard him ask. "You love him, Talia?" My breathing paused.

"Yes," she said, her voice strong and unshakable. "I love him so much, Papa. He saved my life, hell, he *is* my life."

Ivan didn't respond. Then I heard Luka's voice. "You know my decision, Papa. He's Anri's brother. That makes him mine. And I have seen him with Talia. He is for her, like Kisa is for me. He will protect her and give her his loyalty. You have my assurance on that."

I risked a glace up to see that Ivan's head had dropped. He then looked to the Pakhan. The Pakhan shrugged. "He's no threat to us. His family's dead. He's lived his life under Jakhua. And Ivan, he *is* a Kostava. He could strengthen our connections with the Georgians in the future. He's the sole heir, the sole survivor to the biggest clan that existed in Georgia. Many people will be happy he is alive, many will still follow him if he wishes to one day lead. And if he is an ally of the Volkov's, in the family of the Volkov's, it will only ever work in our favor. It makes good business sense. He's contractually a stronger marital match for Talia than any other suitor you could have picked out." The Pakhan shrugged. "Let the boy pledge."

Ivan looked down at me and asked, "Do you have any feelings of hatred for my family?"

I frowned, and I deliberately shook my head. "I have none." I met eyes with Talia and rasped, "I love Talia. I want to be forever with Talia."

"Zaal," Talia whispered, and looked determinedly at her father. "Papa, I won't be without him."

Ivan sighed, and he held out his hand. I took his hand in mine and kissed the back, then brought it to my forehead. Ivan pulled it back and motioned with his fingers for me to rise.

I lifted to my feet. Ivan stepped closer and said, "Prove me wrong about your family name. Prove to me you are as worthy of my daughter as she and my son seem to believe."

"Papa," Talia whispered lovingly from beside me, "thank you."

Ivan opened his arms. Talia went to her father. He kissed her head. "I could not see you miserable, Talia. This man, Zaal, I can see he makes you happy. I refuse to see another child of mine destroyed in this life."

"Thank you," she repeated, and moved back to kiss his cheek.

Talia let go of her father and came to me. She took my hand in hers and said, "We get to be together. A Kostava and a Tolstoi, Zaal. I get to love you."

I pointed to my heart and then to hers. "No names. Just you and me. Because you are . . . for me."

"And I am . . . for you," she declared back. Talia smiled so big and she reached up to run her fingers through my long hair. I lost my breath at the sight.

"Your hair needs washing. Your lovely long hair."

Taking both her hands in mine, I pressed my forehead to hers and said, "I look forward to you cleansing it."

Talia paused, then a laugh escaped her lips. I pressed my fingers to her lips and said, "I should like always to see you smile."

It felt strange to sit at the Tolstoi family table. The Bratva kings were of course at the head of the table. Talia's mother served the food. I didn't really eat, my stomach could not handle it.

I looked round the table. I had to blink at the surreal feeling of being here, and having all this, a new family. My lungs squeezed and a pit formed in my stomach. The last time I had been sitting around a table enjoying food, my family was killed. And I was taken away.

I looked down at my hands and stared. I closed my eyes. I could still feel Anri gripping my right hand as Jakhua walked into the yard. I could still feel Zoya holding my left hand, then crawling into my arms and pressing her nose into my neck.

A lump clogged my throat as those memories surfaced. My breath began to quicken as it hit me precisely what I'd lost. This could've been my life. I could've had my family. Watching them grow, having the same bond.

It was so much. Too much.

I was blindsided by too many memories slamming around my brain. Hearing the laughter from the Russians eating and sharing love was too much. I was going to lose it. I needed to leave the table. I—

Then a soft hand slipped into mine and gently squeezed. My eyes snapped open. Immediately my gaze joined with a dark brown gaze.

Talia.

Her beautiful face looked up at me. I could see the concern in her face. I could feel her worry for me in my heart. Her hand squeezed again, and she leaned in to press a kiss to my cheek. My eyes drifted to a close at her touch. I held on tight. Held on until the pain from the surge of memories stopped.

As I opened my eyes, I felt the stares arcing our way. I looked around the table, Talia's hand still in mine, and I saw all eyes watching us. Talia's mother's eyes were shining as she looked at her daughter. But it was

Luka's face that caught my attention. Exhaling, I met his gaze. I saw something that helped me breathe: his understanding.

Luka sat back in his chair and looked to his father. "I need to take Zaal somewhere."

Ivan placed his fork on his plate. Casting me a wary glance, he nodded his head. Luka stood, and he nudged his head in the direction of the door. Meeting each of the Bratva kings' eyes, I bowed my head and I slowly, respectfully rose from the chair. Talia's hand was still gripping mine. When I looked down at her she got to her feet, too.

Facing her brother, she said, "I've just got him back." Her steely brown eyes met mine. "I go where he goes."

A smile spread on my lips and I brought her hand to my mouth. I kissed her warm skin and Talia's face flushed.

Luka pulled his chair and reached out for Kisa, his wife. "You come, too, *solnyshko*."

Kisa smiled up at her husband and got to her feet. Luka wrapped her in his arm and looked to his father. "Send someone to Durov's place"— he pointed at me—"it's now his."

Ivan clicked his fingers at a guard. "Prepare the apartment."

Luka's eyes met mine. "Let's go."

A car drove us through the streets of Brooklyn. My eyes drank in all the derelict buildings of a place called Brighton Beach, and the people walking about. At times I had to close my eyes. I did not know how to cope with all the new things I was seeing.

But Talia's hand held mine. And when she felt me tense or lose my breath, her palm and lips would meet my cheeks, calming me down.

The car stopped at tall black gates. Luka and Kisa exited the car first, followed by Talia and I. I stared up at the black gates and the green beyond. The grass was filled with rows of stone objects.

The guard unlocked the gates and we walked through. Luka turned to me and said, "Zaal, come with me. I have something to show you."

I nodded. Talia reached up and kissed me on the cheek. "You go with my brother. I'll stay here."

Kisa moved beside Talia. "I'm going to visit my mama, you want to come with me, Tal? I have something to tell you."

Talia nodded at Kisa, then her gaze met mine. "I'll be close." She released my hand and moved off with her friend. I suddenly felt empty. But Luka's hand wrapped around my bicep and he pointed to the far side of the grass.

I followed Luka, passing by stone after stone. At first I struggled to understand what they were, then a memory hit me. Anri and I stood with my papa at a stone. It was my grandpapa's grave.

Ice spiked down my spine when I realized where we were—a graveyard.

Then Luka stopped. I didn't look down. Instead I watched him watch me. Luka ran his hand through his hair, and swallowing, said, "When I escaped the gulag, it was your brother who opened my cell. It was your brother who freed me." Luka rubbed his lips together and stared off at nothing, his eyes losing focus. "He was my friend. I was locked down on the lower floor, but he made sure I got out. He ensured I got my revenge." His eyes then focused back on me. "As we said good-bye, he was heading west to seek his own revenge on the people who put him in the gulag. We were also full of drugs and had no memory of what had happened to us, but he was determined to make those responsible for his imprisonment pay."

My breathing was hard as he spoke of my brother. I could see his loyalty for Anri in his eyes. Thinking of Anri was painful. Painful, but at the same time, Luka knew him. It felt like I knew Anri, too, as Luka spoke about him.

Luka coughed. I knew it was to clear the emotion from his throat. "I didn't see him again until the night we had to fight in the cage here in Brooklyn. He had been recaptured and forced to fight." Luka looked up at me again. "It was by another Georgian crime family. I don't know who. They're keeping themselves under the radar. But one day I'll find out."

My jaw clenched at that, and I vowed that I would help him in this endeavor.

"He died, Zaal. Died under the blades of my 'dusters. It was the most difficult thing I've ever done."

I stared at Luka. A flash of anger swept through me. He had killed my brother, my twin, but when he met my eyes with sadness in his eyes, the anger left me.

"His death haunted me. Has haunted me for months. I didn't know his name, I didn't know who had sent him to the gulag. But now I do. I know it all."

Luka's head turned away and he pointed to the grave. Inhaling, I closed my eyes. I held my breath as I turned, and opening my eyes, stared at a black gravestone. Breath rushed from my lungs as I read:

Anri Kostava
Warrior. Friend.
Brother.
"Be strong. Keep strong."

I read those words. Then read them again, all the time fighting the heavy burning in my chest. I felt Luka stand closer to me.

"He deserved to be honored in my family's graveyard. He deserved to be honored for the brother he was, to both you, and *I*."

I wanted to speak. I fought for words. But they didn't come. I didn't know what to say. What could I say?

But my heart was full as I stared at those words. *"Be strong. Keep strong."*

My hand clenched as I remembered Anri holding my hand, as Jakhua invaded the yard. "Be strong. Keep strong." Remembered him holding my hand as we were strapped to a bed, and the man in the white coat filled us with drugs. He met my eyes and mouthed, "Be strong. Keep strong."

Water dripped from my eyes, and then Jakhua's words replayed in my mind. . . .

. . . *you looked right through him as he begged you to see him. Didn't react as he whispered in your ear . . . and you didn't even shed a tear as he was dragged from the room . . . and you never saw him again. . . .*

Gasping, I remembered his voice in my ear. *"Be strong. Keep strong, brother. I'll come back for you. One day, I'll come and set you free. . . ."*

Anri's voice, his words, circled in my head. I tipped my head back and screamed. I screamed for the brother I had loved, but had forgotten. I screamed for Jakhua stealing my self-control, taking away my good-bye, and I screamed for my brother being gone, for my family, my sister, my little Zoya being gone.

Unable to remain standing, I dropped to my knees. I pressed my hand to the cold stone. I guided my hand over his name. Anri, my brother.

My tears dropped like boulders to the soft grass. I felt Luka still standing behind me. Luka, the man who had killed my brother to save his love. My heart squeezed because I now understood. I understood. I had killed to save my Talia. And I'd do it again in a heartbeat.

Taking a deep breath, I turned to Luka and said, "Thank you for honoring my brother."

Luka kneeled down. He placed a hand on my back. "He was my brother, too, maybe not my blood, but my brother in arms." Luka glanced away, then looking back, said, "As are you."

My heart beat faster and faster as he said those words. I thought back to Anri, in the grass as children. . . .

You're my twin. Grandmama says we share a soul. We'll lead together. We will always be together. We're stronger together. You know this. . . .

Anri had adopted Luka as a brother, and I would do it also. I would honor Anri by following his lead.

Pushing off the grass, I held my hand out to Luka. "My brother took you as a brother. I would be honored to do so, too. A brother in arms. And some day, as a brother-in-law."

Luka exhaled like I had freed him of a demon. He took my hand and I began to slowly exhale.

"Zaal?" Releasing Luka's hand, I turned to see Talia standing behind me.

"Talia," I whispered, and she moved into my arms. I held her close, breathing in her calming scent.

Her hands smoothed over my back and into my hair. "Are you okay, *zolotse*?"

Pulling back, I gazed on the most beautiful face I had ever seen, and said, "I am free. I have you." I glanced to Kisa who was cradled in Luka's arms, and added, "I have a family again." I closed my eyes and allowed myself a smile. I caught Talia's quick inhale of breath, and whispered, "I am no longer alone . . . and my heart is full."

EPILOGUE: TALIA

The evening wind was strong, carrying with it an icy chill.

But all I felt was warmth.

I lay in Zaal's arms, my back flush to his front. We were lying on the soft garden bed on the balcony of our new home, staring at the stars. Only a thin bedsheet covered our naked bodies.

Zaal breathed deeply as his hands traced lazy circles on the back of my hand. My heart swelled with love and adoration, we had found our happiness, such intense and radiant happiness.

Only a few weeks had passed since Luka had returned Zaal to me; since Zaal had sought revenge on Jakhua; since he'd honored his family's deaths—blood for blood with the man who had cast him into slavery.

Luka had arranged for Alik Durov's empty apartment to be given to Zaal, *and* me. My parents hadn't been happy about my leaving their home and moving in with Zaal. My father had insisted we marry first. But like Kisa with Luka, I understood Zaal needed me by his side more than I needed marriage. He was just learning about life, and he refused to let me go.

We hadn't spent a second apart ever since.

Kisa rolled her eyes when I moved in against the grain. She'd always called me the rebel.

And I was glad for it. Zaal and I couldn't get enough of each other. We touched, we bathed, and we made love day and night. I loved him.

I loved him so much that at times I was sure my chest would not be able to contain all the love I had in my heart.

And I knew he loved me, too. It showed in every glance from his jade green eyes, his every gentle touch, and the way he kissed me; gently, softly, like I was his universe.

Like he was the Earth and I was his sun.

Zaal shifted under me, and his hot bare skin smoothed against mine. "I like the stars," he whispered into the silence of the night.

I smiled as my fingers played with the ends of his long black hair. "I like them, too," I replied. And I did. We spent night after night out here on this beautiful rooftop, just watching the night sky. And the daytime, too. Zaal told me that he remembered watching the sky as a child, and after twenty years of nothing but darkness, I wanted to give him his sky. His night and his stars.

I wanted to give him the world.

I had already given him my soul.

My music played softly in the background. I closed my eyes. And I knew. I simply knew that life would never be better than this.

As one song ended, the crackled sound of a familiar song drifted across the rooftop garden. Zaal stilled, his hand halting on the back of mine. Dinah Shore's "I'll Walk Alone" drifted through the French doors. I smiled.

This was our song. A song that meant the world to both of us.

As Dinah's words of a lover's promise sounded, Zaal's mouth moved to my ear and he whispered, "Dance with me."

My heart fluttered at his request. All I'd ever wanted was for a man to hold me as we danced. And Zaal had passed all my expectations.

I nodded my head to his invitation and moved forward, only for Zaal to take me in his strong arms. He lifted me from the bed and carried me into the living room. Sliding me down his body, I gripped his strong arms. I stared into his green eyes.

He looked stunning, breathtaking. His olive skin was golden in the blue light of the full moon shining through the windows.

Silently, Zaal lifted my hand and placed it on his shoulder, then my other in his hand, which he brought to the warmth of his chest. Zaal's free hand wrapped around my waist and he pulled me flush against his hot skin.

Then we began to move.

Zaal led us slowly around the room and I pressed my cheek to his chest. I closed my eyes, letting the old song express to Zaal everything that I felt.

We had found our own peace in our brutal world. And I wouldn't change it for anything. This was my heaven. Zaal was everything.

He owned me.

Possessed me.

Was soldered to me in every possible way.

As the song drew to its close, Zaal's hand on my waist traveled north to rest under my chin. He guided my head up and he fixed his gaze on mine.

Green to brown.

"Talia," he whispered. I nuzzled against his cheek. Zaal's head leaned down and he said, *"Potzeluy menya."* "Kiss me." I smiled wide and a soft contented sigh left his parted lips. Lifting my chin, he crushed his mouth to mine on a low hum. His lips were soft. I felt his love, all of his love, in this one simple touch.

Breaking from my mouth, Zaal pressed his forehead to mine and whispered, "You are . . . for me."

I smiled again. I whispered back with absolute conviction, and tears in my eyes, "I am . . . for you."

They were *our* own words.

Straight from the heart.

Because I was his.

And he was mine.

A Kostava and a Tolstaia.

Heart to heart.

Scarred soul to scarred soul.

Unnamed Female

Manhattan, New York

The door to my apartment burst open. Footsteps pounded down the hallway. I jumped from my seat and faced the door, my heart thumping. Panic quickly consumed me.

Had they found me?

Did they know I was here?

Had they finally come for me?

I held my breath, just waiting, when Avto rounded the corner and ran into the room. I exhaled a long relieved breath at my old friend, then noticed his aged face was flushed, and he was shaking.

Frozen to the spot, fear seizing my limbs, I could feel the incredible heat from the open fire burning my back. Avto fought for breath and I kept waiting, waiting for him to speak.

"Avto?" I whispered in question, eventually drawing lost breath.

I watched him swallow hard and his dark eyes met mine. "He's alive, miss. I've just discovered he's alive."

My eyes widened and my hands joined Avto's in shaking. "Which one?" I asked, voice trembling.

Avto stepped forward, his old body moving slowly. My pulse pounded in my neck when he informed, "Zaal, miss. Zaal is alive."

My knees went weak and I dropped to the floor at the news. Staring at Avto, with tears in my eyes, a single word slipped in a whisper from my lips. . . .

"Sykhaara."

REAP PLAYLIST

The National—"I Need My Girl"
Lorde—"Glory and Gore"
Billie Marten—"In for the Kill"
Emile Haynie—"Come Find Me"
Of Monsters and Men—"I of the Storm"
Lykke Li—"Possibility"
X Ambassadors—"Renegades"
Five Knives—"Savages"
Johnnyswim—"You and I"
Imagine Dragons—"Warriors"
Marina and the Diamonds—"Forget"
NEEDTOBREATHE—"Multiplied"
Emika—"Wicked Game"
WrongChilde—"Love Is a Battlefield (featuring White Sea)"
Sia—"Chandelier (Piano Version)"
Lia Ices—"Love Is Won"
First Aid Kit—"Long Time Ago"
Dinah Shore—"I'll Walk Alone"
Savage Garden—"You Can Still Be Free"

RHODES—"Breathe"

To listen on Spotify:

https://open.spotify.com/user/authortilliecole/playlist
/6ObTTCIweNU6wCguQkzzha

REAP ACKNOWLEDGMENTS

I can't believe I'm writing these acknowledgments.

I feel like I am dreaming. I feel like I am in some kind of fairy tale—as dark as that fairy tale may be—that I never want to wake up from.

To Mam and Dad, thank you for all the support. How crazy is this moment? Love you both.

To my husband. You have been there from day one, and you're still hanging in there with me. I love you to pieces. You are my inspiration, my rock, and my heart.

Sam, Marc, Taylor, Isaac, Archie, and Elias. Love you all.

To my fabulous beta readers, Thessa and Rachel. Your comments and advice were invaluable.

To Liz, my super agent. The best decision I ever made was pairing up with you. You believe in me. You champion me. I wouldn't be here without you.

Eileen, my wonderful editor at St. Martin's Press, thank you so much for believing in my dark and twisted Bratva world. Thank you for loving Kisa and Raze. Thank you for giving Zaal and Talia a chance to live. I CANNOT WAIT to see where this journey will lead.

Tracey-Lee, Thessa, and Kerri, a huge thank-you for running my street teams. And to all of my street team members—LOVE YOU!!!

My FlameWhores on Instagram. You ladies brighten each and every day.

Jodi (the other Mrs. Tolstaia), Alycia, Celesha, and Natasha. Love you, ladies. Your support is everything to me.

Gitte and Jenny. You were the first to ever take a chance on me. I can't thank you enough. Love you.

My IG girls. You can be summed up in three words: fun, amazing, fabulous.

And now my readers. We have been on one hell of a journey these past two years. But in you, I have the best cheerleading squad a person can ask for. Love you. Let's keep trucking.

And finally, to Luka, my Russian boy, my RAZE. You tortured me to give your story life. I resisted, but you broke me down.

I'm forever glad that you did.